"Well?" said I, staring.

" Well ? " said I, staring

(Frontispiece).   See Page 26

THE
BROAD HIGHWAY
A ROMANCE OF KENT
by Jeffery Farnol

With Illustrations by C.E.Brock.R.I.

SAMPSON LOW, MARSTON & Cº Ltd.
LONDON.

𝕿𝖔

SHIRLEY BYRON JEVONS

THE FRIEND OF MY BOYISH AMBITIONS
THIS WORK IS DEDICATED
AS A MARK OF MY GRATITUDE, AFFECTION
AND ESTEEM

J. F.

LONDON, *Oct. 8, 1910*

PREFACE TO NEW ILLUSTRATED EDITION

"O STRONG man that is so weak! O grave Philosopher that is so foolish!" O scholar, pedant, pugilist and—man! Little did we think when we crossed the Atlantic together that we, so soon, should find so warm a reception, or so many kindly hands outstretched to greet us.

But—"as this life of ours is a Broad Highway along which we must all of us pass whether we will or no; as it is a thoroughfare often very hard and cruel in the going, sometimes desolate and hatefully monotonous," as you and I know, Peter; so, even as we hoped, its aspect latterly has changed, and, the stony tract overpassed, the choking dust and heat left behind, we may pause a while beneath the cool and grateful shade of trees; to such a place are we now come, Peter—thou and I.

And, as the years pass, so may this record of thy sufferings, triumphs and failures link us ever closer to that great brotherhood which is Humanity.

And for those to whose kindly judgment, daring all risks, we together owe so much, let these words (though few and inadequate) be the sincere expression of our thanks.

JEFFERY FARNOL.

LONDON, *6th September* 1912.

v

CONTENTS

BOOK I

Contents

Contents

ix

BOOK II.—THE WOMAN

x   Contents

Contents

LIST OF ILLUSTRATIONS

xiii

THE BROAD HIGHWAY

ANTE SCRIPTUM

As I sat of an early summer morning in the shade of a tree, eating fried bacon with a tinker, the thought came to me that I might some day write a book of my own : a book that should treat of the roads and by-roads, of trees, and wind in lonely places, of rapid brooks and lazy streams, of the glory of dawn, the glow of evening, and the purple solitude of night; a book of wayside inns and sequestered taverns ; a book of country things and ways and people. And the thought pleased me much.

" But," objected the Tinker, for I had spoken my thought aloud, " trees and suchlike don't sound very interestin——leastways—not in a book, for after all a tree's only a tree and an inn, an inn ; no, you must tell of other things as well."

" Yes," said I, a little damped, " to be sure there is a highwayman——"

"Come, that's better !" said the Tinker encouragingly.

" Then," I went on, ticking off each item on my fingers, " come Tom Cragg, the pugilist——"

" Better and better ! " nodded the Tinker.

"—a one-legged soldier of the Peninsula, an adventure at a lonely tavern, a flight through woods at midnight pursued by desperate villains, and—a most extraordinary tinker. So far so good, I think, and it all sounds adventurous enough."

" What ! " cried the Tinker. " Would you put me in your book then ? "

" Assuredly."

" Why then," said the Tinker, " it's true I mends kettles, sharpens scissors and such, but I likewise

A   I

peddles books an' nov-els, an' what's more I reads
'em—so, if you must put me in your book, you might
call me a literary cove."

" A literary cove? " said I.

" Ah ! " said the Tinker, " it sounds better—a sight
better—besides, I never read a nov-el with a tinker in
it as I remember, they're generally dooks, or earls, or
barro-nites—nobody wants to read about a tinker."

" That all depends," said I; " a tinker may be
much more interesting than an earl or even a duke."

The Tinker examined the piece of bacon upon his
knife-point with a cold and disparaging eye.

" I've read a good many nov-els in my time," said
he, shaking his head, " and I knows what I'm talking
of," here he bolted the morsel of bacon with much
apparent relish, " I've made love to duchesses, run off
with heiresses, and fought dooels—ah ! by the hundred
—all between the covers of some book or other and
enjoyed it uncommonly well—especially the dooels. If
you can get a little blood into your book, so much the
better, there's nothing like a little blood in a book—
not a great deal, but just enough to give it a ' tang,' so
to speak ; if you could kill your highwayman to start
with it would be a very good beginning to your story."

" I could do that, certainly," said I, " but it would
not be according to fact."

" So much the better," said the Tinker, " who
wants facts in a nov-el ? "

" Hum ! " said I.

" And then again——"

" What more ? " I inquired.

" Love ! " said the Tinker, wiping his knife-blade
on the leg of his breeches.

" Love ? " I repeated.

" And plenty of it," said the Tinker.

" I'm afraid that is impossible," said I after a
moment's thought.

" How impossible ? "

" Because I know nothing about love."

" That's a pity," said the Tinker.

" Under the circumstances, it is," said I.

" Not a doubt of it," said the Tinker, beginning to scrub out the frying pan with a handful of grass, " though to be sure you might learn, you're young enough."

" Yes, I might learn," said I; " who knows?"

" Ah! who knows?" said the Tinker. And after he had cleansed the pan to his satisfaction he turned to me with dexter finger upraised and brow of heavy portent. " Young fellow," said he, " no man can write a good nov-el without he knows summat about love, it aren't to be expected—so the sooner you do learn, the better."

" Hum!" said I.

" And then, as I said afore and I say it again, they wants love in a book nowadays and wot's more they will have it."

" They?" said I.

" The folk as will read your book—after it is written."

" Ah! to be sure," said I, somewhat taken aback, " I had forgotten them."

" Forgotten them?" repeated the Tinker, staring.

" Forgotten that people might want to read it—after it is written."

" But," said the Tinker, rubbing his nose hard, " books are written for people to read, aren't they?"

" Not always," said I.

Hereupon the Tinker rubbed his nose harder than ever.

" Many of the world's greatest books, those master-pieces which have lived and shall live on for ever, were written (as I believe) for the pure love of writing them."

" Oh!" said the Tinker.

" Yes," said I, warming to my theme, " and with little or no idea of the eyes of those unborn genera-tions which were to read and marvel at them; hence it is we get those sublime thoughts untrammelled by passing tastes and fashions, unbounded by narrow creed or popular prejudice."

" Ah?" said the Tinker.

" Many a great writer has been spoiled by fashion and success, for, so soon as he begins to think upon his public, how best to please and hold their fancy (which is ever the most fickle of mundane things) straightway Genius spreads abroad his pinions and leaves him in the mire."

" Poor cove ! " said the Tinker. " Young man, you smile, I think ? "

" No," said I.

" Well, supposing a writer never had no gen'us— how then ? "

" Why then," said I, " he should never dare to write at all."

" Young fellow," said the Tinker, glancing at me from the corners of his eyes, " are you sure you are a gen'us then ? "

Now when my companion said this I fell silent, for the very sufficient reason that I found nothing to say.

" Lord love you ! " said he at last, seeing me thus "hipped "—" don't be downhearted—don't be dashed afore you begin, we can't all be gen'uses—it aren't to be expected, but some on us is a good deal better than most and that's something arter all. As for your book, wot you have to do is to give 'em a little blood now and then with plenty of love and you can't go far wrong ! "

Now whether the Tinker's theory for the writing of a good novel be right or wrong, I will not presume to say. But in this book that lies before you, though you shall read, if you choose, of country things and ways and people, yet, because that part of my life herein recorded was a something hard, rough life, you shall read also of blood ; and, because I came, in the end, to love very greatly, so shall you read of love.

Wherefore, then, I am emboldened to hope that when you shall have turned the last page and closed this book, you shall do so with a sigh.

P. V.

LONDON.

CHAPTER I

" ' AND to my nephew, Maurice Vibart, I bequeath
the sum of twenty thousand pounds in the fervent hope
that it may help him to the devil within the year, or
as soon after as may be.' "

Here Mr Grainger paused in his reading to glance
up over the rim of his spectacles, while Sir Richard lay
back in his chair and laughed loudly. "Gad!" he
exclaimed, still chuckling, "I'd give a hundred pounds
if he could have been present to hear that," and the
baronet went off into another roar of merriment.

Mr Grainger, on the other hand, dignified and
solemn, coughed a short, dry cough behind his hand.

"Help him to the devil within the year," repeated
Sir Richard, still chuckling.

"Pray proceed, sir," said I, motioning towards the
will. . . . But instead of complying, Mr Grainger laid
down the parchment, and removing his spectacles,
began to polish them with a large silk handkerchief.

"You are, I believe, unacquainted with your
cousin, Sir Maurice Vibart?" he inquired.

"I have never seen him," said I; "all my life has
been passed either at school or the university, but I
have frequently heard mention of him nevertheless."

"Egad!" cried Sir Richard, "who hasn't heard of
Buck Vibart—beat Ted Jarraway of Swansea in five
rounds—drove coach and four down Whitehall—on
sidewalk—ran away with a French marquise while
but a boy of twenty, and shot her husband into the
bargain. Devilish celebrated figure in 'sporting
circles,' friend of the Prince Regent——"

"So I understand," said I.

"Altogether as complete a young blackguard as

5

ever swaggered down St James's." Having said which, Sir Richard crossed his legs and inhaled a pinch of snuff.

"Twenty thousand pounds is a very handsome sum," remarked Mr Grainger ponderously and as though more with the intention of saying something rather than remain silent just then.

"Indeed it is," said I, "and might help a man to the devil as comfortably as need be, but——"

"Though," pursued Mr Grainger, "much below his expectations and sadly inadequate to his present needs, I fear."

"That is most unfortunate," said I, "but——"

"His debts," said Mr Grainger, busy at his spectacles again, "his debts are very heavy, I believe."

"Then doubtless some arrangement can be made to —but continue your reading, I beg," said I.

Mr Grainger repeated his short, dry cough and taking up the will, slowly and almost as though unwillingly, cleared his throat and began as follows:

"'Furthermore, to my nephew, Peter Vibart, cousin to the above I will and bequeath my blessing and the sum of ten guineas in cash, wherewith to purchase a copy of Zeno or any other of the stoic philosophers he may prefer.'"

Again Mr Grainger laid down the will, and again he regarded me over the rim of his spectacles.

"Good God!" cried Sir Richard, leaping to his feet, "the man must have been mad. Ten guineas— why, it's an insult—damme!—it's an insult—you'll never take it of course, Peter."

"On the contrary, sir," said I.

"But—ten guineas!" bellowed the baronet; "on my soul now, George was a cold-blooded fish but I didn't think even he was capable of such a despicable trick—no—curse me if I did! Why it would have been kinder to have left you nothing at all—but it was like George—bitter to the end—ten guineas!"

"Is ten guineas," said I, "and when one comes to think of it much may be done with ten guineas."

Sir Richard grew purple in the face, but before he could speak, Mr Grainger began to read again :

" ' Moreover, the sum of five hundred thousand pounds, now vested in the funds, shall be paid to either Maurice or Peter Vibart aforesaid, if either shall, within one calendar year, become the husband of the Lady Sophia Sefton of Cambourne.' "

" Good God ! " exclaimed Sir Richard.

" ' Failing which,' " read Mr Grainger, " ' the said sum, namely, five hundred thousand pounds shall be bestowed upon such charity or charities as the trustees shall select. Signed by me, this tenth day of April, eighteen hundred and——, GEORGE VIBART. Duly witnessed by ADAM PENFLEET, MARTHA TRENT.' "

Here Mr Grainger's voice stopped, and I remember, in the silence that followed, the parchment crackled very loudly as he folded it precisely and laid it on the table before him. I remember also that Sir Richard was swearing vehemently under his breath as he paced to and fro between me and the window.

" And that is all ? " I inquired at last.

" That," said Mr Grainger, not looking at me now, " is all."

" The Lady Sophia," murmured Sir Richard as if to himself, " the Lady Sophia ! " And then, stopping suddenly before me in his walk, " Oh, Peter ! " said he, clapping his hand down upon my shoulder, " oh, Peter, that settles it, you're done for, boy—a crueller will was never made."

" Marriage ! " said I to myself, " Hum ! "

" A damnable iniquity ! " exclaimed Sir Richard, striding up and down the room again.

" The Lady Sophia Sefton of Cambourne ! " said I, rubbing my chin.

" Why, that's just it," roared the baronet ; " she's a reigning toast—most famous beauty in the country, London's mad over her—she can pick and choose from all the finest gentlemen in England. Oh, it's 'good-bye' to all your hopes of the inheritance, Peter, and that's the devil of it."

" Sir, I fail to see your argument," said I.

" What ? " cried Sir Richard, facing round on me, " d'you think you'd have a chance with her then ? "

" Why not ? "

" Without friends, position, or money ? Pish, boy ! don't I tell you that every buck and dandy—every mincing macaroni in the three kingdoms would give his very legs to marry her—either for her beauty or her fortune," spluttered the baronet. " And let me inform you further that she's devilish high and haughty with it all—they do say she even rebuffed the Prince Regent himself."

" But then, sir, I consider myself a better man than the Prince Regent," said I.

Sir Richard sank into the nearest chair and stared at me open-mouthed.

" Sir," I continued, " you doubtless set me down as an egoist of egoists, I freely confess it, so are you, so is Mr Grainger yonder, we are all of us egoists in thinking ourselves as good as some few of our neighbours and better than a great many."

" Deuce take me ! " said Sir Richard.

" Referring to the Lady Sophia, I have heard that she once galloped her horse up the steps of St Paul's Cathedral——"

" And down again, Peter," added Sir Richard.

" Also she is said to be possessed of a temper," I continued, " and is above the average height, I believe, and I have a natural antipathy to termagants, more especially tall ones."

" Termagant ! " cried Sir Richard. " Why, she's the handsomest woman in London, boy. She's none of your milk-and-watery, meek-mouthed misses—curse me, no ! she's all fire and blood and high mettle—a woman, sir—glorious—divine—damme, sir, a black-browed goddess—a positive plum ! "

" Sir Richard," said I, " should I ever contemplate marriage, which is most improbable, my wife must be sweet and shy, gentle eyed and soft of voice, instead of your bold, strong-armed, horse-galloping creature; above all, she must be sweet and clinging——"

"Sweet and sticky, oh, the devil! Hark to the boy, Grainger," cried Sir Richard, "hark to him—and one glance of the glorious Sefton's bright eyes—one glance only, Grainger, and he'd be at her feet—on his knees—on his confounded knees, sir!"

"The question is, how do you propose to maintain yourself in the future?" said Mr Grainger at this point; "life under your altered fortunes must prove necessarily hard, Mr Peter."

"And yet, sir," I answered, "a fortune with a wife tagged on to it must prove a very mixed blessing after all; and then again, there may be a certain amount of satisfaction in stepping into a dead man's shoes, but I, very foolishly, perhaps, have a hankering for shoes of my own. Surely there must be some position in life that I am competent to fill, some position that would maintain me honourably and well; I flatter myself that my years at Oxford were not altogether barren of result——"

"By no means," put in Sir Richard; "you won the High Jump, I believe?"

"Sir, I did," said I, "also 'Throwing the Hammer.'"

"And spent two thousand pounds per annum?" said Sir Richard.

"Sir, I did, but between whiles managed to do fairly well in my studies, to finish a new and original translation of Quintilian, another of Petronius Arbiter and also a literal rendering into the English of the Memoirs of the Sieur de Brantome."

"For none of which you have hitherto found a publisher?" inquired Mr Grainger.

"Not as yet," said I, "but I have great hopes of my Brantome, as you are probably aware this is the first time he has ever been translated into the English."

"Hum!" said Sir Richard, "ha!—and in the meantime what do you intend to do?"

"On that head I have as yet come to no definite conclusion, sir," I answered.

"I have been wondering," began Mr Grainger,

somewhat diffidently, "if you would care to accept a position in my office. To be sure the remuneration would be small at first and quite insignificant in comparison to the income you have been in the receipt of."

"But it would have been money earned," said I, "which is infinitely preferable to that for which we never turn a hand—at least, I think so."

"Then you accept?"

"No, sir," said I, "though I am grateful to you, and thank you most sincerely for your offer, yet I have never felt the least inclination to the practice of law; where there is no interest one's work must necessarily suffer, and I have no desire that your business should be injured by any carelessness of mine."

"What do you think of a private tutorship?"

"It would suit me above all things were it not for the fact that the genus 'Boy' is the most aggravating of all animals and that I am conscious of a certain shortness of temper at times, which might result in pain to my pupil, loss of dignity to myself, and general unpleasantness to all concerned—otherwise a private tutorship would suit most admirably."

Here Sir Richard took another pinch of snuff and sat frowning up at the ceiling, while Mr Grainger began tying up that document which had so altered my prospects. As for me, I crossed to the window and stood staring out at the evening. Everywhere were trees tinted by the rosy glow of sunset, trees that stirred sleepily in the gentle wind, and far away I could see that famous highway, built and paved for the march of Roman Legions, winding away to where it vanished over distant Shooter's Hill.

"And pray," said Sir Richard, still frowning at the ceiling, "what do you propose to do with yourself?"

Now, as I looked out upon this fair evening, I became, of a sudden, possessed of an overmastering desire, a great longing for field and meadow and hedgerow, for wood and coppice and shady stream, for sequestered inns and wide, wind-swept heaths, and ever the broad highway in front. Thus, I answered

Sir Richard's question unhesitatingly, and without turning from the window :

" I shall go, sir, on a walking tour through Kent and Surrey into Devonshire and thence probably to Cornwall."

" And with a miserable ten guineas in your pocket? Preposterous—absurd ! " retorted Sir Richard.

" On the contrary, sir,' said I, " the more I ponder the project, the more enamoured of it I become."

" And when your money is all gone—how then ? "

" I shall turn my hand to some useful employment," said I; " digging, for instance."

" Digging ! " ejaculated Sir Richard, " and you a scholar—and what is more, a gentleman ! "

" My dear Sir Richard," said I, " that all depends upon how you would define a gentleman. To me he would appear, of late years, to have degenerated into a creature whose chief end in life is to spend money he has never earned, to reproduce his species with a deplorable frequency and promiscuity, habitually to drink more than is good for him, and, between whiles, to fill in his time hunting, cock-fighting, or watching entranced while two men pound each other unrecognisable in the prize ring. Occasionally he has the good taste to break his neck in the hunting field, or get himself gloriously shot in a duel, but the generality live on to a good old age, turn their attention to matters political and, following the dictates of their class, damn all reform with a whole-hearted fervour equalled only by their rancour."

" Deuce take me ! " ejaculated Sir Richard feebly, while Mr Grainger buried his face in his pocket-handkerchief.

" To my mind," I ended, " the man who sweats over a spade or follows the tail of a plough is far nobler and higher in the Scheme of Things than any of your young ' bloods ' driving his coach and four to Brighton to the danger of all and sundry."

Sir Richard slowly got up out of his chair, staring at me open mouthed. " Good God ! " he exclaimed at last, " the boy's a Revolutionary."

I smiled and shrugged my shoulders, but, before I could speak, Mr Grainger interposed, sedate and solemn as usual:

"Referring to your proposed tour, Mr Peter, when do you expect to start?"

"Early to-morrow morning, sir."

"I will not attempt to dissuade you, well knowing the difficulty," said he with a faint smile, "but a letter addressed to me at Lincoln's Inn will always find me and receive my most earnest attention." So saying he rose, bowed, and having shaken my hand, left the room, closing the door behind him.

"Peter," exclaimed the baronet, striding up and down, "Peter, you are a fool—sir, a hot-headed, self-sufficient, pragmatical young fool—sir, curse me!"

"I am sorry you should think so," I answered.

"And," he continued, regarding me with a defiant eye, "I shall expect you to draw upon me for any sum that—that you may require for the present—friendship's sake—boyhood and—and all that sort of thing, and—er—oh, damme, you understand, Peter?"

"Sir Richard," said I, grasping his unwilling hand, "I—I thank you from the bottom of my heart."

"Pooh, Peter, dammit!" said he, snatching his hand away and thrusting it hurriedly into his pocket, out of farther reach.

"Thank you, sir," I reiterated; "be sure that should I fall ill or any unforeseen calamity happen to me, I will most gladly, most gratefully accept your generous aid in the spirit in which it is offered, but——"

"But?" exclaimed Sir Richard.

"Until then——"

"Oh, the devil!" said Sir Richard, and ringing the bell ordered his horse to be brought to the door and thereafter stood with his back to the empty fireplace, his fists thrust down into his pockets, frowning heavily and with a fixed intentness at the nearest arm-chair.

Sir Richard Anstruther is tall and broad, ruddy of face, with a prominent nose and great square chin whose grimness is off-set by a mouth singularly sweet and tender, and the kindly light of blue eyes; he is in very truth a gentleman. Indeed, as he stood there in his plain blue coat with its high roll collar and shining silver buttons, his spotless moleskins and heavy, square-toed riding boots he was as fair a type as might be of the English country gentleman. It is such men as he, who, fearless upon the littered quarter-decks of reeling battleships, undismayed amid the smoke and death of stricken fields, their duty well and nobly done, have turned their feet homewards to pass their latter days amid their turnips and cabbages, beating their swords into pruning-hooks, and glad enough to do it.

" Peter," said he suddenly.

" Sir ? " said I.

" You never saw your father to remember, did you ?"

" No, Sir Richard."

" Nor your mother ? "

" Nor my mother . "

" Poor boy—poor boy ! "

" You knew my mother ? "

" Yes, Peter, I knew your mother," said Sir Richard, staring very hard at the chair again, and I saw that his mouth had grown wonderfully tender. " Yours has been a very secluded life hitherto, Peter," he went on after a moment.

" Entirely so," said I, " with the exception of my never-to-be forgotten visits to the Hall."

" Ah yes, I taught you to ride, remember."

" You are associated with every boyish pleasure I ever knew," said I, laying my hand upon his arm. Sir Richard coughed and grew suddenly red in the face.

" Why—ah—you see, Peter," he began, picking up his riding whip and staring at it, " you see your uncle was never very fond of company at any time, whereas I——"

" Whereas you could always find time to remember the lonely boy left when all his companions were gone on their holidays—left to his books and the dreary desolation of the empty schoolhouse, and echoing cloisters——"

" Pooh ! " exclaimed Sir Richard, redder than ever.
" Bosh ! "

" Do you think I can ever forget the glorious day
when you drove over in your coach and four, and
carried me off in triumph, and how we raced the white-
hatted fellow in the tilbury——"

" And beat him ! " added Sir Richard.

" Took off his near wheel on the turn," said I.

" The fool's own fault," said Sir Richard.

" And left him in the ditch, cursing us ! " said I.

" Egad, yes, Peter ! Oh, but those were fine horses
—and though I say it, no better team in the south
country. You'll remember the ' off wheeler ' broke
his leg shortly after and had to be shot, poor devil."

" And later, at Oxford," I began.

" What now, Peter ? " said Sir Richard, frowning
darkly.

" Do you remember the bronze vase that used to
stand on the mantelpiece in my study ? "

" Bronze vase ? " repeated Sir Richard, intent upon
his whip again.

" I used to find bank-notes in it after you had visited
me, and when I hid the vase they turned up just the
same in most unexpected places."

" Young fellow—must have money—necessary—
now and then," muttered Sir Richard.

At this juncture, with a discreet knock, the butler
appeared to announce that Sir Richard's horse was
waiting. Hereupon the baronet, somewhat hastily,
caught up his hat and gloves, and I followed him out
of the house and down the steps.

Sir Richard drew on his gloves, thrust his toe into
the stirrup, and then turned to look at me over his arm.

" Peter," said he.

" Sir Richard ? " said I.

" Regarding your walking tour——"

" Yes ? "

" I think it's all damned tomfoolery ! " said Sir
Richard. After saying which he swung himself into
the saddle with a lightness and ease that many
younger might have envied.

" I'm sorry for that, sir, because my mind is set upon it."

" With ten guineas in your pocket ! "

" That, with due economy, should be ample until I can find some means to earn more."

" A fiddlestick, sir—an accursed fiddlestick ! " snorted Sir Richard. " How is a boy, an unsophisticated, hot-headed young fool of a boy to earn his own living ? "

" Others have done it," I began.

" Pish ! " said the baronet.

" And been the better for it in the end."

" Tush ! " said the baronet.

" And I have a great desire to see the world from the viewpoint of the multitude."

" Bah ! " said the baronet, so forcibly that his mare started, " this comes of your damnable Revolutionary tendencies. Let me tell you, Want is a hard master, and the world a bad place for one who is moneyless and without friends."

" You forget, sir, I shall never be without a friend."

" God knows it, boy," answered Sir Richard, and his hand fell and rested for a moment upon my shoulder. " Peter," said he, very slowly and heavily, " I'm growing old—and I shall never marry—and sometimes, Peter, of an evening I get very lonely and —lonely, Peter." He stopped for a while, gazing away towards the green slopes of distant Shooter's Hill. " Oh, boy ! " said he at last, " won't you come to the Hall and help me to spend my money ? "

Without answering I reached up and clasped his hand; it was the hand which held his whip, and I noticed how tightly he gripped the handle, and wondered.

" Sir Richard," said I at last, "wherever I go I shall treasure the recollection of this moment, but——"

" But, Peter ? "

" But, sir——"

" Oh, dammit ! " he exclaimed, and set spurs to his mare. Yet once he turned in his saddle to flourish his whip to me ere he galloped out of sight.

CHAPTER II

I SET OUT

THE clock of the square-towered Norman church, a mile away, was striking the hour of four as I let myself out into the morning. It was dark as yet, and chilly, but in the east was already a faint glimmer of dawn. Reaching the stables I paused with my hand on the door-hasp, listening to the hiss, hissing that told me Adam, the groom, was already at work within. As I entered he looked up from the saddle he was polishing and touched his forehead with a grimy forefinger.

"You be early abroad, Mr Peter."

"Yes," said I. "I wish to be on Shooter's Hill at sunrise; but first I came to say 'good-bye' to 'Wings.'"

"To be sure, sir," nodded Adam, picking up his lanthorn.

Upon the ensuing interview I will not dwell, it was affecting both to her and to myself, for we were mutually attached.

"Sir," said Adam, when at last the stable door had closed behind us, "that there mare knows as you're a-leaving her."

"I think she does, Adam."

"'Osses be wonderful wise, sir!"

"Yes, Adam."

"This is a bad day for Wings, sir—and all of us, for that matter."

"I hope not, Adam."

"You be a-going away, they tell me, sir?"

"Yes, going away," I nodded.

"Wonder what'll become o' the mare, sir?"

"Ah yes, I wonder," said I.

"Everything to be sold under the will, I think, sir?"

16

" Everything, Adam."

" Excuse me, sir," said he, knuckling his forehead, " you won't be wanting ever a groom, will you ? "

" No, Adam," I answered, shaking my head, " I sha'n't be wanting a groom."

" Nor yet a body servant, sir ? "

" No, Adam, nor yet a body servant."

Here there ensued a silence during which Adam knuckled his right temple again and I tightened the buckle of my knapsack.

" I think, Adam," said I, " I think it is going to be a fine day."

" Yes, sir."

" Good-bye, Adam ! " said I, and held out my hand.

" Good-bye, sir." And, having shaken my hand, he turned and went back into the stable.

So I set off, walking beneath an avenue of trees looming up gigantic on either hand. At the end was the lodge and, ere I opened the gates—for John, the lodgekeeper, was not yet astir—ere I opened the gates, I say, I paused for one last look at the house that had been all the home I had ever known since I could remember. As I stood thus, with my eyes upon the indistinct mass, I presently distinguished a figure running towards me and, as he came up, recognised Adam.

" It ain't much, sir, but it's all I 'ave," said he, and thrust a short, thick, well-smoked clay pipe into my hand—a pipe that was fashioned to the shape of a negro's head. " It's a good pipe, sir," he went on, " a mortal good pipe, and as sweet as a nut ! " saying which he turned about and ran off, leaving me standing there with his parting gift in my hand.

And having put the pipe into an inner pocket, I opened the gate and started off at a good pace along the broad highway.

It was a bleak, desolate world that lay about me, a world of shadows and a white, low-lying mist that filled every hollow and swathed hedge and tree; a lowering earth and a frowning heaven infinitely depressing. But the eastern sky was clear with an

B

CHAPTER III

CONCERNS ITSELF MAINLY WITH A HAT

As the day advanced, the sun beat down with an ever-increasing heat, and what with this and the dust I presently grew very thirsty; wherefore, as I went, I must needs conjure up tantalising visions of ale—of ale that foamed gloriously in tankards, that sparkled in glasses, and gurgled deliciously from the spouts of earthen-pitchers, and I began to look about me for some inn where these visions might be realised and my burning thirst nobly quenched (as such a thirst deserved to be). On I went, through this beautiful land of Kent, past tree and hedge and smiling meadow, by hill and dale and sloping upland, while ever the sun grew hotter, the winding road the dustier, and my mighty thirst the mightier.

At length, reaching the brow of a hill, I espied a small inn or hedge-tavern that stood back from the glare of the road, seeming to nestle in the shade of a great tree, and joyfully I hastened toward it.

As I approached I heard loud voices, raised as though in altercation, and a hat came hurtling through the open doorway and, bounding into the road, rolled over and over to my very feet. And, looking down at it, I saw that it was a very ill-used hat, frayed and worn, dented of crown and broken of brim, yet beneath its sordid shabbiness there lurked the dim semblance of what it had once been, for, in the scratched and tarnished buckle, in the jaunty curl of the brim, it still preserved a certain pitiful air of rakishness; wherefore, I stooped, and, picking it up, began to brush the dust from it as well as I might.

I was thus engaged when there arose a sudden bull-like roar and, glancing up, I beheld a man who reeled backwards out of the inn and who, after staggering a yard or so, thudded down into the road and so lay, staring vacantly up at the sky. Before I could reach him, however, he got upon his legs and, crossing unsteadily to the tree I have mentioned, leaned there and I saw there was much blood upon his face which he essayed to wipe away with the cuff of his coat. Now, upon his whole person, from the crown of his unkempt head down to his broken, dusty boots, there yet clung that air of jaunty, devil-may-care rakishness which I had seen, and pitied in his hat.

Observing, as I came up, how heavily he leaned against the tree, and noting the extreme pallor of his face and the blank gaze of his sunken eyes, I touched him upon the shoulder.

" Sir, I trust you are not hurt ? " said I.

" Thank you," he answered, his glance still wandering, " not in the least—assure you—merely—tap on the nose, sir—unpleasant—damnably, but no more, no more."

" I think," said I, holding out the battered hat, " I think this is yours ? "

His eye encountering it in due time, he reached out his hand somewhat fumblingly, and took it from me with a slight movement of the head and shoulders that might have been a bow.

" Thank you—yes—should know it among a thousand," said he dreamily, " an old friend and a tried— a very much tried one—many thanks." With which words he clapped the much-tried friend upon his head, and with another movement that might have been a bow, turned short round and strode away. And as he went, despite the careless swing of his shoulder, his legs seemed to falter somewhat in their stride and once I thought he staggered; yet, as I watched, half minded to follow after him, he settled his hat more firmly with a light tap upon the crown and, thrusting his hands into the pockets of his threadbare coat, fell to whistling lustily, and so, turning a bend in the road, vanished from my sight.

And presently, my thirst recurring to me, I approached the inn, and descending three steps entered its cool shade. Here I found four men, each with his pipe and tankard, to whom a large, red-faced, big-fisted fellow was holding forth in a high state of heat and indignation.

" Wot's England a-comin' to?—that's wot I wants to know," he was saying, " wot's England a-comin' to when thievin' robbers can come a-walkin' in on you a-stealin' a pint o' your best ale out o' your very own tankard under your very own nose—wot's it a-comin' to?"

" Ah!" nodded the others solemnly. "that's it, Joel—wot?"

" W'y," growled the red-faced innkeeper, bringing his big fist down with a bang, " it's a-comin' to per—dition, that's wot it's a-comin' to!"

" And wot," inquired a rather long, bony man with a face half-hidden in sandy whisker, "wot might per—dition be, Joel, likewise, wheer?"

" You must a danged fule, Tom, my lad!" retorted he whom they called Joel, redder in the face than ever.

" Ay, that ye must!" chorused the others.

" I only axed, wot an' wheer."

" Only axed, did ye?" repeated Joel scornfully.

" Ah," nodded the other, " that's all."

" But you're always a-axin', you are," said Joel gloomily.

" W'ich I notice,' retorted the man Tom, blowing into his tankard, " w'ich I notice as you ain't never over-fond o' answerin'."

" Oh!—I ain't, ain't I?"

" No, you ain't," repeated Tom, " nohow."

Here the red-faced man grew so very red indeed that the others fell to coughing, all together, and shuffling their feet and giving divers other evidences of their embarrassment, all save the unimpressionable Tom.

Seizing the occasion that now presented itself, I knocked loudly upon the floor with my stick, whereupon the red-faced man, removing his eyes slowly and by degrees from the unconcerned Tom, fixed them darkly upon me.

" Supposing," said I, " supposing you are so very obliging as to serve me with a pint of ale ? "

" Then supposin' you show me the colour o' your money ? " he growled, " come, money fust; I aren't takin' no more risks."

For answer I laid the coins before him. And having pocketed the money, he filled and thrust a foaming tankard towards me, which I emptied forthwith and called upon him for another.

" Wheer's your money ? "

" Here," said I, tossing a sixpence to him, " and you can keep the change."

" Why ye see, sir," he began, somewhat mollified, " it be precious 'ard to know who's a gentleman, an' who ain't, who's a thief, an' who ain't these days."

" How so ? "

" Why only a little while ago—just afore you—chap comes a-walkin' in 'ere, no 'account much' to look at, but very 'aughty for all that—comes a-walkin' in 'ere 'e do an' calls for a pint o' ale—you 'eard 'im, all on ye ? " he broke off, turning to the others, " you all 'eard 'im call for a pint o' ale ? "

" Ah—we 'eard 'im," they nodded.

" Comes a-walkin' in 'ere 'e do, bold as brass—calls for a pint o' ale—drinks it off, an'—'ands me 'is 'at; you all seen 'im 'and me 'is 'at ? " he inquired, once more addressing the others.

" Every man of us," the four chimed in with four individual nods.

" ' Wot's this 'ere ? ' says I, turnin' it over. ' It's a 'at, or once was,' says 'e. ' Well, I don't want it,' says I. ' Since you've got it you'd better keep it,' says 'e. ' Wot for ? ' says I. ' Why,' says 'e, ' it's only fair seein' I've got your ale—it's a case of exchange,' says 'e. ' Oh ! is it ? ' says I, an' pitched the thing out into the road an' 'im arter it—an' so it ended. An' wot," said the red-faced man nodding his big head at me, " wot d'ye think o' that now ? "

" Why, I think you were perhaps a trifle hasty," said I.

" Oh, ye do, do ye ? "

" Yes," I nodded.

" An' for why ? "

" Well, you will probably remember that the hat had a band round it——"

" Ay, all wore away it were too——"

" And that in the band was a buckle——"

" Ay, all scratched an' rusty it were—well ? "

" Well, that tarnished buckle was of silver——"

" Silver ! " gasped the man, his jaw falling.

" And easily worth five shillings, perhaps more, so that I think you were, upon the whole, rather hasty." Saying which, I finished my ale and, taking up my staff, stepped out into the sunshine.

CHAPTER IV

I MEET WITH A GREAT MISFORTUNE

THAT day I passed through several villages, stopping only to eat and drink, thus evening was falling as, having left fair Sevenoaks behind, I came to the brow of a certain hill, a long and very steep descent which (I think) is called the River Hill. And here, rising stark against the evening sky, was a gibbet, and standing beneath it a man, a short, square man in a somewhat shabby coat of bottle-green, and with a wide-brimmed beaver hat sloped down over his eyes, who stood with his feet well apart, sucking the knob of a stick he carried, while he stared up at that which dangled by a stout chain from the cross-beam of the gibbet, something black and shrivelled and horrible that had once been human.

As I came up, the man drew the stick from his mouth and touched the brim of his hat with it in salutation.

" An object lesson, sir," said he, and nodded towards the loathsome mass above.

" A very hideous one ! " said I, pausing, " and I think a very useless one."

" He was as fine a fellow as ever thrust toe into stirrup," the man went on, pointing upwards with his stick, " though you'd never think so to look at him now ! "

" It's a horrible sight ! " said I.

" It is," nodded the man, " it's a sight to turn a man's stomach, that is ! "

" You knew him perhaps ? " said I.

" Knew him," repeated the man, staring at me over his shoulder, " knew him—ah—that is, I knew of him."

" A highwayman ? "

" Nick Scrope his name was," answered the man

25

with a nod, " hung at Maidstone assizes last year, and
a very good end he made of it too; and here he be—
hung up in chains all nat'ral and reg'lar, as a warning
to all and sundry."

" The more shame to England," said I; " to my
thinking it is a scandal that our highways should be
rendered odious by such horrors and as wicked as it is
useless."

" 'Od rot me !" cried the fellow, slapping a cloud of
dust from his coat with his stick, " hark to that now."

" What ? " said I, " do you think for one moment
that such a sight, horrible though it is, could possibly
deter a man from robbery or murder whose mind is
already made up to it by reason of circumstances or
starvation ? "

" Well, but it's an old custom, as old as this here
road."

" True," said I, " and that of itself but proves my
argument, for men have been hanged and gibbeted all
these years yet robbery and murder abide with us still,
and are of daily occurrence."

" Why, as to that, sir," said the man, falling into
step beside me as I walked on down the hill, " I won't
say yes and I won't say no, but what I do say is—as
many a man might think twice afore running the
chance of coming to that—look ! " And he stopped to
turn, and point back at the gibbet with his stick.
" Nick can't last much longer, though I've know'd
'em hang a good time—but they made a botch of Nick
—not enough tar, you can see where the sun catches
him there ! "

Once more, though my whole being revolted at the
sight, I must needs turn to look at the thing—the tall,
black shaft of the gibbet, and the grisly horror that
dangled beneath with its chains and iron bands; and
from this, back again to my companion, to find him
regarding me with a curiously twisted smile, and a
long-barrelled pistol held within a foot of my head.

" Well ? " said I, staring.

' Sir," said he, tapping his boot with his stick, " I
must trouble you for the shiner I see a-winking at me

from your cravat, likewise your watch and any small change you may have."

For a moment I hesitated, glancing from his grinning mouth swiftly over the deserted road, and back again.

"Likewise," said the fellow, " I must ask you to be sharp about it." It was with singularly clumsy fingers that I drew the watch from my fob, and the pin from my cravat and passed them to him.

"Now your pockets," he suggested, "turn 'em out."

This command I reluctantly obeyed, bringing to light my ten guineas, which were as yet intact, and which he pocketed forthwith, and two pennies—which he bade me keep.

" For," said he, " 'twill buy you a draught of ale, sir, and there's good stuff to be had at the ' White Hart ' yonder, and there's nothin' like a draught of good ale to comfort a man in any such small adversity like this here. As to that knapsack now," he pursued, eyeing it thoughtfully, " it looks heavy and might hold valleybels, but then, on the other hand, it might not, and those there straps takes time to unbuckle and——" He broke off suddenly for from somewhere on the hill below us came the unmistakable sound of wheels. Hereupon the fellow very nimbly ran across the road, turned, nodded, and vanished among the trees and underbrush that clothed the steep slope down to the valley below.

CHAPTER V

THE BAGMAN

I was yet standing there, half stunned by my loss and the suddenness of it all, when a tilbury came slowly round a bend in the road, the driver of which nodded lazily in his seat while his horse, a sorry, jaded animal, plodded wearily up the steep slope of the hill. As he approached I hailed him loudly, upon which, he suddenly dived down between his knees and produced a brassbound blunderbuss.

"What's to do?" cried he, a thick-set, round-faced, fellow, "what's to do, eh?" and he covered me with the wide mouth of the blunderbuss.

"Thieves!" said I, "I've been robbed, and not three minutes since."

"Ah!" he exclaimed, in a tone of great relief, and with the colour returning to his plump cheeks, "is that the way of it?"

"It is," said I, "and a very bad way, the fellow has left me but twopence in the world."

"Twopence—ah?"

"Come," I went on, "you are armed I see, the thief took to the brushwood, here, not three minutes ago, we may catch him yet——"

"Catch him?" repeated the fellow, staring.

"Yes, don't I tell you he has stolen all the money I possess."

"Except twopence," said the fellow.

"Yes——"

"Well, twopence ain't to be sneezed at, and if I was you——"

"Come, we're losing time," said I, cutting him short.

"But—my mare, what about my mare?"

"She'll stand," I answered; "she's tired enough."

The Bagman, for such I took him to be, sighed,

28

and, blunderbuss in hand, prepared to alight, but, in the act of doing so, paused :

" Was the rascal armed ? " he inquired, over his shoulder.

" To be sure he was," said I.

The Bagman got back into his seat and took up the reins.

" What now ? " I inquired.

" It's this accursed mare of mine," he answered, " she'll bolt again, d'ye see—twice yesterday and once the day before, she bolted, sir, and on a road like this——"

" Then lend me your blunderbuss."

" I can't do that," he replied, shaking his head.

" But why not ? " said I impatiently.

" Because this is a dangerous road and I don't intend to be left unarmed on a dangerous road—I never have been and I never will and there's an end of it, d'ye see ! "

" Then do you mean to say that you refuse your aid to a fellow-traveller—that you will sit there and let the rogue get away with all the money I possess in the world——"

" Oh no ; not on no account, just you get up here beside me and we'll drive to ' The White Hart.' I'm well known at ' The White Hart,' we'll get a few honest fellows at our heels and have this thieving, rascally villain in the twinkling of an——" He stopped suddenly, made a frantic clutch at his blunderbuss, and sat staring. Turning short round I saw the man in the beaver hat standing within a yard of us, fingering his long pistol and with the same twisted smile upon his lips.

" I've a mind," said he, nodding his head at the Bagman, " I've a great mind to blow your face off."

The blunderbuss fell to the roadway, with a clatter.

" Thievin' rascally villain—was it ? Damme ! I think I will blow your face off."

" No—don't do—that," said the Bagman, in a strange, jerky voice, " what 'ud be—the good ? "

" Why that there poor animal wouldn't have to

drag that fat carkiss of yours up and down hills, for
one thing.''

'' I'll get out and walk.''

'' And it might learn ye to keep a civil tongue in
your head.''

'' I—I didn't mean—any—offence.''

'' Then chuck us your purse,'' growled the other,
'' and be quick about it.''   The Bagman obeyed with
wonderful celerity, and I heard the purse chink as the
footpad dropped it into the pocket of his greatcoat.

'' As for you,'' said he, turning to me, '' you get on
your way and never mind me, forget you ever had ten
guineas and don't go a-riskin' your vallyble young
life ; come—up with you ! '' and he motioned me into
the tilbury with his pistol.

'' What about my blunderbuss ? '' expostulated the
Bagman, faintly, as I seated myself beside him, ''you'll
give me my blunderbuss—cost me five pounds it did.''

''More fool you ! '' said the highwayman, and, picking up the unwieldy weapon, he hove it into the ditch.

'' As to our argyment—regardin' gibbetin', sir,''
said he, nodding to me, '' I'm rayther inclined to think
you was in the right on it arter all.''   Then, turning
towards the Bagman : '' Drive on, fat-face ! '' said he,
'' and sharp's the word.''   Whereupon the Bagman
whipped up his horse and, as the tired animal struggled forward over the crest of the hill, I saw the highwayman still watching us with his twisted smile.

Very soon we came in view of '' The White Hart,''
an inn I remembered to have passed on the right hand
side of the road, and, scarce were we driven up to the
door, than down jumped the Bagman, leaving me to
follow at my leisure, and running into the tap, forthwith began recounting his loss to all and sundry, so
that I soon found we were become the centre of a
gaping crowd, much to my disgust.   Indeed, I would
have slipped away, but each time I attempted to do so
the Bagman would appeal to me to corroborate some
statement.

'' Galloping Dick himself, or I'm a Dutchman ! ''
he cried for the twentieth time, '' up he comes, bold as

brass, bless you, and a horse-pistol in each hand.
' Hold hard ! ' says I, and ups with my blunderbuss,
you remember as I ups with my blunderbuss ? " he
inquired, turning to me.

" Quite well," said I.

" Ah, but you should have seen the fellow's face,
when he saw my blunderbuss ready at my shoulder,
green it was—green as grass, for if ever there was
death in a man's face, and sudden death at that, there
was sudden death in mine, when, all at once, my mare,
my accursed mare, jibbed——"

" Yes, yes ? " cried half-a-dozen breathless voices,
" what then ? "

" Why then, gentlemen," said the Bagman, shaking his head and frowning round upon the ring of
intent faces, " why then, gentlemen, being a resolute,
determined fellow, I did what any other man of spirit
would have done—I——"

" Dropped your blunderbuss," said I.

" Ay, to be sure I did——"

" And he pitched it into the ditch," said I.

" Ay," nodded the Bagman dubiously, while the
others crowded nearer.

" And then he took your money, and called you
' Fool ' and ' Fat-face,' and so it ended," said I. With
which I pushed my way from the circle, and, finding a
quiet corner beside the chimney, sat down, and with
my last twopence ordered a tankard of ale.

CHAPTER VI

WHAT BEFELL ME AT " THE WHITE HART "

WHEN a man has experienced some great, and totally unexpected reverse of fortune, has been swept from one plane of existence to another, that he should fail at once to recognise the full magnitude of that change is but natural, for his faculties must of necessity be numbed more or less, by its very suddenness.

Yesterday I had been reduced from affluence to poverty with an unexpectedness that had dazed me for the time being, and, from the poverty of an hour ago, I now found myself reduced to an utter destitution without the wherewithal to pay for the meanest night's lodgment. And, contrasting the careless ease of a few days since with my present lamentable situation, I fell into a gloomy meditation; and the longer I thought it over, the more dejected I became. To be sure, I might apply to Sir Richard for assistance, but my pride revolted at even the thought, more especially at such an early stage, moreover I had determined, beforehand, to walk my appointed road unaided from the first.

From these depressing thoughts I was presently aroused by a loud, rough voice at no great distance, to which, though I had been dimly conscious of it for some time, I had before paid no attention. Now, however, I raised my eyes from the spot upon the floor, where they had rested hitherto, and fixed them upon the speaker.

He was a square-shouldered, bullet-headed fellow, evidently held in much respect by his companions for he occupied the head of the table, and I noticed that whenever he spoke the others held their peace, and hung upon the words with an appearance of much respect.

32

" ' Yes, sirs,' says I," he began, louder than before,
and with a flourish of his long-stemmed pipe, " ' yes
sirs, Tom Cragg's my name and craggy's my natur','
says I, ' I be 'ard, sirs, dey-vilish 'ard an' uncommon
rocky ! ' ' 'Ere's a face as likes good knocks,' I says,
' w'y when I fought Crib Burke o' Bristol 'e broke 'is
'and again' my jaw, so 'e did, an' I scarce knowed 'e'd
'it me till I see 'im 'oppin' wi' the pain of it. Come,
sirs,' says I, ' who'll give me a black eye, a fiver's all I
ask.' Well, up comes a young buck, ready an'
willin'. ' Tom,' says 'e, ' I'll take two flaps at that
figger-head o' yourn for seven guineas, come, what
d'ye say ? ' I says, ' done,' says I. So my fine
gentleman lays by 'is 'at an' cane, strips off 'is right-
'and glove, an' 'eavin' back lets fly at me. Bang
comes 'is fist agin my jaw, an' there's my gentleman
a-dabbin' at 'is broken knuckles wi' 'is 'ankercher.
' Come, my lord,' says I, ' fair is fair, take your other
whack.' ' Damnation ! ' says 'e, ' take your money
an' go to the devil ! ' says 'e ' I thought you was
flesh an' blood, an' not cast iron ! ' ' Craggy, my
lord,' says I, gathering up the rhino, ' Cragg by name
an' craggy by natur', my lord,' says I."

Hereupon ensued a roar of laughter, with much
slapping of thighs, and stamping of feet, while the
bullet-headed man solemnly emptied his tankard,
which was the signal for two or three of those nearest
to vie for its possession, during which Tom Cragg
sucked dreamily at his pipe and stared placidly up at
the ceiling.

" Now, Tom," said a tall, bony individual, chiefly
remarkable in possessing but one eye, and that so
extremely pale and watery as to give one the idea that
it was very much overworked. " Now, Tom," said
he, setting down the refilled tankard at the great man's
elbow with a triumphant flourish, " tell us 'ow you
shook 'ands wi' the Prince Regent."

" Ah ! tell us," chimed the rest.

" Well," said the bullet-headed man, stooping to
blow the froth from his ale, " it was arter I beat Jack
Nolan of Brummagem. The Prince 'e come a-runnin'

c

to me 'e did, as I sat in my corner a-workin' at a loose tusk. ' Tom,' 'e says, ' Tom, you be a wonder.' ' I done Jack Nolan up proper I think, your 'Ighness,' says I. ' Tom,' says 'e, wi' tears in 'is eyes, ' you 'ave; an' if I' ad my way,' says 'e, ' I' d make you Prime Minister to-morrer ! ' 'e says. An' slapped me on the back 'e did, wi' 'is werry own 'and, an' likewise gave me this' ere pin," saying which, he pointed to a flaming diamond horseshoe which he wore stuck through his neckerchief. The stones were extremely large and handsome, looking very much out of place on the fellow's rough person, and seemed in some part to bear out his story. Though, indeed, as regarded his association with the Prince Regent, whose tastes were at all times peculiar (to say the least), and whose love for " the fancy " was notorious, I thought it, on the whole, very probable; for despite Craggy's words, foolishly blatant though they sounded, there was about him in his low, retreating brow, his small, deep-set eyes, his great square jowl and heavy chin, a certain air there was no mistaking. I also noticed that the upper half of one ear was unduly thick and swollen, which is a mark (I believe) of the professional pugilist alone.

" Tom," cried the one-eyed man, " wot's all this we heerd of Ted Jarraway of Swansea bein' knocked out in five rounds by this 'ere Lord Vibbot, up in London ?"

" Vibbot ? " repeated Cragg, frowning into his tankard, " I 'aven't 'eard of no Vibbot, neither lord, earl, nor dook."

" Come, Tom," coaxed the other, " everybody's heerd o' Buck Vibbot, 'im they calls the ' Fightin' Barronite.' "

" If," said Cragg, rolling his bullet head, " if you was to ask me who put Ted Jarraway to sleep, I should answer you, Sir Maurice Vibart, commonly called ' Buck ' Vibart; an' it took ten rounds to do it, not five."

As may be expected at this mention of my cousin's name I pricked up my ears.

" And what's all this 'bout him ' putting out ' Tom Cragg, in three ? " At this there was a sudden silence and all eyes were turned towards the speaker, a small, red-headed fellow, with a truculent eye. " Come," said he, blowing out a cloud of tobacco smoke, " in three rounds ! What d'ye say to that now, come ? "

Cragg had started up in his chair and now sat scowling at his inquisitor open-mouthed; and in the hush I could hear the ticking of the clock in the corner, and the crackle of the logs upon the hearth. Then, all at once, Cragg's pipe shivered to fragments on the floor and he leapt to his feet. In one stride, as it seemed, he reached the speaker, who occupied the corner opposite mine, but, even as he raised his fist, he checked himself before the pocket-pistol which the other held levelled across the table.

" Come, come—none o' that," said the red-headed man, his eye more truculent than ever, " I ain't a fightin' cove myself, and I don't want no trouble—all I asks is, what about Buck Vibart putting out Tom Cragg—in three rounds ? That's a civil question ain't it—what d'ye say now—come ? "

" I says," cried Tom Cragg, flourishing a great fist in the air, " I says as 'e done it—on a foul ! " And he smote the table a blow that set the glasses ringing.

" Done it on a foul ? " cried three or four voices.

" On a foul ! " repeated Cragg.

" Think again," said the red-headed man, " 'twere said as it was a werry clean knock-out."

" An' I say it were done on a foul," reiterated Cragg, with another blow of his fist, " an' wot's more, if Buck Vibart stood afore me—ah, in this 'ere very room, I'd prove my words."

" Humph ! " said the red-headed man, " they do say as he's wonderful quick wi' his 'mauleys,' an' can hit—like a sledge-hammer."

" Quick wi' 'is 'ands 'e may be, an' able to give a goodish thump, but as for beatin' me—it's ' all me eye an' Betty Martin,' an' you can lay to that, my lads. I could put 'im to sleep any time an' anywhere, an' I'd like—ah ! I'd like to see the chap as says contrairy ! " And here the pugilist scowled round upon his hearers (more especially the red-headed man) so blackly that one or two of them shuffled uneasily, and the latter individual appeared to become interested in the lock of his pistol.

"I'd like," repeated Cragg, "ah! I'd like to see the cove as says contrairy."

"No one ain't a-goin' to, Tom," said the one-eyed man soothingly, "not a soul, Lord bless you!"

"I only wish they would," growled Cragg.

"Ain't there nobody to obleege the gentleman?" inquired the red-headed man.

"I'd fight any man as ever was born—wish I may die!" snorted Cragg.

"You always was so fiery, Tom!" purred the one-eyed man, blinking his pale orb.

"I were," cried the prizefighter, working himself into another rage, "ah! an I'm proud of it. I'd fight any man as ever wore breeches—why, burn me! I'd give any man ten shillin' as could stand up to me for ten minutes."

"Ten shillings!" said I to myself, "ten shillings, when one comes to think of it, is a very handsome sum —more especially when one is penniless and destitute!"

"Wish I may die!" roared Cragg, smiting his fist down on the table again, "a guinea—a golden guinea to the man as could stand on 'is pins an' fight me for five minutes—an' as for Buck Vibart—curse im', I say as 'e won on a foul!"

"A guinea," said I to myself, "is a fortune!" And, setting down my empty tankard, I crossed the room and touched Cragg upon the shoulder.

"I will fight you," said I, "for a guinea."

Now, as the fellow's eyes met mine, he rose up out of his chair and his mouth opened slowly, but he spoke no word, backing from me until he was stayed by the table, where he stood, staring at me. And, once again there fell a silence in which I heard the tick of the clock in the corner and the crackle of the logs upon the hearth.

"You?" said he, recovering himself with an effort, "you?" and, as he spoke, I saw his left eyelid twitch suddenly.

" Exactly," I answered, " I think I can stand up to even you—for five minutes." Now, as I spoke, he winked at he again. That it was meant for me was certain, seeing that his back was towards the others, though what he intended to convey I could form no idea, so I assumed as confident an air as possible and waited. Hereupon the one-eyed man broke into a sudden raucous laugh, in which the others joined.

" 'Ark to 'im, lads," he cried, pointing to me with the stem of his pipe, " 'e be a fine un to stand up to Tom Cragg—I don't think."

" Tell 'un to go an' larn hisself to grow whiskers fust ! " cried a second.

" Ay to be sure, 'e aren't got so much as our old cat ! " grinned a third.

" Stay ! " cried the one-eyed man, peering up at me beneath his hand. " Is they whiskers a-peepin' at me over 'is cravat or do my eyes deceive me ? " Which pleasantry called forth another roar of laughter at my expense.

Now, very foolishly perhaps, this nonsense greatly exasperated me, for I was, at that time, painfully conscious of my bare lips and chin. It was, therefore, with an effort that I mastered my quickly rising temper, and once more addressed myself to Cragg :

" I am willing," said I, " to accept your conditions and fight you—for a guinea— or any other man here for that matter, except the humorous gentleman with the watery eye, who can name his own price." The fellow in question stared at me, glanced slowly round and sitting down, buried his face in his tankard.

" Come, Tom Cragg," said I, " a while ago you seemed very anxious for a man to fight, well—I'm your man," and with the words I stripped off my coat and laid it across a chair-back.

This apparent willingness on my part was but a cloak for my real feelings, for I will not here disguise the fact that the prospect before me was anything but agreeable ; indeed my heart was thumping in a most unpleasant manner, and my tongue and lips had become strangely parched and dry, as I fronted Cragg.

Truly, he looked dangerous enough, with his beetling brow, his great depth of chest, and massive shoulders; and the possibility of a black eye or so and general pounding from the fellow's knotted fists, was daunting in the extreme. Still, the chance of earning a guinea, even under such conditions, was not to be lightly thrown away; therefore I folded my arms and waited with as much resolution as I could.

"Sir," said Cragg, speaking in a very altered tone, "sir, you seem oncommon — eager for it."

"I shall be glad to get it over," said I.

"If," he went on slowly, "if I said anything against—you know who, I'm sorry for it—me 'aving the greatest respec' for—you know who—you understand me I think." And herewith he winked, three separate and distinct times.

"No, I don't understand you in the least," said I, "nor do I think it at all necessary; all that I care about is the guinea in question."

"Come, Tom," cried one of the company, "knock 'is 'ead off to begin with."

"Ay, set about 'im, Tom—cut your gab an' finish 'im," and here came the clatter of chairs as the company rose.

"Can't be done," said Cragg, shaking his head, "leastways—not 'ere."

"I'm not particular," said I, "if you prefer, we might manage it very well in the stable with a couple of lanthorns."

"The barn would be the very place," suggested the landlord, bustling eagerly forward and wiping his hands on his apron, "the very place—plenty of room and nice and soft to fall on. If you would only put off your fightin' till to-morrow, we might cry it through the villages, 'twould be a big draw. Ecod! we might make a purse o' twenty pound—if you only would! Think it over—think it over."

"To-morrow I hope to be a good distance from here," said I, "come, the sooner it is over the better, show us your barn." So the landlord called for lanthorns and led the way to a large outbuilding at the back of the inn, into which we all trooped.

"It seems to be a good place and very suitable," said I.

"You may well say that," returned the landlord, "it's many a fine bout as has been brought off in 'ere; the time Jem Belcher beat 'The Young Ruffian' the Prince o' Wales sat in a cheer over in that theer corner—ah, that was a day if you please!"

"If Tom Cragg is ready," said I, turning up the wrist-bands of my shirt, "why so am I." Here it was found to everyone's surprise, and mine in particular, that Tom Cragg was not in the barn. Surprise gave place to noisy astonishment when, after much running to and fro, it was further learned that he had vanished altogether. The inn itself, the stables, and even the haylofts were ransacked without avail. Tom Cragg was gone as completely as though he had melted into thin air, and with him all my hopes of winning the guinea and a comfortable bed.

It was with all my old dejection upon me, therefore, that I returned to the tap-room, and, refusing the officious aid of the One-Eyed Man, put on my coat, readjusted my knapsack and crossed to the door. On the threshold I paused, and looked back.

"If," said I, glancing round the ring of faces, "if there is any man here who is at all willing to fight for a guinea, ten shillings, or even five, I should be very glad of the chance to earn it." But, seeing how each, wilfully avoiding my eye, held his peace, I sighed, and turning by back upon them, set off along the darkening road.

CHAPTER VII

OF THE FURTHER PUZZLING BEHAVIOUR OF TOM
CRAGG, THE PUGILIST

EVENING had fallen, and I walked along in no very happy frame of mind, the more so, as the rising wind and flying wrack of clouds above (through which a watery moon had peeped at fitful intervals) seemed to presage a wild night. It needed but this to make my misery the more complete, for, as far as I could tell, if I slept at all (and I was already very weary), it must, of necessity, be beneath some hedge or tree.

As I approached the brow of the hill, I suddenly remembered that I must once more pass the gibbet, and began to strain my eyes for it. Presently I spied it, sure enough, its grim, gaunt outline looming through the murk, and instinctively I quickened my stride so as to pass it as soon as might be.

I was almost abreast of it when a figure rose from beneath it and slouched into the road to meet me. I stopped there and then, and grasping my heavy staff waited its approach.

" Be that you, sir ? " said a voice, and I recognised the voice of Tom Cragg.

" What are you doing—and there of all places ? "

" Oh—I ain't afeared of 'im," answered Cragg, jerking his thumb towards the gibbet, " I ain't afeard o' none as ever drawed breath—dead or livin'—except it be 'is 'Ighness the Prince Regent."

" And what do you want with me ? "

" I 'opes as theer's no offence, my lord," said he, knuckling his forehead, and speaking in a tone that was a strange mixture of would-be comradeship and cringing servility, " Cragg is my name, an' craggy's my natur', but I know when I'm beat. I knowed ye as soon as I laid my ' peepers ' on ye, an' if I said as

40

it were a foul, why, when a man's in 'is cups, d'ye see,
'e's apt to shoot rayther wide o' the gospel, d'ye see,
an' there was no offence, my lord, strike me blind!
I know you, an' you know me—Tom Cragg by name
an' craggy by——"

"But I don't know you," said I, "and, for that
matter, neither do you know me."

"W'y you ain't got no whiskers, my lord—leastways, not with you now, but——"

"And what the devil has that got to do with it?"
said I angrily.

"Disguises, p'raps!" said the fellow, with a sly
leer, "arter that theer kidnappin'—an' me avin' laid
out Sir Jasper Trent, in Wych Street, accordin' to
your orders, my lord, the Prince give me word to
'clear out'—cut an' run for it, till it blow'd over; an'
I thought, p'raps, knowin' as you an' 'im 'ad 'ad
words, I thought as you 'ad 'cut stick' too——"

"And I think—that you are manifestly drunk," said
I, "if you still wish to fight, for any sum—no matter
how small—put up your hands, if not, get out of my
road." The craggy one stepped aside, somewhat
hastily, which done, he removed his hat and stood
staring and scratching his bullet head as one in sore
perplexity.

"I seen a many rum goes in my time," said he,
"but I never see so rummy a go as this 'ere—strike
me dead!"

So, I left him, and strode on down the hill. As I
went, the moon shot out a feeble ray, through some
rift in the rolling clouds, and, looking back, I saw him
standing where I had left him beneath the gibbet,
still scratching his bullet head, and staring after me
down the hill.

Now, though the whole attitude and behaviour of
the fellow was puzzling to no small degree, my mind
was too full of my own concerns to give much thought
to him—indeed, scarce was he out of my sight but I
forgot him altogether; for, what with my weariness,
the long, dark road before and behind me, and my
empty pockets, I became a prey to great dejection. So

much so that I presently sank wearily beside the way, and, resting my chin in my hands, sat there, miserably enough, watching the night deepen about me.

" And yet," said I to myself, " if, as Epictetus says —' to despise a thing is to possess it,' then am I rich, for I have always despised money ; and if, weary as I am, I can manage to contemn the luxury of a feather bed, then to-night, lying in this grassy ditch beneath the stars, I shall slumber as sweetly as ever I did between the snowy sheets." Saying which, I rose and began to look about for some likely nook in the hedge, where I might pass the night. I was thus engaged when I heard the creak of wheels, and the pleasant rhythmic jingle of harness on the dark hill above, and, in a little while, a great waggon or wain, piled high with hay, hove into view, the driver of which rolled loosely in his seat with every jolt of the wheels, so that it was a wonder he did not roll off altogether. As he came level with me I hailed him loudly, whereupon he started erect and brought his horses to a stand :

" Halloa ! " he bellowed in the loud, strident tone of one rudely awakened, " w'at do 'ee want wi' I ? "

" A lift," I answered, " will you give a tired fellow a lift on his way ? "

" W'y—I dunno—be you a talkin' chap ? "

" I don't think so," said I.

" Because, if you be a talkin' chap, I beant a-goin' to give 'ee a lift, no'ow—not if I knows it ; give a chap a lift, t'other day, I did—took 'im up t'other side o' Sevenoaks, an' 'e talked me up 'ill an' down 'ill, 'e did—dang me ! if I could get a wink o' sleep all the way to Tonbridge ; so if you'm a talkin' chap, my chap, you don't get no lift wi' I."

" I am generally a very silent chap," said I, "besides, I am too tired and sleepy to talk, even if I wished——"

" Sleepy," yawned the man, " then up you get, my chap—I'm sleepy too—I allus am, I am, Lord love ye ! theer's nowt like sleep—up wi' you, my chap." Forthwith, up I clambered, and, laying myself down among the fragrant hay, stretched out my tired limbs, and sighed. Never shall I forget the delicious sense

of restfulness that stole over me as I lay there upon
my back, listening to the creak of the wheels, the
deliberate hoof-strokes of the horses, muffled in the
thick dust of the road, and the gentle snore of the
driver who had promptly fallen asleep again. On we
went as if borne on air, so soft was my bed, now
beneath the far-flung branches of trees, sometimes so
low that I could have touched them with my hand,
now beneath a sky heavy with sombre masses of flying
cloud or bright with the soft radiance of the moon.
On I went, careless alike of destination, of time, and
of future, content to lie there upon the hay, and rest.
And so lulled by the gentle movement, by the sound of
wheels and harness, and the whisper of the soft wind
about me, I presently fell into a most blessed sleep.

CHAPTER VIII

WHICH CONCERNS ITSELF WITH A FARMER'S
WHISKERS AND A WAISTCOAT

How long I slept I have no idea, but when I opened
my eyes it was to find the moon shining down on me
from a cloudless heaven; the wind also had died away;
it seemed my early fears of a wild night were not to
be fulfilled, and for this I was sufficiently grateful.
Now as I lay, blinking up to the moon, I presently
noticed that we had come to a standstill and I listened
expectantly for the jingle of harness and creak of the
wheels to recommence. "Strange!" said I to myself,
after having waited vainly some little time, and,
wondering what could cause the delay, I sat up and
looked about me. The first object my eyes encountered
was a haystack and, beyond that, another, with a little
to one side, a row of barns, and again beyond these, a
great, rambling farmhouse. Evidently the wain had
reached its destination, wherever that might be, and the
sleepy waggoner, forgetful of my presence, had tumbled
off to bed. The which I thought so excellent an example
that I lay down again, and, drawing the loose hay over
me, closed my eyes, and once more fell asleep.

My second awakening was gradual. I at first became
conscious of a sound, rising and falling with a certain
monotonous regularity, that my drowsy ears could
make nothing of. Little by little, however, the sound
developed itself into a somewhat mournful melody or
refrain, chanted by a not unmusical voice. I yawned
and, having stretched myself, sat up to look and listen.
And the words of the song were these:

> " When a man, who muffins cries,
> Cries not, when his father dies
> 'Tis a proof that he would rather
> Have a muffin than his father."

44

The singer was a tall, strapping fellow with a good-tempered face whose ruddy health was set off by a handsome pair of black whiskers. As I watched him, he laid aside the pitch-fork he had been using, and approached the waggon, but, chancing to look up, his eye met mine, and he stopped :

" Hulloa ! " he exclaimed, breaking short off in the middle of a note, " hulloa ! "

" Hallo ! " said I.

" W'at be doin' up theer ? "

" I was thinking," I returned, " that under certain circumstances, I, for one, could not blame the individual, mentioned in your song, for his passionate attachment to muffins. At this precise moment a muffin—or, say, five or six, would be highly acceptable, personally."

" Be you partial to muffins, then ? "

" Yes indeed," said I, " more especially seeing I have not broken my fast since midday yesterday."

" Well, an' w'at be doin' in my hay ? "

" I have been asleep," said I.

" Well, an' what business 'ave ye got a-sleepin' an' a-snorin' in my hay ? "

" I was tired," said I, " and ' Nature her custom holds, let shame say what it will,' still—I do not think I snored."

" 'Ow do I know that—or you, for that matter ? " rejoined the farmer, stroking his glossy whiskers, " hows' ever, if you be quite awake, come on down out o' my hay." As he said this he eyed me with rather a truculent air, likewise he clenched his fist. Thinking it wisest to appear unconscious of this, I nodded affably, and letting myself down from the hay, was next moment standing beside him.

" Supposin' I was to thump 'ee on the nose ? " he inquired.

" What for ? "

" For makin' so free wi' my hay."

" Why then," said I, " I should earnestly endeavour to thump you on yours."

The farmer looked me slowly over from head to foot, with a dawning surprise.

"Thought you was a common tramper, I did,"
said he.

"Why so I am," I answered, brushing the clinging
hay from me.

"Trampers o' the road don't wear gentlemen's
clothes—leastways, I never see one as did." Here his
eyes wandered over me again, from my boots upward.
Half-way up, they stopped, evidently arrested by my
waistcoat, a flowered satin of the very latest cut, for
which I had paid forty shillings in the Haymarket,
scarcely a week before; and, as I looked down at it,
I would joyfully have given it, and every waistcoat
that was ever cut, to have had that forty shillings safe
back in my pocket again.

"That be a mighty fine weskit, sir!"

"Do you think so?" said I.

"Ah, that I do—w'at might be the cost of a weskit
the like o' that, now?"

"I paid forty shillings for it, in the Haymarket, in
London scarcely a week ago," I answered. The fellow
very slowly closed one eye, at the same time striking
his nose three successive raps with his forefinger:

"Gammon!" said he.

"None the less, it's true," said I.

"Any man as would give forty shillin' for a garment as is no mortal good agen the cold—not reachin'
fur enough, even if it do be silk, an' all worked wi'
little flowers—is a dommed fool!"

"Assuredly!" said I, with a nod.

"Howsomever," he continued, "it's a handsome
weskit, there's no denyin', an' well worth a woman's
lookin' at—wi' a proper man inside of it."

"Not a doubt of it," said I.

"I mean," said he, scratching his ear, and staring
hard at the handle of the pitch-fork, "a chap wi' a fine
pair o' whiskers, say."

"Hum!" said I.

"Now, woman," he went on, shifting his gaze to the
top button of his left gaiter, "woman is uncommon fond
o' a good pair o' whiskers—leastways, so I've heerd."

"Indeed," said I, "few women can look upon such

things unmoved I believe, and nothing can set off a pair of fine, black whiskers better than a flowered satin waistcoat."

" That's so ! " nodded the farmer.

" But, unfortunately," said I, passing my hand over my smooth lips and chin, " I have no whiskers."

" No," returned the farmer, with a thoughtful shake of the head, " leastways, none as I can observe."

" Now, you have," said I.

" So they do tell me," he answered modestly.

" And, the natural inference is that you ought to have a flowered waistcoat to go with them."

" Why that's true, to be sure ! " he nodded.

" The price of this one is—fifteen shillings," said I.

" That's a lot o' money, master," said he, shaking his head.

" It's a great deal less than forty," said I.

" An' ten is less than fifteen, an' ten shillin' is my price, what d'ye say ?—come now."

" You drive a hard bargain," said I, " but the waist-coat is yours at your own price," so saying, I slipped off knapsack and coat, and removing the garment in question, having first felt through the pockets, handed it to him, whereupon he slowly counted the ten shillings into my hand ; which done, he sat down upon the shaft of a cart near by, and, spreading out the waistcoat on his knees, looked it over with glistening eyes.

" Forty shillin' you paid for 'un, up to Lunnon," said he, " forty shilling it were, I think ? "

" Forty shillings ! " said I.

" Ecod, it's a sight o' money ! But it's a grand weskit—ah, that it is ! "

" So you believe me now, do you ? " said I, pocketing the ten shillings.

" Well," he answered slowly, " I won't go so fur as that, but 'tis a mighty fine weskit theer's no denyin', an' must ha' cost a sight o' money—a powerful sight ! " I picked up my knapsack and, slipping it on, took my staff, and turned to depart. " Theer's a mug o' home-brewed, an' a slice o' fine roast beef up at th' 'ouse, if you should be so inclined——"

"Why, as to that," said I, over my shoulder, "I neither eat nor drink with a man who doubts my word."

"Meanin' those forty shillin'?"

"Precisely!"

"Well," said he, twisting his whisker with a thoughtful air, "if you could manage to mak' it twenty—or even twenty-five, I might mak' some shift to believe it—though 'twould be a strain, but forty!— no, damme, I can't swaller that!"

"Then, neither can I swallow your beef and ale," said I.

"Wheer be goin'?" he inquired, rising, and following as I made for the gate.

"To the end of the road," I answered.

"Then you be goin' pretty fur—that theer road leads to the sea."

"Why then I'm going to the sea," said I.

"What to do?"

"I haven't the ghost of an idea," I returned.

"Can you work?"

"Yes," said I.

"Can ye thatch a rick?"

"No," said I.

"Shear a sheep?"

"No," said I.

"Guide a plough?"

"No," said I.

"Shoe a 'oss?"

"No," said I.

"Then ye can't work—Lord love me, wheer 'ave 'e been?"

"At a university," said I.

"Anan, master?"

"At a place warranted to turn one out a highly educated incompetent," I explained.

"Why I don't hold wi' eddication nor book-larnin', myself, master. Here I be wi' a good farm, an' money in the bank, an' can't write my own name," said the farmer.

"And here am I, who did fairly at Oxford,

selling my waistcoat that I may eat," said I. Being
come to the gate of the yard, I paused. "There is
one favour you might grant me," said I.

"As what, master?"

"Five minutes under the pump, yonder, and a clean
towel." The farmer nodded, and crossing to one of
the outhouses, presently returned with a towel. And,
resting the towel upon the pump-head, he seized the
handle, and sent a jet of clear, cool water over my
head, and face, and hands.

"You've got a tidy, sizeable arm," said he, as I
dried myself vigorously, "likewise a good strong
back an' shoulders; theer's the makin's of a man in
you as might do summat—say in the plough or smithin'
way, but it's easy to see as you're a gentleman, more's
the pity, an' won't. Hows'ever, sir, if you've a mind
to a cut o' good beef, an' a mug o' fine ale—say the
word."

"First," said I, "do you believe it was forty shillings—yes or no?"

The farmer twisted his whisker, and stared very
hard at the spout of the pump.

"Tell 'ee what," said he at length, "mak' it thirty,
an' I give ye my bible oath to do the best wi' it I can."

"Then I must needs seek my breakfast at the nearest inn," said I.

"An' that is the 'Old Cock,' a mile an' a half
nearer Tonbridge."

"Then the sooner I start the better," said I, "for
I'm mightily sharp set."

"Why as to that," said he, busy with his whisker
again, "I might stretch a pint or two an' call it—
thirty-five, at a pinch—what d'ye say?"

"Why I say 'good morning,' and many of them!"
And, opening the gate, I started off down the road at
a brisk pace. Now, as I went, it began to rain.

D

CHAPTER IX

IN WHICH I STUMBLE UPON AN AFFAIR OF HONOUR

THERE are times (as I suppose) when the most æsthetic of souls will forget the snow of lilies, and the down of a butterfly's wing, to revel in the grosser joys of, say, a beefsteak. One cannot rhapsodise upon the beauties of a sunset, or contemplate the pale witchery of the moon with any real degree of poetic fervour, or any degree of comfort, while hunger gnaws at one's vitals, for comfort is essential to your æsthete, and, after all, soul goes hand in hand with stomach.

Thus, I swung along the road beneath the swaying green of trees, past the fragrant, blooming hedges, paying small heed to the beauties of wooded hill and grassy dale, my eyes constantly searching the road before me for some sign of the " Old Cock " tavern. And presently, sure enough, I espied it, an ugly, flat-fronted building, before which stood a dilapidated horse trough, and a battered sign. Despite its uninviting exterior, I hurried forward, and mounting the three worn steps pushed open the door. I now found myself in a room of somewhat uninviting aspect, though upon the hearth a fire was smouldering which a sulky-faced fellow was kicking into a blaze, to whom I addressed myself.

" Can I have some breakfast here ? " said I.

" Why it's all according, master," he answered, in a surly tone.

" According to what ? " said I.

" According to what you want, master."

" Why, as to that——" I began.

" Because," he went on, administering a particularly vicious kick to the fire, " if you was to ask me for a French hortolon—or even the 'ump of a cam-el—being a very truthful man, I should say—no."

50

" But I want no such things," said I.

" And 'ow am I to know that—'ow am I to know as you ain't set your 'eart on the 'ump of a cam-el ? "

" I tell you I want nothing of the sort," said I, " a chop would do——"

" Chop ! " sighed the man, scowling threateningly at the fire, " chop ! "

" Or steak," I hastened to add.

" Now it's a steak ! " said the man, shaking his head ruefully, and turning upon me a doleful eye, " a steak ! " he repeated ; " of course—it would be ; I s'pose you'd turn up your nose at 'am and eggs—it's only to be expected."

" On the contrary," said I, " ham and eggs will suit me very well, why couldn't you have mentioned them before ? "

" Why, you never axed me as I remember," growled the fellow.

Slipping my knapsack from my shoulders, I sat down at a small table in a corner while the man, with a final kick at the fire, went to give my order. In a few minutes he reappeared with some billets of wood beneath his arm, and followed by a merry-eyed, rosy-cheeked lass, who proceeded, very deftly, to lay a snowy cloth and thereupon, in due season, a dish of savoury ham, and golden-yolked eggs.

" It's a lovely morning ! " said I, lifting my eyes to her comely face.

" It is indeed, sir," said she, setting down the cruet with a turn of her slender wrist.

" Which I make so bold as to deny," said the surly man, dropping the wood on the hearth with a prodigious clatter, " 'ow can any morning be lovely when there ain't no love in it—no, not so much as would fill a thimble ? I say it ain't a lovely morning, not by no manner o' means, and what I says I ain't ashamed on, being a nat'rally truthful man ! " With which words he sighed, kicked the fire again, and stumped out.

" Our friend would seem somewhat gloomy this morning," said I.

"He've been that way a fortnight now, come Saturday," replied the slim lass, nodding.

"Oh?" said I.

"Yes," she continued, checking a smile, and sighing instead; "it's very sad, he've been crossed in love you see, sir."

"Poor fellow!" said I, "can't you try to console him?"

"Me, sir—oh no!"

"And why not? I should think you might console a man for a great deal."

"Why you see, sir," said she, blushing and dimpling very prettily, "it do so happen as I'm the one as crossed him."

"Ah!—I understand," said I.

"I'm to be married to a farmer—down the road yonder; leastways, I haven't quite made up my mind yet."

"A fine, tall fellow?" I inquired.

"Yes—do 'ee know him, sir?"

"With a handsome pair of black whiskers?" said I.

"The very same, sir, and they do be handsome whiskers, though I do say it."

"The finest I ever saw. I wish you every happiness," said I.

"Thankee, sir, I'm sure," said she, and, dimpling more prettily than ever, she tripped away, and left me to my repast.

And when I had assuaged my hunger, I took out the pipe of Adam, the groom, the pipe shaped like a negro's head, and, calling for a paper of tobacco, I filled, and lighted the pipe, and sat staring dreamily out of the window.

Happy is that man who, by reason of an abundant fortune, knows not the meaning of the word hunger; but thrice happy is he who, when the hand of famine pinches, may stay his craving with such a meal as this of mine. Never before, and never since have I tasted just such eggs, and such ham—so tender! so delicate! so full of flavour! It is a memory that can never fade. Indeed sometimes (even now), when I grow hungry, (about dinner-time) I see once more the surly-faced man, the rosy-cheeked waiting-maid, and the gloomy chamber of the "Old Cock" tavern as I saw them upon that early May morning of the year of grace 18—.

So I sat, with a contented mind, smoking my pipe, and staring out at the falling summer rain. And presently, chancing to turn my eyes up the road, I beheld a chaise that galloped in a smother of mud. As I watched its rapid approach, the postilion swung his horses towards the inn, and a moment later had pulled up before the door. They had evidently travelled fast and far, for the chaise was covered with dirt, and the poor horses, in a lather of foam, hung their heads, while their flanks heaved distressfully.

The chaise door was now thrown open, and three gentlemen alighted. The first was a short, plethoric individual, bull-necked and loud of voice, for I could hear him roundly cursing the post-boy for some fault; the second was a tall, languid gentleman, who carried a flat, oblong box beneath one arm, and who paused to fondle his whisker, and look up at the inn with an exaggerated air of disgust; while the third stood mutely by, his hands thrust into the pockets of his greatcoat, and stared straight before him.

The three of them entered the room together, and, while the languid gentleman paused to survey himself in the small, cracked mirror that hung against the wall, the plethoric individual bustled to the fire, and loosening his coats, and neckerchief, spread out his hands to the blaze.

"A good half-hour before our time," said he, glancing towards the third gentleman, who stood looking out of the window with his hands still deep in his pockets, "we did the last ten miles well under the hour—come, what do you say to a glass of brandy?"

At this, his languid companion turned from the mirror, and I noticed that he too, glanced at the silent figure by the window.

"By all means," said he, "though Sir Jasper would hardly seem in a drinking humour," and, with the very slightest shrug of the shoulders, he turned back to the mirror again.

"No, Mr Chester, I am not—in a drinking humour," answered Sir Jasper, without turning round, or taking his eyes from the window.

"Sir Jasper?" said I to myself, "now where, and in what connection, have I heard such a name before?"

He was of a slight build, and seemingly younger than either of his companions by some years, but what struck me particularly about him was the extreme pallor of his face. I noticed also a peculiar habit he had of moistening his lips at frequent intervals with the tip of his tongue, and there was, besides, something in the way he stared at the trees, the wet road, and the grey sky—a strange wide-eyed intensity—that drew, and held, my attention.

"Devilish weather—devilish, on my life and soul!" exclaimed the short, red-faced man, in a loud, peevish tone, tugging viciously at the bell-rope, "hot one day, cold the next, now sun, now rain—— Oh damn it! Now in France—ah, what a climate—heavenly—positively divine; say what you will of a Frenchman, damn him by all means, but the climate, the country, and the women—who would not worship 'em?"

"Exactly!" said the languid gentleman, examining a pimple upon his chin, with a high degree of interest, "always 'dored a Frenchwoman myself; they're so—so—ah—so deuced French, though mark you, Selby," he broke off, as the rosy-cheeked maid appeared with the brandy and glasses, "though mark you, there's much to be said for your English country wenches, after all," saying which, he slipped his arm about the girl's round waist: there was the sound of a kiss, a muffled shriek, and she had run from the room, slamming the door behind her, whereupon the languid gentleman went back to his pimple.

"Oh! as to that, Chester, I quarrel only with the climate. God made England, and the devil sends the weather!"

"Selby," said Sir Jasper, in the same repressed tone that he had used before, and still without taking his

Face Page 54

something this morning, reading these things, but I mean

"Strange, is it?"

something—— conflicting——

how been——something green

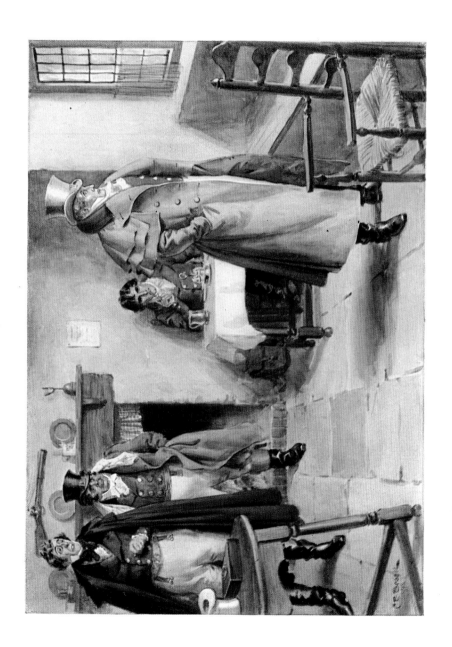

eyes from the grey prospect of sky and tree and winding road, "there is no fairer land, in all the world, than this England of ours; it were a good thing to die—for England, but that is a happiness reserved for comparatively few." And, with the words, he sighed, a strange, fluttering sigh, and thrust his hands deeper into his pockets.

"Die!" repeated the man Selby, in a loud, boisterous way. "Who talks of death?"

"Deuced unpleasant subject!" said the other, with a shrug at the cracked mirror, "something so infernally cold and clammy about it—like the weather."

"And yet it will be a glorious day later. The clouds are thinning already," Sir Jasper went on; "strange, but I never realised, until this morning, how green—and wonderful—everything is!"

The languid Mr Chester forgot the mirror, and turned to stare at Sir Jasper's back, with raised brows, while the man Selby shook his head, and smiled unpleasantly. As he did so, his eye encountered me, where I sat, quietly in my corner, smoking my negro-head pipe, and his thick brows twitched sharply together in a frown.

"In an hour's time, gentlemen," pursued Sir Jasper, "we shall write 'finis' to a more or less interesting incident, and I beg of you, in that hour, to remember my prophecy—that it would be a glorious day, later."

Mr Chester filled a glass, and crossing to the speaker, tendered it to him without a word; as for Selby, he stood stolidly enough, his hands thrust truculently beneath his coat-tails, frowning at me.

"Come," said Mr Chester persuasively, "just a bracer!" Sir Jasper shook his head, but next moment reached out a white, unsteady hand, and raised the brandy to his lips; yet as he drank, I saw the spirit slop over, and trickle from his chin.

"Thanks, Chester," said he, returning the empty glass; "is it time we started yet?"

"It's just half-past seven," answered Mr Chester, consulting his watch, "and I'm rather hazy as to the exact place."

"Deepdene Wood," said Sir Jasper dreamily.

" You know the place ? "

" Oh yes ! "

" Then we may as well start, if you are ready ? "

" Yes, it will be cool, and fresh, outside."

" Settle the bill, Selby, we'll walk on slowly," said Mr Chester, and, with a last glance at the mirror, he slipped his arm within Sir Jasper's, and they went out together.

Mr Selby, meanwhile, rang for the bill, frowning at me all the time.

" What the devil are you staring at ? " he demanded suddenly in a loud, bullying tone.

" If you are pleased to refer to me, sir," said I, " I would say that my eyes were given for use, and that having used them upon you, I have long since arrived at the conclusion that I don't like you."

" Ah ? " said he, frowning fiercer than ever.

" Yes," said I, " though whether it is your person, your manner or your voice that displeases me most, I am unable to say."

" An impertinent young jackanapes ! " said he; " damnation, I think I'll pull your nose ! "

" Why, you may try, and welcome, sir," said I, " though I should advise you not, for should you make the attempt I should be compelled to throw you out of the window."

At this moment, the pretty maid appeared, and tendered him the bill with a curtesy. He glanced at it, tossed some money upon the table, and turned to stare at me again.

" If ever I meet you again——" he began.

" You'd probably know me," I put in.

" Without a doubt," he answered, putting on his hat and buttoning his befrogged surtout; "and should you," he continued, drawing on his gloves, " should you stare at me with those damned, impertinent fishes' eyes of yours, I should, most certainly, pull your nose for you—on the spot, sir."

" And I should as certainly throw you out of the window ! " I nodded.

"An impertinent young jackanapes!" said he again, and went out, banging the door behind him. Glancing from the window, I saw him catch up with the other two, and all three walk on together down the road. Sir Jasper was in the middle, and I noticed that his hands were still deep in his pockets. Now, as I watched their forms getting smaller and smaller in the distance, there grew upon me a feeling that he who walked between would never more come walking back.

And, in a little, having knocked out my negro-head pipe upon my palm, I called for and settled my score. As I rose, the pretty chambermaid picked up my knapsack from the corner, and blushing, aided me to put in on.

"My dear, thank you," said I, and kissed her. This time she neither shrieked nor ran from the room, she merely blushed a trifle rosier.

"Do you think I have fishes' eyes, my dear?"

"La! no, sir—handsome they be, I'm sure, so bright an' black an' wi' little lights a-dancing in them —there, sir, do ha' done, and go along wi' you!"

"By the way," I said, pausing upon the worn steps, and looking back at her, "by the way, how far is it to Deepdene Wood?"

CHAPTER X

WHICH RELATES THE END OF AN HONOURABLE
AFFAIR

SOME half-mile along the road, upon the left hand, was a stile, and beyond the stile, a path—a path that led away over field, and meadow, and winding stream, to the blue verge of distant woods.

Now, midway between these woods and the place where I stood, there moved three figures; and, far away though they were, I could still make out that the middle one walked with his hands—those tremulous, betraying hands—thrust deep within his pockets.

And presently I climbed the stile, and set off along the path.

" Sir Jasper ! " said I to myself. Somewhere in the background of my consciousness I had a vague recollection of having heard mention of such a name before, but exactly when and where I could not, for the life of me, remember.

" Sir Jasper ! " said I to myself again. " It is a very uncommon name, and should be easy to recollect." I had often prided myself on possessing a singularly retentive memory, more especially for names and faces, but, upon the present occasion, the more I pondered the matter, the more hazy I became. So I walked on through the sweet, wet grass, racking my brain for a solution of the problem, but finding none.

When I again looked up, the three figures had vanished where the path took a sharp bend round a clump of pollard oaks, and, determined not to lose them, I hurried my steps; but when I, in turn, rounded the corner, not a soul was in sight.

The path sloped up gently before me, with a thick hedge upon my right, and, after crossing a brawling stream, lost itself in the small wood or coppice, that

58

crowned the ascent. Wondering, I hastened forward, and then, happening to look through the hedge, which grew very thick and high, I stopped all at once.

On the other side of the hedge was a strip of meadow bounded by the brook I have mentioned; now across this stream was a small rustic bridge, and on this bridge was a man. Midway between this man and myself stood a group of four gentlemen, all talking very earnestly together, to judge by their actions, while somewhat apart from these, his head bent, his hands still thrust deep in his pockets, stood Sir Jasper. And from him, for no apparent reason, my eyes wandered to the man upon the bridge—a tall, broad-shouldered fellow, in a buff-coloured great-coat, who whistled to himself, and stared down into the stream, swinging his tasselled riding-boot to and fro. All at once, as if in response to some signal, he rose, and unbuttoning his surtout, drew it off and flung it across the handrail of the bridge.

Mr Chester was on his knees before the oblong box, and I saw the glint of the pistols as he handed them up. The distance had already been paced, and marked out, and now each man took his ground—Sir Jasper, still in his great-coat, his hat over his eyes, his neckerchief lose and dangling, one hand in his pocket, the other grasping his weapon; his antagonist, on the contrary, jaunty and debonnaire, a dandy from the crown of his hat to the soles of his shining boots.

Their arms were raised almost together. The man Selby glanced from one to the other, a handkerchief fluttered, fell, and in that instant came the report of a pistol. I saw Sir Jasper reel backward, steady himself, and fire in return; then, while the blue smoke yet hung in the still air, he staggered blindly, and fell.

Mr Chester, and two or three more, ran forward, and knelt beside him, while his opponent shrugged his shoulders, and, taking off his hat, pointed out the bullet hole to his white-faced second.

And in a little while they lifted Sir Jasper in their arms, but seeing how his head hung, a sudden sickness came upon me, for I knew, indeed, that he would go walking back nevermore. Yet his eyes were wide and staring—staring up at the blue heaven with the same fixed intensity as they had done at the inn.

Then I too looked up at the cloudless sky, and round upon the fair earth; and, in that moment, I for one remembered his prophecy of an hour ago. And, indeed, the day was glorious.

CHAPTER XI

WHICH RELATES A BRIEF PASSAGE-AT-ARMS AT "THE CHEQUERS" INN

In due season I came into Tonbridge town, and following the High Street, presently observed a fine inn upon the right-hand side of the way, which, as I remember, is called "The Chequers." And here were divers loiterers, lounging round the door, or seated upon the benches, but the eyes of all were turned the one way.

And presently, as I paused before the inn, to look up at its snow-white plaster, and massive cross-beams, there issued from the stable yard one in a striped waistcoat, with top-boots and a red face, who took a straw from behind his ear, and began to chew it meditatively; to whom I now addressed myself.

" Good afternoon ! " said I.

" Arternoon ! " he answered.

" A fine day ! " said I.

" Is it ? " said he.

" Why—to be sure it is," said I, somewhat taken aback by his manner; " to be sure it is."

" Oh ! " said he, and shifted the straw very dexterously from one corner of his mouth to the other, by some unseen agency, and stared up the road harder than ever.

" What are you looking at ? " I inquired.

" 'Ill," said he.

" And why do you look at the hill ? "

" Mail," said he.

" Oh ! " said I.

" Ah ! " said he.

" Is it the London coach ? "

" Ah ! " said he.

" Does it stop here ? "

61

" Ah ! " said he.

"Do you ever say anything much beside ' ah ' ? " I inquired.

He stopped chewing the straw, and with his eyes on the distance, seemed to turn this question over in his mind ; having done which, he began to chew again.

" Ah ! " said he.

" Why then you can, perhaps, tell me how many miles it is——"

" Five,' said he.

" I was about to ask how far it was to——"

" The Wells ! " said he.

" Why—yes, to be sure, but how did you know that ? "

" It's use ! " said he.

" What do you mean ? "

" They all ask ! " said he.

" Who do ? "

" Tramps ! " said he.

" Oh ! so you take me for a tramp ? "

" Ah ! " said he.

" And you," said I, " put me in mind of a certain Semiquavering Friar."

" Eh ? " said he, frowning a little at the hill.

" You've never heard of Rabelais, or Panurge, of course," said I. The Ostler took out his straw, eyed it thoughtfully, and put it back again.

" No," said he.

" More's the pity ! " said I, and was about to turn away, when he drew the nearest fist abruptly from his pocket, and extended it towards me.

" Look at that ! " he commanded.

" Rather dirty," I commented, " but otherwise a good, useful member, I make no doubt."

" It's a-goin'," said he, alternately drawing in and shooting out the fist in question, " it's a-goin' to fill your eye up."

" Is it ? " said I.

" Ah ! " said he.

" But what for ? "

" I aren't a Semmy, nor yet a Quaver, an' as for

Friers," said he, very deliberately, "why—Frier yourself, says I."

"Nevertheless," said I, "you are gifted with a
certain terse directness of speech that greatly reminds
me of——"

"Joe!" he called out suddenly over his shoulder.
"Mail, Joe!"

Lifting my eyes to the brow of the hill I could see
nothing save a faint haze, which, however, gradually
grew denser and thicker, and out from this gathering
cloud, soft, and faint with distance, stole the silvery
notes of a horn. Now I saw the coach itself, and, as
I watched it rapidly descending the hill I longed to be
upon it, with the sun above, the smooth road below,
and the wind rushing through my hair. On it came at
a gallop, rocking and swaying, a good fifteen miles an
hour; on it came, plunging into the green shade of
trees, and out into the sun again, with ever the gathering dust cloud behind; while clear, and high, rang the
cheery note of the horn. And now, from the cool
shadows of the inn yard, there rose a prodigious
stamping of hoofs, rattling of chains, and swearing of
oaths, and out came four fresh horses, led by two men,
each of whom wore top-boots, a striped waistcoat, and
chewed upon straws.

And now the coach swung round the bend, and
came thundering down upon "The Chequers," chains
jingling, wheels rumbling, horn braying and, with a
stamp and ring of hoof, pulled up before the inn.

And now, what a running to and fro! what a prodigious unbuckling and buckling of straps, while the
jovial-faced coachman fanned himself with his hat,
and swore jovially at the ostlers, and the ostlers swore
back at the coachman, and the guard, and the coach,
and the horses, individually and collectively; in the
midst of which confusion, down came the window with
a bang, and out of the window came a flask, and a
hand, and an arm, and, last of all, a great, fat face,
round, and mottled, and roaring as it came:

"Oho—I say damn it! damn everybody's eyes and
bones—brandy! O yoho, house—I say brandy!

Guard, landlord, ostlers—brandy, d'ye hear? I say
what the devil! Am I to die for want of a drop of
brandy? Oho!"

Now, little by little, I became conscious (how, I
cannot define) that I was the object of a close and
persistent scrutiny—that I was being watched, and
stared at by someone near by. Shifting my eyes,
therefore, from the mottled face at the coach window,
I cast them swiftly about until they presently met
those of one of the four outside passengers—a tall,
roughly-clad man who leaned far out from the coach
roof, watching me intently; and his face was thin,
and very pale, and the eyes which stared into mine
glowed beneath a jagged prominence of brow.

At the time, though I wondered at the man's expression, and the fixity of his gaze, I paid him no
further heed but turned my attention back to Mottle-
face, who had, by this time, bellowed himself purple.
Howbeit, in due time, the flask having been re-
plenished, and handed to him, he dived back into the
recesses of the coach, jerked up the window, and
vanished as suddenly as he had appeared.

But now the four fresh horses were in, and harnessed,
capering and dancing with an ostler at the head of
each; the Driver tossed off his glass of rum and water,
cast an eye up at the clouds, remarked: " Wind, by
Gemini! " settled his feet against the dashboard, and
gathered up the reins; and now, too, the Guard
appeared, wiping his lips as he came, who also cast
an eye up at the heavens, remarked: " Dust, by
Jingo! " and swung himself up into the rumble.

" All right behind? " sang out the Driver, over his
shoulder.

" All right! " sang back the Guard.

" Then—let 'em go! " cried the Driver. Whereupon
the ostlers jumped nimbly back, the horses threw up
their heads, and danced undecidedly for a moment, the
long whip cracked, hoofs clattered, sparks flew, and,
rumbling and creaking, off went the London Mail with
such a flourish of the horn as woke many a sleepy
echo, near and far. As I turned away, I noticed that

there remained but three outside passengers; the pale-faced man had evidently alighted, yet, although I glanced round for him, he was nowhere to be seen.

Hereupon, being in no mind to undergo the operation of having my eye filled up, and, moreover, finding myself thirsty, I stepped into the " Tap." And there, sure enough, was the Outside Passenger staring moodily out of the window, and with an untouched mug of ale at his elbow. Opposite him sat an old man in a smock frock, who leaned upon a holly-stick, talking to a very short, fat man behind the bar, who took my twopence with a smile, smiled as he drew my ale, and, smiling, watched me drink.

" Be you from Lunnon, sir ? " inquired the old man, eyeing me beneath his hoary brows as I set down my tankard.

" Yes," said I.

" Well, think o' that now—I've been a-goin' to Lunnon this five and forty year—started out twice, I did, but I never got no furder nor Sevenoaks ! "

" How was that ? " I inquired.

" Why, theer's ' The White Hart ' at Sevenoaks, an' they brews fine ale at ' The White Hart,' d'ye see, an' one glass begets another."

" And they sent ye back in the carrier's cart ! " said the fat man, smiling broader than ever.

" Ever see the Lord Mayor a-ridin' in 'is goold coach, sir ? " pursued the old man.

" Yes," said I.

" Ever speak to 'im ? "

" Why, no."

" Ah well, I once knowed a man as spoke to the Lord Mayor o' Lunnon's coachman—but 'e's dead, took the smallpox the year arterwards an' died, 'e did."

At this juncture the door was thrown noisily open, and two gentlemen entered. The first was a very tall man with black hair that curled beneath his hat-brim, and so luxuriant a growth of whisker that it left little of his florid countenance exposed. The second was more slightly built, with a pale, hairless face, wherein

E

were set two small, very bright eyes, rather close together, separated by a high, thin nose with nostrils that worked and quivered when he spoke, a face whose most potent feature was the mouth, coarse and red, with a somewhat protuberant under lip, yet supported by a square, determined chin below—a sensual mouth with more than a suspicion of cruelty lurking in its full curves, and the big teeth which gleamed white and serrated when he laughed. Indeed the whole aspect of the man filled me with an instinctive disgust.

They were dressed in that mixture of ultra-fashionable and horsey styles peculiar to the " Corinthian," or "Buck " of the period, and there was in their air an overbearing yet lazy insolence towards all and sundry that greatly annoyed me.

" Fifteen thousand a year, by gad ! " exclaimed the taller of the two, giving a supercilious sniff to the brandy he had just poured out.

" Yes, ha ! ha !—and a damnably pretty filly into the bargain ! "

" You always were so infernally lucky ! " retorted the first.

" Call it rather the reward of virtue," answered his companion with a laugh that showed his big, white teeth.

" And what of Beverley—poor dey-vil ? " inquired the first.

"Beverley !" repeated the other ; "had he possessed any spirit he would have blown his brains out, like a gentleman ; as it was, he preferred merely to disappear," and herewith the speaker shrugged his shoulders, and drank off his glass with infinite relish and gusto.

" And a—pretty filly, you say ? "

" Oh, I believe you ! Country bred, but devilish well-blooded—trust Beverley for that."

" Egad yes—Beverley had a true eye for beauty or breed, poor dey-vil ! " This expression of pity seemed to afford each of them much subtle enjoyment. " Harking back to this—filly," said the big man, checking his merriment, " how if she jibs, and cuts up rough, kicks over the traces—deyvilish awkward, eh ? "

His companion raised his foot and rested it carelessly upon the settle near by, and upon the heel of his
slim riding-boot I saw a particularly cruel-looking,
long-necked spur.

" My dear Mostyn," said he, his nostrils working,
" for such an emergency there is nothing like a pair
of good sharp ' persuaders,' " here the tapped the
spur lightly with the slender gold-mounted cane he
carried, " and I rather fancy I know just how and
when to use 'em, Mostyn." And once again I saw
the gleam of his big, white teeth.

All this I heard as they lolled within a yard of me,
manifesting a lofty and contemptuous disregard for all
save themselves, waited upon most deferentially by the
smiling fat fellow, and stared at by the aged man with
as much admiring awe as if they had each been nothing
less than a lord mayor of London at the very least.
But now they leaned their heads together and spoke
in lowered tones, but something in the leering eyes of
the one, and the smiling lips of the other, told me that
it was not of horses that they spoke.

" . . . Bring her to reason, by gad ! " said the
slighter of the two, setting down his empty glass with
a bang, " oh, trust me to know their pretty, skittish
ways, trust me to manage 'em—I've never failed yet,
by gad ! "

" Curse me, that's true enough ! " said the other,
and here they sank their voices again.

My ale being finished, I took up my staff, a heavy,
knotted affair, and turned to go. Now, as I did so,
my foot, by accident, came in contact with the gold-
mounted cane I have mentioned, and sent it clattering
to the floor. I was on the point of stooping for it,
when a rough hand gripped my shoulder from behind,
twisting me savagely about, and I thus found myself
staring upon two rows of sharp, white teeth.

" Pick it up ! " said he, motioning imperiously to
the cane on the floor between us.

" Heaven forbid, sir," said I; " ' is thy servant a
dog that he should do this thing ' ? "

" I told you to pick it up," he repeated, thrusting

his head towards me; " are you going to do so, or must I make you?" and his nostrils worked more than ever.

For answer I raised my foot and sent the cane spinning across the room. Somebody laughed, and next moment my hat was knocked from my head. Before he could strike again, however, I raised my staff, but suddenly remembering its formidable weight, I altered the direction of the blow, and thrust it strongly into the very middle of his gaily flowered waistcoat. So strongly did I thrust, indeed, that he would have fallen but for the timely assistance of his companion.

" Come, come," said I, holding him off on the end of my staff, " be calm now, and let us reason together like logical beings. I knocked down your cane by accident, and you, my hat by intent; very well then, be so good as to return me my property, from the corner yonder, and we will call 'quits.' "

" No, by gad! " gasped my antagonist, bending almost double, " wait—only wait until I get—my wind—I'll choke—the infernal life out of you—only wait, by gad! "

" Willingly," said I, " but whatever else you do, you will certainly reach me my hat, otherwise, just so soon as you find yourself sufficiently recovered, I shall endeavour to throw you after it." Saying which, I laid aside my staff, and buttoned up my coat.

" Why," he began, " you infernally low, dusty, ditch-trotting blackguard——". But his companion, who had been regarding me very closely, twitched him by the sleeve, and whispered something in his ear. Whatever it was it affected my antagonist strangely, for he grew suddenly very red, and then very white, and abruptly turned his back upon me.

" Are you sure, Mostyn? " said he in an undertone.

" Certain."

" Well, I'd fight him were he the devil himself! Pistols perhaps would be——"

" Don't be a fool, Harry," cried the other, and seizing his arm, drew him farther away, and, though they lowered their voices I caught such fragments as

" What of George ? " " changes since your time," " ruin your chances at the start," " dead shot."

" Sir," said I, " my hat—in the corner yonder."

Almost to my surprise the taller of the two crossed the room, followed by his friend, to whom he still spoke in lowered tones, stooped, picked up my hat, and, while the other stood scowling, approached, and handed it to me with a bow.

" That my friend, Sir Harry Mortimer, lost his temper is regretted both by him and myself," said he, " but is readily explained by the fact that he has been a long time from London, while I laboured under a— a disadvantage, sir—until your hat was off."

Now, as he spoke, his left eyelid flickered twice in rapid succession.

" I beg you won't mention it," said I, putting on my hat, " but, sir, why do you wink at me ? "

" No, no," cried he, laughing and shaking his head, " ha ! ha !—deyvilish good ! By the way, they tell me George himself is in these parts—incog. of course——"

" George ? " said I, staring.

" Cursed rich, on my life and soul ! " cried the tall gentleman, shaking his head and laughing again, " mum's the word, of course, and I swear a shaven face becomes you most deyvilishly ! "

" Perhaps you will be so obliging as to tell me what you mean ? " said I, frowning.

" Oh, by gad ! " he cried, fairly hugging himself with delight. " Oh, the devil ! this is too rich—too infernally rich, on my life and soul it is ! "

Now all at once there recurred to me the memory of Tom Cragg, the Pugilist; of how he too had winked at me, and of his incomprehensible manner afterwards beneath the gibbet on River Hill.

" Sir," said I, " do you happen to know a pugilist Tom Cragg by name ? "

" Tom Cragg ! well, I should think so, who doesn't, sir ? "

" Because," I went on, " he too seems to labour under the delusion that he is acquainted with me, and——"

" Acquainted ! " repeated the tall gentleman, " acquainted ! Oh, gad ! " and immediately hugged himself in another ecstasy.

" If," said I, " you will have the goodness to tell me for whom you evidently mistake me——"

" Mistake you ! " he gasped, throwing himself upon the settle and rocking to and fro, " ha ! ha !—mistake you ! "

Seeing I did but waste my breath, I turned upon my heel, and made for the door. As I went, my eye, by chance, lighted upon a cheese that stood at the fat landlord's elbow, and upon which he cast amorous glances from time to time.

" That seems a fine cheese ! " said I.

" It is, sir, if I might make so bold, a noble cheese ! " he rejoined, and laid his hand upon it with a touch that was a caress.

" Then I will take three pennyworth of your noble cheese," said I.

" Cheese ! " faintly echoed the gentleman upon the settle, " three pennyworth. Oh, I shall die, positively I shall burst ! "

" Also, a loaf," said I. And when the landlord had cut the cheese, with great nicety—a generous portion—and had wrapped it into a parcel, I put it, together with the loaf, into my knapsack, and giving him " Good-day ! "—strode to the door. As I reached it the tall gentleman rose from the settle, and bowed.

" Referring to George, sir——"

" George ! " said I shortly, " to the devil with George ! "

Now I could not help being struck by the effect of my words, for Sir Harry let fall his cane, and stared open-mouthed, while his companion regarded me with an expression between a frown and wide-eyed dismay.

" Now I wonder," said I to myself as I descended the steps, " I wonder who George can be ? "

Before the inn there stood a yellow-wheeled stanhope with a horse which, from his manner of trembling all over for no conceivable reason, and manifest desire to stand upon his hind legs, I conceived to be a thoroughbred; and, hanging grimly to the bridle, now in the air, now on terra-firma, alternately coaxing and cursing, was my friend the Semiquavering Ostler. He caught sight of me just as a particularly vicious jerk swung him off his legs.

" Damn your liver ! " he cried to the horse, and then, to me : " If you'll jest call Joe to 'old this 'ere black varmin for me I'll—fill yer—eye up."

" Thanks," said I, " but I much prefer to keep it as it is, really there is no need to trouble Joe, and as for you, I wish you good-morning ! "

And when I had gone a little way, chancing to glance back over my shoulder, I saw that the Outside Passenger stood upon the inn steps, and was staring after me.

CHAPTER XII

THE ONE-LEGGED SOLDIER

FOLLOWING the high road I came, in a little, to where the ways divided, the one leading straight before me, the other turning sharp to the left, where (as I remember) is a very steep hill.

And at the parting of the ways was a finger-post with the words: "To LONDON. To TONBRIDGE WELLS. To PEMBRY." Now as I stood beneath the finger-post, debating which road I should take, I was aware of the sound of wheels, and glancing about, saw a carrier's cart approaching. The driver was a fine, tall, ruddy-faced fellow, very spruce as to his person, who held himself with shoulders squared, and bolt upright, and who shouted a cheery greeting to me.

"If so be you are for Pembry, or thereabouts, sir," said he, bringing his horses to a standstill, "why, jump up, sir—that is, if you be so minded."

"My course lies anywhere," said I.

"Then—if you be so minded——?"

"I am so minded," said I.

"Then, sir, jump up," said he.

"Thanks!" said I.

So I climbed upon the seat beside him, and then I saw that he had a wooden leg, and straightway understood his smart bearing, and general neat appearance.

"You have been a soldier?" said I.

"And my name's Tom, and I could tell you a sight about them Spanishers, and Frenchies—that is, if—you be so minded?"

"I am so minded—fire away, Tom."

"Well," he began, fixing his eyes on the "wheeler's" ears, "they Frenchies ain't so bad as is thought, though they do eat frogs, but what I say is—if they be so minded—why frogs let it be!"

" To be sure ! " said I.

" And after all they're well worth fighting, and that's more than you can say for a many ! "

" True," said I, " one generally has a certain respect for the man one fights."

" Then there's Old Bony."

" Have you ever seen him ? "

" I have, sir, I were captured outside the Lines of Torres Vedras, and I saw Old Bony eating his breakfast off a drum-head wi' one hand and a-writing a dispatch wi' the other—a little fat man not so high as my shoulder, look you. There's some as says as Old Bony lives on new-born babies, but I know different. Because why, says you ? Because I've seen with these 'ere ' peepers,' says I—bread it were, and cheese, and garlic, and a uncommon lot at that."

" And where did you lose your leg, Tom ? "

" Vittoria—I 'appened to be carrying my off'cer, Ensign Standish his name, barely eighteen year old. Shot through the lung he were, and a-trying to tell me to put him down and go, the fire being uncommonly 'ot there, you'll understand, sir, and as I say he were trying to tell me to drop him and run for it, and blowing blood-bubbles wi' every word, when all at once I feels a sort of a shock, and there I was on my back and him atop o' me ; and when I went to get up— damme ! there was my leg gone below the knee, and no pleasant sight, neither.'

" And afterward ? "

" Arterwards," he repeated. " Why, that were the end o' my sojerin', ye see ; we lay in the same 'ospital 'im an' me, side by side, and he swore as I'd saved his life—which I 'adn't, look you, and likewise swore as he'd never forget it. And he never 'as either, for here am I wi' my own horse and cart, Tom Price by name, carrier by trade, an' very much at your service, sir, I'm sure."

Thus we climbed the hill of Pembry, by tree and hedge, and lonely cottage, by rolling meadow, and twilit wood, Tom the Soldier and I.

Much he told me of lonely night watches, of death

sudden and sharp, of long, weary marches, and stricken fields, of the bloody doings of the Spanish Guerrillas, of Mina, and his deviltries. And in my ears was the roar of guns, and before my eyes the gleam, and twinkle of bayonets. By the side of Tom the Soldier I waited the thunderous charge of French Dragoons, saw their stern, set faces, and the flash of their brandished steel as they swept down upon our devoted square, swept down to break in red confusion before our bristling bayonets; and the air was full of the screams of smitten horses, and the deep-throated shouts and groans of men. By the side of Tom the Soldier I stormed through many a reeking breach, swept by fire, and slippery with blood; and all for love of it, the munificent sum of eightpence per day, and that which we call "Glory." Bravo, Tom the Soldier!

And presently I became aware that he had stopped his horses, and was regarding me smilingly.

"Tom," said I, "you are a wonderful talker!"

"And you, sir," said he, "are a better listener, and, look you, a good listener is mighty hard to come by. Howsomever, here's the end o' my journey, more's the pity, but if you——"

"Tom," said I suddenly, "you never heard of Tom Cragg, did you?"

"Can't say as I have," he answered, stroking his chin thoughtfully, "though there was a Dick Snagget in the 'Thirty-Ninth,' I remember——"

"And you don't know who 'George' is, of course?" I continued musingly.

"Why, I've knowed a many Georges in my time," said he, "and then there's George, Prince o' Wales, the Prince Regent, as they calls him now."

"George, Prince of Wales!" said I, staring; "by heavens, Tom, I believe you've hit it!" And, with the word, I sprang down from the cart.

"My cottage is near by, sir, and I should be proud for you to eat supper wi' me—that is—if you be so minded?"

"Many thanks," said I, "but I am not so minded, and so, good-bye, Tom!" And, with the words, I

wrung the soldier's honest hand in mine, and went
upon my way.

"George, Prince of Wales!" said I to myself,
"could this be the 'George' they had meant. If so,
then who and what had they supposed me?" Hereupon, as I walked, I fell into a profound meditation in
which I presently remembered how that Tom Cragg
had also mentioned the Prince, giving me to understand that his Highness had actually ordered him
(Tom Cragg) to leave London; and why? "Arter
that theer kidnappin', an' me 'avin' laid out Sir
Jarsper Trent— accordin' to yer order."

Sir Jasper Trent! I stopped stock still in the road.
Sir Jasper Trent! At last I remembered the name
that had eluded me so persistently. Remembered it?
Nay, indeed, it was rather as if the Pugilist had
whispered the words into my ear, and I glanced round
almost expecting to see him.

"Arter that theer kidnappin', an' me 'avin' laid out
Sir Jarsper Trent—accordin' to yer orders!"

According to my orders, or rather, the orders of the
man for whom he (in common with the two gentlemen
at "The Chequers") had mistaken me. But who was
that man? Of him I knew two facts—namely, that he
was much like me in person, and had formerly worn
or possibly still wore, whiskers. And beyond these
two facts I could get no farther, revolve the matter
how I might, so I presently shrugged my shoulders,
and banishing it from my thoughts, for the time
being, set forward at a good pace.

CHAPTER XIII

IN WHICH I FIND AN ANSWER TO MY RIDDLE

THE sun was already westering when I came to a pump beside the way; and seizing the handle I worked it vigorously, then, placing my hollowed hands beneath the gushing spout, drank and pumped, alternately, until I had quenched my thirst. I now found myself prodigiously hungry, and remembering the bread and cheese in my knapsack, looked about for an inviting spot in which to eat.

On one side of the road was a thick hedge, and, beneath this hedge, a deep, dry, grassy ditch; and here, after first slipping off my knapsack, I sat down, took out the loaf and the cheese, and opening my clasp-knife, prepared to fall to.

At this moment I was interrupted in a rather singular fashion, for hearing a rustling close by, I looked up, and into a face that was protruded through a gap in the hedge above me.

It needed but a glance at the battered hat with its jaunty brim, and great silver buckle, and the haggard, devil-may-care face below, to recognise the individual whom I had seen thrown out of the hedge tavern that very morning.

It was a very thin face, as I have said, pale, and hollow-eyed, and framed in black curly hair, whose very blackness did but accentuate the extreme pallor of the skin, which was tight, and drawn above the cheek bones and angle of the jaw. Yet, as I looked at this face, worn and cadaverous though it was, in the glance of the hollow eyes, in the line of the clean-cut mouth I saw that mysterious something which marks a man, what we call for want of a better word, a gentleman.

" Good-evening ! " said he, and lifted the battered hat.

76

" Good-evening ! " said he, and lifted the battered hat

Face Page 76

"Good-evening!" said he, and lifted the battered hat.

Face Page 76

" Good-evening ! " I returned.

" Pardon me," said he, " but I was saluting the bread and cheese."

" Indeed ! " said I.

" Indeed ! " he rejoined, " it is the first edible I have been on speaking terms with, so to speak, for rather more than three days, sir."

" You are probably hungry ? " said I.

" It would be foolish to deny it, sir."

" Then, if you care to eat with me in the ditch here, you are heartily welcome," said I.

" With all the pleasure in life ! " said he, vaulting very nimbly through the hedge; " you shall not ask me twice or the very deuce is in it !—believe me I——". Here he stopped, very suddenly, and stood looking at me.

" Ah ! " said he gently, and with a rising inflection, letting the ejaculation escape in a long-drawn breath.

" Well ? " I inquired. Now as I looked up at him, the whole aspect of the man, from the toes of his broken boots to the crown of the battered hat, seemed to undergo a change, as though a sudden, fierce anger had leapt into life, and been controlled, but by a strong effort.

" On my life and soul, now ! " said he, falling back a step, and eyeing me with a vaguely unpleasant smile, " this is a most unexpected—a most unlooked for pleasure, it is—I vow it is."

" You flatter me," said I.

" No, sir, no; to meet you again—some day—somewhere—alone—quite alone, sir, is a pleasure I have frequently dwelt upon, but never hoped to realise. As it is, sir, having, in my present condition, no chance of procuring better weapons than my fists, allow me to suggest that they are, none the less, entirely at your service; do me the infinite kindness to stand up."

" Sir," I answered, cutting a slice from the loaf, " you are the third person within the last forty-eight hours who has mistaken me for another; it really gets quite wearisome."

" Mistaken you," he broke in, and his smile grew

suddenly bitter, " do you think it possible that I could ever mistake you ? "

" I am sure of it ! " said I. " Furthermore, pray do not disparage your fists, sir. A bout at fisticuffs never did a man any harm that I ever heard ; a man's fists are good, honest weapons supplied by a beneficent Providence—far better than your unnatural swords and murderous hair-triggers ; at least, so I think, being, I trust, something of a philosopher. Still, in this instance, never having seen your face, or heard your voice until to-day, I shall continue to sit here, and eat my bread and cheese, and if you are wise you will hasten to follow my so excellent example while there is any left, for, I warn you, I am mightily sharp set."

" Come, come," said he, advancing upon me threateningly, " enough of this foolery ! "

" By all means," said I, " sit down, like a sensible fellow, and tell me for whom you mistake me."

" Sir, with all the pleasure in life ! " said he, clenching his fists, and I saw his nostrils dilate suddenly, " I take you for the greatest rogue, the most gentlemanly rascal but one, in all England ! "

" Yes," said I, " and my name ? "

" Sir Maurice Vibart ! "

" Sir Maurice Vibart ? " I sprang to my feet, staring at him in amazement. " Sir Maurice Vibart is my cousin," said I.

And so we stood, for a long minute, immobile, and silent, eyeing each other above the bread and cheese.

CHAPTER XIV

FURTHER CONCERNING THE GENTLEMAN IN THE BATTERED HAT

" Sir," said my companion at last, lifting the battered hat, " I tender you my apology, and I shall be delighted to eat with you in the ditch, if you are in the same mind about it ? "

" Then you believe me ? "

" Indubitably, sir," he answered with a faint smile; " had you indeed been Sir Maurice, either he or I, and most probably I, would be lying flat in the road, by this."

So, without more ado, we sat down in the ditch together, side by side, and began to eat. And now I noticed that when he thought my eye was upon him, my companion ate with a due deliberation and nicety, and when he thought it was off, with a voracity that was painful to witness. And after we had eaten awhile in silence, he turned to me with a sigh.

" This is very excellent cheese ! " said he.

" The man from whom I bought it," said I, " called it a noble cheese, I remember."

" I never tasted one of a finer flavour ! " said my companion.

" Hunger is a fine sauce," said I, " and you are probably hungry ? "

" Hungry ! " he repeated, bolting a mouthful and knocking his hat over his eyes with a slap on its dusty crown. " Egad, Mr Vibart ! so would you be—so would any man be who has lived on anything he could beg, borrow or steal, with an occasional meal of turnips—in the digging of which I am become astonishingly expert—and unripe blackberries, which latter I have proved to be a very trying diet in many ways— hungry, oh, damme ! "

And after a while, when there nothing remained of

loaf or cheese save a few scattered crumbs, my companion leaned back, and gave another sigh.

"Sir," said he, with an airy wave of the hand, "in me you behold a highly promising young gentleman ruined by a most implacable enemy—himself, sir. In the first place you must know my name is Beverley——"

"Beverley?" I repeated.

"Beverley," he nodded, "Peregrine Beverley, very much at your service—late of Beverley Place, Surrey, now of Nowhere-in-Particular."

"Beverley," said I again, "I have heard that name before."

"It is highly probable, Mr Vibart—a fool of that name—fortunate or unfortunate as you choose to classify him, lost houses, land, and money in a single night's play. I am that fool, sir, though you have doubtless heard particulars ere now?"

"Not a word!" said I. Mr Beverley glanced at me with a faint mingling of pity and surprise. "My life," I explained, "has been altogether a studious one, with the not altogether unnatural result that I also am bound for Nowhere-in-Particular with just eight shillings and sixpence in my pocket."

"And mine, as I tell you," said he, "has been an altogether riotous one. Thus, each of us, though by widely separate roads—you by the narrow and difficult path of Virtue, and I by the broad and easy road of Folly—have managed to find our way into this Howling Destitution, which we will call Nowhere-in-Particular. Then, how does your path of Virtue better my road of Evil?"

"The point to be considered," said I, "is not so much what we now are, but rather, what we have done, and may ultimately be, and do."

"Well?" said he, turning to look at me.

"For my own achievements, hitherto," I continued, "I have won the High Jump, and Throwing the Hammer, also translated the works of Quintilian, with the Satyricon of Petronius Arbiter, and the Life, Lives, and Memoirs of the Seigneur de Brantome, which last, as you are probably aware, has never before been done into the English."

"Ha!" exclaimed Mr Beverley, sitting up suddenly, with his ill-used hat very much over one eye, "there we have it! Who ever heard of old Quin—What's-his-name, or cared, except, perhaps, a few bald-headed bookworms and withered littérateurs? While you were dreaming of life, and reading the lives of other fellows, I was living it. In my career, episodically brief though it was, I have met, and talked with all the wits, and celebrated men, have drunk good wine, and worshipped beautiful women, Mr Vibart."

"And what has it all taught you?" said I.

"That there are an infernal number of rogues and rascals in the world, for one thing—and that is worth knowing."

"Yes," said I.

"That, though money can buy anything, from the love of a woman to the death of an enemy, it can only be spent once—and that is worth knowing also."

"Yes," said I.

"And that I am a most preposterous ass!—and that last, look you, is more valuable than all the others. Solomon, I think, says something about a wise man being truly wise who knoweth himself a fool, doesn't he?"

"Something of the sort."

"Then," said he, flinging his hat down upon the grass beside him, "what argument can you advance in favour of your 'Narrow and Thorny'?"

"The sum of eight shillings and sixpence, a loaf of bread, and a slice of noble cheese, now no more," said I.

"Egad!" said he, looking at me from the corners of his blue eyes, "the argument is unanswerable, more especially the cheese part, against which I'd say nothing, even if I could." Having remarked which, he lay flat on his back again, staring up at the leaves, and the calm serenity of the sky beyond, while I filled my negro-head pipe from my paper of tobacco, and forthwith began to smoke.

F

And, presently, as I sat alternately watching the blue wreathes of my pipe and the bedraggled figure extended beside me, he suddenly rolled over on his arm, and so lay, watching me.

"On my soul!" he exclaimed at length, "it is positively marvellous."

"What is?" I inquired.

"The resemblance between you and your famous cousin."

"It would appear so," said I, shrugging my shoulders, "though, personally, I was unaware of this fact up till now."

"Do I understand that you have never seen Sir Maurice Vibart, never seen ' Buck ' Vibart?"

"Never!" said I.

"Too much occupied in keeping to the 'Narrow and Thorny,' I suppose? Your cousin's is the Broad and Flowery, with a vengeance."

"So I understand," said I.

"Nevertheless, the resemblance between you, both in face, and figure, is positively astounding! With the sole exception that he wears hair upon his face, and is of a ruddy complexion, while you are pale, and smooth-cheeked as—as a boy——"

"Or yourself!" said I.

"Ah—exactly!" he answered, and passed his fingers across his chin tentatively, and fell again to staring lazily up into the sky. "Do you happen to know anything about that most remarkable species of the ' genus homo ' calling themselves 'Bucks,' or ' Corinthians '?" he inquired' after a while.

"Very little," said I, " and that, only by hearsay."

"Well, up to six months ago, I was one of them, Mr Vibart, until Fortune, and I think now, wisely, decreed it otherwise." And herewith, lying upon his back, looking up through the quivering green of leaves, he told mad tales of a reckless Prince, of the placid Brummel, of the " Dashing " Vibart, the brilliant Sheridan, of Fox, and Grattan, and many others, whose names are now a byword one way or the other. He recounted a story of wild prodigality, of drunken, midnight orgies, of days and nights over the cards, of wine, women, and horses. But, lastly, and very reverently, he spoke of a woman, of her love, and faith, and deathless trust. " Of course," he ended, " I might have starved very comfortably, and much quicker, in London, but when my time comes, I prefer to do my dying beneath some green hedge, or in the shelter of some friendly rick, with the cool, clean wind upon my face. Besides—— She loved the country."

" Then there are some women who can't be bought ? " said I, looking at his glistening eyes.

" Mr Vibart," said he, " so far as I know there are two—the Lady Helen Dunstan and the ' Glorious ' Sefton."

" The Lady Sophia Sefton of Cambourne ? " said I.

" And—the Lady Helen Dunstan," he repeated.

" Do you know the Lady Sophia Sefton ? "

" I have had the honour of dancing with her, frequently," he answered.

" And is she so beautiful as they say ? "

" She is the handsomest woman in London, one of your black-browed, deep-eyed goddesses, tall, and gracious, and most nobly shaped ; though, sir, for my own part, I prefer less fire and ice—a more—gentle beauty."

" As, for instance—the Lady Helen Dunstan ? " said I.

" Exactly ! " nodded Mr Beverley.

" Referring to the Lady Sophia Sefton," I pursued, " she is a reigning toast, I believe ? "

" Gad, yes ! her worshippers are Legion, and chief among them his Royal Highness, and your cousin, Sir Maurice, who has actually had the temerity to enter the field as the Prince's avowed rival—no one but ' Buck ' Vibart could be so madly rash ! "

" A most fortunate lady ! " said I.

" Mr Vibart ! " exclaimed my companion, cocking his battered hat and regarding me with a smouldering eye, " Mr Vibart, I object to your tone ; the noble Sefton's virtue is proud, and high, and above even the breath of suspicion."

" And yet my cousin would seem to be no laggard in love, and as to the Prince—his glance is contamination to a woman."

" Sir," returned Mr Beverley very earnestly, " disabuse your mind of all unworthy suspicions, I beg; your cousin she laughs to scorn, and his Royal Highness she had rebuffed as few women have, hitherto, dared do."

" It would almost seem," said I, after a pause, " that, from what I have inadvertently learned, my cousin has some dirty work afoot, though exactly what, I cannot imagine."

" My dear Mr Vibart, your excellent cousin is for ever up to something or other, and has escaped the well-merited consequences, more than once, owing to his friendship with, and the favour of his friend——"

" George ? " said I.

" Exactly ! " said my companion, raising himself on his elbow, and nodding, " George."

" Have you ever heard mention of Tom Cragg, the Pugilist ? " I inquired, blowing a cloud of smoke into the warm air.

" I won ten thousand guineas when he knocked out Ted Jarraway of Swansea," yawned my companion, " a good fighter, but a rogue—like all the rest of 'em, and a creature of your excellent cousin's."

" I guessed as much," I nodded, and forthwith plunged into an account of my meeting with the " craggy one," the which seemed to amuse Mr Beverley mightily, more especially when I related Cragg's mysterious disappearance.

" Oh, gad ! " cried Beverley, wiping his eyes on the tattered lappel of his coat, " the resemblance served you luckily there; your cousin gave him the thrashing of his life, and poor Tom evidently thought he was in for another. That was the last you saw of him, I'll be bound."

" No, I met him afterwards beneath the gibbet on River Hill, where, among other incomprehensible things, he gave me to understand that he recognised me despite my disguise, assumed, as he supposed, on account of his having kidnapped someone or other,

The Gentleman in the Battered Hat 85

and 'laid out' a certain Sir Jasper Trent in Wych Street according to my orders, or rather, it would seem, my cousin's orders, the author of which outrage Sir Jasper had evidently found out——"

"The devil!" exclaimed Mr Beverley, and sat up with a jerk.

"And furthermore," I went on, "he informed me that the Prince himself had given him the word to leave London until the affair had 'blown over.'"

Now while I spoke Mr Beverley had been regarding me with a very strange expression, his cheeks had gone even paler than before, his eyes seemed to stare through, and beyond me, and his hands were tight-clenched at his sides.

"Mr Beverley," said I, "what ails you?"

For a moment he did not speak, then answered, with the same strange look:

"Sir Jasper Trent—is my cousin, sir!"

My negro-head pipe slipped suddenly, and fell into the grass, happily without injury.

"Indeed!" said I.

"Can you not see what this means, sir?" he went on hurriedly. "Jasper will fight."

"Indeed," said I again, "I fear so."

"Jasper was always a bit of a fish, and with no particular affection for his graceless kinsman, but I am his only relative; and—and he hardly knows one end of a pistol from the other, while your cousin is a dead shot."

"My cousin!" I exclaimed; "then it was he—to be sure I saw only his back."

"Sir Jasper is unmarried—has no relations but myself," my companion repeated with the same fixed intentness of look; "can you appreciate, I wonder, what this would mean to me?"

"Rank, and fortune, and London," said I.

"No, no!" he sprang to his feet, and threw wide his ragged arms with a swift, passionate gesture, "it means Life—and Helen. My God!" he went on, speaking almost in a whisper, "I never knew how much I wanted her—how much I had wilfully tossed aside—till now! I never realised the full misery of it all—till now! I could have starved very well in time, and managed it as quietly as most other ruined fools. But now—to see the chance of beginning again, of coming back to self-respect and—Helen, my God!" And, of a sudden he cast himself upon his face, and so lay, tearing up the grass by handfuls. Then, almost as suddenly, he was upon his feet again, and had caught up his hat. "Sir," said he somewhat shame-facedly, smoothing its ruffled nap with fingers that still quivered, "pray forgive that little ebullition of feeling, it is over—quite over, but your tidings affected me, and I am not quite myself at times—as I have already said, turnips and unripe blackberries are not altogether desirable as a diet."

"Indeed," said I, "you seemed strangely per-turbed."

"Mr Vibart," said he, staring very hard at the battered hat, and turning it round and round, "Mr Vibart, the devil is surprisingly strong in some of us."

"True," said I.

"My cousin, Sir Jasper, is a bookish fellow, and, as I have said, a fool where anything else is in question; if this meeting is allowed to take place I feel that he will most certainly be killed, and his death would mean a new life—more than life to me."

"Yes," said I.

"And for a moment, Mr Vibart, I was tempted to sit down in the ditch again, and let things take their course. The devil, I repeat, is remarkably strong in some of us."

"Then what is your present intention?"

"I am going to London to find Sir Maurice Vibart —to stop this duel."

"Impossible!" said I.

"But you see, sir, it so happens that I am possessed of certain intelligence which might make Sir Maurice's existence in England positively untenable."

"Nevertheless," said I, "it is impossible."

"That remains to be seen, Mr Vibart," said he, and speaking, turned upon his heel.

"One moment," said I, "was not your cousin, Sir Jasper, of the middle height, slim-built and fair-haired, with a habit of plucking at his lips when at all nervous, or excited?"

"Exactly, you know him, sir?"

"No," I answered, "but I have seen him, very lately, and I say again, to stop this duel is an impossibility."

"Do you mean——" he began, and paused. Now, as his eyes met mine the battered hat escaped his fingers, and lay all unheeded. "Do you mean——" he began again, and again stopped.

"Yes," said I, "I mean that you are too late. Sir Jasper was killed at a place called Deepdene Wood, no longer since than to-day at half-past seven in the morning. It was raining at the time, I remember, but the day grew glorious later."

For a long moment Mr Beverley stood silent, with bent head, then, apparently becoming aware of the hat at his feet, he sent it flying with a sudden kick, and watched it describe a wide parabola ere it disappeared into the ditch, some yards away. Which done, he walked after it, and returned, brushing it very carefully with his ragged cuff.

"And—you are sure—quite sure, Mr Vibart?" he inquired, smoothing the broken brim with the greatest solicitude.

"I stood behind a hedge, and watched it done," said I.

"Then—my God!—I am Sir Peregrine Beverley! —I am Sir Peregrine Beverley of Burnham Hall, very much at your service. Jasper—dead!—A knight banneret of Kent, and Justice of the Peace!—how utterly preposterous it all sounds! But to-day I begin life anew, ah yes, a new life, a new life! To-day all things are possible again! The fool has learned wisdom, and, I hope, become a man. But come," said he in a more natural tone, "let us get back to our ditch, and, while you tell me the particulars, if you don't object I should much like to try a whiff at that pipe of yours."

So, while I recounted the affair as briefly as I might, he sat puffing at my pipe, and staring away into the distance. But gradually his head sank lower and lower, until his face was quite hidden from me, and for a long moment after I had ended my narration, there was silence.

"Poor Jasper!" said he at last without raising his head, "poor old Jasper!"

"I congratulate you, Sir Peregrine," said I.

"And I used to pummel him so, when we were boys together at Eton—poor old Jasper!" And, presently, he handed me my pipe and rose. "Mr Vibart," said he, "it would seem that by no effort, or virtue of my own, I am to win free of this howling desolation of Nowhere-in-Particular, after all; believe me, I would gladly take you with me. Had I not met with you it is—rather more than probable—that I—should never have seen another dawn; so if—if ever I can be of—use to you, pray honour me so far, you can always hear of me at Burnham Hall, Pembry. Good-bye, Mr Vibart, I am going to her—in all my rags—for I am a man again."

So, I bade him "good-bye," and, sitting in the ditch, watched him stride away to his new life. Presently, reaching the brow of the hill (there are hills everywhere in the South country), I saw him turn to flourish the battered hat ere he disappeared from my sight.

CHAPTER XV

IN WHICH I MEET WITH A PEDDLER BY THE NAME OF " GABBING " DICK

" You won't be wantin' ever a broom, now? "

I sat up, sleepily, and rubbed my eyes. The sun was gone, and the blue sky had changed to a deep purple, set, here and there, with a quivering star. Yet the light was still strong enough to enable me to distinguish the speaker—a short, thick-set man. Upon his shoulder he carried a bundle of brooms, a pack was slung to his back, while round his neck there dangled a heterogeneous collection of articles—ribbons, laces, tawdry neck chains, and the like; indeed so smothered was he in his wares that, as he stood there, he had more the aspect of some disordered fancy than of a human being.

" You won't be wantin' ever a broom, now? " he repeated, in a somewhat melancholy tone.

" No," said I.

" Nor yet a mop? "

" Nor that either," said I.

" A belt, now," he suggested mournfully, " a fine leather belt wi' a steel buckle made in Brummagem as ever was, and all for a shillin'—what d'ye say to a fine belt ? "

" That I have no need of one, thank you."

" Ah, well ! " said the man, spitting dejectedly at a patch of shadow, " I thought as much, you aren't got the look of a buyer."

" Then why ask me ? "

" Hinstinct ! " said he, " it's jest hinstinct—it comes as nat'ral to me as eatin' or walkin' these 'ere roads."

" Have you come far to-day ? "

" Twenty mile, maybe," he answered, setting down his bundle of brooms.

" Are you tired?"

" 'Course I'm tired!"

" Then why not sit down and rest?"

" Because Id 'ave to get up again, wouldn't I?"

" Are you hungry?"

" 'Ungry aren't the word for it."

" And how is trade?"

" Couldn't be worse!"

" I perceive you are a pessimist," said I.

" No," said he, " I'm a peddler—baptism'l name Richard, commonly known as ' Gabbin' ' Dick."

" At least yours is a fine healthy trade," said I.

" 'Ow so?"

" A life of constant exercise, and fresh air—to-day for instance——"

" 'Ot as a hoven!" said he.

" Yet there was a good, cool wind," said I.

" Ah! an' with dust enough to choke a man! and then there's the lonliness o' these 'ere roads."

" Loneliness?" said I.

" That's the word; sometimes it gets so bad as I'm minded to do away wi' myself——"

" Strange!" I began.

" Not a bit," said he; " when you've been a-walkin' an' a-walkin' all day past hedge and hedge, and tree and tree, it's bad enough, but it's worse when the sun's gone out, an' you foller the glimmer o' the road on and on, past hedges as ain't hedges, and trees as ain't trees, but things as touch you as you pass, and reach out arter you in the dark, behind. Theer's one on 'em, back theer on the Cranbrook road, looks like an oak-tree in the daytime—ah, an' a big 'un—it's nearly 'ad me three times a'ready—once by the leg, once by the arm, and once by the neck. I don't pass it arter dark no more, but it'll 'ave me yet—mark my words—it'll 'ave me one o' these fine nights, and they'll find me a-danglin' in the grey o' the dawn!"

" Do you mean that you are afraid?" I inquired.

" No, not afeared exactly—it's jest the loneliness—the lonely quietness. Why, Lord! you aren't got no

notion o' the tricks the trees and 'edges gets up to a'
nights—nobody 'as but us as tramps the roads. Bill
Nye knowed, same as I know, but Bill Nye's dead—
cut 'is throat 'e did wi' one o' 'is own razors—under a
'edge.''

"And what for?" I inquired, as the Peddler
paused to spit lugubriously into the road again.

"Nobody knowed but me. William Nye 'e were a
tinker, and a rare, merry 'un 'e were—a little man
always up to 'is jinkin' and jokin' and laughin'.
'Dick,' 'e used to say—(but Richard I were baptised,
though they calls me Dick for short), 'Dick,' 'e used
to say, 'd'ye know that theer big oak-tree—the big,
'oller oak as stands at the cross-roads a mile and a 'alf
out o' Cranbrook? A man might do for 'isself very
nice, and quiet, tucked away inside of it, Dick,' says
'e 'it's such a nice, quiet place—so snug and dark, I
wonder as nobody does. I never pass by,' says 'e,
'but I takes a peep inside, jest to make sure as theer
aren't no legs a-danglin', nor nobody 'unched up
dead in the dark. It's such a nice, quiet place,' 'e
used to say, shakin' 'is 'ead, and smilin, sad-like, 'I
wonder as nobody's never thought of it afore.' Well,
one day, sure enough, poor Bill Nye disappeared—
nobody knowed wheer. Bill, as I say, was a merry
sort, always ready wi' a joke, and that's apt to get a
man friends, and they searched for 'im 'igh and low,
but neither 'ide nor 'air o' poor Bill did they find. At
last, one evenin' I 'appened to pass the big oak—the
'oller oak, and mindin' Bill's words, thinks I—'ere's
to see if 'tis empty as Bill said. Goin' up to it I got
down on my 'ands and knees, and strikin' a light,
looked inside—and there, sure enough, was poor Bill
Nye hunched up inside of it wi' a razor in 'is 'and,
and 'is 'ead nigh cut off—and what wi' one thing and
another, a very unpleasant sight he were."

"And why—why did he do it?" I asked.

"Because 'e 'ad to, o' course—it's jest the loneliness.
They'll find me some day—danglin'—I never could
abide blood myself—danglin' to the thing as looks
like a oak-tree in the daytime."

" What do you mean ? " said I.

The Peddler sighed, shook his head, and shouldered his brooms.

" It's jest the loneliness!" said he, and spitting over his shoulder, trudged upon his way.

CHAPTER XVI

HOW I HEARD THE STEPS OF ONE WHO DOGGED
ME IN THE SHADOWS

AND, in a little while, I rose, and buckled on my
knapsack. The shadows were creeping on apace, but
the sky was wonderfuly clear, while, low down upon
the horizon, I saw the full-orbed moon, very broad
and big. It would be a brilliant night later and this
knowledge rejoiced me not a little.

Before me stretched a succession of hills—that chain
of hills which, I believe, is called the Weald, and over
which the dim road dipped, and wound, with, on
either hand, a rolling country, dark with wood, and
coppice—full of mystery. The wind had quite fallen,
but, from the hedges came sudden rustlings, and soft,
unaccountable noises. Once something small, and
dark, scuttered across the road before me, and once a
bird, hidden near by, set up a loud complaint, while,
from the deeps of a neighbouring wood, came the
mournful note of a night-jar.

And, as I walked, I bethought me of poor Bill Nye,
the Tinker. I could picture him tramping upon this
very road, his jingling load upon his back, and the
"loneliness" upon, and around him. A small man,
he would be, with a peaked face, little, round, twinkling eyes, grizzled hair, and a long, blue chin. How I
came to know all this I cannot tell, only it seemed he
must be so. On he went, his chin first upon one
shoulder, and now upon the other, shooting furtive
glances at hedges which were not hedges, and trees
which were not trees. Somewhere there was a "thing"
that looked like a big oak-tree in the daytime—a hollow
oak. On he went through the shadows, on, and on.
Presently he turned out of the road, and there, sure
enough, was the oak itself. Kneeling down, he slipped

93

off his burden, and pushed it through a jagged hole at the root. Then he glanced round him, a long, stealthy look, down at the earth and up at the sky, and crept into the tree. In the dimness I could see him fumble for the thing he wanted, pause to thumb its edge, and, throwing up his chin, raise his hand——

"Folly!" said I aloud, and stopped suddenly in my stride.

The moon's rim was just topping the trees to my left, and its light, feeble though it was as yet, served to show that I had reached a place where four roads met.

Now, casting my eyes about me, they were attracted by a great tree that grew near by, a tree of vast girth, and bigness. And, as I looked, I saw that it was an oak-tree, near the root of which there was a jagged, black hole.

How long I stood staring at this, I cannot say, but, all at once, the leaves of the tree were agitated as by a breath of wind, and rustled with a sound indescribably desolate, and from the dark mass rose the long-drawn, mournful cry of some night bird.

Heedless of my direction, I hurried away, yet, even when I had left it far behind, I glanced back more than once ere its towering branches were lost to my view.

So I walked on through the shadows, past trees that were not trees, and hedges that were not hedges, but frightful phantoms, rather, lifting menacing arms above my head, and reaching after me with clutching fingers. Time and again, ashamed of such weakness, I cursed myself for an imaginative fool, but kept well in the middle of the road, and grasped my staff firmly, notwithstanding.

I had gone, perhaps, some mile or so in this way, alternately rating and reasoning with, myself, when I suddenly fancied I heard a step behind me, and swung round upon my heel, with ready stick; but the road stretched away—empty as far as I could see. Having looked about me on all sides, I presently went on again, yet, immediately, it seemed that the steps began also, keeping time with my own, now slow, now fast, now

slow again, but, whenever I turned, the road behind
was, apparently, as empty and desolate as ever.

I can conceive of few things more nerve-racking than
the knowledge that we are being dogged by something
which we can only guess at, and that all our actions are
watched by eyes which we cannot see. Thus, with
every step, I found the situation grow more intoler-
able, for though I kept a close watch behind me, and
upon the black gloom of the hedges, I could see
nothing. At length, however, I came upon a gap in
the hedge where was a gate, and beyond this, vaguely
outlined against a glimmer of sky, I saw a dim figure.

Hereupon, running forward, I set my hand upon
the gate, and leaping over, found myself face to face
with a man who carried a gun across his arm. If I
was startled at this sudden encounter he was no less
so, and thus we stood eyeing each other as well as we
might in the half light.

"Well," I demanded, at last, "what do you mean
by following me like this?"

"I aren't follered ye," retorted the man.

"But I heard your steps behind me."

"Not mine, master. I've sat and waited 'ere 'arf
an hour, or more, for a poachin' cove——"

"But someone was following me."

"Well, it weren't I, a keeper I be, a-lookin' for a
poachin' cove just about your size, and it's precious
lucky for you as you are a-wearin' that there bell-
crowned 'at!"

"Why so?"

"Because, if you 'adn't 'appened to be a-wearin'
that there bell-crowner, and I 'adn't 'appened to be of
a argifyin' and inquirin' turn o' mind, I should ha'
filled you full o' buckshot."

"Oh?" said I.

"Yes," said he, nodding, while I experienced a
series of cold chills up my spine, "not a blessed doubt
of it. Poachers," he went on, "don't wear bell-crowned
'ats as a rule—I never seed one as did; and so, while I
was a-watchin' of you be'ind this 'ere 'edge, I argies
the matter in my mind. 'Robert,' I says to meself.

'Robert,' I sez, 'did you ever 'appen to see a poachin'
cove in a bell-crowner afore?—no, you never did,'
sez I. 'But, on the other 'and, this 'ere cove is the
very spit o' the poachin' cove as I'm a-lookin' for.
True!' sez I to myself, 'but this 'ere cove is a-wearin'
of a bell-crowner 'at, but the poachin' cove never wore
a bell-crowner—nor never will.' Still, I must say I
come very near pullin' trigger on ye—just to make
sure. So ye see it were precious lucky for you as you
was a-wearin' o' that there——"

" It certainly was," said I, turning away.

"—that there bell-crowner, and likewise as I'm a man
of a nat'ral gift for argiment, and of a inquirin'——"

" Without doubt," said I, vaulting over the gate
into the road once more.

"—turn o' mind, because if I 'adn't 'a' been, and
you 'adn't 'a' wore that there bell-crowner——"

"The consequences are unpleasantly obvious!" said
I over my shoulder, as I walked on down the road.

"—I should ha' shot ye—like a dog!" he shouted,
hanging over the gate to do so.

And, when I had gone on some distance, I took off
that which the man had called a " bell-crowner," and
bestowed upon it a touch, and looked at it as I had
never done before, and there was gratitude in look,
and touch, for to-night it had, indeed, stood my friend.

Slowly, slowly the moon mounted into a cloudless
heaven, at whose advent the starry host " paled their
ineffectual fires," higher and higher, in queenly
majesty, until the dark world was filled with her
glory, and the road before me became transformed
into a silver track splashed here and there with the
inky shadow of hedge, and trees, and leading away
into a land of " Faerie."

Indeed, to my mind, there is nothing more delightful
than to walk upon a country road, beneath a mid-
summer moon, when there is no sound to break the
stillness, save perhaps, the murmur of wind in trees,
or the throbbing melody of some hidden brook. At
such times the world of every-day—the world of
Things Material, the hard, hard world of Common-

sense, seems to vanish quite, and we walk within the
fair haven of our dreams, where Imagination meets,
and kisses us upon the brow. And, at his touch, the
Impossible straightway becomes the Possible, the
Abstract becomes the Concrete, our fondest hopes are
realised, our most cherished visions take form, and
stand before us; surely, at such an hour the gods
come down to walk with us awhile.

From this ecstasy I was suddenly aroused by hearing once more the sound of a footstep upon the road
behind me. So distinct and unmistakable was it that I
turned sharp about, and, though the road seemed as
deserted as ever, I walked back, looking into every
patch of shadow, and even thrust into the denser parts
of the hedges with my staff, but still I found no one.

And yet I knew that I was being followed persistently, step by step, but by whom, and for what
reason?

A little farther on, upon one side of the way, was a
small wood or coppice, and now I made towards this,
keeping well in the shadow of the hedge. The trees
were somewhat scattered, but the underbrush was very
dense, and amongst this I hid myself where I could
watch the road, and waited. Minute after minute
elapsed, and, losing patience, I was about to give up
all hope of thus discovering my unknown pursuer,
when a stick snapped sharply near by, and, glancing
round, I thought I saw a head vanish behind the bole
of an adjacent tree; wherefore I made quickly towards
that tree, but ere I reached it, a man stepped out. A
tall, loose-limbed fellow he was, clad in rough clothes
(that somehow had about them a vague suggestion of
ships, and the sea), and with a moth-eaten fur cap
crushed down upon his head. His face gleamed pale,
and his eyes were deep-sunken, and very bright; also,
I noticed that one hand was hidden in the pocket of
his coat. But most of all, I was struck by the extreme
pallor of his face, and the burning brilliancy of his
eyes.

And, with the glance that showed me all this, I
recognised the Outside Passenger.

G

CHAPTER XVII

HOW I TALKED WITH A MADMAN IN A WOOD
BY MOONLIGHT

" Good-evening, sir ! " he said, in a strange, hurried, sort of way, "the moon, you will perceive, is very nearly at the full to-night." And his voice, immediately, struck me as being at odds with his clothes.

"Why do you stand and peer at me?" said I sharply.

" Peer at you, sir ? "

" Yes, from behind the tree, yonder." As I spoke, he craned his head towards me, and I saw his pale lips twitch suddenly. " And why have you dogged me—why have you followed me all the way from Tonbridge ? "

" Why, sir, surely there is nothing so strange in that. I am a shadow."

" What do you mean by ' a shadow' ? "

" Sir, I am a shadow cast by neither sun, nor moon, nor star—that moves on unceasingly in dark as in light. Sir, it is my fate (in common with my kind), to be ever upon the move—a stranger everywhere without friends or kindred. I have been, during the past year, all over England, east, and west, and north and south ; within the past week, for instance, I have travelled from London to Epsom, from Epsom to Brighton, from Brighton back again to London, and from London here. And I peer at you, sir, because I wished to make certain what manner of man you were before I spoke, and though the moon is bright, yet your hat-brim left your face in shade."

" Well, are you satisfied ? "

" So much so, sir, so very much so, that I should like to talk with you, to—to ask you a question," he answered, passing his hand—a thin, white hand—

98

across his brow, and up over the fur cap that was so out of keeping with the pale face below.

" A question ? "

" If you will be so obliging as to listen, sir; let us sit awhile, for I am very weary." And with the words he sank down upon the grass. After a momentary hesitation, I followed his example, for my curiosity was piqued by the fellow's strange manner, yet, when we were sitting opposite each other, I saw that his hand was still hidden in the pocket of his coat.

" Perhaps, sir," said he in his nervous, hurried manner, " perhaps you would be better able to answer my question were I first to tell you a story—an ordinary, a very commonplace one, I fear, but with the virtue that it is short, and soon told."

" My time is entirely my own," said I, leaning with my shoulders against the tree behind me; " proceed with your story."

" First, then, my name is Strickland—John Strickland ! "

Here he paused, and, though his head was bent, I saw him watching me beneath his brows.

" Well ? " said I.

" I am a super-cargo."

Again he paused expectantly, but seeing I merely nodded, he continued :

" Upon one of my voyages, our vessel was wrecked, and, so far as I know, all save myself and six others— four seamen and two passengers—were drowned. The passengers I speak of were an old merchant—and his daughter, a very beautiful girl—her name was— Angela, sir."

Once again he paused and again he eyed me narrowly.

" Well ? " said I.

" Well, sir," he resumed, speaking in a low, repressed voice, " we seven, after two miserable days in a drifting boat, reached an island where, that same night, the old merchant died. Sir, the sailors were wild, rough men, the island was a desolate one from whence there was seemingly no chance of escape, it lying out of the usual track of ships, and this girl was, as I have said,

very beautiful. Under such conditions her fate would
have been unspeakable degradation, and probably
death; but, sir, I fought and bled for her, not once but
many times, and eventually I killed one of them with
my sheath-knife, and I remember, to this hour, how his
blood gushed over my hands and arms, and sickened
me. After that they waited hourly to avenge his death,
and get me out of their way once and for all, but I had
my long knife, and they but such rude weapons as
they could devise. Day after day, and night after
night, I watched for an opportunity to escape with the
boat, until at last, one day while they were all three
gone inland, not dreaming of any such attempt, for the
sea was very dangerous, and high, with the girl's help
I managed to launch the boat, and so stood out to sea.
And I remember those three sailors came running with
great shouts and cries, and flung themselves down
upon the beach, and crawled upon their knees, praying
to be taken off along with us, and begging us not to
leave them to perish. After three days' buffeting at
the mercy of the seas, we were picked up by a brig
bound for Portsmouth, and, six months later, were in
England. Sir, it is impossible for a man to have lived
beside a beautiful woman day by day, to have fought
for, and suffered with her, not to love her also. Thus,
seeing her friendless and penniless, I wooed, and won
her to wife. We came to London, and for a year our
life was perfect, until, through stress of circumstances,
I was forced to take another position aboard ship.
Well, sir, I bade farewell to my wife, and we set sail.
The voyage, which was to have lasted but three
months, was lengthened out through one misadven-
ture after another, so that it was a year before I saw
my wife again. At first I noticed little difference in
her save that she was paler, but, gradually, I came to
see that she was unhappy. Often I have wakened in
the night to find her weeping silently.

"Oh, sir!" he broke out, "I do not think there is
anything more terrible than to witness in one we love
a sorrow we are unable to reach!" Here he paused,
and I saw that the sweat stood out upon his brow, and

that his hand was tight clenched as he drew it across his temples. "At last, sir," he went on, speaking once more in a low, repressed tone, "returning home one day, I found her—gone."

"Gone?" said I.

"Gone, sir."

"And she left no trace—no letter——?"

"No, she left no letter, sir, but I did find something—a something that had rolled into a corner of the room."

"And what was that?"

"This, sir!" As he spoke, his burning eyes never leaving mine, he thrust a hand into his bosom—his left hand, for his right was where it had been all along, hidden in his pocket—and held out to me a gold seal such as gentlemen wear at their fobs.

"Ah!" I exclaimed.

"Take it!" said the man, thrusting it towards me; "look at it!" Obediently I took the trinket from him, and examining it as well as I might, saw that a letter was engraved upon it, one of those ornamental initials surrounded by rococo scrolls and flourishes.

"What letter does it bear?" asked the man in a strangled voice.

"It looks very like the letter 'Y,'" I answered.

"The letter 'Y'!" cried the man, and then, with a gesture sudden and fierce, he snatched the seal from me, and, thrusting it back into his bosom, laughed strangely.

"Why do you laugh?" said I.

"To be sure," said he harshly, "the light might be better, and yet—well! well! my story is nearly done. I lived on in my lonely house from day to day, and month to month, hoping and waiting for her to come back to me. And one day she did come back to me— just about this hour it was, sir, and on just such another evening, and that same night—she died."

"Good God!" I exclaimed. "Poor fellow!" And, leaning forward, I laid my hand upon his knee, but, at my touch, he drew back so quickly, and with a look so evil, that I was startled.

"Hands off!" said he, and so sat staring at me with his smouldering eyes.

"Are you mad?" said I, and sprang to my feet.

"Not yet," he answered, and once again he passed his hand up, and over his face and brow; "no, not yet, sir." Here he rose, and stood facing me, and I noticed that one hand was still hidden in his pocket, and, thereafter, while I listened to him, I kept my eyes directed thither. "That night—before she—died, sir," he continued, "she told me the name of the man who had destroyed her, and killed my soul, and I have been searching for him ever since—east, and west, and north, and south. Now, sir, here is my question: If I should ever meet that man face to face, as I now see you, should I not be justified in—killing him?"

For a moment I stood with bent head, yet conscious all the while of the burning eyes that scanned my face, then:

"Yes," said I.

The man stood utterly still, his mouth opened as if he would have spoken, but no word came. All at once he turned about, and walked unsteadily five or six paces. Now, as I looked, I saw him suddenly draw his hand from his pocket, then, as he wheeled, I knew, and hurled myself face downward as the pistol flashed.

"Madman!" I cried, and next moment, was on my feet; but, with a sound that was neither a groan, nor a scream, and yet something of both, he leapt into the thickest part of the underbrush, and made off. And standing there, dazed by the suddenness of it all, I heard the snapping of twigs grow fainter and fainter as he crashed through in headlong flight.

CHAPTER XVIII

THE HEDGE-TAVERN

Twigs whipped my face, thorns and brambles dragged at my clothes, hidden obstacles lay in wait for my feet, for the wood grew denser as I advanced, but I pushed on, heedless alike of these and of what direction I took. But, as luck would have it, I presently blundered upon a path which, in a short time, brought me out very suddenly into what appeared to be a small tavern yard, for on either hand was a row of tumble-down stables, and barns, while before me was a low, rambling structure which I judged was the tavern itself. I was yet standing looking about me when a man issued from the stables upon my right, bearing a hammer in one hand, and a lanthorn in the other.

" Hallo ! " said he, staring at me.

" Hallo ! " said I, staring at him.

" You don't chance to 'ave a axle-bolt about you, I suppose ? "

" No," said I.

" Humph ! " he grunted, and, lowering his lanthorn, began searching among the cobblestones.

" Is this it ? " I inquired, picking up a rusty screwbolt at my feet.

" Ah ! " said he, taking it from me with a nod, " know'd I dropped it 'ere some'eres. Ye see," he went on, " couldn't get another round 'ere to-night, and that cussed axle's got to be in place to-morra."

" Yes ? " said I.

" Ah ! " nodded the man, " chaise come in 'ere 'arf-an-hour ago wi' two gentlemen and a lady, in the Lord's own 'urry too. ' Mend this axle, me man,' says one on 'em—a top-sawyer be the looks on 'im, ' mend this axle, and quick about it.' ' Can't be done, my lord,' says I. ' W'ynot ? ' says 'e, showin' 'is

103

teeth savage-like. 'Because it can't,' says I, 'not no'ow, me lord,' says I. Well, after cussin' 'isself well-nigh black in the face 'e orders me to 'ave it ready fust thing to-morra, and if you' adn't found that there bolt for me it wouldn't 'ave been ready fust thing to-morra, which would ha' been mighty bad for me, for this 'ere gentleman's a fire-and-fury out-and-outer, and no error."

"Can I have a bed here, do you think?" I inquired.

"Ah," said he, "I think you can."

"For how much, do you suppose?"

"To you—sixpence."

"Why, that seems reasonable," said I.

"It are," nodded the man, "and a fine feather bed too! But then, Lord, one good turn deserves another——"

"Meaning?"

"This 'ere bolt."

"Are you the landlord, then?"

"I be; and if you feel inclined for a mug o' good ale—say the word."

"Most willingly," said I, "but what of the axle?"

"Plenty o' time for th' axle," nodded the landlord, and setting down his hammer upon a bench hard by, he led the way into the tap. The ale was very strong, and good; indeed this lovely county of Kent is justly famous for such. Finding myself very hungry, the landlord forthwith produced a mighty round of beef, upon which we both fell to, and ate with a will. Which done, I pulled out my negro-head pipe, and the landlord fetching himself another, we sat awhile smoking. And presently, learning I was from London, he began plying me with all manner of questions concerning the great city, of which it seemed he could not hear enough, and I, to describe its wonders as well as I might. At length, bethinking him of his axle, he rose with a sigh. Upon my requesting to be shown my room, he lighted a candle, and led the way up a somewhat rickety stair, along a narrow passage, and throwing open a door at the end, I found myself in a fair-sized chamber with a decent white bed, which he

introduced to my notice by the one word, "feathers."
Hereupon, he pinched off the snuff of the candle with
an expression of ponderous thought.

"And so the Tower o' London ain't *a* tower?" he
inquired at last.

"No," I answered; "it is composed of several
towers surrounded by very strong, battlemented
walls."

"Ah—to—be—sure," said he, "ah, to be sure!
And me 'ave allus thought on it like it was a great big
tower standin' in the midst o' the city, as 'igh as a
mountain. Humph—not a tower—ha! disapp'inted I
be. Humph! good-night, master. Disapp'inted I be
—yes." And having nodded his head ponderously
several times, he turned and went ponderously along
the passage, and down the stair.

At the end of my chamber was a long, low casement, and, drawn thither by the beauty of the night, I
flung open the lattice, and leaned out. I looked down
upon a narrow, deeply-rutted lane, one of those winding, inconsequent byways which it seems out of all
possibility can ever lead the traveller anywhere, and I
was idly wondering what fool had troubled to build a
tavern in such a remote, out-of-the-way spot, when my
ears were saluted by the sound of voices. Now, immediately beneath my window there was a heavy
porch, low, and squat, from which jutted a beam with
a broken signboard, and it was from beneath this
porch that the voices proceeded, the one loud and
hectoring, the other gruff and sullen. I was about to
turn away when a man stepped out into the moonlight.
His face was hidden in the shadow of his hat-brim,
but from his general air and appearance I judged him
to be one of the gentlemen whose chaise had broken
down. As I watched him he walked slowly round the
angle of the house, and disappeared. In a little while,
I drew in my head from the casement, and having removed my dusty boots, together with my knapsack
and coat, blew out the candle, and composed myself to
sleep.

Now it seemed to me that I was back upon the road,

standing once more beside the great oak-tree. And, as I watched, a small, hunched figure crept from the jagged opening in the trunk, a figure with a jingling pack upon its back, at sight of which I turned and ran, filled with an indescribable terror. But, as I went, the Tinker's pack jingled loud behind me, and when I glanced back, I saw that he ran with head dangling in most hideous fashion, and that his right hand grasped a razor. On I sped faster and faster, but with the Tinker ever at my heels, until I had reached this tavern; the door crashed to, behind me, only just in time, and I knew, as I lay there, that he was standing outside, in the moonlight, staring up at my casement with his horrible, dead face.

Here I, very mercifully, awoke, and lay, for a while, blinking in the ghostly radiance of the moon, which was flooding in at the window directly upon me. Now whether it was owing to the vividness of my dream, I know not, but as I lay, there leapt up within me a sudden conviction that somebody *was* indeed standing outside in the lane, staring up at my window. So firmly was I convinced of this that, moved by a sudden impulse, I rose, and cautiously approaching the window, peered out. And there, sure enough, his feet planted wide apart, his hands behind his back, stood a man staring up at my window. His head was thrown back so that I could see his face distinctly—a fleshy face with small, close-set eyes, and thick lips, behind which I caught the gleam of big, white teeth. This was no tinker, but as I looked, I recognised him as the slenderer of the two " Corinthians " with whom I had fallen out at " The Chequers." Hereupon, I got me back to bed, drowsily wondering what should bring the fellow hanging about a dilapidated hedge-tavern at such an hour. But gradually my thoughts grew less coherent, my eyes closed, and in another moment I should have been asleep, when I suddenly came to my elbow, broad awake, and listening, for I had heard two sounds, the soft creak of a window opened cautiously near by, and a stealthy footstep outside my door.

CHAPTER XIX

IN WHICH I BECOME A SQUIRE OF DAMES

WHO does not recognise the solemn majesty of Night —that season of awesome stillness when tired mankind lies supine in that strange inertia so like death; when the soul, quitting the wearied body for a space, flies hence—but whither?

What wonder is it if, at such an hour as this, we are prone to magnify trifles, or that the most insignificant thing becomes an omen full of ghastly meaning and possibilities? The creak of a door in the silence, a rustle in the dark, become to us of infinitely greater moment than the crash of falling empires.

Thus, for a space, I lay, with ears on the stretch, and every nerve tingling, waiting for—I knew not what.

In a little, I became conscious of yet another sound, indescribably desolate : the low, repressed sound of a woman's sobbing.

Once more I rose, and looking down into the lane, found it deserted; the watcher had vanished. I also noticed that the casement next to mine had been opened wide, and it was from here, as it seemed, that the weeping proceeded.

After some little hesitation, I knocked softly upon the wall, at which the weeping was checked abruptly, save for an occasional sob, whereupon I presently rapped again. At this, after a moment or so, I saw a very small, white hand appear at the neighbouring window, and next moment, was looking into a lovely, flushed face framed in bright hair, with eyes woefully swelled by tears—but a glance showed me that she was young, and of a rare and gentle beauty.

Before I could speak she laid her finger upon her lip with a warning gesture.

107

"Help me—oh, help me!" she whispered hurriedly; "they have locked me in here, and I dare not go to bed, and—and—oh, what shall I do?"

"Locked you in?" I exclaimed.

"Oh, what shall I do?" she sobbed. "I tell you I am afraid of him—his hateful, wicked eyes!" Here a tremor seemed to shake her, and she covered her face with her hands. "To-night, when I found the key gone from the door, and remembered his look as he bade me 'Good-night'—I thought I should have died. I waited here, close beside the window—listening, listening. Once I thought I heard a step outside my door, and opened the casement to throw myself out— he shall not find me here when he comes."

"No," said I, "he shall not find you here when he comes."

All this she had imparted to me in broken whispers, and with her face still hidden, but, at my words, she peeped at me through her fingers.

"You mean?"

"You must run away."

"But the door is locked."

"There remains the window."

"The window!" she repeated, trembling.

"You would find it easy enough with my help."

"Quick, then!" she exclaimed, and held out her hand.

"Wait," said I, and turned back into my room. Hereupon, having locked the door, I got into my boots, slipped on my coat and knapsack, and, last of all, threw my blackthorn staff out of the window (where I was sure of finding it), and climbed out after it.

The porch I have mentioned, upon which I now stood, sloped steeply down upon two sides, so that I had no little difficulty in maintaining my foothold; on the other hand, it was no great distance from the ground, and I thought that it would be easy enough of descent.

At this moment the lady reappeared at the lattice.

"What is it?" I whispered, struck by the terror in her face.

" Quick ! " she cried, forgetting all prudence in her fear, " quick—they are coming—I hear someone upon the stair. Oh, you are too late ! " and, sinking upon her knees, she covered her face with her hands. Without more ado I swung myself up, and clambered over the sill into the room beside her. I was looking round for something that might serve me for a weapon when my eye encountered a tall oak press, a heavy, cumbersome affair, but, save the bed, the only furniture the room possessed. Setting my shoulder to it therefore, I began to urge it towards the door. But it was soon apparent that I could not get there in time, for the creeping footstep was already close outside, and, next moment, a key was softly inserted in the lock.

" Quick ! hide yourself ! " I whispered, over my shoulder, and stepping back from the door to give myself room, I clenched my fists. There was a faint creak as the key turned, the door was opened cautiously, and a man's dim figure loomed upon the threshold.

He had advanced two or three paces on tip-toe before he discovered my presence, for the room was in shadow, and I heard his breath catch, suddenly, and hiss between his teeth ; then, without a word, he sprang at me. But as he came, I leapt aside, and my fist took him full and squarely beneath the ear. He pitched sideways, and falling heavily, rolled over upon his back, and lay still.

As I leaned above him, however (for the blow had been a heavy one), he uttered a groaning oath, whereupon, pinning him forthwith by the collar, I dragged him out into the passage, and whipping the key from the lock, transferred it to the inside and, closing the door, locked it. Waiting for no more I scrambled back through the casement, and reached up my hand to the lady.

" Come," said I, and (almost as quickly as it takes to set it down here) she was beside me upon the roof of the porch, clinging to my arm. Exactly how it was managed I am unable to say, all that I remember being the vision of a slender foot, and ankle, and an excellently shaped leg.

Our farther descent to the ground proved much more difficult than I had supposed, but, though I could feel her trembling, my companion obeyed my whispered instructions, and yielded herself implicitly to my guidance, so that we were soon standing in the lane before the house, safe and sound except for a few rents to our garments.

" What is it ? " she whispered, seeing me searching about in the grass.

" My staff,' said I, " a faithful friend, I would not lose it."

" But they will be here in a minute—we shall be seen."

" I cannot lose my staff," said I.

" Oh, hurry ! hurry ! " she cried, wringing her hands. And, in a little while, having found my staff, we turned our backs upon the tavern, and began to run up the lane, side by side. As we went came the slam of a door behind us—a sudden clamour of voices, followed, a moment later, by the sharp report of a pistol, and, in that same fraction of time, I stumbled over some unseen obstacle, and my hat was whisked from my head.

" Are you hurt ? " panted my companion.

" No," said I, " but it was a very excellent shot nevertheless !" For, as I picked up my hat I saw a small round hole that pierced it through and through, midway between crown and brim.

The lane wound away between high hedges, which rendered our going very dark, for the moon was getting low, and difficult by reason of the deep wheel-ruts, but we hurried forward notwithstanding, urged on by the noise of the chase. We had traversed some half mile, thus, when my ears warned me that our pursuers were gaining upon us, and I was inwardly congratulating myself that I had stopped to find my staff, and wondering how much execution such a weapon might reasonably be capable of, when I found that my companion was no longer at my side. As I

" Come," said I, and (almost as quickly as it takes to set it down here) she was beside me upon the roof of the porch

Face Page 110

"Come," said I, and (almost as if
takes to set it down here) she was beside me upon
the roof of the porch

Face Page 110

paused, irresolute, her voice reached me from the shadow of the hedge.

" This way," she panted.

" Where ? " said I.

" Here ! " and, as she spoke, her hand slipped into mine, and so she led me through a small gate, into a broad, open meadow beyond. But, to attempt crossing this would be little short of madness, for (as I pointed out) we could not go a yard without being seen.

" No no," she returned, her breath still labouring, " wait—wait till they are past." And so, hand in hand, we stood there in the shadow, screened very effectively from the lane by the thick hedge, while the rush of our pursuers' feet drew nearer and nearer; until we could hear a voice that panted out curses upon the dark lane, ourselves, and everything concerned; at sound of which, my companion seemed to fall into a shivering fit, her clasp tightened upon my hand, and she drew closer to me. Thus we remained until voices and footsteps had grown faint with distance, but, even then, I could feel that she was trembling still. Suddenly she drew her fingers from mine, and covered her face with her hands.

" Oh, that man ! " she exclaimed in a whisper, " I didn't quite realise till now—what I have escaped. Oh, that beast ! "

" Sir Harry Mortimer ? " said I.

" You know him ? " she cried.

" Heaven forbid ! " I answered, " but I have seen him once before at ' The Chequers ' inn at Tonbridge, and I never forget names or faces—especially such as his."

" How I hate him ! " she whispered.

" An unpleasant animal, to be sure," said I. " But come, it were wiser to get as far from here as possible, they will doubtless be returning soon."

So we started off again, running in the shadow of the hedge. We had thus doubled back upon our pursuers, and, leaving the tavern upon our left, soon gained the kindly shadow of those woods through which I had passed in the early evening.

Borne to us upon the gentle wind was the haunting perfume of hidden flowers, and the sinking moon sent long shafts of silvery light to pierce the leafy gloom, and make the shadows more mysterious.

The path we followed was very narrow, so that sometimes my companion's knee touched mine, or her long, silken hair brushed my brow or cheek, as I stooped to lift some trailing branch that barred her way, or open a path for her through the leaves.

So we journeyed on through the mysteries of the woods together.

CHAPTER XX

CONCERNING DÆMONS IN GENERAL AND ONE IN PARTICULAR

In certain old books you shall find strange mention of witches, warlocks, succubæ, spirits, dæmons, and a thousand other powers of darkness, whose pronounced vocation was the plague of poor humanity. Within these books you may read (if you will) divers wondrous accounts, together with many learned disquisitions upon the same, and most minute and particular descriptions of witch-marks and the like.

Aforetime, when a man committed some great offence against laws human or divine, he was said to be possessed of a dæmon—that is to say, he became the medium and instrument through, and by which, the evil was wrought; thus, when in due season he came to be hanged, tortured, or burned, it was inflicted not so much as a punishment upon him, the man, as to exorcise, once and for all, the devil which possessed him.

In these material, common-sense days, we are wont to smile the superior smile at the dark superstitions and deplorable ignorance of our forefathers; yet life is much the same now as then, the devil goeth up and down in the world, spirits, dæmons, and the thousand powers of darkness abide with us still, though to-day they go by different names, for there is no man in this smug, complacent age of ours, but carries within him a power of evil greater or less, according to his intellect. Scratch off the social veneer, lift but a corner of the very decent cloak of our civilisation, and behold! there stands the Primal Man in all his old, wild savagery, and with the devil leering upon his shoulder. Indeed, to-day as surely as in the dim past, we are all possessed of a devil great or small, weaker or stronger as the case may be; a dæmon which, though he sometimes seems to slumber, is yet watchful, and ever ready to spring up, and possess us to the undoing of ourselves and others.

Thus, as I followed my companion through the wood, I was conscious of a Dæmon that ran beside me, leaping and gambolling at my elbow, though I kept my eyes straight before me. Anon, his clutching fingers were upon my arm, and fain I would have shaken him off, but could not; while, as I watched the swing, and grace of the lithe, feminine body before me, from the little foot to the crowning glory of her hair, she seemed a thousand times more beautiful than I had supposed. And I had saved her to-night—from what? There had been the fear of worse than death in her eyes when that step had sounded outside her chamber door. Hereupon, as I walked I began to recall much that I had read in the old romances of the gratitude of rescued ladies.

"Truly," said I to myself, "in olden days a lady well knew how to reward her rescuer!"

"Woman is woman—the same to-day as then—try her, try her!" chuckled the Dæmon. And now, as I looked more fully at this Dæmon, he seemed no dæmon at all, but rather, a jovial companion who nodded, and winked, and nudged me slyly with his elbow. "What are pretty faces for but to be admired?" said he in my ear; "what are slender waists for but to be pressed; and as for a kiss or two in a dark wood, with no one to spy—they like it, you dog, they like it!"

So we traversed the alleys of the wood, now in shadow, now in moonlight, the Lady, the Dæmon, and I, and always the perfume of hidden flowers seemed sweeter, and stronger, the gleam of her hair and the sway of her body the more alluring, and always the voice at my ear whispered: "Try her, you dog, try her."

At last, being come to a broad, grassy glade, the lady paused, and, standing in the full radiance of the dying moon, looked up at me with a smile on her red lips.

" They can never find us now ! " she said.

" No, they can never find us now," I repeated, while the Dæmon at my elbow chuckled again.

" And—oh, sir ! I can never, never thank you," she began.

" Don't," said I, not looking at her ; " don't thank me till—we are out of the wood."

" I think," she went on slowly, "that you—can guess from—from what you saved me, and can understand something of my gratitude, for I can never express it all."

" Indeed," said I, " indeed you overestimate my service."

" You risked your life for me, sir," said she, her eyes glistening, " surely my thanks are due to you for that ? And I do thank you—from my heart ! " and with a swift, impulsive gesture, she stretched out her hands to me. For a brief moment I hesitated, then seized them, and drew her close. But, even as I stooped above her, she repulsed me desperately ; her loosened hair brushed my eyes and lips—blinded, maddened me ; my hat fell off, and all at once her struggles ceased.

" Sir Maurice Vibart ! " she panted, and I saw a hopeless terror in her face. But the Dæmon's jovial voice chuckled in my ear :

" Ho, Peter Vibart, act up to your cousin's reputation, who's to know the difference ? " My arms tightened about her, then I loosed her suddenly, and, turning, smote my clenched fist against a tree ; which done, I stooped and picked up my hat and blackthorn staff.

" Madam," said I, looking down upon my bleeding knuckles, " I am not Sir Maurice Vibart. It seems my fate to be mistaken for him wherever I go. My name is Peter, plain and unvarnished, and I am very humbly your servant." Now as I spoke it seemed that the Dæmon, no longer the Jovial Companion, was himself again, horns, hoof, and tail—nay, indeed, he seemed a thousand times more foul and hideous than before, as he mouthed, and jibed at me in baffled fury; wherefore, I smiled, and turned my back upon him.

"Come," said I, extending my hand to the trembling girl, "let us get out of these dismal woods." For a space she hesitated, looking up at me beneath her lashes, then reached out, and laid her fingers in mine, and, as we turned away, I knew that the Dæmon had cast himself upon the ground, and was tearing at the grass in a paroxysm of rage and bafflement.

"It is strange," said I, after we had gone some little distance, "very strange that you should only have discovered this resemblance here, and now, for surely you saw my face plainly enough at the inn."

"No; you see. I hardly looked at you."

"And, now that you do look at me, am I so very much like Sir Maurice?"

"Not now," she answered, shaking her head, "for though you are of his height, and though your features are much the same as his, your expression is different. But a moment ago—when your hat fell off——"

"Yes?" said I.

"Your expression—your face looked——"

"Demoniac?" I suggested.

"Yes," she answered.

"Hum!" said I.

So we went upon our way, nor paused until we had left the Dæmon and the dark woods behind us. Then I looked from the beauty of the sweet, pure earth to the beauty of her who stood beside me, and I saw that her glance rested upon the broken knuckles of my right hand. Meeting my eyes her own drooped, and a flush crept into her cheeks, and, though of course she could not have seen the Dæmon, yet I think that she understood.

CHAPTER XXI

" JOURNEYS END IN LOVERS' MEETINGS "

THE moon was fast sinking below the tree-tops to our left, what time we reached a road, or rather cart-track that wound away up a hill. Faint and far a church clock slowly chimed the hour of three, the solemn notes coming sweet and silvery with distance.

" What chimes are those ? " I inquired.

" Cranbrook Church."

" Is it far to Cranbrook ? "

" One mile this way, but two by the road yonder."

" You seem very well acquainted with these parts," said I.

" I have lived here all my life—those are the Cambourne Woods over there——"

" Cambourne Woods ! " said I.

" Part of the Sefton estates," she continued ; " Cambourne village lies to the right, beyond."

" The Lady Sophia Sefton of Cambourne ! " said I thoughtfully.

" My dearest friend," nodded my companion.

" They say she is very handsome," said I.

" Then they speak truth, sir."

" She has been described to me," I went on, " as a Peach, a Goddess, and a Plum ; which should you consider the most proper term ! " My companion shot an arch glance at me from the corners of her eyes, and I saw a dimple come and go, beside the curve of her mouth.

" Goddess, to be sure," said she ; " peaches have such rough skins, and plums are apt to be sticky."

" And goddesses," I added, " were all very well upon Olympus, but, in this matter-of-fact age, must be sadly out of place. Speaking for myself——"

" Have you ever seen this particular Goddess ? " inquired my companion.

117

" Never."

" Then wait until you have, sir."

The moon was down now, yet the summer sky was wonderfully luminous and in the east I almost fancied I could detect the first faint gleam of day. And after we had traversed some distance in silence, my companion suddenly spoke, but without looking at me.

" You have never once asked who I am," she said, almost reproachfully I thought, " nor how I came to be shut up in such a place—with such a man."

"Why, as to that," I answered, "I make it a general rule to avoid awkward subjects when I can, and never to ask questions that it will be difficult to answer."

" I should find not the least difficulty in answering either," said she.

" Besides," I continued, " it is no affair of mine, after all."

" Oh ! " said she, turning away from me ; and then, very slowly : " No, I suppose not."

" Certainly not," I added ; " how should it be ? "

" How indeed ! " said she over her shoulder. And then I saw that she was angry, and wondered.

" And yet," I went on, after a lapse of silence, " I think I could have answered both questions the moment I saw you at your casement."

" Oh ! " said she—this time in a tone of surprise, and her anger all gone again, for I saw that she was smiling ; and again I wondered.

" Yes," I nodded.

" Then," said she, seeing I was silent, " whom do you suppose me ? "

" You are, to the best of my belief, the Lady Helen Dunstan." My companion stood still, and regarded me for a moment in wide-eyed astonishment.

" And how, sir, pray, did you learn all this ? " she demanded with the dimple once more peeping at me slyly from the corner of her pretty mouth.

" By the very simple method of adding two and two together," I answered ; " moreover, no longer since than yesterday I broke bread with a certain Mr Beverley——"

I heard her breath come in a sudden gasp, and next moment she was peering up into my face while her hands beat upon my breast with soft, quick little taps.

" Beverley ! " she whispered. " Beverley !—no, no —why, they told me—Sir Harry told me that Peregrine lay dying—at Tonbridge.

" Then Sir Harry Mortimer lied to you," said I, " for no longer ago than yesterday afternoon I sat in a ditch eating bread and cheese with a Mr Peregrine Beverley."

" Oh !—are you sure—are you sure ? "

" Quite sure. And, as we ate, he told me many things, and among them, of a life of wasted opportunities—of foolish riot, and prodigal extravagance, and of its logical consequence—want."

" My poor Perry ! " she murmured.

" He spoke also of his love for a very beautiful and good woman, and its hopelessness."

" My dear, dear Perry ! " said she again.

" And yet," said I, " all this is admittedly his own fault, and, as I think Heraclitus says : ' Suffering is the inevitable consequence of Sin, or Folly.' "

"And he is well ? " she asked ; " quite—quite well ? "

" He is," said I.

" Thank God ! " she whispered. " Tell me," she went on, " is he so very, very poor—is he much altered ? I have not seen him for a whole, long year."

"Why, a year is apt to change a man," I answered. " Adversity is a hard school, but, sometimes, a very good one."

" Were he changed, no matter how—were he a beggar upon the roads, I should love him—always ! " said she, speaking in that soft, caressing voice which only the best of women possess.

" Yes, I had guessed as much," said I, and found myself sighing.

" A year is a long, long time, and we were to have been married this month, but my father quarrelled with him, and forbade him the house, so poor Perry went back to London. Then we heard he was ruined, and I almost died with grief—you see, his very

poverty only made me love him the more.   Yesterday
—that man——"

" Sir Harry Mortimer ? " said I.

" Yes (he was a friend of whom I had often heard
Perry speak); and he told me that my Perry lay at
Tonbridge, dying, and begging to see me before the
end. He offered to escort me to him, assuring me that
I could reach home again long before dusk.   My
father, who I knew would never permit me to go, was
absent, and so—I ran away. Sir Harry had a carriage
waiting, but, almost as soon as the door was closed
upon us, and we had started, I began to be afraid of
him and—and——"

" Sir Harry, as I said before, is an unpleasant
animal," I nodded.

" Thank Heaven," she pursued, " we had not gone
very far before the chaise broke down ! And—the
rest you know."

The footpath we had been following now led over
a stile into a narrow lane or byway. Very soon we
came to a high stone wall wherein was set a small
wicket. Through this she led me, and we entered a
broad park where was an avenue of fine old trees,
beyond which I saw the gables of a house, for the
stars had long since paled to the dawn, and there was
a glory in the east.

" Your father will be rejoiced to have you safe back
again," said I.

" Yes," she nodded, " but he will be very angry."
And, hereupon, she stopped and began to pull, and
twist, and pat her shining hair with dexterous white
fingers, talking thus the while :

" My mother died at my birth, and since then father
has worshipped her memory, and his face always
grows wonderfully gentle when he looks upon her
portrait. They say I'm greatly like her—though she
was a famous beauty in her day. And, indeed, I think
there must be some truth in it, for, no matter how I
may put him out, my father can never be very angry
when my hair is dressed so."

With the word, she turned, and truly, I thought the

face peeping out from its clustered curls even more lovely and bewitching than before.

" I very much doubt if any man could," said I.

As we approached the house, I saw that the smooth gravel was much cut up as though by the coming and going of many wheels, and horses, and also that one of the windows still shone with a bright light, and it was towards this window that my companion led me. In a while, having climbed the terrace steps, I noticed that this was one of those French windows opening to the ground. Now, looking through into the room beyond, I beheld an old man who sat bowed down at a table, with his white head pillowed upon his arms, sitting so very still that he might have been asleep but for the fierce grip of his twitching hands. Now upon the table, at no great distance from him, between the guttering candles, lay a hat—a very ill-used, battered-looking object which I thought I recognised, where-fore, looking about, I presently espied its owner lean-ing against the mantel. He was powdered with dust from head to foot, and his worn garments looked more ragged than ever; and, as he stood there, in the droop of his head, and the listless set of his shoulders, there was an air of the most utter dejection, and hopeless-ness, while upon his thin cheek I saw the glisten of a great, solitary tear. But, as I looked, the window was burst suddenly open :

" Perry ! "

Love, surprise, joy, pity—all were summed up in that one short word—yet deeper than all was love. And, at that cry, the white head was raised, raised in time to see a vision of loveliness caught up in two ragged arms.

" Father ! "

And now the three heads—the white, the golden, and the black, were drawn down together, drawn, and held close in an embrace that was indeed reunion.

Then, seeing my presence was become wholly un-necessary, I turned away, and was soon, once more, deep among the trees. Yet, as I went, I suddenly heard voices that called upon my name, but I kept on, and, in due season, came out upon the broad highway.

And, in a little, as I went, very full of thought, the sun rose up. So I walked along through a world all glorious with morning.

" Father ! "

Face Page 122

CHAPTER XXII

IN WHICH I MEET WITH A LITERARY TINKER

EVEN in that drowsy, semi-conscious state, that most delightful borderland which lies midway between sleeping and waking, I knew it could not be the woodpecker who, as I judged from sundry manifest signs, lodged in the tree above me. No woodpecker that ever pecked could originate such sounds as these—two quick, light strokes, followed by another, and heavier, thus: Tap, tap—TAP; a pause, and then, tap, tap—TAP again, and so on.

Whatever doubts I may have yet harboured on the subject, however, were presently dispelled by a fragrance sweeter, to the nostrils of a hungry man, than the breath of flowers, the spices of the East, or all the vaunted perfumes of Arabia—in a word, the odour of frying bacon.

Hereupon, I suddenly realised how exceedingly keen was my appetite, and sighed, bethinking me that I must first find a tavern before I could satisfy my craving, when a voice reached me from no great distance, a full, rich, sonorous voice, singing a song. And the words of the song were these:

> "A tinker I am, O a tinker am I,
> A tinker I'll live, and a tinker I'll die;
> If the King in his crown would change places wi' me
> I'd laugh so I would, and I'd say unto he:
> 'A tinker I am, O a tinker am I,
> A tinker I'll live, and a tinker I'll die.'"

It was a quaint air, with a shake at the end of the two first and two last lines, which, altogether, I thought very pleasing. I advanced, guided by the voice, until I came out into a grassy lane. Seated upon an artfully-contrived folding stool, was a man. He was a very small man despite his great voice, who held a kettle between his knees, and a light hammer in his hand, while a little to one side of him there blazed a crackling fire of twigs upon which a hissing frying-pan was balanced. But what chiefly drew and held my attention was the man's face; narrow and peaked, with little, round, twinkling eyes set deep in his head, close black hair, grizzled at the temples, and a long, blue chin.

And presently, as I stood staring at him, he finished his song, and chancing to raise his eyes stared back at me.

"Good-morning!" said he at last, with a bright nod.

"So then you didn't cut your throat in the Hollow Oak, after all?" said I.

"Nor likely to either, master," he answered, shaking his head. "Lord love your eyes and limbs, no!"

"But," said I, "some day or so ago I met a man——"

"Ah!" nodded the Tinker, "to be sure you did."

"A peddler of brooms, and ribands——"

"Gabbing Dick!" nodded the Tinker.

"Who told me very seriously——"

"That I'd been found in the big holler oak wi' my throat cut," nodded the Tinker.

"But what did he mean by it?"

"Why, y'see," explained the Tinker, leaning over to turn a frizzling bacon-rasher very dexterously with the blade of a jack-knife, "y'see, Gabbing Dick is oncommon fond of murders, hangings, sooicides, and such like—it's just a way he's got."

"A very unpleasant way!" said I.

"But very harmless when all's done, and said," added the Tinker.

"You mean?"

"A leetle weak up here," explained the Tinker, tapping his forehead with the handle of the jack-knife. "His father was murdered the day afore he were born, d'ye see, which druv his poor mother out of her mind, which conditions is apt to make a man a leetle strange."

"Poor fellow!" said I, while the Tinker began his tap-tapping again.

"Are you hungry?" he inquired suddenly, glancing up at me with his hammer poised.

"Very hungry!" said I. Hereupon, he set down his hammer, and turning to a pack at his side, proceeded to extract therefrom a loaf of bread, a small tin of butter, and a piece of bacon, from which last he cut sundry slices with the jack-knife. He now lifted the hissing rashers from the pan to a tin plate, which he set upon the grass at my feet, together with the bread and the butter, and having produced a somewhat battered knife and fork, handed them to me with another bright nod.

"You are very kind!" said I.

"Why, I'm a man as is fond o' company, y'see—especially of one who can think, and talk, and you have the face of both. I am—as you might say—a literary cove, being fond o' books, nov-els, and such like." And in a little while, the bacon being done to his liking, we sat down together, and began to eat.

"That was a strange song of yours," said I, after a while.

"Did you like it?" he inquired with a quick tilt of his head.

"Both words and tune," I answered.

"I made the words myself," said the Tinker

"And do you mean it?"

"Mean what?" asked the Tinker.

"That you would rather be a tinker than a king?"

"Why, to be sure I would," he rejoined. "Bein' a literary cove I know summat o' history, and a king's life weren't all lavender—not by no manner o' means, nor yet a bed o' roses."

"Yet there's much to be said for a king."

"Very little, I think," said the Tinker.

"A king has great advantages."

"Which he generally abuses," said the Tinker.

"There have been some great and noble kings."

"But a great many more bad 'uns!" said the Tinker. "And then, look how often they got theirselves pisoned, or stabbed, or 'ad their 'eads chopped off ! No—if you axes me, I prefer to tinker a kettle under a hedge."

" Then you are contented ? "

" Not quite," he answered, his face falling; " me being a literary cove (as I think I've mentioned afore), it has always been my wish to be a scholar."

" Far better be a tinker," said I.

" Young fellow," said the Tinker, shaking his head reprovingly, " you're off the mark there—knowledge is power; why, Lord love my eyes and limbs ! what's finer than to be able to read in the Greek and Latin ? "

" To possess the capacity of earning an honest livelihood," said I.

" Why, I tell you," continued the Tinker, unheeding my remark, " I'd give this here left hand o' mine to be able to read the very words of such men as Plato, Aristotle, Epictetus, Xenophon, and all the rest of 'em."

" There are numerous translations," said I.

" Ah, to be sure ! " sighed the Tinker, " but then, they are translations."

"There are good translations as well as bad," said I.

" Maybe," returned the Tinker, " maybe, but a translation's only a echo, after all, however good it be." As he spoke, he dived into his pack and brought forth a book, which he handed to me. It was a smallish volume in battered leathern covers, and had evidently seen much long and hard service. Opening it at the title-page I read :

Epictetus
his
ENCHIRIDION
with
Simplicius
his
COMMENT:
Made English from the Greek
By
George Stanhope, late Fellow
Of King's College in Camb.
LONDON
Printed for Richard Sare at Gray's Inn Gate in Holborn
and Joseph Hindmarsh against the Exchange in Cornhill:
1694

" You've read Epictetus, perhaps ? " inquired the Tinker.

" I have."

" Not in the Greek, of course."

" Yes," said I, smiling, " though by dint of much labour."

The Tinker stopped chewing to stare at me wide-eyed, then swallowed his mouthful at one gulp.

" Lord love me ! " he exclaimed, " and you so young, too ! "

" No," said I ; " I'm twenty-five."

" And Latin, now—don't tell me you can read the Latin."

" But I can't make a kettle, or even mend one, for that matter," said I.

" But you are a scholar, and it's a fine thing to be a scholar ! "

" And I tell you again, it is better to be a tinker," said I.

" How so ? "

" It is a healthier life, in the first place," said I.

" That, I can believe," nodded the Tinker.

" It is a happier life, in the second place."

" That, I doubt," returned the Tinker.

" And, in the third place, it pays much better."

" That, I don't believe," said the Tinker.

" Nevertheless," said I, " speaking for myself, I have, in the course of my twenty-five years, earned but ten shillings, and that—but by the sale of my waistcoat."

" Lord love me ! " exclaimed the Tinker, staring.

" A man," I pursued, " may be a far better scholar than I—may be full of the wisdom of the Ancients, and the teachings of all the great thinkers and philos-ophers, and yet starve to death—indeed frequently does ; but who ever heard of a starving Tinker ? "

" But a scholar may write great books," said the Tinker.

" A scholar rarely writes a great book," said I, shaking my head, " probably for the good and suffici-ent reason that great books never *are* written."

"Young fellow," said the Tinker, staring, "what do you mean by that?"

"I mean that truly great books only happen, and very rarely."

"But a scholar may happen to write a great book," said the Tinker.

"To be sure—he may; a book that nobody will risk publishing, and if so—a book that nobody will trouble to read, nowadays."

"Why so?"

"Because this is an eminently unliterary age, incapable of thought, and therefore, seeking to be amused. Whereas the writing of books was once a painful art, it has of late become a trick very easy of accomplishment, requiring no regard for probability, and little thought, so long as it is packed sufficiently full of impossible incidents through which a ridiculous heroine, and a more absurd hero, duly sigh their appointed way to the last chapter. Whereas books were once a power, they are, of late, degenerated into things of amusement with which to kill an idle hour, and be promptly forgotten the next."

"Yet the great books remain," said the Tinker.

"Yes," said I; "but who troubles their head over Homer or Virgil these days—who cares to open Steele's 'Tatler,' or Addison's 'Spectator' while there is the latest novel to be had, or ' Bell's Life ' to be found on any coffee-house table?"

"And why," said the Tinker, looking at me over a piece of bacon skewered upon the point of his jack-knife, "why don't you write a book?"

"I probably shall, some day," I answered.

"And supposing," said the Tinker, eyeing the piece of bacon thoughtfully, "supposing nobody ever reads it?"

"The worse for them!" said I.

Thus we talked of books, and the making of books (something of which I have already set down in another place), until our meal was at an end.

"You are a rather strange young man, I think," said the Tinker, as, having duly wiped knife, and fork, and plate upon a handful of grass, I handed them back.

"Yet you are a stranger tinker."

"How so?"

"Why, who ever heard of a tinker who wrote verses, and worked with a copy of Epictetus at his elbow?"

"Which I don't deny as I'm a great thinker," nodded the Tinker; "to be sure, I think a powerful lot."

"A dangerous habit," said I, shaking my head, "and a most unwise one!"

"Eh?" cried the Tinker, staring.

"Your serious, thinking man," I explained, "is seldom happy—as a rule has few friends, being generally regarded askance, and is always misunderstood by his fellows. All the world's great thinkers, from Christ down, were generally misunderstood, looked at askance, and had very few friends."

"But these were all great men," said the Tinker.

"We think so now, but in their day they were very much despised, and who was more hated, by the very people He sought to aid, than Christ?"

"By the evil-doers, yes," nodded the Tinker.

"On the contrary," said I, "his worst enemies were men of learning, good citizens, and patterns of morality, who looked upon him as a dangerous zealot, threatening the destruction of the old order of things, hence they killed him—as an agitator. Things are much the same to-day. History tells us that Christ, or the spirit of Christ, has entered into many men who have striven to enlighten and better the conditions of their kind, and they have generally met with violent deaths, for Humanity is very gross and blind."

The Tinker slowly wiped his clasp-knife upon the leg of his breeches, closed it, and slipped it into his pocket.

"Nevertheless," said he at last, "I am convinced that you are a very strange young man."

"Be that as it may," said I, "the bacon was de-

I

licious. I have never enjoyed a meal so much—except once at an inn called 'The Old Cock.'"

"I know it," nodded the Tinker; "a very poor house."

"But the ham and eggs are beyond praise," said I; "still, my meal here under the trees with you will long remain a pleasant memory."

"Good-bye, then," said the Tinker. "Good-bye, young man, and I wish you happiness."

"What is Happiness?" said I. The Tinker removed his hat, and having scratched his head, put it on again.

"Happiness," said he; "Happiness is the state of being content with one's self, the world, and everything in general."

"Then," said I, "I fear I can never be happy."

"And why not?"

"Because, supposing I ever became contented with the world, and everything in general, which is highly improbable, I shall never, never be contented with myself."

CHAPTER XXIII

CONCERNING HAPPINESS, A PLOUGHMAN, AND SILVER BUTTONS

Now as I went, pondering on true Happiness, and the nature of it, I beheld a man ploughing in a field hard by, and, as he ploughed, he whistled lustily. And drawing near to the field, I sat down upon a gate, and watched, for there are few sights and sounds I am fonder of than the gleam of the ploughshare and the sighing whisper it makes as it turns the fragrant loam.

"A truly noble occupation!" said I to myself, "dignified by the ages—ay—old, well nigh, as the green earth itself, no man need be ashamed to guide a plough."

And indeed a fine sight it made, the straining horses, the stalwart figure of the Ploughman, with the blue sky, the long brown furrows, and, away and beyond, the tender green of leaves; while the jingle of the harness, the clear, merry, whistled notes, and the song of a skylark, high above our heads, all blended into a chorus it was good to hear.

As he came up to where I sat upon the gate, the Ploughman stopped, and wiping the glistening moisture from his brow, nodded good-humouredly.

"A fine morning!" said I.

"So it be, sir, now you come to mention it, it do be a fine day sure-ly."

"You, at least, seem happy," said I.

"Happy?" he exclaimed, staring.

"Yes," said I.

"Well, I bean't."

"And why not?" The Ploughman scratched his ear, and carried his glance from my face up to the sky, and down again.

"I dunno," he answered, "but I bean't."

131

"Yet you whistle gaily enough."

"Why, a man must do summat."

"Then you seem strong and healthy."

"Yes, I do be fine an' hearty."

"And sleep well?"

"Like a blessed log."

"And eat well?"

"Eat!" he exclaimed, with a mighty laugh. "Lord! I should think so—why, I'm always eatin' or thinkin' of it. Oh, I'm a fine eater, I am—an' I bean't no chicken at drinkin' neither."

"Then you ought to be happy."

"Ah!—but I bean't!" he repeated, shaking his head.

"Have you any troubles?"

"None as I can think on."

"You earn good money every week?"

"Ten shillin'."

"You are not married?"

"Not me."

"Then," said I, "you must be happy." The Ploughman pulled at his ear again, looked slowly all round the field, and, finally, shook his head.

"Well," said he, "I bean't."

"But why not?" His eye roved slowly up from my boots to the buttons on my coat.

"Them be fine buttons!" said he.

"Do you think so?"

"Look like silver!"

"They are silver," said I.

"Lord!" he exclaimed, "you wouldn't part wi' they buttons, I suppose?"

"That depends!"

"On what?"

"On how much you would give for them." The Ploughman thrust a hand into a deep pocket, and brought up five shillings.

"I were a-goin' to buy a pair o' boots, on my way 'ome," he explained, "but I'd rayther 'ave they buttons, if five shillin'll buy 'em."

"The boots would be more serviceable," said I.

" Maybe, sir, but then, everybody wears boots, but there bean't many as can show buttons the like o' them—so if you're willin——"

" Lend me your knife," said I. And, forthwith, I sawed off the eight silver buttons, and dropped them into his palm, whereupon he handed me the money with great alacrity.

" And now," said I, " tell me why you are not happy."

" Well," returned the Ploughman, back at his ear again, " ye see it bein' as you ask so sudden-like, I can't 'zackly say, but if you was to pass by in a day or two, why, maybe I could tell ye."

So, pocketing the buttons, he whooped cheerily to his horses, and plodded off, whistling more merrily than ever.

CHAPTER XXIV

WHICH INTRODUCES THE READER TO THE ANCIENT

THE sun was high when I came to a place where the ways divided, and, while I stood hesitating which road to take, I heard the cool plash and murmur of a brook at no great distance. Wherefore, being hot, and thirsty, I scrambled through the hedge, and coming to the brook, threw myself face down beside it, and catching up the sweet pure water in my hands, drank my fill; which done, I bathed my feet, and hands, and face, and became much heartened and refreshed thereby. Now because I have ever loved the noise of running waters, in a little while, I rose and walked on beside the stream, listening to its blithesome melody. So, by devious ways, for the brook wound prodigiously, I came at length to a sudden declivity down which the water plunged in a miniature cascade, sparkling in the sun, and gleaming with a thousand rainbow hues. On I went, climbing down as best I might, until I found myself in a sort of green basin, very cool after the heat and glare of the roads, for the high, tree-clad sides afforded much shade. On I went, past fragrant thickets, and bending willows, with soft lush grass underfoot and leafy arches overhead, and the brook singing and chattering at my side; albeit a brook of changeful mood, now laughing and dimpling in some fugitive ray of sunshine, now sighing, and whispering in the shadows, but ever moving upon its appointed way, and never quite silent. So I walked on beside the brook, watching the fish that showed like darting shadows on the bottom, until, chancing to raise my eyes, I stopped. And there, screened by leaves, shut in among the green, stood a small cottage, or hut. My second glance showed it to be tenantless, for the thatch was partly gone, the windows were broken, and the door had long since fallen from its hinges. Yet, despite its forlornness and desolation, despite the dilapidation of broken door, and fallen chimney, there was something in the air of the place that drew me strangely. It was somewhat roughly put together, but still very strong, and seemed, save for the roof, weather-fast.

" A man might do worse than live here," thought I, " with the birds for neighbours, and the brook to sing him to sleep at night. Indeed a man might live very happily in such a place."

I was still looking at the hut, with this in my mind, when I was startled by hearing a thin, quavering voice behind me :

" Be you'm a-lookin' at t' cottage, master ? "

Turning sharp round, I beheld a very ancient man in a smock frock, who carried a basket on one arm, and leaned upon a stick.

" Yes," I answered; " I was wondering how it came to be built in such an out-of-the-world spot."

" Why, 'twere built by a wanderin' man o' the roads."

" It's very lonely ! " said I.

" Ye may well say so, sir—haunted it be tu."

" Haunted ? " said I.

" Haunted as ever was ! " answered the old man with a sprightly nod strangely contrasting with his wrinkled face and tremulous limbs ; " no one ventur's nigh the place arter dark, an' few enough in the daytime, for that matter."

" On account of the ghost ? "

" Ah ! " nodded the Ancient, " moans 'e du, an' likewise groans. Theer's some as says 'e twitters tu, an' shakes chains."

" Then nobody has lived here of late ? "

" Bless 'ee no—nor wouldn't, no, not if ye paid 'em tu. Nobody's come a-nigh the place, you may say, since 'twere built by the wanderin' man. Lived 'ere all alone, 'e did—killed 'isself 'ere likewise."

" Killed himself ! " said I.

" Ah !—'ung 'isself—be'ind th' door yonder, sixty

an' six year ago come August, an' 'twere me as found
'im. Ye see," said the old man, setting down his
basket, and seating himself with great nicety on the
moss-grown doorstep, " ye see, 'twere a tur'ble storm
that night—rain, and wind, wi' every now an' then a
gert, cracklin' flame o' lightnin'. I mind I'd been up
to th' farm a-courtin' o' Nancy Brent—she'm dead
now, poor lass, years an' years ago, but she were a
fine, buxom maid in those days, d'ye see. Well, I
were comin' 'ome, and what wi' one thing an' another,
I lost my way. An' presently, as I were stumblin'
along in the dark, comes another crackle o' lightnin',
an' lookin' up, what should I see but this 'ere cottage.
'Twere newer-lookin' then, wi' a door, an' winders,
but the door was shut, an' the winders was dark—so
theer I stood in the rain, not likin' to disturb the
stranger, for 'e were a gert, fierce, unfriendly kind o'
chap, an' uncommon fond o' bein' left alone. How-
s'ever, arter a while, up I goes to th' door, an' knocks
(for I were a gert, strong, strappin', well-lookin' figure
o' a man myself, in those days, d'ye see, an' could
give a good buffet, an' tak' one tu), so up I goes to th'
door, an' knocks wi' my fist clenched, all ready (an' a
tidy, sizable fist it were in those days)—but Lord!
nobody answered, so, at last, I lifted the latch." Here
the Ancient paused to draw a snuff-box from his
pocket, with great deliberation, noting my awakened
interest with a twinkling eye.

" Well?" I inquired.

" Well," he continued slowly, " I lifted th' latch,
an' give a push to the door, but it would only open a
little way—an inch, p'r'aps, an' stuck." Here he
tapped, and opened his snuff-box.

" Well?" I inquired again.

" Well," he went on, " I give it a gert, big push wi'
my shoulder (I were a fine, strong chap in those days),
an', just as it flew open, comes another flash o' lightnin', an' the fust thing I seen was—a boot."

" A boot!" I exclaimed.

" A boot as ever was," nodded the Ancient, and
took a pinch of snuff with great apparent gusto.

He pointed to a rusty iron staple that had been driven deep into the beam above the door

" Go on," said I, " go on."

" Oh !—it's a fine story, a fine story !" he chuckled, " theer bean't many men o' my age as 'as fund a 'ung man in a thunderstorm ! Well, as I tell ye, I seen a boot, likewise a leg, an' theer were this 'ere wanderin' man o' the roads a-danglin' be'ind th' door from a stapil—look ye ! " he exclaimed, rising with some little difficulty, and hobbling into the hut, " theer be th' very stapil, so it be ! " and he pointed up to a rusty iron staple that had been driven deep into the beam above the door.

" And why," said I, " why did he hang himself ? "

" Seein' 'e 'ad no friends, and never told nobody— nobody never knowed," answered the old man, shaking his head, " but on that theer stapil 'e 'ung 'isself an' on that theer stapil I fund 'im, on a stormy night sixty and six year ago come August."

" You have a wonderful memory ! " said I.

" Ay, to be sure ; a wunnerful mem'ry, a wunnerful mem'ry ! "

" Sixty and six years is an age," said I.

" So it be," nodded the Ancient, " I were a fine young chap in those days, tall I were, an' straight as a arrer. I be a bit different now."

" Why, you are getting old," said I.

" So's t' stapil yonder, but t' stapil looks nigh as good as ever."

" Iron generally wears better than flesh and blood," said I ; " it's only natural."

" Ay, but 'e can't last for ever," said the Ancient, frowning, and shaking his head at the rusty staple. " I've watched un, month in an' month out, all these years, an' seen un growin' rustier an' rustier, an' : ' I'll last 'ee out yet,' I've said tu un—'e knows it— 'e've heerd me many an' many a time—' I'll last 'ee out yet ! " I've said, an' so I will, tu—'e can't last for ever an' I be a vig'rus man—a mortal vig'rus man— bean't I ? "

" Wonderfully ! " said I.

" An' so strong as a bull ? "

" To be sure."

" An' t' stapil can't last much longer—eh, maister ? —so old an' rusty as 'e be ? "

" One would hardly think so."

" Not so long as a tur'ble vig'rus man, like I be ? " he inquired with a certain wistful appeal in his eyes.

" No," I answered impulsively.

" I knowed it—I knowed it," he chuckled, feebly brandishing his stick, " such a poor old stapil as 'tis, all eat up wi' rust. Every time I come 'ere a-gatherin' watercress, I come in an' give un a look, an' watch un rustin' away, an' rustin' away ; I'll see un go fust, arter all, so I will ! " and, with another nod at the staple, he turned, and hobbled out into the sunshine.

And seeing how, despite his brave showing, he laboured to carry the heavy basket, I presently took it from him, disregarding his protests, and set off by his side ; yet, as we went, I turned once to look back at the deserted hut.

" You'm thinkin' 'tis a tur'ble bad place at night ? " said the old man.

" On the contrary," I answered, " I was thinking it might suit a homeless man like me very well indeed."

" D'ye mean—to live there ? " exclaimed the Ancient.

" Yes," said I.

" Then you bean't afraid o' the ghost ? "

" No," I answered.

" P'r'aps you be one o' they fules as think theer bean't no ghosts ? "

" As to that," I answered, " I don't know, but I don't think I should be much afraid, and it is a great blessing to have some spot on this unfriendly world that we can call ' home '—even though it be but a hut, and haunted."

In a little while the path we followed led up a somewhat steep ascent which, though not so precipitous as the place where I had entered the hollow, was a difficult climb, notwithstanding : seeing which, I put out a hand to aid my aged companion. But he repulsed me almost sharply :

" Let be," he panted, " let be, nobody's never 'elped me up this 'ere path, an' nobody never shall ! "

So up we went, the Ancient and I, side by side, and very slowly, until, the summit being reached, he seated himself, spent and breathless, upon a fallen tree, which had doubtless served this purpose many times before, and mopped at his wrinkled brow with a trembling hand.

" Ye see," he cried, as soon as he had recovered his breath sufficiently, " ye see, I be wunnerful spry an' active—could dance ye a hornpipe any day, if I was so minded."

" On my word," said I, " I believe you could ! But where are you going now ? "

" To Siss'n'urst ! "

" How far is that ? "

" 'Bout a mile acrost t' fields, you can see the pint o' Joel Amos's oast-'ouse above the trees yonder."

" Is there a good inn at Sissinghurst ? "

" Ay, theer's ' The Bull,' comfortable, an' draws fine ale ! "

" Then I will go to Sissinghurst."

" Ay, ay," nodded the old man, " if it be good ale an' a comfortable inn you want you need seek no further nor Siss'n'urst ; ninety an' one years I've lived there, an' I know."

" Ninety-one years ! " I repeated.

" As ever was ! " returned the Ancient, with another nod. " I be the oldest man in these parts 'cept David Relf, an' 'e died last year."

" Why then, if he's dead, you must be the oldest," said I.

" No," said the Ancient, shaking his head, " ye see it be this way : David were my brother, an' uncommon proud 'e were o' bein' the oldest man in these parts, an' now that 'e be dead an' gone it du seem a poor thing—ah ! a very poor thing !—to tak' 'vantage of a dead man, an' him my own brother ! " Saying which, the Ancient rose, and we went on together, side by side, towards Sissinghurst village.

CHAPTER XXV

OF BLACK GEORGE, THE SMITH, AND HOW WE THREW THE HAMMER

"THE BULL" is a plain, square, white-washed building, with a sloping roof, and before the door an open portico, wherein are set two seats on which one may sit of a sunny afternoon with a mug of ale at one's elbow and watch the winding road, the thatched cottages bowered in roses, or the quiver of distant trees where the red, conical roof of some oast-house makes a vivid note of colour amid the green. Or one may close one's eyes and hark to the chirp of the swallows under the eaves, the distant lowing of cows, or the clink of hammers from the smithy across the way.

And presently, as we sat there drowsing in the sun, to us came one from the "tap," a bullet-headed fellow, small of eye, and nose, but great of jaw, albeit he was become somewhat fat and fleshy—who, having nodded to me, sat him down beside the Ancient, and addressed him as follows:

"Black Jarge be 'took' again, Gaffer!"

"Ah! I knowed 'twould come soon or late, Simon," said the Ancient, shaking his head, "I knowed as 'e'd never last the month out."

"Seemed goin' on all quiet and reg'lar, though," said the bullet-headed man, whom I discovered to be the landlord of "The Bull"—"seemed nice and quiet, and nothin' out o' the way, when, 'bout an hour ago it were, 'e ups and heaves Sam out into the road."

"Ah!" said the old man, nodding his head again, "to be sure, I've noticed, Simon, as 'tis generally about the twentieth o' the month as Jarge gets 'took.'"

"'E've got a wonderful 'ead, 'ave the Gaffer!" said Simon, turning to me.

140

" Yes," said I, " but who is Black George; how comes he to be ' taken,' and by what ? "

" Gaffer," said the Innkeeper, " you tell un."

" Why, then," began the Ancient, nothing loth, "Black Jarge be a gert, big, strong man—the biggest, gertest, and strongest in the South Country, d'ye see (a'most as fine a man as I were in my time), and, off and on, gets took wi' tearin's, and rages, at which times 'e don't mind who 'e 'its——"

" No—nor wheer ! " added the Innkeeper.

" Oh, 'e be a bad man, be Black Jarge when 'e's took, for 'e 'ave a knack, d'ye see, of takin' 'old o' the one nighest to un, and a-heavin' of un over 'is 'ead."

" Extremely unpleasant ! " said I.

" Just what he done this marnin' wi' Sam," nodded the Innkeeper—" hove un out into the road, 'e did."

" And what did Sam do ? " I inquired.

" Oh ! Sam were mighty glad to get off so easy."

" Sam must be a very remarkable fellow—undoubtedly a philosopher," said I.

" 'E be nowt to look at ! " said the Ancient.

Now at this moment there came a sudden deep bellow, a hoarse, bull-like roar from somewhere near by, and, looking round in some perplexity, through the wide doorway of the smithy opposite, I saw a man come tumbling, all arms and legs, who, having described a somersault, fell, rolled over once or twice, and sitting up in the middle of the road, stared about him in a dazed sort of fashion.

" That's Job ! " nodded the Ancient.

"Poor fellow !" said I, and rose to go to his assistance.

"Oh, that weren't nothin'," said the Ancient, laying a restraining hand upon my arm, " nothin' at all, Job bean't 'urt, why, I've seen 'em fall further nor that afore now, but y'see Job be pretty heavy handlin' —even for Black Jarge."

And, in a little while, Job arose from where he sat in the dust, and limping up, sat himself down on the opposite bench, very black of brow and fierce of eye. And, after he had sat there silent for maybe five minutes, I said that I hoped he wasn't hurt.

" ' 'Urt ? '' he repeated, with a blank stare. " 'Ow should I be 'urt ? ''

" Why, you seemed to fall rather heavily," said I.

At this Job regarded me with a look half resentful, half reproachful, and immediately turned his back upon me; from which, and sundry winks, and nods, and shakes of the head from the others, it seemed that my remark had been ill-judged. And after we had sat silent for maybe another five minutes, the Ancient appeared to notice Job's presence for the first time.

" Why, you bean't workin' 's arternoon then, Job ? '' he inquired solemnly.

" Noa ! ''

" Goin' to tak' a 'olleyday, p'r'aps ? ''

" Ah ! I'm done wi' smithin'—leastways, for Black Jarge.''

" And him wi' all that raft o' work in, Job ? Pretty fix 'e'll be in wi' no-one to strike for 'im ! '' said Simon.

" Sarves un right tu ! '' retorted Job, furtively rubbing his left knee.

" But what'll 'e do wi' out a 'elper ! '' persisted Simon.

" Lord knows ! '' returned the Ancient ; " unless Job thinks better of it.''

" Not me,'' said that individual, feeling his right elbow with tender solicitude. " I'm done wi' Black Jarge, I am. 'E nigh broke my back for me once afore, but this is the last time—I never swing a sledge for Black Jarge again—danged if I du ! ''

" And 'im to mend th' owd church screen up to Cranbrook Church,'' sighed the Ancient ; " a wunnerful screen, a wunnerful screen ! older nor me—ah ! a sight older—hunneds and hunneds o' years older— they wouldn't let nobody touch it but Black Jarge.''

" 'E be the best smith in the South Country ! '' nodded Simon.

" Ay, an' a bad man to work for as ever was ! '' growled Job ; " I'll work for 'e no more, my mind's made up, an' when my mind's made up theer bean't no movin' me—like a rock I be ! ''

" 'Twould ha' been a fine thing for a Siss'n'urst man to ha' mended t' owd screen ! '' said the Ancient.

" 'Twould that ! " nodded Simon, " a shame it is as it should go to others."

Hereupon, having finished my ale, I rose.

" Be you'm a-goin', young maister ? " inquired the Ancient.

" Why, that depends," said I. " I understand that this man, Black George, needs a helper, so I have decided to go and offer my services."

" You ! " exclaimed Job, staring in open-mouthed amazement, as did also the other two.

" Why not ? " I rejoined. " Black George needs a helper, and I need money."

" My chap," said Job warningly, " don't ye do it. You be a tidy, sizable chap, but Black Jarge 'ud mak' no more o' you than I should of a babby—don't ye do it."

" Better not," said Simon.

" On the contrary," I returned, " better run a little bodily risk, and satisfy one's hunger, rather than lie safe but famishing beneath some hedge or rick— what do you think, Ancient ? "

The old man leaned forward and peered up at me sharply beneath his hanging brows.

" Well ? " said I.

" You'm right ! " he nodded, " and a man wi' eyes the like o' yourn bean't one as 'tis easy to turn aside, even though it do be Black Jarge as tries."

" Then," said Job, as I took up my staff, " if your back's broke, my chap—why, don't go for to blame me, that's all ! You be a sight too cocksure—ah, that you be ! "

" I'm thinkin' Black Jarge would find this chap a bit different to Job," remarked the Ancient. " What do 'ee think, Simon ? "

" Looks as if 'e might take a good blow, ah ! and give one, for that matter," returned the Innkeeper, studying me with half-closed eyes, and his head to one side, as I have seen artists look at pictures. " He be pretty wide in the shoulders, and full in the chest, and, by the look of him, quick on 'is pins."

" You've been a fightin' man, Simon, and you ought to know—but he've got summat better still."

" And what might that be, Gaffer ? " inquired the Innkeeper.

" A good, straight, bright eye, Simon, wi' a look in it as says, ' I will ! ' "

" Ah ! but what o' Jarge ? " cried Job, " Black Jarge don't mind a man's eyes, 'cept to black frequent, 'e don't mind nothin', nor nobody."

" Job," said the Ancient, tapping his snuff-box, " theer's some things as is better nor gert, big muscles, and gert, strong fists—if you wasn't a danged fule you'd know what I mean. Young man," he went on, turning to me, " you puts me in mind o' what I were at your age—though, to be sure, I were taller'n you by about five, or six inches, maybe more—but don't go for to be too cocksure for all that. Black Jarge aren't to be sneezed at."

" And, if you must 'it un," added the Innkeeper, " why, go for the chin—theer aren't a better place to 'it a man than on the chin, if so be you can thump it right—and 'ard enough. I mind 'twas so I put out Tom Brock o' Bedford—a sweet, pretty blow it were too, though I do say it."

" Thank you ! " said I; " should it come to fighting, which Heaven forfend, I shall certainly remember your advice." Saying which, I turned away, and crossed the road to the open door of the smithy, very conscious of the three pairs of eyes that watched me as I went.

Upon the threshold of the forge I paused to look about me, and there, sure enough, was the smith. Indeed a fine, big fellow he was, with great shoulders, and a mighty chest, and arms whose bulging muscles showed to advantage in the red glow of the fire. In his left hand he grasped a pair of tongs wherein was set a glowing iron scroll upon which he beat with the hammer in his right. I stood watching until, having beaten out the glow from the iron, he plunged the scroll back into the fire, and fell to blowing with the bellows. But now, as I looked more closely at him, I almost doubted if this could be Black George, after all, for this man's hair was of a bright gold, and

curled in tight rings upon his brow, while, instead of
the black, scowling visage I had expected, I beheld a
ruddy, open, well-featured face out of which looked a
pair of eyes of a blue you may sometimes see in a
summer sky at evening. And yet again, his massive
size would seem to proclaim him the famous Black
George, and no other. It was with something of
doubt in my mind, nevertheless, that I presently
stepped into the smithy and accosted him.

"Are you Black George?" I inquired. At the
sound of my voice he let go the handle of the bellows,
and turned; as I watched, I saw his brows draw suddenly together, while the golden hairs of his beard
seemed to curl upward.

"Suppose I be?"

"Then I wish to speak with you."

"Be that what you'm come for?"

"Yes."

"Be you come far?"

"Yes."

"That's a pity."

"Why?"

"'Cause you'll 'ave a good way to go back again."

"What do you mean?"

"Well, for one thing, I means as I don't like your
looks, my chap."

"And why don't you like my looks?"

"Lord!" exclaimed the smith, "'ow should I
know—but I don't—of that I'm sartin sure."

"Which reminds me," said I, "of a certain unpopu-
lar gentleman of the name of Fell, or Pell, or Snell."

"Eh?" said the smith, staring.

"There is a verse, I remember, which runs, I think,
in this wise:

"'I do not love thee, Doctor Fell, or Pell, or Snell,
For reasons which I cannot tell;
But this, I know, and know full well,
I do not love thee, Doctor Fell, or Pell, or Snell.'"

"So you'm a poet, eh?"

"No," said I, shaking my head.

K

" Then I'm sorry for it; a man don't meet wi' poets every day," saying which, he drew the scroll from the fire, and laid it, glowing, upon the anvil. " You was wishful to speak wi' me, I think?" he inquired.

" Yes," I answered.

"Ah!" nodded the smith, "to be sure," and, forth-with, began to sing most lustily, marking the time very cleverly with his ponderous hand-hammer.

" If," I began, a little put out at this, " if you will listen to what I have to say——" But he only ham-mered away harder than ever, and roared his song the louder; and, though it sounded ill enough at the time, it was a song I came to know well later, the words of which are these :

> " Strike ! ding ! ding !
> Strike ! ding ! ding !
> The iron glows,
> And loveth good blows
> As fire doth bellows.
> Strike ! ding ! ding !"

Now seeing he was determined to give me no chance to speak, I presently seated myself close by, and fell to singing likewise. Oddly enough, the only thing I could recall, on the moment, was the Tinker's song, and that but very imperfectly; yet it served my pur-pose well enough. Thus we fell to it with a will, the different notes clashing, and filling the air with a most vile discord, and the words all jumbled up together, something in this wise :

> " Strike ! ding ! ding !
> A tinker I am, O
> Strike ! ding ! ding !
> A tinker am I
> The iron it glows,
> A tinker I'll live
> And loveth good blows
> And a tinker I'll die.
> As fire doth bellows.
> If the King in his crown
> Strike ! ding ! ding !
> Would change places with me
> Strike ! ding ! ding !"   And so forth.

The louder he roared, the louder roared I, until the place fairly rang with the din, in so much that, chancing to look through the open doorway, I saw the Ancient, with Simon, Job, and several others, on the opposite side of the way, staring, open-mouthed, as well they might. But still the smith and I continued to howl at each other with unabated vigour until he stopped all at once, and threw down his hammer with a clang.

"Dang me if I like that voice o' yourn!" he exclaimed.

"Why, to be sure, I don't sing very often," I answered.

"Which, I mean to say, is a very good thing; ah! a very good thing!"

"Nor do I pretend to sing——"

"Then why do 'ee try now?"

"For company's sake."

"Well, I don't like it—I've 'ad enough of it."

"Then," said I, "suppose you listen to what I have to say?"

"Not by no manner o' means."

"Then what do you propose to do?"

"Why," said the smith, rising, and stretching himself, "since you ax me, I'm a-goin' to pitch you out o' yon door."

"You may try, of course," said I, measuring the distance between us with my eye, "but if you do, seeing you are so much the bigger and stronger man, I shall certainly fetch you a knock with this staff of mine which I think you will remember for many a day."

So saying, I rose, and stepped out into the middle of the floor. Black George eyed me slowly up from the soles of my boots to the crown of my hat and down again, picked up his hammer in an undecided fashion, looked it over as if he had never seen such a thing before, tossed it into a corner, and, seating himself on the anvil, folded his arms. All at once a merry twinkle leapt into the blue depths of his eyes, and I saw the swift gleam of a smile.

"What do 'ee want—man?" said he.

Now hereupon, with a sudden gesture, I pitched my
staff out through the open doorway into the road,
and folded my arms across my chest, even as he.

" Why did 'ee do that ? " he inquired, staring.

" Because I don't think I shall need it after all."

" But suppose I was to come for 'ee now ? "

" But you won't."

" You be a strange sort o' chap ! " said he, shaking
his head.

" So they tell me."

" And what does the like o' you want wi' the likes
o' me ? "

" Work ! "

" Know anythin' about smithin' ? "

" Not a thing."

" Then why do 'ee come 'ere ? "

" To learn."

" More fool you ! " said the smith.

" Why ? "

" Because smithin' is 'ard work, and dirty work, and
hot work, and work as is badly paid nowadays."

" Then why are you a smith ? "

" My feyther was a smith afore me."

" And is that your only reason ? "

" My only reason."

" Then you are the greater fool."

" You think so, do ye ? "

" Certainly."

" Supposin'," said Black George, stroking his
golden beard reflectively, " supposin' I was to get up
and break your neck for that."

" Then you would, at least, save me from the folly
of becoming a smith."

" I don't," said Black George, shaking his head,
" no, I do not like you."

" I am sorry for that."

" Because," he went on, " you've got the gift o' the
gab, and a gabbing man is worse than a gabbing
woman."

" You can gab your share, if it comes to that,"
said I.

" Can I ? "

" You can."

" My chap," he growled, holding up a warning hand,
" go easy now, go easy, don't get me took again."

" Not if I can help it," I returned.

" I be a quiet soul till I gets took—a very quiet soul
—lambs bean't quieter, but I won't answer for that
neck o' yourn if I do get took—so look out ! "

" I understand you have an important piece of work
on hand," said I, changing the subject.

" Th' owd church screen, yes."

" And are in need of a helper ? "

" Ah ! to be sure—but you aren't got the look o' a
workin' cove. I never see a workin' cove wi' 'ands the
like o' yourn, so white as a woman's they be."

" I have worked hard enough in my time, nevertheless," said I.

" What might you 'ave done, now ? "

" I have translated Petronius Arbiter, also Quintilian, with a literal rendering into the English of the
Memoires of the Sieur de Brantome."

" Oh," exclaimed the smith, " that sounds a lot !
anything more ? "

" Yes," I answered; " I won the High Jump, and
Throwing the Hammer."

" Throwin' th' 'ammer ! " repeated Black George
musingly; " was it anything like that theer ? " and he
pointed to a sledge near by.

" Something," I answered.

" And you want work ? "

" I do."

" Tell 'ee what, my fellow, if you can throw that
theer 'ammer further nor me, then I'll say, ' Done,'
and you can name your own wages, but if I beat you,
and I'm fair sure I can, then you must stand up to me
for ten minutes, and I'll give 'ee a good trouncin' to
ease my mind—what d'ye say ? "

After a momentary hesitation, I nodded my head.

" Done ! " said I.

" More fool you ! " grinned the smith, and catching
up his sledge-hammer, he strode out into the road.

Before "The Bull" a small crowd had gathered, all
newly come from field or farmyard, for most of them
carried rake, or pitchfork, having doubtless been
drawn thither by the hellish outcry of Black George
and myself. Now I noticed that, while they listened
to the Ancient, who was holding forth, snuff-box in
hand, yet every eye was turned towards the smithy,
and in every eye was expectation. At our appearance,
however, I thought they seemed, one and all, vastly
surprised and taken aback, for heads were shaken, and
glances wandered from the smith and myself to the
Ancient, and back again.

"Well, I'll be danged!" exclaimed Job.

"I knowed it!—I knowed it!" cried the Ancient,
rubbing his hands and chuckling.

"Knowed what, Gaffer?" inquired Black George,
as we came up.

"Why, I knowed as this young chap would come
out a-walkin' 'pon his own two legs, and not like Job,
a-rollin' and a-wallerin' in the dust o' th' road—like a
hog."

"Why, y'see, Gaffer," began the smith, almost
apologetically it seemed to me, "it do come sort o'
nat'ral to heave the likes o' Job about a bit—Job's
made for it, y' might say, but this chap's different."

"So 'e be, Jarge—so 'e be!" nodded the Ancient.

"Though, mark me, Gaffer, I aren't nohow in love
wi' this chap neither—'e gabs too much to suit me, by
a long sight!"

"'E do that!" chimed in Job, edging nearer;
"what I sez is, if 'e do get 'is back broke, 'e aren't got
nobody to blame but 'isself—so cocksure as 'e be."

"Job," said the Ancient, "hold thee tongue."

"I sez 'e's a cocksure cove," repeated Job doggedly,
"an' a cocksure cove 'e be, what do 'ee think, Jarge?"

"Job," returned the smith, "I don't chuck a man
into t' road and talk wi' 'im both in the same day."

In this conversation I bore no part, busying myself
in drawing out a wide circle in the dust, a proceeding
watched by the others with much interest, and not a
few wondering comments.

"What be goin' to du wi' 'ammer, Jarge?"
inquired the Ancient.

"Why," explained the smith, "this chap thinks 'e
can throw it further nor me." At this there was a
general laugh. "If so be 'e can," pursued Black
George, "then 'e comes to work for me at 'is own
price, but if I beat 'im, then 'e must stand up to me
wi' is fists for ten minutes."

"Ten minutes!" cried a voice; "'e won't last five
—see if 'e do."

"Feel sorry for un," said a second, "'e do be so
pale as a sheet a'ready."

"So would you be if you was in 'is shoes!" chimed
in a third; whereat there was a general laugh.

Indeed, as I looked round the ring of grinning, un-
responsive faces, it was plain to see that all sympathy
was against the stranger, as is the way of bird, beast,
fish, but especially man, the world over—and I experienced a sudden sense of loneliness which was, I
think, only natural. Yet, as I put up my hand to
loose the strap of my knapsack, I encountered another
already there, and, turning, beheld Simon the
Innkeeper.

"If it do come to fightin'," he whispered close in
my ear, "if it do come to fightin', and I'm fair sure it
will, keep away as much as you can—you look quick
on your pins—moreover, whatever you do, watch 'is
right, and when you do see a chance to strike, go for
'is chin—a little to one side and strike danged 'ard!"

"Many thanks for your friendly advice," said I,
with a grateful nod, and, slipping off my coat, would
have handed it to him but that the Ancient hobbled
up, and, taking it from me, folded it ostentatiously
across his arm.

"Mark my words, Simon," said he, "this young
chap is as like what I were at his age as one pea is to
another—I says so, and I means so."

"Come," said Black George, at this juncture, "I've
work waitin' to be done, and my forge fire will be out."

"I'm quite ready," said I, stepping forward. It was
now arranged that, standing alternately within the

circle, we should each have three throws—whoever should make the two best throws to win.

Hereupon, the smith took his place within the circle, hammer in hand.

"Wait," said I, "the advantage usually lies with the last thrower, it would be fairer to you were we to toss for it."

"No," answered Black George, motioning the on-lookers to stand back, "I've got th' 'ammer, and I'll throw first."

Now, as probably everyone knows, it is one thing to swing a sledge-hammer in the ordinary way but quite another to throw it any distance, for there is required, beside the bodily strength, a certain amount of know-ledge, without which a man is necessarily handi-capped. Thus, despite my opponent's great strength of arm, I was fairly sanguine of the result.

Black George took a fresh grip upon the hammer-shaft, twirled it lightly above his head, swung it once, twice, thrice—and let it go.

With a shout, Job, and two or three others, ran down the road to mark where it had fallen, and presently returned, pacing out the distance.

"Fifty-nine!" they announced.

"Can 'ee beat that?" inquired Black George com-placently.

"I think I can," I answered as, taking up the hammer, I, in turn, stepped into the ring. Gripping the shaft firmly, I whirled it aloft, and began to swing it swifter and swifter, gaining greater impetus every moment, till, like a flash, it flew from my grasp. Panting, I watched it rise, rise, rise, and then plunge down to earth in a smother of dust.

"'E've beat it!" cried the Ancient, flourishing his stick excitedly. "Lord love me, 'e've beat it!"

"Ay, 'e've beat it, sure-ly," said a man who carried a rake that was for ever getting in everybody's way.

"An' by a goodish bit tu!" shouted another.

"Ah! but Jarge aren't got 'is arm in yet," retorted a third; "Jarge can do better nor that by a long sight!" But now all voices were hushed as Job paced up.

"Eighty-two!" he announced. Black George looked hard at me, but, without speaking, stepped sulkily into the ring, moistened his palms, looked at me again, and seizing the hammer, began to whirl it as he had seen me. Round and round it went, faster and faster, till, with a sudden lurch, he hurled it up and away. Indeed it was a mighty throw! Straight and strong it flew, describing a wide parabola ere it thudded into the road.

The excitement now waxed high, many started off to measure the distance for themselves, shouting one to another as they went. As for the smith, he stood beside me, whistling, and I saw that the twinkle was back in his eyes again.

"One hunner and twenty!" cried half-a-dozen voices.

"And a half," corrected Job, thrusting the hammer into my hand, and grinning.

"Can 'ee beat that?" inquired Black George again.

"Ay, can 'ee beat that?" echoed the crowd.

"It was a marvellous throw!" said I, shaking my head. And indeed, in my heart I knew I could never hope to equal, much less beat, such a mighty cast. I therefore decided on strategy, and, with this in mind, proceeded, in a leisurely fashion, once more to mark out the circle, which was oblitered in places, to flatten the surface underfoot, to roll up my sleeves, and tighten my belt; in fine, I observed all such precautions as a man might be expected to take before some supreme effort.

At length, having done everything I could think of to impress this idea upon the onlookers, I took up the hammer.

"Means to do it this time!" cried the man with the rake, knocking off Job's hat in his excitement, as, with a tremendous swing, I made my second throw. There was a moment's breathless silence as the hammer hurtled through the air, then, like an echo to its fall, came a shout of laughter, for the distance was palpably far short of the giant smith's last. A moment later Job came pacing up, and announced:

"Eighty-seven!" Hereupon arose a very babel of voices:

" You've got un beat a'ready, Jarge ! "

" Well, I knowed it from the start ! "

" Let un alone," cried Simon, " 'e've got another chance yet."

" Much good it'll do 'im ! "

" Ah ! might as well give in now, and take 'is thrashin' and ha' done wi' it."

That my ruse had succeeded with the crowd was evident; they—to a man—believed I had done my best, and already regarded me as hopelessly beaten. My chance of winning depended upon whether the smith, deluded into a like belief, should content himself with just beating my last throw, for, should he again exert his mighty strength to the uttermost, I felt that my case was indeed hopeless.

It was with a beating heart, therefore, that I watched him take his place for the last throw. His face wore a confident smile, but nevertheless he took up the hammer with such a businesslike air that my heart sank, and, feeling a touch upon my arm, I was glad to turn away.

"I be goin' to fetch a sponge and water," said Simon.

" A sponge and water ! "

" Ah !—likewise some vinegar—theer's nothin' like vinegar, and remember—the chin, a little to one side preferred."

" So then you think I shall be beaten ? "

"Why, I don't say that, but it's best to be prepared, aren't it now ? "

And, with a friendly nod, the Innkeeper turned away. In that same minute there arose another shout from the crowd as they greeted Black George's last throw, and, Job, striding up, announced :

" Ninety-eight ! "

Then, while the air still echoed with their plaudits, I stepped into the ring, and, catching up the hammer, swung it high above my head, and, at the full length of my arms, began to wheel it. The iron spun faster and faster till, setting my teeth, with the whole force of every fibre, every nerve, and muscle of my body, I let it fly.

The blood was throbbing at my temples and my breath coming fast at I watched its curving flight. And now all voices were hushed so that the ring of the iron could be plainly heard as it struck the hard road, and all eyes watched Job as he began pacing towards us. As he drew nearer I could hear him counting to himself, thus :

"Ninety-one, ninety-two, ninety-three, ninety-four, ninety-five, ninety-six, ninety-seven, ninety-eight, ninety-nine, one hundred, one hundred and one, one hundred and two—one hundred and two ! "

Next moment, as it seemed to me, an inarticulate Ancient was desperately trying to force me into my coat, wrong side first, and Simon was shaking my hand.

"You tricked me ! " cried a voice, and turning, I found Black George confronting me with clenched fists.

"And how did I trick you ? "

"I could ha' chucked farther nor that."

"Then why didn't you ? "

"Because I thought you was beat. I say you tricked me."

"And I tell you the match was a fair one from start to finish ! "

"Put up your hands ! " said the smith, advancing in a threatening manner.

"No," said I, "a bargain is a bargain," and turning my back upon him, I fell to watching the man with the rake, who, not content with Job's word, was busily pacing out the distance for himself.

"Put up your hands ! " repeated Black George hoarsely.

"For the last time, no," said I over my shoulder. "Strike me if you will," I went on, seeing him raise his fist, " I shall not defend myself, but I tell you this, Black George, the first blow you strike will brand you coward, and no honest man."

"Coward, is it ? " cried he, and, with the word, had seized me in a grip that crushed my flesh, and nigh swung me off my feet—" coward is it," he repeated.

" Yes," said I, " none but a coward would attack an unresisting man." So, for a full minute we stood thus, staring into each other's eyes, and once again I saw the hairs of his golden beard curl up, and outwards.

What would have been the end I cannot say, but there came upon the stillness the sound of flying footsteps, the crowd was burst asunder, and a girl stood before us, a tall, handsome girl with raven hair, and great flashing black eyes.

" Oh !—you, Jarge, think shame on yourself—think shame on yourself, Black Jarge. Look ! " she cried, pointing a finger at him, " look at the great, strong man—as is a coward ! "

I felt the smith's grip relax, his arms dropped to his sides, while a deep, red glow crept up his cheeks till it was lost in the clustering curls of gleaming, yellow hair.

" Why, Prue——" he began, in a strangely altered voice, and stopped. The fire was gone from his eyes as they rested upon her, and he made a movement as though he would have reached out his hand to her, but checked himself.

" Why, Prue——" he said again, but choked suddenly, and turning away, strode back towards his forge without another word. On he went, looking neither to right nor left, and I thought there was something infinitely woe-begone and pitiful in the droop of his head.

Now as I looked from his forlorn figure to the beautiful, flushed face of the girl, I saw her eyes grow wonderfully soft, and sweet, and brim over with tears. And, when Black George had betaken himself back to his smithy, she also turned, and crossing swiftly to the inn, vanished through its open doorway.

" She've a fine sperrit, 'ave that darter o' yourn, Simon, a fine sperrit. Oh ! a fine sperrit as ever was ! " chuckled the Ancient.

" Prue aren't afeard o' Black Jarge—never was," returned Simon ; " she can manage un—allus could, you'll mind she could allus tame Black Jarge wi' a look, Gaffer."

" You tricked me" cried a voice, and turning, I found Black George confronting me with clenched fists

Face Page 156

"You tricked me," cried a voice, and turning, I found Black George confronting me with clenched fists

Face Page 150

"Ah! she'm a gran'-darter to be proud on be Prue," nodded the Ancient, "an' proud I be tu!"

"What," said I, "is she your daughter, Simon?"

"Ay, for sure."

"And your granddaughter, Ancient?"

"Ay, that she be, that she be."

"Why then, Simon must be your son."

"Son as ever was!" nodded the old man, "and a goodish son 'e be tu—oh, I've seen worse."

"And now," added Simon, "come in, and you shall taste as fine a jug of ale as there be in all Kent."

"Wait," said the old man, laying his hand upon my arm, " I've took to you, young chap, took to you amazin'—what might your name be?"

"Peter," I answered.

"A good name, a fine name," nodded the old man, "Peter—Simon,' said he, glancing from one to the other of us. "Simon—Peter, minds me o' the disciple of our blessed Lord, it du—a fine name be Peter."

So Peter I became to him thenceforth, and to the whole village.

CHAPTER XXVI

WHEREIN I LEARN MORE CONCERNING THE GHOST OF THE RUINED HUT

AND after the Ancient and Simon and I had, very creditably, emptied the jug between us, I rose to depart.

" Peter " said the Ancient, " wheer be goin' ? "

" Home ! " said I.

" And wheer be that ? "

" The cottage in the Hollow," said I.

" What—th' 'aunted cottage ? " he cried, staring.

" Yes," I nodded; " from what I saw of it, I think, with a little repairing, it might suit me very well."

" But the ghost ? " cried the old man; " have ye forgot the ghost ? "

" Why, I never heard of a ghost really harming anyone yet," I answered.

" Peter," said Simon quietly, " I wouldn't be too sure o' that. I wouldn't go a-nigh the place, myself—once is enough for me."

" Simon," said I, " what do you mean by 'once' ? "

Now when I asked him this, Simon breathed hard, and shuffled uneasily in his chair.

" I mean, Peter, as I've heerd un," he replied slowly.

" Heard him ! " I repeated incredulously; " you ?—are you sure ? "

" Sure as death, Peter. I've heerd un a-shriekin' and a-groanin' to 'isself, same as Gaffer 'as, and lots of others. Why, Lord bless 'ee ! theer be scarce a man in these parts but 'as 'eerd un one time or another."

" Ay—I've 'eerd un, and seen un tu ! " croaked the Ancient excitedly. " A gert, tall thing 'e be, wi' a 'orn on 'is 'ead, and likewise a tail; some might ha' thought 'twas the Wanderin' Man o' the Roads as I found 'angin' on t' stapil—some on 'em du, but I knowed better—I knowed 'twere Old Nick 'isself, all

158

flame, and brimstone, an' wi' a babby under 'is arm ! "

" A baby ? " I repeated.

" A babby as ever was," nodded the Ancient.

" And you say you have heard it too, Simon ? " said I.

" Ay," nodded the Innkeeper ; " I went down into th' 'Oller one evenin'—'bout six months ago, wi' Black Jarge, for we 'ad a mind to knock th' owd place to pieces, and get rid o' the ghost that way. Well, Jarge ups wi' 'is 'ammer, and down comes the rotten old door wi' a crash. Jarge 'ad swung up 'is 'ammer for another blow when, all at once, theer comes a scream." Here Simon shivered involuntarily, and glanced uneasily over his shoulder, and round the room.

" A scream ? " said I.

"Ah ! " nodded Simon, " but 'twere worse nor that." Here he paused again, and looking closer at him, I was surprised to see that his broad, strong hands were shaking, and that his brow glistened with moisture.

" What was it like ? " I inquired, struck by this apparent weakness in one so hardy and full of health.

" 'Twere a scream wi' a bubble in it," he answered, speaking with an effort, " 'twere like somebody shriekin' out wi' 'is throat choked up wi' blood. Jarge and me didn't wait for no more—we run. And as we run, it follered, groanin' arter us till we was out upon the road, and then it shrieked at us from the bushes. Ecod ! it do make me cold to talk of it, even now. Jarge left 'is best sledge be'ind 'im, and I my crowbar, and we never went back for them, nor never shall, no." Here Simon paused to mop the grizzled hair at his temples. " I tell 'ee, Peter, that place aren't fit for no man at night. If so be you'm lookin' for a bed, my chap, theer's one you can 'ave at ' The Bull,' ready and willin'."

" An' gratus ! " added the Ancient, tapping his snuff-box.

" Thank you," said I, " both of you, for the offer, but I have a strange fancy to hear, and, if possible, see this ghost for myself."

"Don't 'ee du it," admonished the Ancient, "so dark an' lonesome as it be, don't 'ee du it, Peter."

"Why, Ancient," said I, "it isn't that I doubt your word, but my mind is set on the adventure. So, if Simon will let me have threepenny worth of candles, and some bread and meat—no matter what—I'll be off, for I should like to get there before dusk."

Nodding gloomily, Simon rose, and went out, whereupon the Ancient leaned over and laid a yellow, clawlike hand upon my arm.

"Peter," said he, "Peter, I've took to you amazin' —just a few inches taller—say a couple— an' you'd be the very spit o' what I were at your age—the very spit."

"Thank you, Ancient!" said I, laying my hand on his.

"Now, Peter, 'twould be a hijious thing—a very hijious thing if, when I come a-gatherin' watercress in the marnin', I should find you a-danglin' on t' stapil, cold and stiff—like t' other, or lyin' a corp wi' your throat cut—'twould be a hijious—hijious thing, Peter, but oh! 'twould mak' a fine story in the tellin'."

In a little while Simon returned with the candles, a tinder-box, and a parcel of bread and meat, for which he gloomily but persistently refused payment. Last of all he produced a small, brass-bound pistol, which he insisted on my taking.

"Not as it'll be much use agin' a ghost," said he with a gloomy shake of the head, "but a pistol's a comfortable thing to 'ave in a lonely place—'specially if that place be very dark." Which last, if something illogical, may be none the less true.

So, having shaken each by the hand, I bade them "Good-night," and set off along the darkening road.

CHAPTER XXVII

WHICH TELLS HOW AND IN WHAT MANNER I SAW THE GHOST

Now, as I went, my mind was greatly exercised as to a feasible explanation of what I had just heard. That a man so old as the Ancient should " see things " I could readily believe, by reason of his years, for great age is often subject to such hallucinations, but with Simon, a man in the prime of his life, it was a different matter altogether. That he had been absolutely sincere in his story I had read in his dilating eye and the involuntary shiver that had passed over him while he spoke. Here indeed, though I scouted all idea of supernatural agency, there lay a mystery that piqued my curiosity not a little.

Ghosts!—pshaw! what being endowed with a reasoning mind could allow himself to think, let alone believe in, such folly?—ghosts—fiddle-de-dee, sir!

Yet here, and all at once, like an enemy from the dark, old stories leaped at and seized me by the throat : old tales of spectres grim and bloody, of goblins, and haunted houses from whose dim desolation strange sounds would come ; tales long since heard, and forgot —till now.

Ghosts!—why, the road was full of them, they crowded upon my heels, they peered over my shoulders, I felt them brush my elbows, and heard them gibbering at me from the shadows.

And the sun was setting already !

Ghosts! And why not? " ' There are more things in heaven and earth than are dreamed of in your philosophy.' "

Involuntarily I hastened my steps, but the sun had set ere I reached the Hollow. Yes, the sun had set, and the great basin, below me, was already brimful of

shadows which, as I watched, seemed to assume
shapes—vast, nebulous, and constantly changing—
down there amid the purple gloom of the trees. Indeed, it looked an unholy place in the half light, a pit
framed for murders, and the safe hiding of tell-tale
corpses, the very haunt of horrid goblins and spectres,
grim and ghastly.

So evilly did the place impress me that it needed an
effort of will ere I could bring myself to descend the
precipitous slope. Bats flitted to and fro across my
path, now and then, emitting their sharp, needlelike
note, while, from somewhere in the dimness beyond,
an owl hooted.

By the time I reached the cottage it had fallen quite
dark, here in the Hollow, though the light still lingered
in the world above, so I took out my tinder-box, and
one of the candles, which, after several failures, I
succeeded in lighting, and, stepping into the cottage
began to look about me.

The place was small, as I think I have before said,
and comprised two rooms shut off from each other by
a strong partition with a door midway. Lifting the
candle, I glanced at the staple on which the builder of
the cottage had choked out his life so many years ago,
and, calling to mind the Ancient's fierce desire to out-
last it, I even reached up my hand and gave it a shake;
but, despite the rust of years, the iron felt as strong
and rigid as ever, so that it seemed the old man's
innocent wish must go unsatisfied after all. The
second room appeared much the same size as the first,
and like it in all respects, till, looking upwards, I
noticed a square trap door in a corner, while under-
neath, against the wall, hung a rough ladder. This I
proceeded to lift down, and mounting, cautiously
lifted the trap. Holding the candle above my head to
survey this chamber, or rather garret, the first object
my eye encountered was a small tin pannikin, and
beyond that a stone jar, or demijohn. Upon closer
inspection I found this last to be nearly full of water
quite sweet and fresh to the taste, which, of itself, was
sufficient evidence that someone had been here very

lately. I now observed a bundle of hay in one corner, which had clearly served for a bed, beside which were a cracked mug, a tin plate, a pair of shoes, and an object I took to be part of a flute or wind instrument of some kind. But what particularly excited my interest were the shoes, which had evidently seen long and hard service, for they were much worn, and had been roughly patched here and there. Very big they were, and somewhat clumsy, thick-soled, and square of toe, and with a pair of enormous silver buckles.

These evidences led me to believe that whoever had been here before was likely to return, and, not doubting that this must be he who had played the part of ghost so well, I determined to be ready for him.

So, leaving all things as I found them, I descended, and having closed the trap, hung up the ladder as I had found it.

In the first of the rooms there was a rough fireplace built into one corner, and as the air struck somewhat damp and chill, I went out and gathered a quantity of twigs and dry wood, and had soon built a cheerful, crackling fire. I now set about collecting armfuls of dry leaves, which I piled against the wall for a bed. By the time this was completed to my satisfaction the moon was peeping above the tree-tops, filling the Hollow with far-flung shadows.

I now lay down upon my leafy couch, and fell to watching the fire, and listening to the small, soft song of the brook outside. In the opposite wall was a window, the glass of which was long since gone, through which I could see a square of sky, and the glittering belt of Orion. My eyes wandered from this to the glow of the fire many times, but gradually my head grew heavier and heavier, until, at length, the stars became confused with the winking sparks upon the hearth, and the last that I remember was that the crackle of the fire sounded strangely like the voice of the Ancient croaking :

" A hijious thing, Peter, a hijious thing ! "

I must have slept for an hour, or nearer two (for the room was dark, save for a few glowing embers on the

hearth, and the faint light of the stars at the window),
when I suddenly sat bolt upright, with every tingling
nerve straining as if to catch something which had,
but that very moment, eluded me. I was yet wondering what this could be, when, from somewhere close
outside the cottage, there rose a sudden cry—hideous
and appalling—a long-drawn-out, bubbling scream
(no other words can describe it), that died slowly down
to a wail only to rise again higher and higher, till it
seemed to pierce my very brain. Then all at once it
was gone and silence rushed in upon me—a
silence fraught with fear and horror unimagin-
able.

I lay rigid, the blood in my veins jumping with
every throb of my heart till it seemed to shake me
from head to foot. And then the cry began again,
deep and hoarse at first, but rising, rising until the
air thrilled with a scream such as no earthly lips could
utter.

Now the light at the window grew stronger and
stronger, and, all at once, a feeble shaft of moonlight
crept across the floor. I was watching this most
welcome beam when it was again obscured by a
something, indefinable at first, but which I gradually
made out to be very like a human head peering in at
me, but, if this was so, it seemed a head hideously
mis-shapen—and there—sure enough, rising from the
brow, was a long, pointed horn.

As I lay motionless, staring at this thing, my hand,
by some most fortunate chance, encountered the pistol
in my pocket; and, from the very depths of my soul, I
poured benedictions upon the honest head of Simon
the Innkeeper, for its very contact seemed to restore
my benumbed faculties; with a single bound I was
upon my feet, and had the weapon levelled at the
window.

"Speak!" said I, "speak, or I'll shoot." There
was a moment of tingling suspense, and then:
"Oh man, dinna do that!" said a voice.
"Then come in and show yourself!"
Herewith the head incontinent disappeared, there

was the sound of a heavy step, and a tall figure loomed in the doorway.

" Wait ! " said I, as, fumbling about, I presently found tinder-box, and candle, having lighted which I turned, and beheld a man—an exceedingly tall man, clad in the full habit of a Scottish Highlander. By his side hung a long, straight, basket-hilted sword, beneath one arm he carried a bagpipe, while upon his head was—not a horn—but a Scots bonnet with a long eagle's feather.

" Oh, man," said he, eyeing me with a somewhat wry smile, " I'm juist thinkin' ye're no' afear'd o' bogles, whateffer ! "

CHAPTER XXVIII

THE HIGHLAND PIPER

" Who are you? " said I, in no very gentle tone.

" Donal's my name, sir, an' if ye had an e'e for the tartan, ye'd ken I was a Stuart."

" And what do you want here, Donald Stuart? "

" The verra question she'd be askin' ye'sel'—wha' gars ye tae come gowkin' an' spierin' about here at sic an hour? "

" It is my intention to live here, for the future," said I.

" Hoot toot! ye'll be no meanin' it? "

" But I do mean it," said I.

" Eh, man! but ye maun ken the place is no canny, what wi' pixies, an' warlocks, an' kelpies, forbye——"

" Indeed, they told me it was haunted, but I determined to see for myself."

" Weel? "

" Well, I am glad to find it haunted by nothing worse than a wandering Scots piper.

The Highlander smiled his wry smile, and taking out a snuff-box, inhaled a pinch, regarding me the while.

" Ye're the first as ever stayed—after they'd heard the first bit squeakie, tae find out if 'twere a real bogle or no."

" But how in the world did you make such awful sounds? "

" I'm thinkin' it's the bit squeakie ye'll be meanin'? " he inquired.

" Yes; how did you do it? "

" Oh, it's juist the pipes! " he answered, patting them affectionately, " will I show ye the noo? "

" Pray do," said I. Hereupon he set the mouth-piece to his lips, inflated the bag, stopped the vents

" *Oh, man,*" *said he, eyeing me with a somewhat wry smile,* " *I'm juist thinkin' ye're no' afear'd o' bogles, whateffer !* "

Face Page 166

"Oh, man," said he, eyeing me with a somewhat wry smile, "I'm just thinkin' ye're no afear'd o' bogles, whatever?"

Face Page 106

with his fingers, and, immediately, the air vibrated
with the bubbling scream I have already attempted
to describe.

"Oh, man!" he exclaimed, laying the still groaning instrument gently aside, "oh, man! is it no juist
won'erful?"

"But what has been your object in terrifying people
out of their wits in this manner?"

"Sir, it's a' on account o' the snuff."

"Snuff!" I repeated.

"Juist that!" he nodded.

"Snuff," said I again; "what do you mean?"

The Piper smiled again—a slow smile, that seemingly
dawned only to vanish again; it was, indeed, if I may
so express it, a grave and solemn smile, and his nearest
approach to mirth, for not once in the days which followed did I ever see him give vent to a laugh. I here
also take the opportunity to say that I have greatly
modified his speech in the writing, for it was so broad
that I had much ado to grasp his meaning at times.

The Piper smiled, then, and, unwinding the plaid
from his shoulder, spread it upon the floor, and sat
down.

"Ye maun ken," he began, "that I hae muckle
love for the snuff, an' snuff is unco expenseeve in
these parts."

"Well?" said I.

"Ye maun ken, in the second place, that ma brither
Alan canna' abide the snuff."

"Your brother Alan!" said I wondering.

"Ma brither Alan," he nodded gravely.

"But what of him, what has he to do with——"

"Man, bide a wee. I'm comin' tae that."

"Go on, then," said I, "I'm listening."

"Weel, I'd hae ye tae ken I'm a braw, bonnie piper,
an' ma brither Alan, he's a bonnie piper too—no sic a
fair graund piper as me, bein' somewhat uncertain wi'
his 'warblers,' ye ken, but a bonnie piper, whateffer.
Aweel, mebbe a year syne, I fell in love wi' a lassie,
which wad ha' been a' richt if ma brither Alan hadna'
fallen in love wi' her too, so that she, puir lassie,

didna' ken which tae tak'. 'Donal',' says Alan, 'can ye no love anither lassie; she can no marry the twa o' us, that's sure!' 'Then Alan,' says I, 'we'll juist play for her.' Which I think ye'll own was a graund idee, only the lassie couldna' juist mak' up her mind which o' us piped the best. So the end of it was we agreed, ma brither Alan an' I, to pipe oor way through England for a year, an' the man wha came back wi' the maist siller should wed the lassie."

"And a very fair proposal," said I, "but——"

"Wheest, man! juist here's where we come to the snuff, for, look ye, every time I bought a paper o' snuff I minded me that ma brither Alan, not takkin' it himself, was so much siller tae the gude—an'—oh, man! it used tae grieve me sair—till, one day, I lighted on this bit hoosie."

"Well?" said I.

"What, d'ye no see it?"

"No, indeed," I answered.

"Eh, man! ma brither Alan doesna' buy the snuff, but he must hae a roof tae shelter him an' a bed tae lie in o' nights, an' pay for it too, ye ken, fourpence, or a bawbee, or a shillin', as the case may be, whiles here I hae baith for the takkin'. An', oh, man! many's the nicht I've slept the sweeter for thinkin' o' that saxpence or shillin' that Alan's a-partin' wi' for a bed little better than mine. So, wishfu' tae keep this bit hoosie tae mysel'—seein' 'twas haunted as they ca' it—I juist kep' up the illusion on account o' trampers, wanderin' gypsies, an' sic-like dirty tykes. Eh! but 'twas fair graund tae see 'em rinnin' awa' as if the de'il were after them, spierin', back o'er their shoulders, an' a' by reason of a bit squeakie o' the pipes, here. An' so, sir, ye hae it."

I now proceeded to build and relight the fire, during which the Scot drew a packet of bread and cheese from his sporran, together with a flask which, having uncorked, he held out to me with the one word, "Whuskey!"

"Thank you, Donald, but I rarely drink anything stronger than ale," said I.

"Aweel!" said he, "if ye winna', ye winna' an' there's but a wee drappie left, tae be sure." Whereupon, after two or three generous gulps, he addressed himself to his bread and cheese, and I, following his example, took out the edibles Simon had provided.

"An' ye're minded tae bide here, ye tell me?" he inquired after a while.

"Yes," I nodded, "but that need not interfere with you—two can live here as easily as one, and, now that I have had a good look at you, I think we might get along very well together."

"Sir," said he solemnly, "my race is royal—I am a Stuart—here's a Stuart's hand," and he reached out his hand to me across the hearth with a gesture that was full of a reposeful dignity. Indeed, I never remember to have seen Donald anything but dignified.

"How do you find life in these parts?" I inquired.

"Indeefferent, sir—vera indeefferent! Tae be sure, at fairs an' sic-like I've often had as much as ten shillin' in ma bonnet at a time; but it's juist the kilties that draw 'em—they hae no real love for the pipes, whateffer! A rantin' reel pleases 'em well eneugh, but eh! they hae no hankerin' for the gude music."

"That is a question open to argument, Donald," said I; "can anyone play real music on a bagpipe, think you?"

"Sir," returned the Scot, setting down the empty flash and frowning darkly at the fire, "the pipes is the king of a' instruments, 'tis the sweetest, the truest, the oldest, whateffer!"

"True, it is very old," said I thoughtfully; "it was known, I believe, to the Greeks, and we find mention of it in the Latin as: 'tibia utricularia,' Suetonius tells us that Nero promised to appear publicly as a bagpiper. Then, too, Chaucer's Miller played a bagpipe, and Shakespeare frequently mentions the 'drone of a Lincolnshire Bagpipe.' Yes, it is certainly a very old, and, I think, a very barbarous instrument."

"Hoot toot! the man talks like a muckle fule," said Donal', nodding to the fire.

"For instance," I continued, "there can be no comparison between a bagpipe and a—fiddle, say."

"A fiddle!" exclaimed Donal' in accents of withering scorn, and still addressing the fire. "Ye can juist tell him tae gang tae the de'il wi' his fiddle."

"Music is, I take it, the expression of one's mood or thought, a dream translated into sound," said I thoughtfully, "therefore——"

"Hae ye ever heard the pipes?"

"Why, yes, but long ago."

"Then," said Donal', "ye shall juist hear 'em again." So saying, he wiped his mouth, took up his instrument, and began slowly inflating it.

Then, all at once, from drones and chanter there rushed forth such a flood of melody as seemed to sweep me away upon its tide.

First I seemed to hear a roar of wind through desolate glens, a moan of trees, and a rush of sounding waters; yet softly, softly there rises above the flood of sound a little rippling melody which comes, and goes, and comes again, growing ever sweeter with repetition. And now the roar of wind is changed to the swing of marching feet, the tread of a mighty host whose step is strong and free; and lo! they are singing, as they march, and the song is bold and wild, wild, wild. Again and again, beneath the song, beneath the rhythm of marching feet, the melody rises, very sweet but infinitely sad, like a silver pipe or an angel's voice tremulous with tears. Once again the theme changes, and it is battle, and death, sudden, and sharp; there is the rush and shock of charging ranks, and the surge and tumult of conflict, above whose thunder, loud and clear and shrill, like some battle-cry, the melody swells, one moment triumphant, and the next is lost again.

But now the thunder rolls away, distant and more distant—the day is lost, and won; but, sudden and clear, the melody rings out once more, fuller now, richer, and complete, the silver pipe has become a golden trumpet. And yet, what sorrow, what anguish unspeakable rings through it, the weeping and wailing of a nation! So the melody sinks slowly, to die away in one long-drawn, minor note, and Donal' is looking across at me with his grave smile, and I will admit both his face and figure are sadly blurred.

"Donald," said I, after a little, "Donald, I will never speak against the pipes again, they are indeed the king of all instruments—played as you play them."

"Ou ay, I'm a bonnie piper, I'll no deny it!" he answered. "I'm glad ye like it, for, Sassenach though ye be, it proves ye hae the music. 'Tis a bit pibroch I made tae Wullie Wallace—him as the damned Sassenach murdered—black be their fa'. Aweel! 'twas done afore your time or mine—so—gude-nicht tae ye, Southeron!" saying which he rose, saluted me stiffly, and stalked majestically to bed.

CHAPTER XXIX

HOW BLACK GEORGE AND I SHOOK HANDS

THE world was full of sunshine, the blithe song of birds, and the sweet, pure breath of waking flowers as I rose next morning, and coming to the stream, threw myself down beside it and plunged my hands and arms and head into the limpid water whose contact seemed to fill me with a wondrous gladness in keeping with the world about me.

In a little while I rose, with the water dripping from me, and having made shift to dry myself upon my neckcloth, nothing else being available, returned to the cottage.

Above my head I could hear a gentle sound rising and falling with a rhythmic measure, that told me Donal' still slept; so, clapping on my hat and coat, I started out to my first day's work at the forge, break-fastless, for the good and sufficient reason that there was none to be had, but full of the glad pure beauty of the morning; and I bethought me of the old Psalmist's deathless words : " Though sorrow endure for a night, yet joy cometh in the morning "—(brave, true words which shall go ringing down the ages to bear hope and consolation to many a wearied, troubled soul); for now as I climbed the steep path where bats had hovered last night and turned to look back at the pit which had seemed a place of horror—behold ! it was become a very paradise of quivering green, spangled with myriad jewels where the dew yet clung.

Indeed, if any man would experience the full ecstasy of being alive—the *joi de vivre* as the French have it —let him go out into the early morning, when the sun is young, and look about him with a seeing eye.

So, in a little while, with the golden song of a

172

blackbird in my ears, I turned village-wards, very hungry, yet, therewithal, content.

Long before I reached the smithy I could hear the ring of Black George's hammer, though the village was not yet astir, and it was with some trepidation as to my reception that I approached the open doorway.

There he stood, busy at his anvil, goodly to look upon in his bare-armed might, and with the sun shining in his yellow hair, a veritable son of Anak. He might have been some hero, or demigod come back from that dim age when angels wooed the daughters of men, rather than a village blacksmith, and a very sulky one at that; for though he must have been aware of my presence, he never glanced up or gave the slightest sign of welcome, or the reverse.

Now, as I watched I noticed a certain slowness—a heaviness in all his movements, together with a listless, slipshod air which, I judged was very foreign to him; moreover, as he worked, I thought he hung his head lower than was quite necessary.

"George!" George went on hammering. "George!" said I again. He raised the hammer for another stroke, hesitated, then lifted his head with a jerk, and immediately I knew why he had avoided my eye.

"What do 'ee want wi' me?"

"I have come, for two reasons," said I; "one is to begin work——"

"Then ye'd best go away again," he broke in, "ye'll get no work here."

"And the second," I went on, "is to offer you my hand. Will you take it, George, and let bygones be bygones?"

"No," he burst out vehemently—"No, I tell 'ee. Ye think to come 'ere an' crow o'er me, because ye beat me, by a trick, and because ye heerd—her—" His voice broke, and, dropping his hammer, he turned his back upon me. "Called me 'coward'! she did," he went on after a little while, "you heerd her—they all heerd her! I've been a danged fule!" he said, more as if speaking his thoughts aloud —than addressing me, "but a man can't help lovin' a lass—like Prue, and when 'e loves 'e can't 'elp hopin'. I've hoped these three years an' more, and last night—she called me—coward." Something bright and glistening splashed down upon the anvil, and there ensued a silence broken only by the piping of the birds and the stirring of the leaves outside.

"A fule I be!" said Black George at last, shaking his head, "no kind o' man for the likes o' her—too big I be—and rough. And yet—if she'd only given me the chance!"

Again there fell a silence wherein, mingled with the bird-chorus, came the tap, tapping of a stick upon the hard road, and the sound of approaching footsteps, whereupon George seized the handle of the bellows and fell to blowing the fire vigorously; yet once I saw him draw the back of his hand across his eyes with a quick, furtive gesture. A moment after, the Ancient appeared, quaint, befrocked figure, framed in the yawning doorway and backed by the glory of the morning. He stood awhile to lean upon his stick, and peer about, his old eyes still dazzled by the sunlight he had just left, owing to which he failed to see me where I sat in the shadow of the forge.

"Marnin', Jarge!" said he, with his quick, bright nod. The smith's scowl was blacker and his deep voice gruffer than usual as he returned the greeting; but the old man seemed to heed it not at all, but taking his snuff-box from the lining of his tall, broad-brimmed hat (its usual abiding place), he opened it, with his most important air.

"Jarge," said he, "I'm thinkin' ye'd better tak' Job back to strike for ye again if you'm goin' to mend t' owd screen."

"What d'ye mean?" growled Black George.

"Because," continued the old man, gathering a pinch of snuff with great deliberation, "because, Jarge, the young feller as beat ye at the throwin'—'im as was to 'ave worked for ye at 'is own price—be dead."

"What!" cried Black George, starting.

"Dead!" nodded the old man, "a corp' 'e be—eh! such a fine, promisin' young chap, an' now—a corp'." Here the Ancient nodded solemnly again, three times, and inhaled his pinch of snuff with great apparent zest and enjoyment.

"Why——" began the amazed George, "what——" and broke off to stare, open-mouthed.

"Last night, as ever was," continued the old man, "'e went down to th' 'aunted cottage—'tweren't no manner o' use tryin' to turn 'im—no, not if I'd gone down to 'im on my marrer-bones—'e were that set on it—so off he goes, 'bout sundown, to sleep in th' 'aunted cottage—I knows, Jarge, 'cause I follered un, an' seen for myself; so now I'm a-goin' down to find 'is corp'——"

He had reached thus far, when his eye, accustomed to the shadows, chancing to meet mine, he uttered a gasp, and stood staring at me with dropped jaw.

"Peter!" he stammered at last. "Peter—be that you, Peter?"

"To be sure it is," said I.

"Bean't ye—dead, then?"

"I never felt more full of life."

"But ye slep' in th' 'aunted cottage last night."

"Yes."

"But—but—the ghost, Peter?"

"Is a wandering Scotsman."

"Why then I can't go down and find ye corp' arter all?"

"I fear not, Ancient."

The old man slowly closed his snuff-box, shaking his head as he did so.

"Ah, well! I won't blame ye, Peter," said he magnanimously; "it bean't your fault, lad, no—but what's come to the ghost!"

"The ghost," I answered, "is nothing more dreadful than a wandering Scotsman!"

"Scotsman!" exclaimed the Ancient sharply. "Scotsman!"

"Yes, Ancient."

"You'm mazed, Peter—ah! mazed ye be!—what,

aren't I heerd un moanin' an' groanin' to isself—ah !
an' twitterin' tu ? "

" As to that," said I, " those shrieks and howls he
made with his bagpipe, very easy for a skilled player
such as he."

Someone was drawing water from a well across the
road, for I heard the rattle of the bucket, and the
creak of the winch, in the pause which now ensued,
during which the Ancient, propped upon his stick,
surveyed me with an expression that was not exactly
anger, nor contempt, nor sorrow, and yet something
of all three. At length he sighed, and shook his head
at me mournfully.

" Peter," said he, " Peter, I didn't think as you'd
try to tak' 'vantage of a old man wi' a tale the like o'
that—such a very, very old man, Peter—such a old,
old man ! "

" But I assure you, it's the truth," said I earnestly.

" Peter, I seen Scotchmen afore now," said he, with
a reproachful look, " ah ! that I 'ave, many's the time,
an' Scotchmen don't go about wi' tails, nor yet wi'
'orns on their 'eads—leastways I've never seen one as
did. An', Peter, I know what a bagpipe is, I've heerd
'em often an' often—squeak they do, yes—but a squeak
bean't a scream, Peter, nor yet a groan—no." Having
delivered himself of which, the Ancient shook his
head at me again, and, turning his back, hobbled away.

When I turned to look at George it was to find him
regarding me with a strange expression.

" Sir," said he ponderously, " did you sleep in th'
'aunted cottage last night ? "

" Yes, though, as I have tried to explain, and unsuccessfully it seems, it is haunted by nothing more
alarming than a Scots Piper.

" Sir," said George in the same slow, heavy way,
" I couldn't go a-nigh the place myself—'specially
arter dark—I'd be—ah ! I'd be afeard to ! I did go
once, and then not alone, and I ran away. Sir, you'm
a better man nor me—you done what I durstn't do.
Sir, if so be as you'm in the same mind about it—I
should like to—to shake your hand."

So there, across the anvil which was to link our lives together thenceforth, Black George and I clasped hands, looking into each other's eyes.

"George," said I at last, "I've had no breakfast."

"Nor I!" said George.

"And I'm mightily hungry!"

"So am I," said George.

"Then come, and let us eat," and I turned to the door.

"Why, so we will—but not at—'The Bull'—she be theer. Come to my cottage, it be close by—that is, if you care to, sir?"

"With all my heart!" said I, "and my name is—Peter."

"What do you say to 'am and eggs—Peter?"

"Ham and eggs will be most excellent!" said I.

M

" Peter," said he, fixing me with his eye, " were it
a Scotchman or were it not ? "

" Why, to be sure it was," I answered, " a Scotch
piper, as I told you, and——"

" Peter," said the Ancient, tapping his snuff-box,
" it weren't no ghost, then—ay or no."

" No," said I, " nothing but a——"

" Peter ! " said the Ancient, nodding solemnly,
" Peter, I 'ates ye ! " and, turning sharp about, he
tottered away upon his stick.

" So—that's it ! " said I, staring after the old man's
retreating figure.

" Why, ye see," said George, somewhat diffidently,
" ye see, Peter, Gaffer be so old !—and all 'is friends
be dead, and he've come to look on this 'ere ghost as
belongin' to 'im a'most. Loves to sit an' tell about it,
'e do, it be all 'e've got left to live for, as ye might
say, and now you've been and gone and said as theer
bean't no ghost arter all, d'ye see ? "

" Ah yes, I see," I nodded, " I see. But you don't
still believe in this ghost, do you, George ? "

" N-o-o-o—not 'xactly," answered George, hesitating upon the word, " can't say as I believe 'xactly,
and yet, Lord ! 'ow should I know ? "

" Then you do still believe in the ghost ? "

" Why, y'see, Peter, we do know as a man 'ung
'isself theer, 'cause Gaffer found un—likewise I've
heerd it scream—but as for believin' in it, since you
say contrarywise—why, 'ow should I know ? "

" But why should I deny it, George—why should I
tell you all of a Scotchman ? "

" Why, y'see, Peter," said George, in his heavy
way, " you be such a strange sort o' chap ! "

" George," said I, " let us get back to work."

Yet, in a little while, I set aside the hammer, and
turned to the door.

" Peter, wheer be goin' ? "

" To try and make my peace with the Ancient," I
answered, and forthwith crossed the road to " The
Bull." But with my foot on the step I paused,
arrested by the sound of voices and laughter within

the tap, and, loudest of all, was the voice of the
pseudo blacksmith, Job.

" If I were only a bit younger ! " the Ancient was
saying. Now, peeping in through the casement, a
glance at his dejected attitude, and the blatant bearing
of the others, explained to me the situation then and
there.

" Ah ! but you ain't," retorted old Amos, " you'm a
old, old man an' gettin' older wi' every tick o' the
clock, you be, an gettin' mazed-like wi' years."

" Haw ! haw ! " laughed Job and the five or six
others.

" Oh, you—Job ! if my b'y Simon was 'ere 'e'd
pitch 'ee out into the road, so 'e would—same as
Black Jarge done," quavered the Ancient.

" P'r'aps, Gaffer, p'r'aps ! " returned Job, " but I
sez again, I believe what Peter sez, an' I don't
believe there never was no ghost at all."

" Ay lad, but I tell 'ee theer was—I seed un ! "
cried the old man eagerly, " seed un wi' these two
eyes, many's the time. You, Joel Amos—you've
'eerd un a-moanin' an' a-groanin'—you believe as I
seed un, don't 'ee now—come ? "

" He ! he ! " chuckled Old Amos, " I don't know if
I du, Gaffer—ye see you'm gettin' that old——"

" But I did—I did—oh, you chaps, I tell 'ee I
did ! "

" You'm gettin' old, Gaffer," repeated Amos,
dwelling upon the theme with great unction, " very,
very old——"

" But so strong as a bull, I be ! " added the Ancient,
trying manfully to steady the quaver in his voice.

" Haw ! haw ! " laughed Job and the others, while
Old Amos chuckled shrilly again.

" But I tell 'ee I did see un, I—I see'd un plain as
plain," quavered the Ancient, in sudden distress,
" Old Nick it were, wi' 'orns, an' a tail."

" Why, Peter told us 'twere only a Scottish man
wi' a bagpipe, returned Job."

" Ay, for sure," nodded Old Amos, " so 'e did."

" A lie, it be—a lie a lie ! " cried the Ancient,

" 'twere Old Nick, I see un—plain as I see you."

" Why, ye see, you'm gettin' dre'fful old an' 'elp-less, Gaffer," chuckled Old Amos again, " an' your eyes plays tricks wi' you."

" Ah, to be sure they do ! " added Job ; whereupon Old Amos chuckled so much that he was taken by a violent fit of coughing.

" Oh ! you chaps, you as I've seen grow up from babbies—aren't theer one o' ye to tak' the old man's word an' believe as I seen un ? " The cracked old voice sounded more broken than usual, and I saw a tear crawling slowly upon the Ancient's furrowed cheek. Nobody answered, and there fell a silence broken only by the shuffle and scrape of heavy boots and the setting down of tankards.

" Why, ye see, Gaffer," said Job at last, " theer's been a lot o' talk o' this 'ere ghost, an' some 'as even said as they 'eerd it, but, come to think on it, nobody's never laid eyes on it but you, so——"

" There you are wrong, my fellow," said I, stepping into the room. " I also have seen it."

" You ? " exclaimed Job, while half-a-dozen pairs of eyes stared at me in slow wonderment.

" Certainly I have."

" But you said as it were a Scotchman, wi' a bag-pipe, I heerd ye—we all did."

" And believed it—like fools ! "

" Peter ! " cried the Ancient, rising up out of his chair, " Peter, do 'ee mean it ? "

" To be sure I do."

" Do 'ee mean it were a ghost, Peter, do 'ee ? "

" Why, of course it was," I nodded, " a ghost, or the devil himself, hoof, horns, tail, and all—to say nothing of the fire and brimstone."

" Peter," said the Ancient, straightening his bent old back proudly, " oh, Peter !—tell 'em I'm a man o' truth, an' no liar—tell 'em, Peter."

" They know that," said I ; " they know it without my telling them, Ancient."

" But," said Job, staring at me aghast, " do 'ee

mean to say as you live in a place as is 'aunted by the—devil 'isself ? ''

" Oh, Lord bless 'ee ! '' cried the old man, laying his hand upon my arm, " Peter don't mind Old Nick no morn'n I do—Peter aren't afeard of' im. 'Cause why ? 'Cause 'e 'ave a clean 'eart, 'ave Peter. You don't mind Old Nick, do 'ee lad ? ''

" Not in the least,'' said I, whereupon those nearest instinctively shrank farther from me, while Old Amos rose and shuffled towards the door.

" I've heerd o' folk sellin' theirselves to the devil afore now ! '' said he.

" You be a danged fule, Joel Amos !.'' exclaimed the Ancient angrily.

" Fule or no—I never see a chap wi' such a tur'ble dark-lookin' face afore, an' wi' such eyes—so black, an' sharp, an' piercin' as needles, they be—ah ! goes through a man like two gimlets, they do ! '' Now, as he spoke, Old Amos stretched out one arm towards me with his first and second fingers crossed : which fingers he now opened wide apart, making what I believe is called " the horns,'' and an infallible safe-guard against this particular form of evil.

" It's the ' Evil Eye,' '' said he in a half whisper, " ' the Evil Eye ' ! '' and, turning about, betook himself away.

One by one the others followed, and, as they passed me, each man averted his eyes and I saw that each had his fingers crossed.

So it came to pass that I was, thenceforward, regarded askance, if not openly avoided, by the whole village, with the exception of Simon and the Ancient, as one in league with the devil, and possessed of the " Evil Eye.''

CHAPTER XXXI

IN WHICH DONAL' BIDS ME FAREWELL

HALCYON days! my masters, happy, care-free, halcyon days! To waken to the glory of a summer's morning, and shaking off dull sleep, like a mantle, to stride out into a world all green and gold, breathing a fragrant air laden with sweet, earthy smells. To plunge within the clear, cool waters of the brook whose magic seemed to fill one's blood with added life and lust of living. Anon, with Gargantuan appetite, to sit and eat until even Donal' would fall a-marvelling; and so, through shady coppice and sunny meadow, betimes to work.

Halcyon days! my masters, happy, care-free, halcyon days! with the ringing hammers, the dancing sparks mounting upon the smoke, the sweat, the toil, yet all lightened with laugh and song and good-fellowship.

And then, the labour done, the fire dead—Black George to his lonely cottage, and I to "The Bull"—there to sit between Simon and the Ancient, waited upon by the dexterous hands of sweet-eyed Prudence. What mighty rounds of juicy beef, washed down by draughts of good brown ale! What pies and puddings, prepared by those same slender, dexterous hands! And later, pipe in mouth, what grave discussions upon men and things—peace and war—the dead and the living—the rise and fall of nations—and Simon's new litter of pigs! At last, the "Goodnight" being said—homeward through the twi-lit lanes, often pausing to look upon the shadowy woods, to watch some star, or hearken to the mournful note of a night-jar, soft with distance.

What wonder if, at this time, my earlier dreams and ambitions faded from my ken—what wonder that Petronius Arbiter, and the jolly Sieur de Brantome lay neglected in my dusty knapsack.

184

Go to! Petronius, go to! How "stale, flat, and unprofitable" were all thy vaunted pleasures, compared with mine. Alas! for thy noble intellect draggled in the mire to pander to an Imperial Swine, and for all thy power and wise statecraft which yet could not save thee from untimely death.

And thou, Brantome! old gossip, with all thy scandalous stories of ladies, always and ever "très belle, et fort honneste" couldst not find time among them all to note the glories of the world wherein they lived, and moved, and had their "fort honneste" being?

But let it not be thought my leisure hours were passed in idle dreaming and luxurious ease; on the contrary, I had, with much ado, rethatched the broken roof of my cottage as well as I might, mended the chimney, fitted glass to the casements and a new door upon its hinges. This last was somewhat clumsily contrived, I grant you, and of a vasty strength quite unnecessary, yet a very excellent door I considered it, nevertheless.

Having thus rendered my cottage weather-proof, I next turned my attention to furnishing it. To which end I, in turn, and with infinite labour, constructed a bedstead, two elbow-chairs, and a table; all to the profound disgust of Donal', who could by no means abide the rasp of my saw, so that, reaching for his pipes, he would fill the air with eldrich shrieks and groans, or drown me in a torrent of martial melody.

It was about this time—that is to say, my second bedstead was nearing completion, and I was seriously considering the building of a press with cupboards to hold my crockery, also a shelf for my books—when, chancing to return home somewhat earlier than usual, I was surprised to see Donal' sitting upon the bench I had set up beside the door, polishing the buckles of that identical pair of square-toed shoes that had once so piqued my curiosity.

As I approached he rose, and came to meet me with the brogues in his hand.

"Man, Peter," said he, "I maun juist be gangin'."

"Going!" I repeated; "going where?"

"Back tae Glenure—the year is a'most up, ye ken, an' I wadna' hae ma brither Alan afore me wi' the lassie, forbye he's an unco braw an' sonsy man, ye ken, an' a lassie's mind is aye a kittle thing."

"True," I answered, "what little I know of woman would lead me to suppose so; and yet—Heaven knows! I shall be sorry to lose you, Donal'."

"Ay—I ken that fine, an' ye'll be unco lonesome wi'out me an' the pipes, I'm thinkin'."

"Very!"

"Eh, Peter, man! if it wasna' for the lassie I'd no hae the heart tae leave ye. Ye'll no be forgettin' the 'Wullie Wallace Lament'?"

"Never!" said I.

"Oh, man, Peter! it's in my mind ye'll no hear sic pipin' again, forbye there's nae man—Hielander nor Lowlander—has juist the trick o' the 'warblers' like me, an' it's no vera like we shall e'er meet again i' this warld, man, Peter. But I'll aye think o' ye—away there in Glenure, when I play the 'Wullie Wallace' bit tune—I'll aye think o' ye, Peter, man."

After this we stood awhile, staring past each other into the deepening shadows.

"Peter," said he at last, "it's no a vera genteel present tae be makin' ye, I doot," and he held up the battered shoes. "They're unco worn, an' wi' a clout here an there, ye'll notice, but the buckles are guid siller, an' I hae naething else to gi'e ye. Ay, man! but it's many a weary mile I've marched in these at the head o' the Ninety-Second, an' it's mony a stark fecht they've been through—Vittoria, Salamanca, Talavera, tae Quatre Bras an' Waterloo; tak' 'em, Peter, tak' 'em—tae mind ye sometimes o' Donal' Stuart. An' now—gi'e us a grup o' ye hand. Gude keep ye, Peter, man!"

So saying, he thrust the brogues upon me, caught and squeezed my hand, and turning sharp about, strode away through the shadows, his kilt swaying, and tartans streaming gallantly.

And, presently, I went and sat me down upon the

bench beside the door, with the war-worn shoes upon my knee. Suddenly, as I sat there, faint and fainter with distance, and unutterably sad, came the slow, sweet music of Donal's pipes playing the " Wallace Lament." Softly the melody rose and fell, until it died away in one long-drawn, wailing note.

Now, as it ended, I rose, and uncovered my head, for I knew this was Donal's last farewell.

Much more I might have told of this strange yet lovable man who was by turns the scarred soldier, full of stirring tales of camp and battlefield; the mischievous child delighting in tricks and rogueries of all sorts; and the stately Hieland gentleman. Many wild legends he told me of his native glens, with strange tales of the " second sight "—but here, perforce, must be no place for such. So here then I leave Donal' and hurry on with my narrative.

CHAPTER XXXII

IN WHICH THIS FIRST BOOK BEGINS TO DRAW TO A CLOSE

> " Strike ! ding ! ding !
> Strike ! ding ! ding !
> The iron glows,
> And loveth good blows
> As fire doth bellows.
> Strike ! ding ! ding !"

OUT beyond the smithy door a solitary star twinkles low down in the night sky, like some great jewel; but we have no time for star-gazing, Black George and I, for to-night we are at work on the old church screen, which must be finished to-morrow.

And so the bellows roar hoarsely, the hammers clang, and the sparks fly, while the sooty face of Black George, now in shadow, now illumed by the fire, seems like the face of some Fire-god or Salamander. In the corner, perched securely out of reach of stray sparks, sits the Ancient, snuff-box in hand as usual.

To my mind, a forge is at its best by night, for, in the red, fiery glow, the blackened walls, the shining anvil, and the smith himself, bare-armed and bare of chest, are all magically transfigured, while, in the hush of night, the drone of the bellows sounds more impressive, the stroke of the hammers more sonorous and musical, and the flying sparks mark plainly their individual courses, ere they vanish.

I stand, feet well apart, and swing the great " sledge " to whose diapason George's hand-hammer beats a tinkling melody, coming in after each stroke with a ring and clash exact and true, as is, and has been, the way of masters of the smithing craft all the world over from time immemorial.

" George," said I, during a momentary lull, leaning

188

my hands upon the long hammer-shaft, "you don't sing."

"No, Peter."

"And why not?"

"I think, Peter."

"But surely you can both think and sing, George?"

"Not always, Peter."

"What's your trouble, George?"

"No trouble, Peter," said he, above the roar of the bellows.

"Then sing, George."

"Ay, Jarge, sing," nodded the Ancient; "'tis a poor 'eart as never rejices, an' that's in the Scripters—so sing, Jarge."

George did not answer, but, with a turn of his mighty wrist, drew the glowing iron from the fire. And once more the sparks fly, the air is full of the clink of hammers, and the deep-throated Song of the Anvil, in which even the Ancient joins, in a voice somewhat quavery, and generally a note or two behind, but with great gusto and goodwill notwithstanding:

> "Strike! ding! ding!
> Strike! ding! ding!"

in the middle of which I was aware of one entering to us, and presently, turning round, espied Prudence with a great basket on her arm. Hereupon hammers were thrown aside, and we straightened our backs, for in that basket was our supper.

Very fair and sweet Prudence looked, lithe and vigorous, and straight as a young poplar, with her shining black hair curling into little tight rings about her ears, and with great, shy eyes, and red, red mouth. Surely a man might seek very far ere he found such another maid as this brown-cheeked, black-eyed village beauty.

"Good-evening, Mr Peter!" said she, dropping me a curtsey with a grace that could not have been surpassed by any duchess in the land; but, as for poor George, she did not even notice him, neither did he raise his curly head nor glance toward her.

"You come just when you are most needed, Prudence," said I, relieving her of the heavy basket, "for here be two hungry men."

"Three!" broke in the Ancient; "so 'ungry as a lion, *I* be!"

"Three hungry men, Prudence, who have been hearkening for your step this half-hour and more."

Quoth Prudence shyly: "For the sake of my basket?"

"Ay, for sure!" croaked the Ancient; "so ravenous as a tiger I be!"

"No," said I, shaking my head, "basket or no basket, you are equally welcome, Prudence—how say you, George?" But George only mumbled in his beard. The Ancient and I now set to work putting up an extemporised table, but as for George, he stood staring down moodily into the yet glowing embers of the forge.

Having put up the table, I crossed to where Prudence was busy unpacking her basket.

"Prudence," said I, "are you still at odds with George?" Prudence nodded.

"But," said I, "he is such a splendid fellow! His outburst the other day was quite natural, under the circumstances—surely you can forgive him, Prudence."

"There be more nor that betwixt us, Mr Peter," sighed Prue. "'Tis his drinkin'; six months ago he promised me never to touch another drop—an' he broke his word wi' me."

"But surely good ale, in moderation, will harm no man—nay, on the contrary——"

"But Jarge bean't like other men, Mr Peter!"

"No; he is much bigger, and stronger!" said I, "and I never saw a handsomer fellow."

"Yes," nodded the girl, "so strong as a giant, an' so weak as a little child!"

"Indeed, Prudence," said I, leaning nearer to her in my earnestness, "I think you are a little unjust to him. So far as I know him, George is anything but weak-minded, or liable to be led into anything——"

Hearing the Ancient chuckle gleefully, I glanced up to find him nodding and winking to Black George, who stood with folded arms and bent head, watching us from beneath his brows, and, as his eyes met mine, I thought they gleamed strangely in the firelight.

"Come, Prue," said the Ancient, bustling forward, "table's ready—let's sit down an' eat—faintin' an' famishin' away, I be!".

So we presently sat down, all three of us, while Prudence carved, and supplied our wants, as only Prudence could.

And after a while, our hunger being appeased, I took out my pipe, as did the Ancient and George theirs likewise, and together we filled them, slowly and carefully, as pipes should be filled, while Prudence folded a long, paper spill wherewith to light them, the which she proceeded to do, beginning at her grandfather's churchwarden. Now, while she was lighting mine Black George suddenly rose, and, crossing to the forge, took thence a glowing coal with the tongs, thus doing the office for himself. All at once I saw Prue's hand was trembling, and the spill was dropped or ever my tobacco was well alight; then, she turned swiftly away, and began replacing the plates and knives and forks in her basket.

"Be you'm a-goin', Prue?" inquired the Ancient mumblingly, for his pipe was in full blast.

"Yes, gran'fer."

"Then tell Simon as I'll be along in 'arf an hour or so, will 'ee, lass?"

"Yes, gran'fer!" Always with her back to us.

"Then kiss ye old grandfeyther as loves 'ee, an' means for to see 'ee well bestowed, an' wed, one o' these fine days!" Prudence stooped, and pressed her fresh, red lips to his wrinkled old cheek and, catching up her basket, turned to the door, yet not so quickly but that I had caught the gleam of tears beneath her lashes. Black George half rose from his seat, and stretched out his hand towards her burden, then sat down again as, with a hasty "Good-night," she vanished through the yawning doorway. And, sitting

there, we listened to her quick, light footstep cross the
road to "The Bull."

"She'll make some man a fine wife, some day!"
exclaimed the Ancient, blowing out a cloud of smoke,
"ay, she'll mak' some man as fine a wife as ever was,
some day."

"You speak my very thought, Ancient," said I,
"she will indeed—what do you think, George?" But
George's answer was to choke suddenly, and, thereafter, to fall a-coughing.

"Smoke go t' wrong way, Jarge?" inquired the
Ancient, fixing him with his bright eye.

"Ay," nodded George.

"Ha!" said the old man, and we smoked for a
time in silence.

"So 'andsome as a picter she be!" said the Ancient
suddenly.

"She is fairer than any picture," said I impulsively,
"and what is better still, her nature is as sweet and
beautiful as her face!"

"'Ow do 'ee know that?" said George, turning
sharply upon me.

"My eyes and ears tell me so, as yours surely must
have done long ago," I answered.

"Ye do think as she be a purty lass, then, Peter?"
inquired the Ancient.

"I think," said I, "that she is the prettiest lass I
ever saw—don't you think so, George?" But again
George's only answer was to choke.

"Smoke again, Jarge?" inquired the Ancient

"Ay," said George, as before.

"'Tis a fine thing to be young," said the Ancient,
after a somewhat lengthy pause, and with a wave of
his long pipe-stem, "a very fine thing!"

"It is," said I, "though we generally realise it all
too late."

As for George, he went on smoking.

"When you are young," pursued the Ancient, "you
eats well, an' enjys it, you sleeps well an' enjys it—
your legs is strong, your arms is strong, an' you
bean't afeard o' nothin' nor nobody. Oh! life's a very

fine thing when you're young; but youth's tur'ble
quick a-goin'—the years roll slow at first, but gets
quicker'n quicker, till, one day, you wakes to find
you'm an old man; an' when you'm old, the way gets
very 'ard, an' toilsome, an' lonely."

" But there is always memory," said I.

" You'm right theer, Peter, so theer be—so theer be
—why, I be a old, old man, wi' more years than 'airs
on my 'ead, an' yet it seems but yesterday as I were
a-holdin' on tu my mother's skirt, an' wonderin' 'ow
the moon got lighted. Life be very short, Peter, an'
while we 'ave it 'tis well to get all the 'appiness out of
it we can."

" The wisest men of all ages preached the same,"
said I, " only they all disagreed as to how happiness
was to be gained."

" More fules they ! " said the Ancient.

" Eh ? " I exclaimed, sitting up.

" More fules they ! " repeated the old man with a
solemn nod.

" Why, then, do you know how true happiness may
be found ? "

" To be sure I du, Peter,"

" How ? "

" By marriage, Peter, an' 'ard work !—an' they
allus goes together."

" Marriage ! " said I.

" Marriage as ever was, Peter."

" There I don't agree with you," said I.

" That," retorted the Ancient, stabbing at me with
his pipe-stem, " that's because you never was married,
Peter."

" Marriage ! " said I; " marriage brings care, and
great responsibility, and trouble for one's self means
trouble for others."

" What o' that ? " exclaimed the Ancient. " 'Tis
care and 'sponsibility as mak' the man, an' if you
marry a good wife she'll share the burden wi' ye, an'
ye'll find what seemed your troubles is a blessin' arter
all. When sorrer comes, 'tis a sweet thing—oh ! a
very sweet thing—to 'ave a woman to comfort ye an'

N

'old your 'and in the dark hour—an' theer's no sympathy so tender as a woman's, Peter. Then, when ye be old, like me, an' full o' years—'tis a fine thing to 'ave a son o' your own—like Simon—an' a grand-darter—like my Prue—'tis worth 'aving lived for, Peter, ay, well worth it. It's a man's dooty to marry, Peter, 'is dooty to 'isself an' the world. Don't the Bible say summat about it not bein' good for a man to live alone? Every man as is a man should marry—the sooner the better."

" But," said I, " to every happy marriage there are scores of miserable ones."

" 'Cause why, Peter? 'Cause people is in too much o' a hurry to marry, as a rule. If a man marries a lass arter knowin' 'er a week—'ow is 'e goin' to know if she'll suit 'im all 'is days? Nohow, Peter, it aren't nat'ral—woman tak's a lot o' knowin' ' Marry in 'aste, an' repent in leisure!' That aren't in the Bible, but it ought to be."

" And your own marriage was a truly happy one, Ancient?"

" Ah! that it were, Peter, 'appy as ever was—but then, ye see, there was a Providence in it. I were a fine young chap in them days, summat o' your figure only bigger—ah! a sight bigger—an' I were sweet on several lassies, an' won't say as they wer'n't sweet on me—three on 'em, most especially so. One was a tall, bouncin' wench wi' blue eyes, an' golden 'air—like sunshine it were, but it wer'n't meant as I should buckle up wi' 'er."

" Why not?"

" 'Cause, it so 'appened as she married summun else."

" And the second?"

" The second were a fine, pretty maid tu, but I couldn't marry she."

" Why?"

" 'Cause Peter, she went an' took an' died afore I could ax 'er."

" And the third, you married."

" No, Peter, though it come to the same thing in the

end—she married I. Ye see, though I were allus at 'er beck an' call, I could never pluck the courage to up an' ax 'er right out. So things went on for a year or so, maybe, till one day—she were makin' apple-dumplings, Peter—'Martin,' says she, lookin' at me sideways out of 'er black eyes—just like Prue's they were—'Martin,' says she, 'you'm uncommon fond o' apple-dumplings?' 'For sure,' says I, which I were, Peter. 'Martin,' says she, 'shouldn't 'ee like to eat of 'em whenever you wanted to, at your very own table, in a cottage o' your own?' 'Ah! if you'd mak' 'em!' says I, sharp like. 'I would if you'd ax me, Martin,' says she. An' so we was married, Peter, an' as you see, theer was a Providence in it, for, if the first one 'adn't married some'un else, an' the second 'adn't died, I might ha' married one o' they, an' repented it all my days, for I were young then, an' fulish, Peter, fulish.'' So saying, the Ancient rose, sighing, and knocked the ashes from his pipe.

"Talkin' 'bout Prue," said he, taking up his hat and removing his snuff-box therefrom ere he set it upon his head, "talkin' 'bout Prue," he repeated, with a pinch of snuff at his nostrils.

"Well?" The word seemed shot out of George involuntarily.

"Talkin' 'bout Prue," said the Ancient again, glancing at each of us in turn, "theer was some folks as used to think she were sweet on Jarge theer, but I, bein' 'er lawful gran'feyther, knowed different—didn't I, Jarge?"

"Ay," nodded the smith.

"Many's the time I've said to you a-sittin' in this very corner, 'Jarge,' I've said, 'mark my words, Jarge—if ever my Prue does marry some'un—which she will—that there some'un won't be you.' Them be my very word, bean't they, Jarge?"

"Your very words, Gaffer," nodded George.

"Well then," continued the old man, "'ere's what I was a-comin' to—Prue's been an' fell in love wi' some'un at last."

Black George's pipe shivered to fragments on the

floor, and as he leaned forward I saw that his great hands were tightly clenched.

"Gaffer," said he, in a strangled voice, "what do 'ee mean?"

"I mean what I says, Jarge."

"How do 'ee know?"

"Bean't I the lass's gran'feyther?"

"Be ye sure, Gaffer—quite sure?"

"Ay—sartin sure—twice this week, an' once the week afore she forgot to put any salt in the soup—an' that speaks wollums, Jarge, wollums!" Here, having replaced his snuff-box, the Ancient put on his hat, nodded, and hobbled away. As for Black George, he sat there, staring blindly before him long after the tapping of the Ancient's stick had died away, nor did he heed me when I spoke, wherefore I laid my hand upon his shoulder.

"Come, George," said I, "another hour, and the screen will be finished." He started, and, drawing from my hand, looked up at me very strangely.

"No, Peter," he mumbled, "I aren't a-goin' to work no more to-night," and as he spoke he rose to his feet.

"What—are you going?" said I, as he crossed to the door.

"Ay, I'm a-goin'." Now, as he went towards his cottage, I saw him reel, and stagger, like a drunken man.

CHAPTER XXXIII

IN WHICH WE DRAW YET NEARER TO THE END OF THIS FIRST BOOK

IT is not my intention to chronicle all those minor happenings that befell me, now or afterward, lest this history prove wearisome to the reader (on the which head I begin to entertain grave doubts already). Suffice it then that as the days grew into weeks, and the weeks into months, by perseverance I became reasonably expert at my trade, so that, some two months after my meeting with Black George, I could shoe a horse with any smith in the country.

But, more than this, the people with whom I associated day by day—honest, loyal, and simple-hearted as they were, contented with their lot, and receiving all things so unquestioningly and thankfully, filled my life, and brought a great calm to a mind that had, hitherto, been somewhat self-centred and troubled by pessimistic doubts and phantastic dreams culled from musty pages.

What book is there to compare with the great Book of Life—whose pages are for ever a-turning, wherein are marvels and wonders undreamed; things to weep over, and some few to laugh at, if one but has eyes in one's head to see withal?

To walk through the whispering cornfields, or the long, green alleys of the hop-gardens with Simon, who combines innkeeping with farming, to hear him tell of fruit and flower, of bird and beast, is better than to read the Georgics of Virgil.

To sit in the sunshine and watch the Ancient, pipe in mouth, to hearken to his animadversions upon Life, and Death, and Humanity, is better than the cynical wit of Rochefoucauld, or a page out of honest old Montaigne.

To see the proud poise of sweet Prue's averted head,
and the tender look in her eyes when George is near,
and the surge of the mighty chest and the tremble of
the strong man's hand at the sound of her light foot-
fall, is more enthralling than any written romance,
old or new.

In regard to these latter, I began, at this time, to
contrive schemes and to plot plots for bringing them
together—to bridge over the difficulty which separated
them, for, being happy, I would fain see them happy
also. Now, how I succeeded in this self-imposed task,
the reader (if he trouble to read far enough) shall see
for himself.

" George," said I, on a certain Saturday morning,
as I washed the grime from my face and hands, " are
you going to the Fair this afternoon ? "

" No, Peter, I aren't."

" But Prudence is going," said I, drying myself
vigorously upon the towel.

" And how," inquired the smith, bending in turn
above the bucket in which we performed our ablutions,
" and how might you know that, Peter ? "

" Because she told me so."

" Told you so, did she ? " said George, and immediately plunged his head into the bucket.

" She did," I answered.

" And supposing," said George, coming up very
red in the face, and with the water streaming from his
sodden curls, " supposing she is goin' to the Fair,
what's that to me ? I don't care wheer she comes, no,
nor wheer she goes, neither ! " and he shook the water
from him as a dog might.

" Are you quite sure, George ? "

" Ah ! sartin sure. I've been sure of it now ever
since she called me——"

" Pooh, nonsense, man ! she didn't mean it—women
—especially young ones—often say things they do not
mean—at least, so I am given to understand."

" Ay, but she did mean it," said George, frowning
and nodding his head, " but it ain't that, Peter, no, it
aren't that, it's the knowin' as she spoke truth when

she called me ' coward,' and despisin' me for it in 'er
heart, that's wheer it is, Peter."

" Nevertheless, I'm sure she never meant it,
George."

" Then let 'er come and tell me so."

" I don't think she'll do that," said I.

" No more do I, Peter," saying which he fell to
work with the towel even as I had done.

" George," said I after a silence.

" Well, Peter ? "

" Has it ever struck you that Prudence is an uncommonly handsome girl ? "

" To be sure it 'as, Peter—I were blind else."

" And that other men may see this too ? "

" Well, Peter ? "

" And someone—even tell her so ? " His answer
was a long time coming, but come it did at last :

" Well, Peter ? "

" And—ask her to marry him, George ? " This
time he was silent so long that I had tied my neckerchief and drawn on my coat ere he spoke, very heavily
and slowly, and without looking at me.

" Why, then, Peter, let 'im. I've told 'ee afore, I
don't care wheer she comes nor wheer she goes, she
bean't nothin' to me no more, nor I to she. If so be
some man 'as a mind to ax 'er for 'isself, all open an'
above board, I say again—let 'im. And now, let's
talk o' summat else."

" Willingly. There's to be boxing, and single-
stick, and wrestling at the Fair, I understand."

" Ay."

" And, they tell me there is a famous wrestler
coming all the way from Cornwall to wrestle the best
man for ten guineas."

" Ay, so there be."

" Well ? "

" Well, Peter ? "

" They were talking about it at ' The Bull ' last
night——"

" ' The Bull '—to be sure—you *was* at ' The Bull '
last night—well ? "

"They were saying that you were a mighty wrestler, George, that you were the only man in these parts who could stand up to this Cornishman."

" Ay, I can wrastle a bit, Peter," he replied, speaking in the same heavy, listless manner; "what then?"

" Why then, George, get into your coat, and let's be off."

" Wheer to?"

" The Fair."   Black George shook his head.

" What, you won't?"

" No, Peter."

" And why not?"

" Because I aren't got the mind to—because I aren't never goin' to wrastle no more, Peter—so theer's an end on't."   Yet, in the doorway I paused and looked back.

" George."

" Peter?"

" Won't you come—for friendship's sake?"

Black George picked up his coat, looked at it, and put it down again.

" No, Peter!"

CHAPTER XXXIV

WHICH DESCRIBES SUNDRY HAPPENINGS AT THE FAIR, AND ENDS THIS FIRST BOOK

" I say, young cove, where are you a-pushing of ? "

The speaker was a very tall individual whose sharp-pointed elbow had, more than once, obtruded itself into my ribs. He was extremely thin and bony, with a long, drooping nose set very much to one side, and was possessed of a remarkable pair of eyes—that is to say, one eyelid hung continually lower than the other, thus lending to his otherwise sinister face an air of droll and unexpected waggery that was quite startling to behold.

All about us were jostling throngs of men and women in snowy smock frocks, and holiday gowns, who pushed, or were pushed, laughed, or frowned, according to their several natures; while above the merry hubbub rose the blare of trumpets, the braying of horns, and the crash, and rattle of drums—in a word, I was in the middle of an English Country Fair.

" Now then, young cove," repeated the man I have alluded to, " where are you a-pushing of ? Don't do it again, or mind your eye ! " And, saying this, he glared balefully at me with one eye and leered jocosely with the other, and into my ribs came his elbow again.

" You seem to be able to do something in that way yourself," I retorted.

" Oh—do I ? "

" Yes," said I ; " suppose you take your elbow out of my waistcoat."

" ' Elber,' " repeated the man, " what d'ye mean by ' elber ' ? "

" This," said I, catching his arm in no very gentle grip.

" If it's a fight you're wantin'——" began the man.

201

" It isn't ! " said I.

" Then leggo my arm ! "

" Then keep your elbow to yourself."

" 'Cod ! I never see such a hot-headed cove ! "

" Nor I a more bad-tempered one."

This altercation had taken place as we swayed to and fro in the crowd, from which we now slowly won free, owing chiefly to the dexterous use of the man's bony elbows, until we presently found ourselves in a veritable jungle of carts and waggons of all kinds and sorts, where we stopped, facing each other.

" I'm inclined to think, young cove, as you'd be short-tempered if you been shied at by your feller-man from your youth up," said the man.

" What do you mean by ' shied at ' ? "

" What I sez !—some perfessions is easy, and some is 'ard—like mine."

" And what is yours ? "

" I'm a perfessional Sambo."

" A what ? "

" Well—a ' Nigger-head,' then—blacks my face—sticks my 'ead through a 'ole, and let's 'em shy at me —three shies a penny—them as 'its me gets a cigar—a big 'un—them as don't—don't ! "

" Yours is a very unpleasant profession," said I.

" A man must live ! "

" But," said I, " supposing you get hit ? "

" Them as 'its me gets a cigar ! "

" Doesn't it hurt you ? "

" Oh ! you gets used to it—though, to be sure, they don't 'it me very often, or it would be a loss ; cigars is expensive—leastways, they costs money."

" But surely a wooden image would serve your turn just as well."

" A wooden image ! " exclaimed the man dis-gustedly. " James !—you must be a fool, you must ! Who wants to throw at a wooden image—you can't 'urt a wooden image, can you—if you throwed 'eavens 'ard at a wooden image that there wooden image wouldn't flinch, would it ? When a man throws at anything 'e likes to 'it it—that's 'uman—and when 'e 'its it 'e likes to see it flinch—that's 'uman too, and when it flinches, why—'e rubs 'is 'ands, and takes another shot—and that's the 'umanest of all. So you see, young cove, you're a fool with your wooden image.''

Now, as he ended, I stooped, very suddenly, and caught hold of his wrist—and then I saw that he held my purse in his hand. It was a large hand with bony knuckles, and very long fingers, upon one of which, was a battered ring. He attempted, at first, to free himself of my grip, but, finding this useless, stood glowering at me with one eye and leering with the other.

" Ha ! " said I.

" Hallo ! " said he.

" A purse ! " said I.

" Why, so it is," he nodded; " leastways, it looks uncommonly like one, don't it ? "

" What's more, it looks like mine ! "

" Does it ? "

" I could swear to it anywhere."

" Could you ? "

" I could."

" Then p'r'aps you'd better take it, young cove, and very welcome, I'm sure."

" So you've been picking my pocket ! " said I.

" Never picked a pocket in my life—should scorn to."

I put away my recovered property, and straightway shifted my grip to the fellow's collar.

" Now," said I, " come on."

" Why, what are you a-doing of ? "

" What does one generally do with a pickpocket ? "

But I had hardly uttered the words when, with a sudden, cunning twist, he broke my hold, and, my foot catching in a guy-rope, I tripped, and fell heavily, and ere I could rise he had made good his escape. I got to my feet, somewhat shaken by the fall, yet congratulating myself on the recovery of my purse, and, threading my way among the tents, was soon back among the crowd. Here were circuses and shows of all kinds, where one might behold divers strange beasts, the usual Fat Women and Skeleton Men (who ever heard of the order being reversed?); and before the shows were fellows variously attired, but each being purplish of visage, and each possessing the lungs of a Stentor—more especially one, a round-bellied, bottle-nosed fellow in a white hat, who alternately roared and beat upon a drum—a red-haired man he was, with a fiery eye, which eye, chancing to single me out in the crowd, fixed itself pertinaciously upon me, thenceforth, so that he seemed to address himself exclusively to me, thus:

"O my stars! [young man]." (Bang goes the drum.) "The wonderful wild, 'airy, and savage man from Bonhoola, as eats snakes alive, and dresses his-self in sheeny serpents! O my eye! step up! [young man]." (Bang!) "Likewise the ass-tonishin' and beautiful Lady Paulinolotti, as will swaller swords, sabres, bay'nets, also chewin' up glass, and bottles quicker than you can wink [young man]." (Bang!) "Not to mention Catamaplasus, the Fire Fiend, what burns hisself with red-hot irons, and likes it, drinks liquid fire with gusto—playfully spittin' forth the same, together with flame and sulphurous smoke, and all for sixpence [young man]." (Bang!) "O my stars! step up [young man] and all for a tanner." (Bang!)

Presently, his eye being off me for the moment, I edged my way out of the throng and so came to where a man stood mounted upon a cart. Beside him was a fellow in a clown's habit who blew loudly three times upon a trumpet, which done, the man took off his hat and began to harangue the crowd, something in this wise:

"I come before you, ladies and gentlemen, not for vulgar gain—or, as I might say—kudos, which is Eyetalian for the same—not to put my hands into your pockets and rifle 'em of your honestly earned money; no, I come before you for the good of each one of you, for the easing of suffering mankind—as I might say—the ha-melioration of stricken humanity. In a word, I am here to introduce to you what I call my Elixir

Anthropos—Anthropos, ladies and gentlemen, is an old and very ancient Egyptian word meaning man— or woman, for that matter," etc.

During this exordium I had noticed a venerable man in a fine blue surtout and a wide-brimmed hat, who sat upon the shaft of a cart and puffed slowly at a great pipe. And as he puffed, he listened intently to the quack-salver's address, and from time to time his eyes would twinkle and his lips curve in an ironic smile. The cart, upon the shaft of which he sat, stood close to a very small, dirty, and disreputable-looking tent, towards which the old gentleman's back was turned. Now, as I watched, I saw the point of a knife gleam through the dirty canvas, which, vanishing, gave place to a hand protruded through the slit thus made—a very large hand with bony knuckles, and long fingers, upon one of which was a battered ring. For an instant the hand hovered undecidedly, then darted forward—the long skirts of the old gentleman's coat hardly stirred, yet, even as I watched, I saw the hand vanish with a fat purse in its clutches.

Skirting the tent, I came round to the opening, and stooping, peered cautiously inside. There, sure enough, was my pickpocket gazing intently into the open purse, and chuckling as he gazed. Then he slipped it into his pocket, and out he came—where I immediately pinned him by the neckerchief.

And, after a while, finding he could not again break my hold, he lay still, beneath me, panting, and, as he lay, his one eye glared more balefully and his other leered more waggishly than ever, as I, thrusting my hand into his pocket, took thence the purse, and transferred it to my own.

"Halves, mate!" he panted, "halves, and we'll cry 'quits.'"

"By no means," said I, rising to my feet, but keeping my grip upon him.

"Then what's your game?"

"I intend to hand you over as a pickpocket."

"That means 'Transportation'!" said he, wiping

the blood from his face, for the struggle, though short, had been sharp enough.

"Well?" said I.

"It'll go 'ard with the babby."

"Baby!" I exclaimed.

"Ah!—or the hinfant, if you like it better—one as I found in a shawl, a-laying on the steps o' my van one night, sleeping like a alderman—and it were snowing too."

"Yet you are a thief!"

"We calls it 'faking.'"

"And ought to be given up to the authorities."

"And who's to look arter the babby?"

"Are you married?"

"No."

"Where is the baby?"

"In my van."

"And where is that?"

"Yonder!" and he pointed to a gaily-painted caravan that stood near-by. "'E's asleep now, but if you'd like to take a peep at 'im——"

"I should," said I. Whereupon the fellow led me to his van, and, following him up the steps, I entered a place which, though confined, was wonderfully neat and clean, with curtains at the open windows, a rug upon the floor, and an ornamental brass lamp pendant from the roof. At the far end was a bed, or rather, berth, curtained with chintz, and upon this bed, his chubby face pillowed upon a dimpled fist, lay a very small man indeed. And, looking up from him to the very large, bony man, bending over him, I surprised a look upon the hardened face—a tenderness that seemed very much out of place.

"Nice and fat, ain't 'e?" said the man, touching the baby's apple-like cheek with a grimy finger.

"Yes."

"Ah—and so 'e should be, James! But you should see 'im eat, a alderman's nothing to Lewis—I calls 'im Lewis, for 'twere at Lewisham I found 'im, on a Christmas Eve—snowing it was, but, by James! it didn't bother 'im—not a bit."

For an instant the hand hovered undecidedly

Face Page 206

"And why did you keep him?—there was the parish."

"Parish!" repeated the man bitterly. "I were brought up by the parish myself—and a nice job they made o' me!"

"Don't you find him a great trouble?"

"Trouble!" exclaimed the man. "Lewis ain't no trouble—not a bit—never was, and he's great company when I'm on the move from one town to another—larning to talk a'ready."

"Now," said I, when we had descended from the van, "I propose to return this purse to the owner, if he is to be found; if not, I shall hand it to the proper authorities."

"Walker!" exclaimed the man.

"You shall yourself witness the restitution," said I unheeding his remark, "after which——"

"Well!" said he, glancing back toward his caravan, and moistening his lips as I tightened my grip upon his arm, "what about me?"

"You can go—for Lewis's sake—if you will give me your word to live honestly henceforth."

"You have it, sir—I swear it—on the Bible if you like."

"Then let us seek the owner of this purse." So, coming in a while to where the quack doctor was still holding forth—there, yet seated upon the shaft of the cart, puffing at his great pipe, was the venerable man. At sight of him the pickpocket stopped and caught my arm.

"Come, master," said he, "come, you never mean to give up all that good money—there's fifty guineas, and more, in that purse!"

"All the more reason to return it," said I.

"No, don't—don't go a-wasting good money like that—it's like throwing it away!" But shaking off the fellow's importunate hand, I approached, and saluted the venerable man.

"Sir," said I, "you have had your pocket picked."

He turned and regarded me with a pair of deep-set, very bright eyes, and blew a whiff of smoke slowly into the air.

"Sir," he replied, "I found that out five minutes ago."

"The fact seems to trouble you very little," said I.

"There, sir, being young, and judging exteriorly, you are wrong. There is recounted somewhere in the classics an altogether incredible story of a Spartan youth and a fox : the boy, with the animal hid beneath his cloak, preserved an unruffled demeanour despite the animal's tearing teeth, until he fell down and died. In the same way, young sir, no man can lose fifty-odd guineas from his pocket and remain unaffected by the loss."

"Then, sir," said I, "I am happy to be able to return your purse to you." He took it, opened it, glanced over its contents, looked at me, took out two guineas, looked at me again, put the money back, closed the purse, and, dropping it into his pocket, bowed his acknowledgment. Having done which, he made room for me to sit beside him.

"Sir," said he, chuckling, "hark to that lovely rascal in the cart, yonder—hark to him, Galen was an ass and Hippocrates a dunce beside this fellow—hark to him."

"There's nothing like pills!" the Quack-salver was saying at the top of his voice; "place one upon the tip o' the tongue—in this fashion—take a drink o' water, beer, or wine, as the case may be, give a couple o' swallers, and there you are. Oh, there's nothing in the world like pills, and there's nothing like my Elixir Anthropos—for coughs, colds, and the rheumatics— for sore throats, sore eyes, sore backs—good for the croup, measles, and chicken-pox—a certain cure for dropsy, scurvy, and the king's evil—there's no disease or ailment, discovered or invented, as my pills won't soothe, heal, ha-meliorate, and charm away, and all I charge is one shilling a box. Hand 'em round, Jonas." Whereupon the fellow in the clown's dress, stepping down from the cart, began handing out the boxes of pills and taking in the shillings as fast as he conveniently could.

"A thriving trade!" said my venerable companion,

" it always has been, and always will, for Humanity is a many-headed fool, and loves to be ' bamboozled.' These honest folk are probably paying for bread pellets compounded with a little soap, yet will go home, swallow them in all good faith, and think themselves a great deal better for them."

" And therefore," said I, " probably derive as much benefit from them as from any drug yet discovered."

" Young man," said my companion, giving me a sharp glance, " what do you mean ? "

" Plainly, sir, that a man who believes himself cured of a disease is surely on the high road to recovery."

" But a belief in the efficacy of that rascal's bread pellets cannot make them anything but bread pellets."

" No," said I, " but it may effect great things with the disease."

" Young man, don't tell me that you are a believer in Faith Healing, and such-like tomfoolery—disease is a great and terrible reality, and must be met, and overcome, by a real means."

" On the contrary, sir, may it not be rather the outcome of a preconceived idea—of a belief that has been held universally for many ages and generations of men ? I do not deny disease—who could ? but suffering and disease have been looked upon from the earliest days as punishments wrought out upon a man for his sins. Now, may not the haunting fear of this retributive justice be greatly responsible for suffering and disease of all kinds—since the mind unquestionably reacts upon the body ? "

" Probably, sir, probably, but—since disease is with us, how would you propose to remedy it ? "

" By disbelieving in it; by regarding it as something abnormal and utterly foreign to the divine order of things."

" Pooh ! " exclaimed my venerable companion. " Bah !—quite, quite impracticable ! "

" They say the same of ' The Sermon on the Mount,' sir," I retorted.

" Can a man, wasting away in a decline, discredit the fact that he is dying with every breath he draws ? "

o

" Had you, or I, or any man, the Christ-power to
teach him a disbelief in his sickness, then would he be
hale and well. The Great Physician healed all diseases
thus, without the aid of drugs, seeking only to implant
in the mind of each sufferer the knowledge that he was
whole and sound—that is to say, a total disbelief in his
malady. How many times do we read the words :
'Thy faith hath made thee whole'? All He demanded
of them was faith—or, as I say, a disbelief in their
disease."

" Then the cures of Christ were not miracles ? "

" No more so than any great and noble work is a
miracle."

" And do you," inquired my companion, removing
his pipe from his lips, and staring at me very hard,
" do you believe that Jesus Christ was the Son of
God ? "

" Yes," said I, " in the same way that you and I
are, and the Quack-salver, yonder."

" But was He divine ? "

" Surely a mighty thinker—a great teacher whose
hand points the higher way, whose words inspire
Humanity to nobler ends and aims, is, of necessity,
divine."

" You are a very bold young man, and talk, I think,
a little wildly."

" Heterodoxy has been styled so before, sir."

" And a very young, young man."

" That, sir, will be amended by time." Here,
puffing at his pipe, and finding it gone out, he looked
at me in surprise.

" Remarkable ! " said he.

" What is, sir ? "

" While I listened to you I have actually let my pipe
go out—a thing which rarely happens with me." As
he spoke he thrust one hand into his pocket, when he
glanced slowly all round, and back once more to me.

" Remarkable ! " said he again.

" What now, sir ? "

" My purse has gone again ! "

" What !—gone ! " I ejaculated.

"Vanished!" said he, and, to prove his words, turned inside out first one pocket and then the other.

"Come with me," said I, springing up, "there is yet a chance that we may possibly recover it." Forthwith I led him to where had stood a certain gaily-painted caravan, but it was gone—vanished as utterly as my companion's purse.

"Most annoying!" said he, shaking his venerable head, "really most exasperating—I particularly wished to secure a sample of that fellow's pills—the collection of quack remedies is a fad of mine—as it is——"

"My purse is entirely at your disposal, sir," said I, "though to be sure, a very——" But there I stopped, staring, in my turn, blankly at him.

"Ha?" he exclaimed, his eyes twinkling.

"Yes," I nodded, "the rascal made off with my purse also—we are companions in misfortune."

"Then as such, young sir, come and dine with me, my habitation is but a little way off."

"Thank you, sir, but I am half expecting to meet with certain good friends of mine, though I am none the less honoured by your offer."

"So be it, young sir, then permit me to wish you a very 'Good-day'" and, touching the brim of his hat with the long stem of his pipe, the Venerable Man turned and left me.

Howbeit, though I looked diligently on all hands, I saw nothing of Simon or the Ancient; thus evening was falling as, bending my steps homeward, I came to a part of the Fair where drinking-booths had been set up, and where they were preparing to roast an ox whole, as is the immemorial custom. Drinking was going on, with its usual accompaniment of boisterous merriment and rough horseplay—the vulgarity of which ever annoys me. Two or three times I was rudely jostled as I made my way along, so that my temper was already something the worse, when, turning aside to avoid all this, I came full upon two fellows, well-to-do farmers, by their look, who held a struggling girl between them—to each of whom I reached out a hand, and, gripping them firmly by their collars, brought their two heads together with a sounding crack—and then I saw that the girl was Prudence. Next moment we were running, hand in hand, with the two fellows roaring in pursuit. But Prudence was wonderfully fleet and light of foot, wherefore, doubling and turning among carts, tents, and booths, we had soon outstripped our pursuers, and rid ourselves of them altogether. In spite of which Prudence still ran on till, catching her foot in some obstacle, she tripped, and would have fallen, but for my arm.

And looking down into her flushed face, glowing through the sweet disorder of her glossy curls, I could not but think how lovely she was. But, as I watched, the colour fled from her cheeks, her eyes dilated, and she started away from me.

Now, turning hastily, I saw that we were standing close by a certain small, dirty, and disreputable-looking tent, the canvas of which had been slit with a knife—and my movement had been quick enough to enable me to see a face vanish through the canvas. And, fleeting though the glimpse had been, yet, in the lowering brow, the baleful glare of the eye, and the set of the great jaw, I had seen—Death.

And, after we had walked on a while together, looking at Prue, I noticed that she trembled.

"Oh, Mr Peter," she whispered, glancing back over her shoulder, "did ye see?"

"Yes, Prudence, I saw." And, speaking, I also glanced back towards the villainous little tent, and though the face appeared no more, I was aware, nevertheless, of a sudden misgiving that was almost like a foreboding of evil to come; for in those features, disfigured though they were with black rage and passion, I had recognised the face of Black George.

A WORD TO THE READER

REMEMBERING the very excellent advice of my friend the Tinker as to the writing of a good " nov-el," I am perturbed, and not a little discouraged, upon looking over these pages, to find that I have, as yet, described no desperate hand-to-hand encounters, no hairbreadth escapes (unless a bullet through one's hat may be justly so regarded), and, above all—not one word of LOVE!

You, sir, who have expectantly borne with me thus far, may be tempted to close the book in a huff, and, hurling it from you, with a deep-voiced anathema, clap on your hat, and sally forth into the sunshine.

Or you, madam, breathing a sigh o'er hopes deferred, may take up needle, and silk, and turn you, once again, to that embroidery which has engaged your dainty fingers this twelvemonth and more, yet which, like Penelope's Web, would seem no nearer completion.

Ah well, sir! exercise, especially walking, is highly beneficial to the liver, they tell me—and nothing, madam, believe me (unless it be playing the harp), can show off a pretty hand, or the delicate curves of a shapely wrist and arm to such advantage as that self-same embroidery. But since needlework (like books and all sublunary things) is apt to grow monotonous, you may, perchance, for lack of better occupation, be driven to address yourself, once more, to this, my Narrative.

And since you, sir, no matter how far you walk, must, of necessity, return to your chair and chimney-corner, it is possible that, having dined adequately, and lighted your pipe (and being therefore in a more charitable and temperate frame of mind), you may lift my volume from the dusty corner where it has lain all this while, and (though probably with sundry grunts

213

and snorts, indicative that the thing is done under
protest, as it were) reopen these pages.

In the which hope, dear madam, and you, noble
sir, I here commence this, my Second Book—which,
as you see, is headed thus:

THE WOMAN

BOOK II

THE WOMAN

BOOK II

THE WOMAN

CHAPTER I

OF STORM, AND TEMPEST, AND OF THE COMING OF CHARMIAN

I WAS at sea in an open boat. Out of the pitch black heaven there rushed a mighty wind, and the pitch black seas above me rose high, and ever higher, flecked with hissing white; wherefore I cast me face downwards in my little boat, that I might not behold the horror of the waters; and above their ceaseless, surging thunder there rose a long-drawn cry :
" Charmian ! "
I stood upon a desolate moor, and the pitiless rain lashed me, and the fierce wind buffeted me; and, out of the gloom where frowning earth and heaven met—there rose a long-drawn cry :
" Charmian ! "
I started up in bed, broad awake, and listening; yet the tumult was all about me still—the hiss and beat of rain, and the sound of a rushing, mighty wind—a wind that seemed to fill the earth—a wind that screamed about me, that howled above me, and filled the woods, near and far, with a deep booming, pierced, now and then, by the splintering crash of snapping bough or falling tree. And yet, somewhere in this frightful pandemonium of sound, blended in with it, yet not of it, it seemed to me that the cry still faintly echoed :
" Charmian ! "
So appalling was all this to my newly-awakened senses, that I remained, for a time, staring into the darkness as one dazed. Presently, however, I rose,

and, donning some clothes, mended the fire which still smouldered upon the hearth, and, having filled and lighted my pipe, sat down to listen to the awful voices of the storm.

What brain could conceive—what pen describe that elemental chorus, like the mighty voice of persecuted Humanity, past and present, crying the woes, and ills, the sorrows and torments, endured of all the ages? To-night, surely, the souls of the un-numbered dead rode within the storm, and this was the voice of their lamentation.

From the red mire of battlefields are they come, from the flame and ravishment of fair cities, from dim and reeking dungeons, from the rack, the stake, and the gibbet, to pierce the heavens once more with the voice of their agony.

Since the world was made, how many have lived and suffered, and died, unlettered and unsung—snatched by a tyrant's whim from Life to Death, in the glory of the sun, in the gloom of night, in blood and flame, and torment? Indeed, their name is " Legion."

But there is a great and awful Book, whose leaves are countless, yet every leaf of which is smirched with blood, and fouled with nameless sins, a record, howsoever brief and inadequate, of human suffering, wherein as " through a glass, darkly," we may behold horrors unimagined; where Murder stalks, and rampant Lust, where Treachery creeps with curving back, smiling mouth, and sudden, deadly hand, where Tyranny, fierce-eyed, and iron-lipped, grinds the nations beneath a bloody heel. Truly, Man hath no enemy like man. And Christ is there, and Socrates, and Savonarola—and there, too, is a cross of agony, a bowl of hemlock, and a consuming fire.

O noble martyrs! by whose blood, and agony, the world is become a purer and better place for us, and those who shall come after us—O glorious, innumerable host! thy poor, mained bodies were dust ages since, but thy souls live on in paradise, and thy memory abides, and shall abide in the earth, for ever.

Ye Purblind, ye Pessimists, existing with no hope

of a Resurrection, bethink you of these matters; go, open the great and awful Book, and read and behold these things for yourselves—for what student of History is there but must be persuaded of Man's Immortality—that, though this poor flesh be mangled, torn asunder, burned to ashes, yet the soul, rising beyond the tyrant's reach, soars triumphant above Death and this sorry world, to the refuge of " the everlasting arms "; for God is a just God!

Now, in a while, becoming conscious that my pipe was smoked out and cold, I reached up my hand to my tobacco-box upon the mantelshelf. Yet I did not reach it down, for, even as my fingers closed upon it, above the wailing of the storm, above the hiss and patter of driven rain, there rose a long-drawn cry :

" Charmian ! "

So, remembering the voice I had seemed to hear calling in my dream, I sat there with my hand stretched up to my tobacco-box, and my face screwed round to the casement behind me, that, as I watched, shook and rattled beneath each wind-gust, as if some hand strove to pluck it open.

How long I remained thus, with my hand stretched up to my tobacco-box, and my eyes upon this window, I am unable to say, but, all at once, the door of the cottage burst open with a crash, and immediately the quiet room was full of rioting wind and tempest; such a wind as stopped my breath, and sent up a swirl of smoke and sparks from the fire. And, borne upon this wind, like some spirit of the storm, was a woman with flying draperies and long, streaming hair, who turned, and with knee and shoulder, forced to the door, and so leaned there, panting.

Tall she was, and nobly shaped, for her wet gown clung, disclosing the sinuous lines of her waist and the bold, full curves of hip and thigh. Her dress, too, had been wrenched and torn at the neck, and, through the shadow of her fallen hair, I caught the ivory gleam of her shoulder, and the heave and tumult of her bosom.

Here I reached down my tobacco-box and mechanically began to fill my pipe, watching her the while.

Suddenly she started, and seemed to listen. Then, with a swift, stealthy movement, she slipped from before the door, and I noticed that she hid one hand behind her.

" Charmian ! "

The woman crouched back against the wall, with her eyes towards the door, and always her right hand was hidden in the folds of her petticoat. So we remained, she watching the door, and I, her.

" Charmian ! "

The voice was very near now, and, almost immediately after, there came a loud " view hallo," and a heavy fist pounded upon the door.

" Oh, Charmian, you're there—yes, yes—inside—I know you are. I swore you should never escape me, and you sha'n't—by God ! " A hand fumbled upon the latch, the door swung open, and a man entered. As he did so I leapt forward, and caught the woman's wrist. There was a blinding flash, a loud report, and a bullet buried itself somewhere in the rafters overhead. With a strange, repressed cry, she turned upon me so fiercely that I fell back before her.

The new-comer, meantime, had closed the door, latching it very carefully, and now, standing before it, folded his arms, staring at her with bent head. He was a very tall man, with a rain-sodden, bell-crowned hat crushed low upon his brows, and wrapped in a long, many-caped overcoat, the skirts of which were woefully mired and torn. All at once he laughed, very softly and musically.

" So, you would have killed me, would you, Charmian—shot me—like a dog ? " His tone was soft as his laugh and equally musical, and yet neither was good to hear. " So you thought you had lost me, did you, when you gave me the slip, a while ago ? Lose me ? Escape me ? Why, I tell you, I would search for you day and night—hunt the world over until I found you, Charmian—until I found you," said he, nodding his head and speaking almost in a whisper. " I would, by God ! "

*With knee and shoulder, forced to the door, and
so leaned there, panting*

Face Page 220

The woman neither moved nor uttered a word, only her breath came thick and fast, and her eyes gleamed in the shadow of her hair.

They stood facing each other, like two adversaries, each measuring the other's strength, without appearing to be conscious of my presence; indeed, the man had not so much as looked toward me even when I had struck up the pistol.

Now, with every minute I was becoming more curious to see this man's face, hidden as it was in the shadow of his dripping hat-brim. Yet the fire had burned low.

"You always were a spitfire, weren't you, Charmian?" he went on in the same gentle voice; "hot, and fierce, and proud—the flame beneath the ice—I knew that, and loved you the better for it; and so I determined to win you, Charmian—to win you whether you would or no. And—you are so strong—so tall, and glorious, and strong, Charmian!"

His voice had sunk to a murmur again, and he drew a slow step nearer to her.

"How wonderful you are, Charmian! I always loved your shoulders and that round, white throat. Loved? Worshipped them, worshipped them! And to-night——?" He paused, and I felt, rather than saw, that he was smiling. "And to-night you would have killed me, Charmian—shot me—like a dog! But I would not have it different. You have flouted, coquetted, scorned, and mocked me—for three years, Charmian, and to-night you would have killed me—and I—would not have it otherwise, for surely you can see that this of itself must make your final surrender—even sweeter."

With a gesture utterly at variance with his voice, so sudden, fierce, and passionate was it, he sprang toward her with outstretched arms. But, quick as he, she eluded him, and, before he could reach her, I stepped between them.

"Sir," said I, "a word with you."

"Out of my way, bumpkin!" he retorted, and, brushing me aside, made after her. I caught him by the skirts of his long, loose coat, but, with a dexterous twist, he had left it in my grasp. Yet the check, momentary though it was, enabled her to slip through the door of that room which had once been Donal's, and, before he could reach it, I stood upon the threshold. He regarded me for a moment beneath his hatbrim, and seemed undecided how to act.

" My good fellow," said he at last, " I will buy your cottage of you—for to-night—name your price."

I shook my head. Hereupon he drew a thick purse from his pocket, and tossed it, chinking, to my feet.

" There are two hundred guineas, bumpkin, maybe more—pick them up, and—go," and turning, he flung open the door.

Obediently I stooped, and, taking up the purse, rolled it in the coat which I still held, and tossed both out of the cottage.

" Sir," said I, " be so very obliging as to follow your property."

" Ah !" he murmured, " very pretty, on my soul ! " And, in that same moment, his knuckles caught me fairly between the eyes, and he was upon me swift, and fierce, and lithe as a panther.

I remember the glint of his eyes and the flash of his bared teeth, now to one side of me, now to the other, as we swayed to and fro, overturning the chairs, and crashing into unseen obstacles. In that dim and narrow place small chance was there for feint or parry, it was blind, brutal work, fierce, and grim, and silent. Once he staggered, and fell heavily, carrying the table crashing with him, and I saw him wipe blood from his face as he rose; and once I was beaten to my knees, but was up before he could reach me again, though the fire upon the hearth spun giddily round and round, and the floor heaved oddly beneath my feet.

Then, suddenly, hands were upon my throat, and I could feel the hot pant of his breath in my face, breath that hissed and whistled between clenched teeth. Desperately I strove to break his hold, to tear his hands asunder, and could not, only the fingers tightened and tightened.

Up and down the room we staggered, grim and voiceless—out through the open door—out into the whirling blackness of the storm. And there, amid the tempest, lashed by driving rain and deafened by the roaring rush of wind, we fought—as our savage forefathers may have done, breast to breast, and knee to knee—stubborn and wild, and merciless—the old, old struggle for supremacy and life.

I beat him with my fists, but his head was down between his arms; I tore at his wrists, but he gripped my throat the tighter; and now we were down, rolling upon the sodden grass, and now we were up, stumbling and slipping, but ever the gripping fingers sank the deeper, choking the strength and life out of me. My eyes stared up into a heaven streaked with blood and fire, there was the taste of sulphur in my mouth, my arms grew weak and nerveless, and the roar of wind seemed a thousand times more loud. Then—something clutched and dragged us by the feet, we tottered, swayed helplessly, and plunged down together. But, as we fell, the deadly, gripping fingers slackened for a moment, and, in that moment I had broken free, and, rolling clear, stumbled up to my feet. Yet, even then I was still encumbered, and stooping down, found the skirts of the overcoat twisted tightly about my foot and ankle. Now, as I loosed it, I inwardly blessed that tattered garment, for it seemed that to it I owed my life.

So I stood, panting, and waited for the end. I remember a blind groping in the dark, a wild hurlyburly of random blows, a sudden sharp pain in my right hand—a groan, and I was standing with the swish of the rain about me, and the moaning of the wind in the woods beyond.

How long I remained thus I cannot tell, for I was as one in a dream, but the cool rain upon my face refreshed me, and the strong, clean wind in my nostrils was wonderfully grateful. Presently, raising my arm stiffly, I brushed the wet hair from my eyes, and stared round me into the pitchy darkness, in quest of my opponent.

" Where are you ? " said I at last, and this was the first word uttered during the struggle; " where are you ? "

Receiving no answer I advanced cautiously (for it was, as I have said, black dark), and so, presently, touched something yielding with my foot.

" Come—get up ! " said I, stopping to lay a hand upon him, " get up, I say." But he never moved; he was lying upon his face, and, as I raised his head, my fingers encountered a smooth, round stone, buried in the grass, and the touch of that stone thrilled me from head to foot with sudden dread. Hastily I tore open waistcoat and shirt, and pressed my hand above his heart. In that one moment I lived an age of harrowing suspense, then breathed a sigh of relief, and, rising, took him beneath the arms and began to half drag, half carry him towards the cottage.

I had proceeded thus but some dozen yards or so when, during a momentary lull in the storm, I thought I heard a faint " Hallo," and looking about, saw a twinkling light that hovered to and fro, coming and going, yet growing brighter each moment. Setting down my burden, therefore, I hollowed my hands about my mouth, and shouted.

" This way ! " I called; " this way ! "

" Be that you, sir ? " cried a man's voice at no great distance.

" This way ! " I called again, " this way ! " The words seemed to reassure the fellow, for the light advanced once more, and as he came up, I made him out to be a postilion by his dress, and the light he carried, the lanthorn of a chaise.

" Why—sir ! " he began, looking me up and down, by the light of his lanthorn, " strike me lucky if I'd ha' knowed ye ! you looks as if—oh, Lord ! "

" What is it ? " said I, wiping the rain from my eyes again. The Postilion's answer was to lower his lanthorn towards the face of him who lay on the ground between us, and point. Now, looking where he pointed, I started suddenly backwards, and shivered, with a strange stirring of the flesh.

For I saw a pale face with a streak of blood upon the cheek—there was blood upon my own; a face framed in lank hair, thick and black—as was my own; a pale, aquiline face, with a prominent nose, and long, cleft chin—even as my own. So, as I stood looking down upon this face, my breath caught, and my flesh crept, for indeed, I might have been looking into a mirror— the face was the face of myself.

CHAPTER II

THE POSTILION

" GOOD Lord ! " exclaimed the Postilion, and fell back a step.

" Well ? " said I, meeting his astonished look as carelessly as I might.

" Lord love me ! " said the Postilion.

" What now ? " I inquired.

" I never see such a thing as this 'ere," said he, alternately glancing from me down to the outstretched figure at my feet, " if it's bewitchments, or only enchantments, I don't like it—strike me pink if I do ! "

" What do you mean ? "

" Eyes," continued the Postilion slowly and heavily, and with his glance wandering still—" eyes, same—nose, i-dentical—mouth, when not bloody, same—hair, same—figure, same—no, I don't like it—it's onnat'ral ! that's what it is."

" Come, come," I broke in, somewhat testily, " don't stand there staring like a fool—you see this gentleman is hurt."

" Onnat'ral's the word ! " went on the Postilion, more as though speaking his thoughts aloud than addressing me, " it's a onnat'ral night to begin with—seed a many bad 'uns in my time, but nothing to ekal this 'ere, that I lost my way aren't to be wondered at ; then him, and her a-jumping out o' the chaise and a-running off into the thick o' the storm—that's onnat'ral in the second place ! and then, his face, and your face—that's the most onnat'rallest part of it all—likewise, I never see one man in two suits o' clothes afore, nor yet a-standing up, and a-laying down both at the same i-dentical minute—onnat'ral's the word—and—I'm a-going."

" Stop ! " said I, as he began to move away.

" Not on no account ! "

" Then I must make you," said I, and doubled my fists.

The Postilion eyed me over from head to foot, and paused, irresolute.

" What might you be wanting with a peaceable, civil-spoke cove like me? " he inquired.

" Where is your chaise? "

" Up in the lane, som'eres over yonder," answered he, with a vague jerk of his thumb over his shoulder.

" Then, if you will take this gentleman's heels we can carry him well enough between us—it's no great distance."

" Easy ! " said the Postilion, backing away again, " easy, now—what might be the matter with him, if I might make so bold—ain't dead, is he? "

" Dead—no, fool ! " I rejoined angrily.

" Voice like his, too ! " muttered the Postilion, backing away still farther; " yes, onnat'ral's the word —strike me dumb if it ain't ! "

"Come, will you do as I ask, or must I make you?"

" Why, I ain't got no objection to taking the gent's 'eels, if that's all you ask, though mind ye, if ever I see such damned onnat'ralness as this 'ere in all my days, why—drownd me ! "

So, after some delay, I found the overcoat and purse (which latter I thrust into the pocket ere wrapping the garment about him), and lifting my still unconscious antagonist between us, we started for the lane; which we eventually reached, with no little labour and difficulty. Here, more by good fortune than anything else, we presently stumbled upon a chaise and horses, drawn up in the gloom of sheltering trees, in which we deposited our limp burden as comfortably as might be, and where I made some shift to tie up the gash in his brow.

" It would be a fine thing," said the Postilion moodily as I, at length, closed the chaise door, " it would be a nice thing if 'e was to go a-dying."

" By the looks of him," said I, " he will be swearing your head off in the next ten minutes or so."

Without another word the Postilion set the lanthorn back in its socket, and swung himself into the saddle.

"Your best course would be to make for Tonbridge, bearing to the right when you strike the high road."

The Postilion nodded, and, gathering up the reins, turned to stare at me, once more, while I stood in the gleam of the lanthorn.

"Well?" I inquired.

"Eyes," said he, rubbing his chin very hard, as one at a loss, "eyes, identical—nose, same—mouth, when not bloody, same—'air, same—everything, same —Lord love me!"

"Pembry would be nearer," said I, "and the sooner he is between the sheets the better."

"Ah!" exclaimed the Postilion with a slow nod, and drawing out the word unduly, "and talking o' sheets and beds—what about my second passenger? I started wi' two, and 'ere's only one—what about Number Two—what about—'er?"

"Her!" I repeated.

"'Er as was with 'im—Number One—'er what was a-quarrelling wi' Number One all the way from London—'er as run away from Number One into the wood, yonder, what about Number Two—'er?"

"Why, to be sure—I had forgotten her!"

"Forgotten?" repeated the Postilion, "Oh, Lord, yes!" and leaning over, he winked one eye, very deliberately; "forgotten 'er—ah!—to be sure—of course!" and he winked again.

"What do you mean?" I demanded, nettled by the fellow's manner.

"Mean?" said he, "I means as of all the damned onnat'ralness as come on a honest, well-meaning, civil-spoke cove—why, I'm that there cove, so 'elp me!" Saying which, he cracked his whip, the horses plunged forward, and, almost immediately, as it seemed, horses, chaise, and Postilion had lurched into the black murk of the night, and vanished.

CHAPTER III

WHICH BEARS AMPLE TESTIMONY TO THE STRENGTH
OF THE GENTLEMAN'S FISTS

CONSIDERING all that had befallen, during the last half-hour or so, it was not very surprising, I think, that I should have forgotten the very existence of this woman Charmian, even though she had been chiefly instrumental in bringing it all about, and to have her recalled to my recollection thus suddenly (and, moreover, the possibility that I must meet with and talk to her) perturbed me greatly, and I remained, for some time, quite oblivious to wind and rain, all engrossed by the thought of this woman.

"A dark, fierce, Amazonian creature!" I told myself, who had (abhorrent thought) already attempted one man's life to-night; furthermore, a tall woman, and strong (therefore unmaidenly), with eyes that gleamed wild in the shadow of her hair. And yet my dismay arose not so much from any of these as from the fact that she was a woman, and, consequently, beyond my ken.

Hitherto I had regarded the sex very much from a distance, and a little askance, as creatures naturally illogical, and given to unreasoning impulse; delicate, ethereal beings whose lives were made up of petty trifles and vanities, who were sent into this gross world to be admired, petted, occasionally worshipped, and frequently married.

Indeed, my education, in this direction, had been shockingly neglected, thus far, not so much from lack of inclination (for who can deny the fascination of the Sex?) as for lack of time and opportunity; for, when, as a young gentleman of means, and great expectations, I should have been writing sonnets to the eyebrow of some "ladye fayre," or surreptitiously wooing some farmer's daughter, in common with my kind, I was hearkening to the plaint of some Greek or Roman lover, or chuckling over old Brantome.

Thus, women were to me practically an unknown quantity, as yet, and hence it was with no little trepidation that I now started out for the cottage and this truly Amazonian Charmian, unless she had disappeared as suddenly as she had come (which I found myself devoutly hoping).

As I went, I became conscious that I was bleeding copiously above the brow, that my throat was much swollen, and that the thumb of my right hand pained exceedingly at the least touch; added to which was a dizziness of the head, and a general soreness of body, that testified to the strength of my opponent's fists.

On I stumbled, my head bent low against the stinging rain, and with uncertain, clumsy feet, for reaction had come, and with it, a deadly faintness. Twigs swung out of the darkness to lash at and catch me as I passed, invisible trees creaked and groaned above and around me, and once, as I paused to make more certain of my direction, a dim, vague mass plunged down athwart my path with a rending crash.

On I went (wearily enough, and with the faintness growing upon me, a sickness that would not be fought down), guiding my course by touch rather than sight, until, finding myself at fault, I stopped again, staring about me beneath my hand. Yet, feeling the faintness increase with inaction, I started forward, groping before me as I went; I had gone but a few paces, however, when I tripped over some obstacle, and fell heavily. It wanted but this to complete my misery, and I lay where I was, overcome by a deadly nausea.

Now presently, as I lay thus, spent and sick, I became aware of a soft glow, a brightness that seemingly played all around me, wherefore, lifting my heavy head, I beheld a ray of light that pierced the gloom, a long, gleaming vista jewelled by falling raindrops, whose brilliance was blurred, now and then, by the flitting shapes of wind-tossed branches. At sight of this my strength revived, and rising, I staggered on towards this welcome light, and thus I saw that it streamed from the window of my cottage. Even then, it seemed, I journeyed miles before I felt the latch beneath my fingers, and fumbling, opened the door, stumbled in and closed it after me.

For a space I stood dazed by the sudden light, and then, little by little, noticed that the table and chairs had been righted, that the fire had been mended, and that candles burned brightly upon the mantel. All this I saw but dimly for there was a mist before my eyes, yet I was conscious that the girl had leapt up on my entrance, and now stood fronting me across the table.

"You!" said she, in a low, repressed voice—"you?"

Now, as she spoke, I saw the glitter of steel in her hand.

" Keep back ! " she said, in the same subdued tone, " keep back—I warn you ! " But I only leaned there against the door, even as she had done; indeed, I doubt if I could have moved just then, had I tried. And, as I stood thus, hanging my head, and not answering her, she stamped her foot suddenly, and laughed a short, fierce laugh.

" So—he has hurt you ? " she cried; " you are all blood—it is running down your face—the Country Bumpkin has hurt you ! Oh, I am glad ! glad ! glad !" and she laughed again. " I might have run away," she went on mockingly, "but you see—I was prepared for you," and she held up the knife, " prepared for you—and now—you are pale, and hurt, and faint— yes, you are faint—the Country Bumpkin has done his work well. I shall not need this, after all—see ! " And she flung the knife upon the table.

" Yes—it is better—there," said I, " and I think— madam—is—mistaken."

" Mistaken ? " she cried, with a sudden catch in her voice, " what—what do you mean ? "

" That I—am—the Bumpkin ! " said I.

Now, as I spoke, a black mist enveloped all things, my knees loosened suddenly, and stumbling forward, I sank into a chair.

" I am—very—tired ! " I sighed, and so, as it seemed, fell asleep.

CHAPTER IV

WHICH, AMONG OTHER MATTERS, HAS TO DO WITH
BRUISES AND BANDAGES

SHE was on her knees beside me, bathing my battered face, talking all the while in a soft voice that I thought wonderfully sweet to hear.

" Poor boy ! " she was saying, over and over again, "poor boy ! " And after she had said it, perhaps, a dozen times, I opened my eyes, and looked at her.

" Madam, I am twenty-five ! " said I. Hereupon, sponge in hand, she drew back and looked at me.

A wonderful face—low-browed, deep-eyed, full-lipped. The eyes were dark, and swiftly changeful, and there was a subtle witchery in the slanting shadow of their lashes.

" Twenty-five ! " she repeated, " can it really be ? "

" Why not, madam ? "

" So very young ? "

" Why——" I began, greatly taken aback. " Indeed, I—that is——"

But here she laughed and then she sighed, and sighing, shook her head.

" Poor boy ! " said she, " poor boy ! " And, when I would have retorted, she stopped me with the sponge.

" Your mouth is cut," said she, after a while, " and there is a great gash in your brow."

" But the water feels delicious ! " said I.

" And your throat is all scratched and swollen ! "

" But your hands are very gentle and soothing ! "

" I don't hurt you, then ? "

" On the contrary, the—the pain is very trifling, thank you."

" Yet you fainted a little while ago."

" Then it was very foolish of me."

" Poor——" she hesitated, and looking up at her

through the trickling water, I saw that she was smiling.

"—fellow!" said she. And her lips were very sweet, and her eyes very soft and tender—for an Amazon.

And, when she had washed the blood from my face, she went to fetch clean water from where I kept it in a bucket in the corner.

Now, at my elbow, upon the table, lay the knife, a heavy, clumsy contrivance I had bought to use in my carpentry, and I now, mechanically, picked it up. As I did so the light gleamed evilly upon its long blade.

" Put it down ! " she commanded, " put it away—it is a hateful thing ! "

" For a woman's hand," I added, " so hideously unfeminine ! "

" Some men are so hatefully—hideously—masculine ! " she retorted, her lip curling. " I expected—him—and you are terribly like him."

" As to that," said I, " I may have the same coloured eyes, and hair, and be something of the same build——"

" Yes," she nodded, " it was your build, and the colour of your eyes and hair, that—startled me."

" But, after all," said I, " the similarity is only skin-deep, and goes no farther."

" No," she answered, kneeling beside me again; " no, you are—only twenty-five ! " And, as she said this, her eyes were hidden by her lashes.

" Twenty-five is—twenty-five ! " said I, more sharply than before. " Why do you smile ? "

" The water is all dripping from your nose and chin !—stoop lower over the basin."

" And yet," said I, as well as I could on account of the trickling water, for she was bathing my face again, " and yet, you must be years younger than I."

" But then, some women always feel older than a man—more especially if he is hurt."

" Thank you," said I, " thank you; with the exception of a scratch, or so, I am very well ! " But, as I moved, I caught my thumb clumsily against the table-edge, and winced with the sudden pain of it.

" What is it—your hand ? "

" My thumb."

" Let me see ? " Obediently I stretched out my hand to her.

" Is it broken ? "

" Dislocated, I think."

" It is greatly swollen ! "

" Yes," said I, and taking firm hold of it, with my left hand, I gave it a sudden pull which started the sweat upon my temples, but sent it back into joint.

" Poor——"

" Well ? " said I, as she hesitated.

"—man ! " said she, and touched the swollen hand very tenderly with her fingers.

" You do not fear me any longer ? "

" No."

" In spite of my eyes and hair ? "

" In spite of your eyes, and hair—you see, a woman knows instinctively whom she must fear and whom not to fear."

" Well ? "

" And you are one I do not fear, and, I think, never should."

" Hum ! " said I, rubbing my chin, " I am only twenty-five ! "

" Twenty-five is—twenty-five ! " said she demurely.

" And yet, I am very like—him—you said so yourself ! "

" Him ! " she exclaimed, starting. " I had forgotten all about him. Where is he—what has become of him ? " and she glanced apprehensively towards the door.

" Half way to Tonbridge—or should be by now."

" Tonbridge ! " said she, in a tone of amazement, and turned to look at me again.

" Tonbridge ! " I repeated.

" But he is not the man to—to run away," said she doubtfully—" even from you."

" No, indeed ! " said I, shaking my head, " he

certainly did not run away, but circumstances—and a stone, were too much—even for him.''

'' A stone ? ''

'' Upon which he—happened to fall, and strike his head—very fortunately for me.''

'' Was he—much hurt ? ''

'' Stunned only,'' I answered.

She was still kneeling beside my chair, but now she sat back, and turned to stare into the fire. And, as she sat, I noticed how full and round and white her arms were, for her sleeves were rolled high, and that the hand, which yet held the sponge, was likewise very white, neither big nor little, a trifle wide, per- haps, but with long, slender fingers. Presently, with a sudden gesture, she raised her head and looked at me again—a long, searching look.

'' Who are you ? '' she asked suddenly.

'' My name,'' said I, '' is Peter.''

'' Yes,'' she nodded, with her eyes still on mine.

'' Peter—Smith,'' I went on, '' and, by that same token, I am a blacksmith—very humbly at your ser- vice.''

'' Peter—Smith ! '' she repeated, as though trying the sound of it, hesitating at the surname exactly as I had done. '' Peter—Smith !—and mine is Charmian, Charmian—Brown,'' and here again was a pause between the two names.

'' Yours is a very beautiful name,'' said I, '' especi- ally the Charmian ! ''

'' And yours,'' she retorted, '' is a beautifully—ugly one ! ''

'' Yes ? ''

'' Especially the—Peter ! ''

'' Indeed, I quite agree with you,'' said I, rising, '' and now, if I may trouble you for the towel—thank you ! '' Forthwith I began to dry my face as well as I might on account of my injured thumb, while she watched me with a certain elusive merriment peeping from her eyes, and quivering at me round her lips, an expression half mocking, half amused, that I had seen there more than once already. Wherefore, to hide from her my consciousness of this, I fell to towelling myself vigorously, so much so, that, forgetting the cut in my brow, I set it bleeding faster than ever.

" Oh, you are very clumsy ! " she cried, springing up, and snatching the towel from me she began to stanch the blood with it. " If you will sit down, I will bind it up for you."

" Really, it is quite unnecessary," I demurred.

" Quite ! " said she; " is there anything will serve as a bandage ? "

" There is the towel ! " I suggested.

" Not to be thought of ! "

" Then you might tear a strip off the sheet," I said, nodding towards the bed.

" Ridiculous ! " said she, and proceeded to draw a handkerchief from the bosom of her dress, and having folded it with great nicety and moistened it in the bowl, she tied it about my temples.

Now, to do this, she had, perforce, to pass her arms about my neck, and this brought her so near that I could feel her breath upon my lips, and there stole to me, out of her hair, or out of her bosom, a perfume very sweet, that was like the fragrance of violets at evening. But her hands were all too dexterous, and, quicker than it takes to write, the bandage was tied, and she was standing before me, straight, and tall.

" There—that is more comfortable, isn't it ? " she inquired, and with the words, she bestowed a final little pat to the bandage, a touch so light—so ineffably gentle—that it might almost have been the hand of that long-dead mother whom I had never known. " That is better, isn't it ? " she demanded.

" Thank you—yes, very comfortable ! " said I. But, as the word left me, my glance, by accident, encountered the pistol near by, and at sight of it a sudden anger came upon me, for I remembered that, but for my intervention, this girl was a murderess; wherefore, I would fain have destroyed the vile thing, and reached for it impulsively, but she was before me, and snatching up the weapon, hid it behind her as she had done once before.

"Give it to me," said I, frowning, "it is an accursed thing!"

"Yet it has been my friend to-night," she answered.

"Give it to me!" I repeated. She threw up her head, and regarded me with a disdainful air, for my tone had been imperative.

"Come," said I, and held out my hand. So, for a while, we looked into each other's eyes, then, all at once she dropped the weapon on the table before me, and turned her back to me.

"I think——" she began, speaking with her back still turned to me.

"Well?" said I.

"—that you have——"

"Yes?" said I.

"—very unpleasant—eyes!"

"I am very sorry for that," said I, dropping the weapon out of sight, behind my row of books, having done which, I drew both chairs nearer the fire, and invited her to sit down.

"Thank you, I prefer to stand," said she loftily.

"As you will," I answered, but, even while I spoke, she seemed to change her mind, for she sank into the nearest chair, and, chin in hand, stared into the fire.

"And so," said she, as I sat down opposite her, "and so your name is Peter Smith, and you are a blacksmith?"

"Yes, a blacksmith."

"And make horseshoes?"

"Naturally, yes."

"And do you live here?"

"Yes."

"Alone?"

"Quite alone!"

"And how long have you lived here alone?"

"Not so long that I am tired of it."

"And is this cottage yours?"

"Yes—that is, it stands on the Sefton estates, I believe, but nobody hereabouts would seem anxious to dispute my right of occupying the place."

" Why not ? "

" Because it is generally supposed to be haunted."

" Oh ! "

" It was built by some wanderer of the roads," I explained, " a stranger to these parts, who lived alone here, and eventually died alone here."

" Died here ? "

" Hanged himself on the staple above the door, yonder."

" Oh ! " said she again, and cast a fearful glance towards the deep-driven, rusty staple.

" The country folk believe his spirit still haunts the place," I went on, " and seldom, or never, venture foot within the Hollow."

" And are you not afraid of this ghost ? "

" No," said I.

" It must be very lonely here."

" Delightfully so."

" Are you so fond of solitude ? "

" Yes, for solitude is thought, and to think is to live."

" And what did you do with the—pistol ? "

" I dropped it out of sight behind my books, yonder."

" I wonder why I gave it to you."

" Because, if you remember, I asked you for it."

" But I usually dislike doing what I am asked, and your manner was—scarcely courteous."

" You also objected to my eyes, I think ? "

" Yes," she nodded.

" Hum ! " said I.

The dark night, outside, was filled with malignant dæmons now, who tore at the rattling casements, who roared and bellowed down the chimney, or screamed furiously round the cottage ; but here, in the warm fire-light, I heeded them not at all, watching, rather, this woman, where she sat, leaning forward, gazing deep into the glow. And where the light touched her hair it woke strange fires, red and bronze. And it was very rebellious hair, with little tendrils that gleamed, here and there, against her temples, and small, defiant curls that seemed to strive to hide behind her ear, or, bold and wanton, to kiss her snowy neck—out of sheer bravado.

As to her dress, I, little by little, became aware of two facts, for whereas her gown was of a rough, coarse material such as domestic servants wear, the stockinged foot that peeped at me beneath its hem (her shoes were drying on the hearth) was clad in a silk so fine that I could catch, through it, the gleam of the white flesh beneath. From this apparent inconsistency I deduced that she was of educated tastes, but poor— probably a governess, or, more likely still taking her hands into consideration, with their long, prehensile fingers, a teacher of music, and was going on to explain to myself her present situation as the outcome of Beauty, Poverty, and the Devil, when, she sighed, glanced toward the door, shivered slightly, and reaching her shoes from the hearth prepared to slip them on.

" They are still very wet ! " said I deprecatingly.

" Yes," she answered.

" Listen to the wind ! " said I.

" It is terribly high."

" And it rains very hard ! " said I.

" Yes," and she shivered again.

" It will be bad travelling for anyone to-night," said I.

Charmian stared into the fire.

" Indeed, it would be madness for the strongest to stir abroad on such a night."

Charmian stared into the fire.

" What with the wind and the rain the roads would be utterly impassable, not to mention the risks of falling trees or shattered boughs."

Charmian shivered again.

" And the inns are all shut, long ago; to stir out, therefore, would be the purest folly."

Charmian stared into the fire.

" On the other hand, here are a warm room, a good fire, and a very excellent bed."

She neither spoke nor moved, only her eyes were raised suddenly and swiftly to mine.

"Also," I continued, returning her look, "here, most convenient to your hand, is a fine sharp knife, in case you are afraid of the ghost or any other midnight visitant—and so—good-night, madam!" Saying which, I took up one of the candles and crossed to the door of that room which had once been Donal's, but here I paused to glance back at her. "Furthermore," said I, snuffing my candle with great nicety, "madam need have no further qualms regarding the colour of my hair and eyes—none whatever."

Whereupon I bowed somewhat stiffly on account of my bruises, and going into my chamber, closed the door behind me.

Having made the bed (for since Donal's departure I had occupied my two beds alternately) I undressed slowly, for my thumb was very painful, also I paused frequently to catch the sound of the light, quick foot-step beyond the door. and the whisper of her garments as she walked.

"Charmian!" said I to myself when at length all was still, "Charmian!" And I blew out my candle.

Outside, the souls of the unnumbered dead still rode the storm, and the world was filled with their woeful lamentation. But, as I lay in the dark, there came to me a faint perfume as of violets at evening-time, elusive and very sweet, breathing of Charmian herself; and putting up my hand, I touched the handkerchief that bound my brow.

"Charmian!" said I to myself again, and so, fell asleep.

CHAPTER V

IN WHICH I HEAR ILL NEWS OF GEORGE

THE sun was pouring in at my lattice when I awoke next morning to a general soreness of body that at first puzzled me to account for. But as I lay in that delicious state between sleeping and waking I became aware of a faint, sweet perfume, and, turning my head, espied a handkerchief upon the pillow beside me. And immediately I came to my elbow, with my eyes directed to the door, for now indeed I remembered all, and beyond that door, sleeping or waking, lay a woman.

In the early morning things are apt to lose something of the glamour that was theirs over night; thus I remained propped upon my elbow, gazing apprehensively at the door, and with my ears on the stretch, hearkening for any movement from the room beyond that should tell me she was up, but I heard only the early chorus of the birds, and the gurgle of the brook, swollen with last night's rain. In a while I rose and began to dress somewhat awkwardly, on account of my thumb, yet with rather more than my usual care, stopping occasionally to hear if She was yet astir. Being at last fully dressed, I sat down to wait until I should hear her footstep. But I listened vainly, for minute after minute elapsed until, rising at length, I knocked softly. And having knocked thrice, each time louder than before, without effect, I lifted the latch and opened the door.

My first glance showed me that the bed had never even been slept in, and that save for myself the place was empty. And yet the breakfast-table had been neatly set, though with but one cup and saucer.

Now beside this cup and saucer was one of my few books, and picking it up, I saw that it was my Virgil.

Q   241

Upon the fly-leaf, at which it was open, I had, years ago, scrawled my name thus:

PETER VIBART

But lo! close under this, written in a fine Italian hand, were the following words:

"To Peter Smith, Esq. [the "Smith" underlined] Blacksmith. Charmian Brown ["Brown" likewise underlined] desires to thank Mr Smith, yet because thanks are so poor and small, and his service so great, needs must she remember him as a gentleman, yet oftener as a blacksmith, and most of all, as a man. Charmian Brown begs him to accept this little trinket in memory of her; it is all she has to offer him. He may also keep her handkerchief."

Upon the table, on the very spot where the book had lain, was a gold heart-shaped locket, very quaint and old-fashioned, upon one side of which was engraved the following posy:

"Hee who myne heart would keepe for long
Shall be a gentil man and strong."

Attached to the locket was a narrow blue riband, wherefore, passing this riband over my head, I hung the locket about my neck. And having read through the message once more, I closed the Virgil, and, replacing it on the shelf, set about brewing a cup of tea, and so presently sat down to breakfast.

I had scarcely done so, however, when there came a timid knock at the door, whereat I rose expectantly, and immediately sat down again.

"Come in!" said I. The latch was slowly raised, the door swung open, and the Ancient appeared. If I was surprised to see him at such an hour, he was even more so, for, at sight of me, his mouth opened, and he stood staring speechlessly, leaning upon his stick.

"Why, Ancient," said I, "you are early abroad this morning!"

"Lord!" he exclaimed, scarcely above a whisper.

"Come in and sit down," said I.

"Lord! Lord!" he murmured, "an' a-eatin' 'is breakfus' tu. Lordy, Lord!"

"Yes," I nodded, "and, such as it is, you are heartily welcome to share it—sit down," and I drew up my other chair.

"A-eatin' 'is breakfus' as ever was!" repeated the old man, without moving.

"And why not, Ancient?"

"Why not?" he repeated disdainfully. "'Cause breakfus' can't be ate by a corp', can it?"

"A corpse, Ancient, what do you mean?"

"I means as a corp' aren't got no right to eat a breakfus'—no!"

"Why, I—no, certainly not."

"Consequently, you aren't a corp', you'll be tellin' me."

"I?—no, not yet, God be thanked!"

"Peter," said the Ancient, shaking his head, and mopping his brow with a corner of his neckerchief, "you du be for ever a-givin' of me turns, that ye du."

"Do I, Ancient?"

"Ay—that ye du, an' me such a aged man tu—such a very aged man. I wonders at ye, Peter, an' me wi' my white 'airs—oh, I wonders at ye!" said he, sinking into the chair I had placed for him and regarding me with a stern, reproving eye.

"If you will tell me what I have been guilty of——?" I began.

"I come down 'ere, Peter—so early as it be, tu—I come down 'ere to look for your corp', arter the storm an' what 'appened last night. I comes down 'ere, and what does I find?—I finds ye a-eatin' your breakfus'—just as if theer never 'adn't been no storm at all—no nor nothin' else."

"I'm sure," said I, pouring out a second cup of tea, "I'm sure I would sooner you should find my corpse than anyone else, and am sorry to have disappointed you again, but really, Ancient——"

"Oh, it aren't the disapp'intment, Peter—I found one corp', an' that's enough, I suppose, for an aged man like me—no, it aren't that—it's findin' ye eatin'

your breakfus'—just as if theer 'adn't been no storm—
no, nor yet no devil, wi' 'orns, an' a tail, a-runnin' up
an' down in the 'Oller 'ere, an' a-roarin' an' a-bellerin',
as John Pringle said, last night."

"Ah! and what else did John Pringle say?" I
inquired, setting down my cup.

"Why, 'e come into 'The Bull' all wet an' wild-
like, an' wi' 'is two eyes a-stickin' out like goose-
berries! 'E comes a-bustin' into the 'tap'—an' never
says a word till 'e's emptied Old Amos's tankard—
that bein' nighest. Then—'By Goles!' says 'e,
lookin' round on us all, 'by Goles! I jest seen the
ghost!' 'Ghost!' says all on us, sittin' up, ye may
be sure, Peter. 'Ay,' says John, lookin' over 'is
shoulder, scared-like, 'seed un wi' my two eyes, I did,
an' what's more, I heerd un tu!' 'Wheer?' says all
on us, beginnin' to look over our shoulders likewise.
'Where?' says John, 'wheer should I see un but in
that theer ghashly 'Oller. I see a light, fust of all,
a-leapin' an' a-dancin' about 'mong the trees—ah! an'
I 'eerd shouts as was enough to curdle a man's good
blood.' 'Pooh! what's lights?' says Joel Amos,
cockin' 'is eye into 'is empty tankard; 'that bean't
much to frighten a man, no, nor shouts neither.'
'Aren't it?' says John Pringle, fierce-like; 'what if I
tell ye the place be full o' flamin' fire—what if I tell ye
I see the devil 'isself, all smoke, an' sparks, an' brim-
ston' a-floatin' an' a-flyin', an' draggin' a body
through the tops o' the trees?' 'Lord!' says everybody, an' well they might, Peter, an' nobody says
nothin' for a while. 'I wonder,' says Joel Amos at
last, 'I wonder who 'e was a-draggin' through the
tops o' the trees—an' why?' 'That'll be poor Peter
bein' took away,' says I, 'I'll go an' find the poor
lad's corp' in the mornin——an' 'ere I be."

"And you find me not dead, after all your trouble,"
said I.

"If," said the Ancient, sighing, "if your arms was
broke, or your legs was broke, now—or if your 'air
was singed, or your face all burned an' blackened wi'
sulphur, I could ha' took it kinder; but to find ye

a-sittin' eatin', an' drinkin'—it aren't what I expected of ye, Peter, no." Shaking his head moodily, he took from his hat his never-failing snuff-box, but, having extracted a pinch, paused suddenly in the act of inhaling it, to stare at me very hard. " But," said he, in a more hopeful tone, " but your face be all bruised, an' swole up, to be sure, Peter."

" Is it, Ancient ? "

" Ah ! that it be—that it be," he cried, his eyes brightening, " an' your thumb all bandaged tu."

" Why, so it is, Ancient."

" An'—Peter—— ! " The pinch of snuff fell, and made a little brown cloud on the snow of his smock-frock as he rose, trembling, and leaned towards me, across the table.

" Well, Ancient ? "

" Your throat—— ! "

" Yes—what of it ? "

" It—be all marked—scratched it be—tore, as if—as if—claws 'ad been at it, Peter, long—sharp—claws ! "

" Is it, Ancient ? "

"Peter—oh, Peter ! " said he, with a sudden quaver in his voice, " who was it—what was it, Peter ? " and he laid a beseeching hand upon mine. " Peter ! " his voice had sunk almost to a whisper, and the hand plucked tremulously at my sleeve, while in the wrinkled old face was a look of pitiful entreaty. "Oh, Peter ! oh, lad ! 'twere Old Nick as done it—'twere the devil as done it, weren't it—oh ! say 'twere the devil, Peter." And, seeing that hoary head all a-twitch with eagerness as he waited my answer, how could I do other than nod ?

" Yes, it was the devil, Ancient." The old man subsided into his chair, embracing himself exultantly.

" I knowed it ! I knowed it ! " he quavered. "" 'Twere the devil flyin' off wi' Peter,' says I, an' they fules laughed at me, Peter, ay, laughed at me they did, but they won't laugh at the old man no more—not they ; old I be, but they won't laugh at me no more, not when they see your face an' I tell 'em." Here he paused to fumble for his snuff-box, and, opening it, held it towards me.

" Tak' a pinch wi' me, Peter."

" No, thank you, Ancient."

" Come, 'twould be a wonnerful thing to tell as I'd took snuff out o' my very own box wi' a man as 'ad fou't wi' the devil—come—tak' a pinch, Peter," he pleaded. Whereupon, to please him, I did so, and immediately fell most violently a-sneezing.

" And," pursued the old man when the paroxysm was over, " did ye see 'is 'orns, Peter, an' 'is——'

" Why, no, Ancient; you see, he happened to be wearing a bell-crowned hat, and a long coat."

" A 'at an' coat ! " said the old man in a disappointed tone—" a 'at, Peter ? "

" Yes," I nodded.

" To be sure, the Scripters say as 'e goeth up an' down like a ravening lion seekin' whom 'e may devour."

" Yes," said I, " but more often, I think, like a fine gentleman ! "

" I never heerd tell o' the devil in a bell-crowned 'at afore, but p'r'aps you'm right, Peter—tak' another pinch o' snuff."

" No more," said I, shaking my head.

" Why, it's apt to ketch you a bit at first, but, Lord ! Peter, for a man as 'as fou't wi' the devil——"

" One pinch is more than enough, Ancient."

" Oh, Peter, 'tis a wonnerful thing as you should be alive this day ! "

" And yet, Ancient, many a man has fought the devil before now and lived—nay, has been the better for it."

" Maybe, Peter, maybe, but not on sech a tur'ble wild night as last night was." Saying which, the old man nodded emphatically and, rising, hobbled to the door, yet there he turned and came back again. " I nigh forgot, Peter, I have noos for ye."

" News ? "

" Noos as ever was—noos as'll surprise ye, Peter."

" Well ? " I inquired.

" Well, Peter, Black Jarge be ' took ' again."

" What ? " I exclaimed.

"Oh! I knowed 'twould come—I knowed 'e couldn't last much longer. I says to Simon, day afore yesterday it were, ' Simon,' I says, ' mark my words, 'e'll never last the month out—no.' "

" How did it happen, Ancient ? "

" Got tur'ble drunk, 'e did, over to Cranbrook— throwed Mr Scrope, the Beadle, over the churchyard wall—knocked down Jeremy Tullinger, the Watchman, an' then—went to sleep. While 'e were asleep they managed, cautious-like, to tie 'is legs an' arms, an' locked 'im up, mighty secure, in the vestry. 'Ows'ever, when 'e woke up 'e broke the door open, an' walked out, an' nobody tried to stop 'im—not a soul, Peter."

" And when was all this ? "

" Why, that's the very p'int," chuckled the Ancient, " that's the wonnerful part of it, Peter. It all 'appened on Sat'day night, day afore yesterday as ever was—the very same day as I says to Simon, ' mark my words, 'e won't last the month out.' "

" And where is he now ? "

" Nobody knows, but theer's them as says they see 'im makin' for Sefton Woods." Hereupon, breakfast done, I rose, and took my hat.

" Wheer away, Peter ? "

" To the forge; there is much work to be done, Ancient."

" But Jarge bean't theer to 'elp ye."

" Yet the work remains, Ancient."

" Why then, if you'm goin' I'll go wi' ye, Peter." So we presently set out together.

All about us, as we walked, were mute evidences of the fury of last night's storm : trees had been uprooted, and great branches torn from others as if by the hands of angry giants ; and the brook was a raging torrent. Down here, in the Hollow, the destruction had been less, but in the woods, above, the giants had worked their will, and many an empty gap showed where, erstwhile, had stood a tall and stately tree.

" Trees be very like men," said the Ancient, nodding to one that lay prone beside the path, " 'ere

to-day an' gone to-morrer, Peter—gone to-morrer.
The man in the Bible, 'im as was cured of 'is blind-
ness by our blessed Lord, 'e said as men was like
trees walkin', but, to my mind, Peter, trees is much
more like men a-standing still.   Ye see, Peter, trees
be such companionable things; it's very seldom as
you see a tree growin' all by itself, an' when you do,
if you look at it you can't 'elp but notice 'ow lonely
it do look—why, its very leaves seem to 'ave a down-
'earted sort o' droop.   I knowed three on 'em once—
elm-trees they was—growin' all close together, so
close that their branches used to touch each other
when the wind blew, jest as if they was a-shakin'
'ands wi' one another, Peter.   You could see as they
was uncommon fond of each other, wi' half an eye.
Well, one day, along comes a storm and blows one on
'em down—kills it dead, Peter; an' a little while later,
they cuts down another—Lord knows why—an' theer
was the last one, all alone an' solitary.   Now, I used
to watch that theer tree—an' here's the cur'us thing,
Peter—day by day I see that tree a-droopin' an'
droopin', a-withering—an' a-pinin' for them other
two—brothers you might say—till one day I come
by, an' theer it were, Peter, a-standin' up so big an'
tall as ever—but dead !   Ay, Peter, dead it were, an'
never put forth another leaf, an' never will, Peter—
never.   An', if you was to ax me, I should say as
it died because its 'eart were broke, Peter.   Yes, trees
is very like men, an' the older you grow the more
you'll see it."

It was thus we talked, or rather, the Ancient talked
and I listened, until we reached Sissinghurst.   At the
door of the smithy we stopped.

" Peter," said the old man, staring very hard at a
button on my coat.

" Well, Ancient ? "

" What about that theer—poor, old, rusty—stapil ?"

" Why, it is still above the door, Ancient, you must
have seen it this morning."

" Oh, ah ! I seed it, Peter, I seed it," answered the
old man, shifting his gaze to a rolling white cloud

above. " I give it a glimp' over, Peter, but what do
'ee think of it ? "

" Well," said I, aware of the fixity of his gaze and
the wistful note in his voice, " it is certainly older and
rustier than it was."

" Rustier, Peter ? "

" Much rustier ! " Very slowly, a smile dawned on
the wrinkled old face, and very slowly the eyes were
lowered till they met mine.

" Eh, lad ! but I be glad o' that—we be all growin'
older, Peter, an'—though I be a wonnerful man for
my age, an' so strong as a cart-'orse, Peter, still, I du
sometimes feel like I be growin' rustier wi' length o'
days, an' 'tis a comfort to know as that theer stapil's
a-growin' rustier along wi' me. Old I be, but t'
stapil's old too, Peter, an' I be waitin' for the day
when it shall rust itself away altogether; an' when
that day comes, Peter, then I'll say, like the patriarch
in the Bible : ' Lord, now lettest thou thy servant
depart in peace ! ' Amen, Peter ! "

" Amen ! " said I. And so, having watched the old
man totter across to " The Bull," I turned into the
smithy and set about lighting the fire.

CHAPTER VI

IN WHICH I LEARN OF AN IMPENDING DANGER

I AM at the forge, watching the deepening glow of the coals as I ply the bellows; and, listening to their hoarse, not unmusical drone, it seems like a familiar voice (or the voice of a familiar), albeit a somewhat wheezy one, speaking to me in stertorous gasps, something in this wise:

"Charmian Brown—desires to thank—Mr Smith—but because thanks—are so poor and small—and his service so great—needs must she remember him——"

"Remember me!" said I aloud, and, letting go the shaft of the bellows the better to think this over, it naturally followed that the bellows grew suddenly dumb, whereupon I seized the handle and recommenced blowing with a will.

"—remember him as a gentleman," wheezed the familiar.

"Psha!" I exclaimed.

"—yet oftener as a smith——"

"Hum!" said I.

"—and most of all—as a man."

"As a man!" said I, and, turning my back upon the bellows, I sat down upon the anvil and, taking my chin in my hand, stared away to where the red roof of old Amos's oast-house peeped through the swaying green of leaves.

"As a man?" said I to myself again, and so fell a-dreaming of this Charmian. And, in my mind, I saw her, not as she had first appeared, tall and fierce, and wild, but as she had been when she stooped to bind up the hurt in my brow—with her deep eyes brimful of tenderness, and her mouth sweet and compassionate. Beautiful eyes she had, though whether they were blue, or brown, or black, I could not for the life of me remember; only I knew I could never forget the look they had held when she gave that final pat to the bandage. And here I found that I was turning a little locket round and round in my fingers, a little, old-fashioned heart-shaped locket with its quaint inscription :

> " Hee who myne heart would keepe for long
>   Shall be a gentil man, and strong."

I was sitting thus, plunged in a reverie, when a shadow fell across the floor, and looking up I beheld Prudence, and straightway, slipping the locket back into the bosom of my shirt, I rose to my feet, somewhat shamefaced to be caught thus idle.

Her face was troubled, and her eyes red, as from recent tears, while in her hand she held a crumpled paper.

" Mr Peter——" she began, and then stopped, staring at me.

" Well, Prudence ? "

" You—you've seen him ! "

" Him—whom do you mean ? "

" Black Jarge ! "

" No ; what should make you think so ? "

" Your face be all cut—you've been fightin' ! "

" And supposing I have—that is none of George's doing ; he and I are very good friends—why should we quarrel ? "

" Then—then it weren't Jarge ? "

" No—I have not seen him since Saturday."

" Thank God ! " she exclaimed, pressing her hand to her bosom as if to stay its heaving. " But you must go," she went on breathlessly. " Oh, Mr Peter ! I've been so fearful for 'ee, and—and—you might meet each other any time, so—so you must go away."

"Prudence," said I, "Prudence, what do you mean ?"

For answer, she held out the crumpled paper, and, scrawled in great, straggling characters, I read these words :

" PRUDENCE,—I'm going away, I shall kill him else, but I shall come back. Tell him not to cross my path, or God help him, and you, and me.   GEORGE."

" What does it all mean, Prudence ? " said I, like a
fool.

Now, as I spoke, glancing at her I saw her cheeks,
that had seemed hitherto more pale than usual, grow
suddenly scarlet, and, meeting my eyes, she hid her
face in her two hands. Then, seeing her distress, in
that same instant I found the answer to my question,
and so stood, turning poor George's letter over and
over, more like a fool than ever.

" You must go away—you must go away ! " she
repeated.

" Hum ! " said I.

" You must go soon, he means it, I—I've seen
death in his face," she said, shuddering ; " go to-day
—the longer you stay here the worse for all of us—
go now."

" Prudence ! " said I.

" Yes, Mr Peter ! " from behind her hands.

" You always loved Black George, didn't you ? "

" Yes, Mr Peter."

" And you love him still, don't you ? " A moment's
silence, then :

" Yes, Mr Peter."

" Excellent ! " said I. Her head was raised a trifle,
and one tearful eye looked at me over her fingers. " I
had always hoped you did," I continued, " for his
sake, and for yours, and in my way, a very blundering
way as it seems now, I have tried to bring you two
together." Prudence only sobbed. " But things are
not hopeless yet. I think I can see a means of
straightening out this tangle."

" Oh, if we only could ! " sobbed Prudence. " Ye
see, I were very cruel to him, Mr Peter ! "

" Just a little, perhaps," said I, and, while she
dabbed at her pretty eyes with her snowy apron, I
took pen and ink from the shelf where I kept them,
which, together with George's letter, I set upon the
anvil. " Now," said I, in answer to her questioning
look, " write down just here, below where George
signed his name, what you told me a moment ago."

" You mean, that I——"

" That you love him, yes."

" Oh, Mr Peter ! "

" Prudence," said I, " it is the only way, so far as I can see, of saving George from himself ; and no sweet, pure maid need be ashamed to tell her love, especially to such a man as this, who worships the very ground that little shoe of yours has once pressed."

She glanced up at me, under her wet lashes, as I said this, and a soft light beamed in her eyes, and a smile hovered upon her red lips.

" Do he—really, Mr Peter ? "

" Indeed he does, Prudence, though I think you must know that without my telling you." So she stooped above the anvil, blushing a little, and sighing a little, and crying a little, and, with fingers that trembled somewhat, to be sure, wrote these four words :

" George, I love you."

" What now, Mr Peter ? " she inquired, seeing me begin to unbuckle my leather apron.

" Now," I answered, " I am going to look for Black George."

" No !—no ! " she cried, laying her hands upon my arm, " no ! no ! if 'ee do meet him he—he'll kill 'ee ! "

" I don't think he will," said I, shaking my head.

" Oh, don't go !—don't go ! " she pleaded, shaking my arm in her eagerness ; " he be so strong, and wild, and quick—he'll give 'ee no chance to speak—'twill be murder ! "

" Prudence," said I, " my mind is set on it. I am going—for your sake, for his sake, and my own," saying which I loosed her hands gently and took down my coat from its peg.

" Dear God ! " she exclaimed, staring down at the floor with wide eyes, " if he were to kill 'ee——! "

" Well," said I, " my search would be ended and I should be a deal wiser in all things than I am to-day."

" And he—would be hanged ! " said Prudence, shuddering.

" Probably—poor fellow ! " said I. At this she

glanced quickly up, and once again the crimson dyed
her cheeks.

"Oh, Mr Peter, forgive me! I—I were only
thinkin' of Jarge, and——"

"And quite right too, Prudence," I nodded; "he is
indeed worth any good woman's thoughts; let it be
your duty to think of him, and for him, henceforth."

"Wait!" said she, "wait!" And turning, she
fled through the doorway and across the road, swift
and graceful as any bird, and presently was back
again, with something hidden in her apron.

"He be a strong man, and terrible in his wrath,"
said she, "and I—love him, but—take this wi' you,
and if it—must be—use it, because I *do* love him."
Now, as she said this, she drew from her apron that
same brass-bound pistol that had served me so well
against the "ghost" and thrust it into my hand.
"Take it, Mr Peter—take it, but—oh!"—here a great
sob choked her voice—"don't—don't use it—if—if
you can help it, for my sake."

"Why, Prue!" said I, touching her bowed head
very tenderly, "how can you think I would go up
against my friend with death in my hand—Heaven
forbid!" So I laid aside the weapon and, clapping
on my hat, strode out into the glory of the summer
morning, but left her weeping in the shadows.

CHAPTER VII

WHICH NARRATES A SOMEWHAT REMARKABLE CONVERSATION

To find a man in Cambourne Woods, even so big a man as Black George, would seem as hard a matter as to find the needle in the proverbial " bottle of hay "; the sun crept westwards, the day declined into evening, yet, hungry though I was, I persevered in my search, not so much in the hope of finding him (in the which I knew I must be guided altogether by chance) as from a disinclination to return, just yet, to the cottage. " It would be miserable there at this hour," I told myself, " miserable and lonely."

Yet why should I be lonely, I, who had gloried in my solitude hitherto. Whence then had come this change?

While I stood thus, seeking an answer to this self-imposed question and finding none, I heard someone approach, whistling, and, looking about, beheld a fellow with an axe upon his shoulder, who strode along at a good pace, keeping time to his whistle. He gave me a cheery greeting as he came up, but without stopping.

" You seem in a hurry," said I.

" Ah ! " grinned the man, over his shoulder, " 'cause why ?—'cause I be goin' 'ome."

" Home ! " said I.

" To supper," he nodded, and, forthwith, began to whistle again while I stood listening till the clear notes had died away.

" Home ! " said I for the second time, and there came upon me a feeling of desolation such as I had never known even in my neglected boyhood's days.

Home ! truly a sweet word, a comfortable word, the memory of which has been as oil and wine to many a sick and weary traveller upon this Broad Highway of

255

life; a little word, and yet one which may come betwixt a man and temptation, covering him like a shield. "Roof and walls, be they cottage or mansion, do not make home," thought I, "rather is it the atmosphere of mutual love, the intimacies of thought, the joys and sorrows endured together, and the never-failing sympathy—that bond invisible yet stronger than death."

And, because I had, hitherto, known nothing of this, I was possessed of a great envy for this axe-fellow as I walked on through the wood.

Now as I went, it was as if there were two voices arguing together within me, whereof ensued the following triangular conversation :

MYSELF. Yet I have my books—I will go to my lonely cottage and bury myself among my books.

FIRST VOICE. Assuredly! Is it for a philosopher to envy a whistling axe-fellow—go to!

SECOND VOICE. Far better a home and loving companionship than all the philosophy of all the schools; surely Happiness is greater than Learning, and more to be desired than Wisdom!

FIRST VOICE. Better rather that Destiny had never sent her to you.

MYSELF (rubbing my chin very hard, and staring at nothing in particular). Her?

SECOND VOICE. Her!—to be sure, she who has been in your thoughts all day long.

FIRST VOICE (with lofty disdain). Crass folly!—a woman utterly unknown, who came heralded by the roar of wind and the rush of rain—a creature born of the tempest, with flame in her eyes and hair, and fire in the scarlet of her mouth; a fierce, passionate being, given to hot impulse—even to the taking of a man's life!

("But," said I, somewhat diffidently, "the fellow was a proved scoundrel!")

FIRST VOICE (bellowing). Sophistry! sophistry!—even supposing he was the greatest of villains, does that make her less a murderess in intent?

MYSELF. Hum!

FIRST VOICE (roaring). Of course not! Again,

can this woman even faintly compare with your ideal of what a woman should be—this shrew!—this termagant! Can a woman whose hand has the strength to level a pistol, and whose mind the will to use it, be of a nature gentle, clinging, sweet——

SECOND VOICE (sotto). And sticky!

FIRST VOICE (howling). Of course not!—preposterous!

(Hereupon, finding no answer, I strode on through the alleys of the wood; but, when I had gone some distance, I stopped again, for there rushed over me the recollection of the tender pity of her eyes and the gentle touch of her hand as when she had bound up my hurts.

"Nevertheless," said I doggedly, "her face can grow more beautiful with pity, and surely no woman's hand could be lighter or more gentle.")

FIRST VOICE (with withering contempt). Our Peter fellow is like to become a preposterous ass.

(But, unheeding, I thrust my hand into my breast, and drew out a small handful of cambric, whence came a faint perfume of violets. And, closing my eyes, it seemed that she was kneeling before me, her arms about my neck, as when she had bound this handkerchief about my bleeding temples.

"Truly," said I, "for that one sweet act alone, a woman might be worth dying for!")

SECOND VOICE. Or better still—living for!

FIRST VOICE (in high indignation). Balderdash, sir!—sentimental balderdash!

SECOND VOICE. A truth incontrovertible!

("Folly!" said I, and threw the handkerchief from me. But next moment, moved by a sudden impulse, I stooped and picked it up again.)

FIRST VOICE. Our Peter fellow is becoming the fool of fools!

MYSELF. No, of that there is not the slightest fear, because—she is— gone.

And thus I remained staring at the handkerchief for a great while.

R

CHAPTER VIII

IN WHICH I SEE A VISION IN THE GLORY OF THE MOON, AND EAT OF A POACHED RABBIT

THE moon was rising as, hungry and weary, I came to that steep descent I have mentioned more than once, which leads down into the Hollow, and her pale radiance was already upon the world—a sleeping world wherein I seemed alone. And as I stood to gaze upon the wonder of the heavens, and the serene beauty of the earth, the clock in Cranbrook Church chimed nine.

All about me was a soft stirring of leaves, and the rustle of things unseen, which was as the breathing of a sleeping host. Borne to my nostrils came the scent of wood, and herb, and dewy earth, while up-stealing from the shadow of the trees below, the voice of the brook reached me, singing its never-ending song—now loud and clear, now sinking to a rippling murmur—a melody of joy and sorrow, of laughter and tears, like the greater melody of Life.

And, presently, I descended into the shadows, and walking on beside the brook, sat me down upon a great boulder; and, straightway, my weariness and hunger were forgotten, and I fell a-dreaming.

Truly it was a night to dream in—a white night, full of the moon and the magic of the moon. Slowly she mounted upwards, peeping down at me through whispering leaves, checkering the shadows with silver, and turning the brook into a path of silver for the feet of fairies. Yes, indeed, the very air seemed fraught with a magic whereby the unreal became the real and things impossible the manifestly possible.

And so, staring up at the moon's pale loveliness, I dreamed the deathless dreams of long-dead poets and romancers, wherein were the notes of dreamy lutes, the soft whisper of trailing garments, and sighing voices

258

that called beneath the breath. Between Petrarch's Laura and Dante's Beatrice came one as proud, and gracious, and beautiful as they, deep-bosomed, broad-hipped, with a red, red mouth, and a subtle witchery of the eyes. I dreamed of nymphs and satyrs, of fauns and dryads, and of the young Endymion who, on just such another night, in just such another leafy bower, waited the coming of his goddess.

Now as I sat thus, chin in hand, I heard a little sound behind me, the rustling of leaves, and, turning my head, beheld one who stood half in shadow, half in moonlight, looking down at me beneath a shy languor of drooping lids, with eyes hidden by their lashes—a woman tall, and fair, and strong as Dian's self.

Very still she stood, and half wistful, as if waiting for me to speak, and very silent I sat, staring up at her as she had been the embodiment of my dreams conjured up by the magic of the night, while, from the mysteries of the woods, stole the soft, sweet song of a nightingale.

"Charmian?" said I at last, speaking almost in a whisper. Surely this was the sweet goddess herself, and I, the wondering shepherd on Mount Ida's solitude.

"Charmian!" said I again, "you—have come then?" With the words I rose. "You have come, then?" I repeated.

But now she sighed a little, and turning her head away, laughed very sweet and low—and sighed again.

"Were you expecting me?"

"I—I think I was—that is—I—I don't know!" I stammered.

"Then you were not—very surprised to see me?"
"No."

"And you are not—very sorry to see me?"
"No."

"And—are you not very—glad to see me?"
"Yes."

Here there fell a silence between us, yet a silence that was full of leafy stirrings, soft night noises, and the languorous murmur of the brook. Presently

Charmian reached out a hand, broke off a twig of willow and began to turn it round and round in her white fingers, while I sought vainly for something to say.

" When I went away this morning," she began at last, looking down at the twig, " I didn't think I should ever come back again."

" No, I—I supposed not," said I awkwardly.

" But, you see, I had no money."

" No money ? "

" Not a penny. It was not until I had walked a long, long way, and was very tired, and terribly hungry, that I found I hadn't enough to buy even a crust of bread."

" And there was three pounds, fifteen shillings, and sixpence in Donal's old shoe," said I.

" Sevenpence ! " she corrected.

" Sevenpence ? " said I, in some surprise.

" Three pounds, fifteen shillings, and sevenpence. I counted it."

" Oh ! " said I.

She nodded. " And in the other I found a small, very curiously shaped piece of wood."

" Ah—yes, I've been looking for that all the week. You see, when I made my table, by some miscalculation, one leg persisted in coming out shorter than the others, which necessitated its being shored up by a book until I made that block."

" Mr Peter Vibart's Virgil book ! " she said, nodding to the twig.

" Y-e-s ! " said I, somewhat disconcerted.

" It was a pity to use a book," she went on, still very intent upon the twig, " even if that book does belong to a man with such a name as Peter Vibart."

Now presently, seeing I was silent, she stole a glance at me, and looking, laughed.

" But," she continued more seriously, " this has nothing to do with you, of course, nor me, for that matter, and I was trying to tell you how hungry—how hatefully hungry I was, and I couldn't beg, could I, and so—and so I—I——"

" You came back," said I.

" I came back."

" Being hungry."

" Famishing ! "

" Three pounds, fifteen shillings, and—sevenpence is not a great sum," said I, " but perhaps it will enable you to reach your family."

" I'm afraid not; you see I have no family:"

" Your friends, then."

" I have no friends; I am alone in the world."

" Oh ! " said I, and turned to stare down into the brook, for I could think only that she was alone, and solitary, even as I, which seemed like an invisible bond between us, drawing us each nearer the other, whereat I felt ridiculously pleased that this should be so.

" No," said Charmian, still intent upon the twig, " I have neither friends, nor family, nor money, and so—being hungry—I came back here, and ate up all the bacon."

"Why, I hadn't left much, if I remember."

" Six slices ! "

Now, as she stood, half in shadow, half in moonlight, I could not help but be conscious of her loveliness. She was no pretty woman; beneath the high beauty of her face lay a dormant power that is ever at odds with prettiness, and before which I felt vaguely at a loss. And yet, because of her warm beauty, because of the elusive witchery of her eyes, the soft, sweet column of the neck and the sway of the figure in the moonlight—because she was no goddess, and I no shepherd in Arcadia, I clasped my hands behind me, and turned to look down into the stream.

" Indeed," said I, speaking my thoughts aloud, " this is no place for a woman, after all."

" No," said she very softly.

"No—although, to be sure, there are worse places."

" Yes," said she, " I suppose so."

"Then again, it is very far removed from the world, so that a woman must needs be cut off from all those little delicacies and refinements that are supposed to be essential to her existence."

" Yes," she sighed.

" Though what," I continued, " what on earth would be the use of a—harp, let us say, or a pair of curling-irons in this wilderness, I don't know."

" One could play upon the one and curl one's hair with the other, and there is a deal of pleasure to be had from both," said she.

" Then also," I pursued, " this place, as I told you, is said to be haunted—not," I went on, seeing that she was silent, " not that you believe in such things, of course? But the cottage is very rough, and ill and clumsily furnished—though, to be sure, it might be made comfortable enough, and——"

" Well? " she inquired, as I paused.

" Then——" said I, and was silent for a long time, watching the play of the moonbeams on the rippling water.

" Well? " said she again at last.

" Then," said I, " if you are friendless, God forbid that I should refuse you the shelter of even such a place as this—so—if you are homeless, and without money—stay here—if you will—so long as it pleases you."

I kept my eyes directed to the running water at my feet as I waited her answer, and it seemed a very long time before she spoke.

" Are you fond of stewed rabbit? "

" Rabbit! " said I, staring.

" With onions! "

" Onions? "

" Oh, I can cook a little, and supper is waiting."

" Supper? "

" So if you are hungry——"

" I am ravenous! "

" Then why not come home and eat it? "

" Home? "

" Instead of echoing my words and staring the poor moon out of countenance? Come," and, with the word, she turned and led the way to the cottage. And behold, the candles were lighted, the table was spread with a snowy cloth, and a pot simmered upon the hob :

a pot that gave forth an odour delectable, and over which Charmian bent forthwith, and into which she gazed with an anxious brow and thrust an inquiring fork.

" I think it's all right ! "

" I'm sure of it," said I, inhaling the appetising aroma—" but pray, where did you get it ? "

" A man sold it to me—he had a lot of them."

" Hum ! " said I, " probably poached."

" I bought this for sixpence—out of the old shoe."

" Sixpence ?—then they certainly were poached. These are the Cambourne Woods, and everything upon them, fish, flesh, or fowl, living or dead, belongs to the Lady Sophia Sefton of Cambourne."

" Then—perhaps we had better not eat it," said she, glancing at me over her shoulder—but, meeting my eye, she laughed. And so we presently sat down to supper and, poached though it may have been, that rabbit made a truly noble end, notwithstanding.

CHAPTER IX

WHICH RELATES SOMEWHAT OF CHARMIAN BROWN

WE were sitting in the moonlight.

"Now," said Charmian, staring up at the luminous heaven, "let us talk."

"Willingly," I answered; "let us talk of stars."

"No—let us talk of ourselves."

"As you please."

"Very well, you begin."

"Well—I am a blacksmith."

"Yes, you told me so before."

"And I make horseshoes——"

"He is a blacksmith, and makes horseshoes!" said Charmian, nodding at the moon.

"And I live here, in this solitude, very contentedly; so that it is only reasonable to suppose that I shall continue to live here, and make horseshoes—though, really," I broke off, letting my eyes wander from my companion's upturned face back to the glowing sky, once more, "there is little I could tell you about so commonplace a person as myself that is likely to interest you."

"No," said Charmian, "evidently not!" Here my gaze came down to her face again so quickly that I fancied I detected the ghost of a smile upon her lips.

"Then," said I, "by all means let us talk of something else."

"Yes," she agreed; "let us talk of the woman Charmian—Charmian—Brown." A tress of hair had come loose, and hung low above her brow, and in its shadow her eyes seemed more elusive, more mocking than ever, and, while our glances met, she put up a hand and began to wind this glossy tress round and round her finger.

"Well?" said she.

" Well," said I, " supposing you begin."

" But is she likely to interest you ? "

" I think so—yes."

" Aren't you sure, then ? "

" Quite sure—certainly."

" Then why don't you say so ? "

" I thought you would take that for granted."

" A woman should take nothing for granted, sir."

" Then," said I, " supposing you begin."

" I've half a mind not to," she retorted, curling the tress of hair again, and then, suddenly : " What do you think of Charmian Brown ? "

" I think of her as little as I can."

" Indeed, sir ! "

" Indeed," said I.

" And why, pray ? "

" Because," said I, knocking the ashes from my pipe, " because the more I think about her the more incomprehensible she becomes."

" Have you known many women ? "

" Very few," I confessed, " but——"

" But ? "

" I am not altogether unfamiliar with the sex—for I have known a great number—in books."

" Our blacksmith," said Charmian, addressing the moon again, " has known many women—in books ! His knowledge is, therefore, profound ! " and she laughed.

" May I ask why you laugh at me ? "

" Oh ! " said she, " don't you know that women in books and women out of books are no more the same than day and night, or summer and winter ? "

" And yet there are thousands of women who exist for us in books only, Laura, Beatrice, Trojan Helen, Aspasia, the glorious Phryne, and hosts of others," I demurred.

" Yes ; but they exist for us only as their historians permit them, as their biographers saw, or imagined them. Would Petrarch ever have permitted Laura to do an ungracious act, or anything which, to his masculine understanding, seemed unfeminine ; and would Dante have mentioned it had Beatrice been guilty of one? A man can no more understand a woman from the reading of books than he can learn Latin or Greek from staring at the sky."

" Of that," said I, shaking my head, " of that I am not so sure."

" Then—personally—you know very little concerning women?" she inquired.

" I have always been too busy," said I. Here Charmian turned to look at me again.

" Too busy?" she repeated, as though she had not heard aright; " too busy?"

" Much too busy!" Now, when I said this, she laughed, and then she frowned, and then she laughed again.

" You would much rather make a—horseshoe than talk with a woman, perhaps?"

" Yes, I think I would."

" Oh!" said Charmian, frowning again, but this time she did not look at me.

" You see," I explained, turning my empty pipe over and over, rather aimlessly, " when I make a horseshoe I take a piece of iron and, having heated it, I bend and shape it, and with every hammer-stroke I see it growing into what I would have it—I am sure of it, from start to finish; now, with a woman it is—different."

" You mean that you cannot bend, and shape her, like your horseshoe?" still without looking towards me.

" I mean that—that I fear I should never be quite sure of a—woman, as I am of my horseshoe."

" Why, you see," said Charmian, beginning to braid the tress of hair, " a woman cannot, at any time, be said to resemble a horseshoe—very much, can she?"

" Surely," said I, " surely you know what I mean——?"

" There is Laura, and Beatrice, and Helen, and Aspasia, and Phyrne, and hosts of others," said Charmian, nodding to the moon again. " Oh yes—our blacksmith has read of so many women in books that he has no more idea of women out of books than I of Sanscrit."

And, in a little while, seeing I was silent, she con-descended to glance towards me :

" Then I suppose, under the circumstances, you have never been—in love ? "

" In love ? " I repeated, and dropped my pipe.

" In love."

" The Lord forbid ! "

" Why, pray ? "

" Because Love is a disease—a madness, coming between a man and his life's work. Love ! " said I, " it is a calamity ! "

" Never having been in love himself, our black-smith, very naturally, knows all about it ! " said Charmian to the moon.

" I speak only of such things as I have read——" I began.

" More books ! " she sighed.

"—words of men, much wiser than I—poets and philosophers, written——"

" When they were old and grey-headed," Charmian broke in ; " when they were quite incapable of judging the matter—though many a grave philosopher loved ; now didn't he ? "

" To be sure," said I, rather hipped, " Dionysius Lambienus, I think, says somewhere, that a woman with a big mouth is infinitely sweeter in the kissing—and——"

" Do you suppose he read that in a book ? " she inquired, glancing at me sideways.

" Why, as to that," I answered, " a philosopher may love, but not for the mere sake of loving."

" For whose sake then, I wonder ? "

" A man who esteems trifles for their own sake is a trifler, but one who values them, rather, for the deductions that may be drawn from them—he is a philosopher."

Charmian rose, and stood looking down at me very strangely.

" So ! " said she, throwing back her head, " so, throned in lofty might, superior Mr Smith thinks Love a trifle, does he ? "

" My name is Vibart, as I think you know," said I, stung by her look, or her tone, or both.

" Yes," she answered, seeming to look down at me from an immeasurable altitude, " but I prefer to know him, just now, as Superior Mr Smith."

" As you will," said I, and rose also; but, even then, though she had to look up to me, I had the same inward conviction that her eyes were regarding me from a great height; wherefore I attempted—quite unsuccessfully—to light my pipe.

And after I had struck flint and steel vainly, perhaps a dozen times, Charmian took the box from me, and, igniting the tinder, held it for me while I lighted my tobacco.

" Thank you ! " said I, as she returned the box, and then I saw that she was smiling. " Talking of Charmian Brown——" I began.

" But we are not."

" Then suppose you begin ? "

" Do you really wish to hear about that—humble person ? "

" Very much ! "

" Then you must know, in the first place, that she is old, sir, dreadfully old ! "

" But," said I, " she really cannot be more than—twenty-three—or four at the most."

" She is just twenty-one ! " returned Charmian, rather hastily, I thought.

" Quite a child ! "

" No, indeed—it is experience that ages one—and by experience she is quite—two hundred ! "

" The wonder is that she still lives."

" Indeed it is ! "

" And, being of such a ripe age, it is probable that she at any-rate has—been in love."

" Scores of times ! "

" Oh ! " said I, puffing very hard at my pipe.

" Or fancied so," said Charmian.

" That," I replied, " that is a very different thing ! "

" Do you think so ? "

" Well—isn't it ? "

" Perhaps."

" Very well, then, continue, I beg."

" Now, this woman," Charmian went on, beginning to curl the tress of hair again, " hating the world about her with its shams, its hypocrisy, and cruelty, ran away from it all, one day, with a villain."

" And why with a villain?"

" *Because* he was a villain!"

" That," said I, turning to look at her, " that I do not understand!"

" No, I didn't suppose you would," she answered.

" Hum!" said I, rubbing my chin. " And why did you run away *from* him?"

" Because he *was* a villain."

" That was very illogical!" said I.

" But very sensible, sir." Here there fell a silence between us, and, as we walked, now and then her gown would brush my knee, or her shoulder touch mine, for the path was very narrow.

" And—did you——" I began suddenly, and stopped.

" Did I—what, sir?"

" Did you love him?" said I, staring straight in front of me.

" I—ran away from him."

" And—do you—love him?"

" I suppose," said Charmian, speaking very slowly, " I suppose you cannot understand a woman hating and loving a man, admiring and despising him, both at the same time?"

" No, I can't."

" Can you understand one glorying in the tempest that may destroy her, riding a fierce horse that may crush her, or being attracted by a will strong, and masterful, before which all must yield or break?"

" I think I can."

" Then," said Charmian, " this man is strong, and wild, and very masterful, and so—I ran away with him."

" And do you—love him?" We walked on some distance ere she answered :

" I—don't know."

" Not sure, then? "

" No."

After this we fell silent altogether, yet once, when I happened to glance at her, I saw that her eyes were very bright beneath the shadow of her drooping lashes, and that her lips were smiling; and I pondered very deeply as to why this should be.

Re-entering the cottage, I closed the door, and waited the while she lighted my candle.

And, having taken the candle from her hand, I bade her " Good-night," but paused at the door of my chamber.

" You feel—quite safe here? "

" Quite safe! "

" Despite the colour of my hair and eyes—you have no fear of—Peter Smith? "

" None! "

" Because he is neither fierce nor wild, nor master-ful! "

" Because he is neither fierce nor wild," she echoed.

" Nor masterful! " said I.

" Nor masterful! " said Charmian, with averted head. So I opened the door, but, even then, must needs turn back again.

" Do you think I am so very—different—from him? "

" As different as day from night, as the lamb from the wolf," said she, without looking at me. " Good-night, Peter! "

" Good-night! " said I, and so, going into my room, I closed the door behind me.

" A lamb! " said I, tearing off my neckcloth, and sat, for some time, listening to her footstep and the soft rustle of her petticoats going to and fro.

" A lamb! " said I again, and slowly drew off my coat. As I did so, a little cambric handkerchief fell to the floor, and I kicked it, forthwith, into a corner.

" A lamb! " said I, for the third time, but, at this moment, came a light tap upon the door.

" Yes? " said I, without moving.

" Oh, how is your injured thumb? "

" Thank you, it is as well as can be expected."

" Does it pain you very much?"

" It is not unbearable!" said I.

" Good-night, Peter!" and I heard her move away. But presently she was back again.

" Oh, Peter?"

" Well?"

" Are you frowning?"

" I—I think I was—why?"

" When you frown, you are very like—him, and have the same square set of the mouth and chin, when you are angry—so don't, please don't frown, Peter—Good-night!"

" Good-night, Charmian!" said I, and stooping, I picked up the little handkerchief and thrust it under my pillow.

CHAPTER X

I AM SUSPECTED OF THE BLACK ART

" VIBART ! "

The word had been uttered close behind me, and very softly, yet I started at this sudden mention of my name and stood for a moment with my hammer poised above the anvil ere I turned and faced the speaker. He was a tall man with a stubbly growth of grizzled hair about his lank jaws, and he was leaning in at that window of the smithy which gave upon a certain grassy back lane.

" You spoke, I think ! " said I.

" I said, ' Vibart ' ! "

" Well ? "

" Well ? "

" And why should you say ' Vibart ' ? "

" And why should you start ? " Beneath the broad, flapping hat his eyes glowed with a sudden intensity as he waited my answer.

" It is familiar," said I.

" Ha ! familiar ? " he repeated, and his features were suddenly contorted as with a strong convulsion, and his teeth gleamed between his pallid lips.

My hammer was yet in my grasp, and, as I met this baleful look, my fingers tightened instinctively about the shaft.

" Familiar ? " said he again.

" Yes," I nodded; " like your face, for it would almost seem that I have seen you somewhere before, and I seldom forget faces."

" Nor do I ! " said the man.

Now, while we thus fronted each other, there came the sound of approaching footsteps, and John Pringle, the Carrier, appeared, followed by the pessimistic Job.

" Marnin', Peter !—them 'orseshoes," began John, pausing just outside the smithy door, " you was to finish 'em 's arternoon; if so be as they bean't done, you bein' short-'anded wi'out Jarge, why, I can wait." Now, during this speech, I was aware that both his and Job's eyes had wandered from my bandaged thumb to my bare throat, and become fixed there.

"Come in and sit down," said I, nodding to each, as I blew up the fire, "come in." For a moment they hesitated, then John stepped gingerly into the smithy, closely followed by Job, and watching them beneath my brows as I stooped above the shaft of the bellows, I saw each of them furtively cross his fingers.

"Why do you do that, John Pringle?" said I.

"Do what, Peter?"

"Cross your fingers."

"Why, ye see, Peter," said John, glancing in turn at the floor, the rafters, the fire, and the anvil, but never at me, "ye see, it be just a kind o' way o' mine."

"But why does Job do the same?"

"An' why do 'ee look at a man so sharp an' sudden-like?" retorted Job sullenly; "dang me! if it aren't enough to send cold shivers up a chap's spine— I never see such a pair o' eyes afore—no—nor don't want to again."

"Nonsense!" said I; "my eyes can't hurt you."

"An' 'ow am I to know that, 'ow am I to be sure o' that, an' you wi' your throat all torn wi' devil's claws an' demon's clutches—it bean't nat'ral—Old Amos says so, an' I sez so."

"Pure folly!" said I, plucking the iron from the fire, and beginning to beat and shape it with my hammer, but presently, remembering the strange man who had spoken my name, I looked up, and then I saw that he was gone. "Where is he?" said I involuntarily.

"Where's who?" inquired John Pringle, glancing about uneasily.

"The fellow who was talking to me as you came up?"

"I didn't see no fellow!" said Job, looking at John and edging nearer the door.

"Nor me neither!" chimed in John Pringle, looking at Job.

s

" Why, he was leaning in at the window, here, not a minute ago," said I, and plunging the half-finished horseshoe back into the fire I stepped out into the road, but the man was nowhere to be seen.

" Very strange ! " said I.

" What might 'e 'ave been like, now ? " inquired John.

" He was tall and thin, and wore a big flapping hat."

John Pringle coughed, scratched his chin, and coughed again.

" What is it, John ? " I inquired.

" Why, then, you couldn't 'appen to notice—'im wearin' 'is 'at—you couldn't 'appen to notice if 'e 'ad ever a pair o' 'orns, Peter ? "

" Horns ! " I exclaimed.

" Or a—tail, Peter ? "

" Or even a—'oof, now ? " suggested Job.

" Come," said I, looking from one to the other, " what might you be driving at ? "

" Why, ye see, Peter," answered John, coughing again, and scratching his chin harder than ever, " ye see, Peter, it aren't nat'ral for a 'uman bein' to go a-vanishin' away like this 'ere—if 'twere a man as you was a-talkin' to——"

" Which I doubts ! " muttered Job.

" If 'twere a man, Peter, then I axes you—where is that man ? "

Before I could answer this pointed question, old Joel Amos hobbled up, who paused on the threshold to address someone over his shoulder.

" Come on, James, 'ere 'e be—come for'ard, James, like a man."

Thus adjured, another individual appeared : a somewhat flaccid-looking individual, with colourless hair and eyes, one who seemed to exhale an air of apology, as it were, from the hobnailed boot upon the floor to the grimy forefinger that touched the straw-like hair in salutation.

" Marnin', Peter ! " said Old Amos, " this yere is —Dutton."

" How do you do ? " said I, acknowledging the introduction, " and what can I do for Mr Dutton ? " The latter, instead of replying, took out a vivid belcher handkerchief, and apologetically mopped his face.

" Speak up, James Dutton," said Old Amos.

" Lord ! " exclaimed Dutton, " Lord ! I du be that 'ot !—you speak for I, Amos, du."

" Well," began Old Amos, not ill-pleased, " this 'ere Dutton wants to ax 'ee a question, 'e du, Peter."

" I shall be glad to answer it, if I can," I returned.

" You 'ear that ?—well, ax your question, James Dutton," commanded the old man.

" W'y, ye see, Amos," began Dutton, positively reeking apology, " I du be that on-common 'ot—you ax un."

" W'y then, Peter," began Amos, with great unction, " it's 'is pigs ! "

" Pigs ? " I exclaimed, staring.

" Ah ! pigs, Peter," nodded Old Amos, " Dutton's pigs; 'is sow farrowed last week—at three in the marnin'—nine of 'em ! "

" Well ? " said I, wondering more and more.

" Well, Peter, they was a fine 'earty lot, an' all a-doin' well—till last Monday."

" Indeed ! " said I.

" Last Monday night, four on 'em sickened, an' died ! "

" Most unfortunate ! " said I.

" An' the rest 'as never been the same since."

" Probably ate something that disagreed with them," said I, picking up my hammer and laying it down again. Old Amos smiled and shook his head.

" You know James Dutton's pigsty, don't ye, Peter ? "

" I really can't say that I do."

" Yet you pass it every day on your way to the 'Oller—it lays just be'ind Simon's oast-'ouse, as James 'isself will tell 'ee."

" So it du," interpolated Dutton, with an apologetic nod, " which, leastways, if it don't, can't be no'ow ! " having delivered himself of which, he buried his face in the belcher handkerchief.

" Now, one evenin', Peter," continued Old Amos, " one evenin' you leaned over the fence o' that theer pigsty an' stood a-lookin' at they pigs for, p'r'aps, ten minutes."

"Did I?"

"Ay, that ye did—James Dutton see ye, an' 'is wife, she see ye tu, and I see ye."

"Then," said I, "probably I did. Well?"

"Well," said the old man, looking round upon his hearers, and bringing out each word with the greatest unction, "that theer evenin' were last Monday evenin' as ever was—the very same hour as Dutton's pigs sickened and died!" Hereupon John Pringle and Job rose simultaneously from where they had been sitting, and retreated precipitately to the door.

"Lord!" exclaimed John.

"I might ha' knowed it!" said Job, drawing a cross in the air with his finger.

"An' so James Dutton wants to ax ye to tak' it off, Peter," said Old Amos.

"To take what off?"

"Why, the spell, for sure." Hereupon I gave free play to my amusement, and laughed, and laughed, while the others watched me with varying expressions.

"And so you think that I bewitched Dutton's pigs, do you?" said I, at last, glancing from Old Amos to the perspiring Apology (who immediately began to mop at his face and neck again). "And why," I continued, seeing that nobody appeared willing to speak, "why should you think it of me?"

"W'y, Peter, ye bean't like ordinary folk, your eyes goes through an' through a man. An' then, Peter, I mind as you come a-walkin' into Siss'n'urst one night from Lord knows wheer, all covered wi' dust, an' wi' a pack on your back."

"You are wrong there, Amos," said I, "it was afternoon when I came, and the Ancient was with me."

"Ah! an' wheer did 'e find ye, Peter?—come, speak up an' tell us."

"In the Hollow," I answered.

"Ay, 'e found 'ee in the very spot wheer the Wanderer o' the Roads 'ung 'isself, sixty an' six years ago."

"There is nothing very strange in that!" said I.

*" An' so James Dutton wants to ax ye to tak' it off,
Peter," said Old Amos. " To take what off?"
" Why, the spell, for sure." Hereupon I gave
free play to my amusement*

Face Page 276

"Ay, so James Dutton wants to ax ye to tak 't off,
Peter," said Old Amos. "To take what off?"
"Why, the spell, for sure." Hereupon I gave
free play to my amusement.

Face Page 326

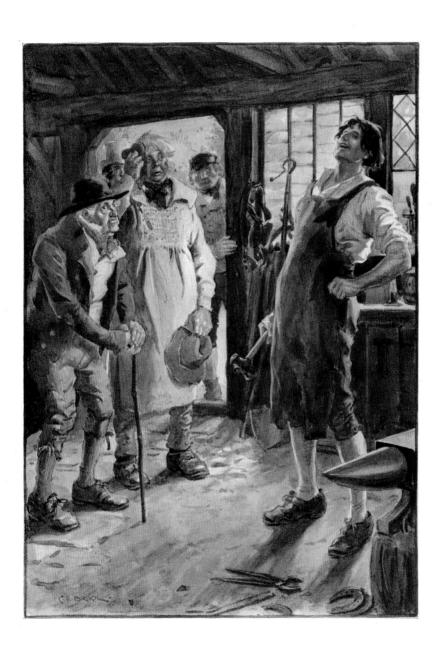

" What's more, you come into the village an' beat Black Jarge throwin' th' 'ammer, an' 'im the strongest man in all the South Country ! "

" I beat him because he did not do his best—so there is nothing strange in that either."

" An' then, you lives all alone in that theer ghashly 'Oller—an' you fights, an' struggles wi' devils an' demons, all in the wind, and rain, an' tearin' tempest— an' what's most of all—you comes back—alive, an' what's more yet, wi' devil-marks upon ye an' your throat all tore wi' claws. Old Gaffer be over proud o' findin' ye, but old Gaffer be dodderin'—dodderin' 'e be, an' fulish wi' years ; 'e'd ha' done much better to ha' left ye alone—I've heerd o' folk sellin' theirselves to the devil afore now, I've likewise heerd o' the ' Evil Eye ' afore now—ah ! an' knows one when I sees it."

"Nonsense !" said I sternly, "nonsense ! This talk of ghosts and devils is sheer folly. I am a man, like the rest of you, and could not wish you ill—even if I would—come, let us all shake hands, and forget this folly ! " and I extended my hand to Old Amos.

He glanced from it to my face, and immediately, lowering his eyes, shook his head.

" 'Tis the ' Evil Eye ' ! " said he, and drew a cross upon the floor with his stick, " the ' Evil Eye ' ! "

" Nonsense ! " said I again ; " my eye is no more evil than yours or Job's. I never wished any man harm yet, nor wronged one, and I hope I never may. As for Mr Dutton's pigs, if he take better care of them, and keep them out of the damp, they will probably thrive better than ever—come, shake hands ! "

But, one by one, they edged their way to the door after Old Amos, until only John Pringle was left ; he, for a moment, stood hesitating, then, suddenly reaching out, he seized my hand, and shook it twice.

" I'll call for they 'orseshoes in the marnin', Peter," said he, and vanished.

" Arter all," I heard him say, as he joined the others, " 'tis summat to ha' shook 'ands wi' a chap as fights wi' demons ! "

CHAPTER XI

A SHADOW IN THE HEDGE

OVER the uplands, to my left, the moon was peeping at me, very broad, and yellow, as yet, casting long shadows athwart my way. The air was heavy with the perfume of honeysuckle abloom in the hedges—a warm, still air wherein a deep silence brooded, and in which leaf fluttered not and twig stirred not; but it was none of this I held in my thoughts as I strode along, whistling softly as I went. Yet, in a while, chancing to lift my eyes, I beheld the object of my reverie coming towards me through the shadows.

" Why—Charmian ! " said I, uncovering my head.

" Why—Peter ! "

" Did you come to meet me ? "

" It must be nearly nine o'clock, sir."

" Yes, I had to finish some work."

" Did anyone pass you on the road ? "

" Not a soul."

" Peter, have you an enemy ? "

" Not that I know of, unless it be myself. Epictetus says somewhere that——"

" Oh, Peter, how dreadfully quiet everything is ! " said she, and shivered.

" Are you cold ? "

" No—but it is so dreadfully—still."

Now in one place the lane, narrowing suddenly, led between high banks crowned with bushes, so that it was very dark there. As we entered this gloom Charmian suddenly drew closer to my side and slipped her hand beneath my arm and into my clasp, and the touch of her fingers was like ice.

" Your hand is very cold ! " said I. But she only laughed, yet I felt her shiver as she pressed herself close against me.

278

And now it was she who talked and I who walked in silence, or answered at random, for I was conscious only of the clasp of her fingers and the soft pressure of hip and shoulder.

So we passed through this place of shadows, walking neither fast nor slow, and ever her cold fingers clasped my fingers, and her shoulder pressed my arm while she talked, and laughed, but of what, I know not, until we had left the dark place behind. Then she sighed deeply and turned, and drew her arm from mine, almost sharply, and stood looking back, with her two hands pressed upon her bosom.

" What is it? "

" Look ! " she whispered, pointing, " there—where it is darkest—look ! " Now, following the direction of her finger, I saw something that skulked amid the shadows—something that slunk away, and vanished as I watched.

" A man ! " I exclaimed, and would have started in pursuit, but Charmian's hands were upon my arm, strong and compelling.

" Are you mad ? " cried she angrily; " would you give him the opportunity I prevented ? He was waiting there to—to shoot you, I think ! "

And, after we had gone on some little way, I spoke.

" Was that why you—came to meet me ? "

" Yes."

" And—kept so close beside me.'"

" Yes."

" Ah yes, to be sure ! " said I, and walked on in silence; and now I noticed that she kept as far from me as the path would allow.

" Are you thinking me very—unmaidenly again, sir ? "

" No," I answered; " no."

" You see, I had no other way. Had I told you that there was a man hidden in the hedge you would have gone to look, and then—something dreadful would have happened."

" How came you to know he was there ? "

" Why, after I had prepared supper I climbed that

steep path which leads to the road and sat down upon the fallen tree that lies there, to watch for you, and, as I sat there, I saw a man come hurrying down the road."

" A very big man ? "

" Yes, very tall he seemed, and, as I watched, he crept in behind the hedge. While I was wondering at this, I heard your step on the road, and you were whistling."

" And yet I seldom whistle."

" It was you—I knew your step."

" Did you, Charmian ? "

" I do wish you would not interrupt, sir."

" I beg your pardon," said I humbly.

" And then I saw you coming, and the man saw you too, for he crouched suddenly; I could only see him dimly in the shadow of the hedge, but he looked murderous, and it seemed to me that if you reached his hiding-place before I did—something terrible would happen, and so——"

" You came to meet me."

" Yes."

" And walked close beside me, so that you were between me and the shadow in the hedge ? "

" Yes."

" And I thought——" I began, and stopped.

" Well, Peter ? " Here she turned, and gave me a swift glance beneath her lashes.

"—that it was because—you were—perhaps—rather glad to see me." Charmian did not speak, indeed she was so very silent that I would have given much to have seen her face just then, but the light was very dim, as I have said, moreover she had turned her shoulder towards me. " But I am grateful to you," I went on, " very grateful, and—it was very brave of you ! "

" Thank you, sir," she answered in a very small voice, and I more than suspected that she was laughing at me.

" Not," I therefore continued, " that there was any real danger."

" What do you mean ? " she asked quickly.

" I mean that, in all probability, the man you saw was Black George, a very good friend of mine, who, though he may imagine he has a grudge against me, is too much of a man to lie in wait to do me hurt."

" Then why should he hide in the hedge ? "

" Because he committed the mistake of throwing the town Beadle over the churchyard wall, and is, consequently, in hiding, for the present."

" He has an ill-sounding name."

" And is the manliest, gentlest, truest, and worthiest fellow that ever wore the leather apron."

Seeing how perseveringly she kept the whole breadth of the path between us I presently fell back and walked behind her; now her head was bent, and thus I could not but remark the little curls and tendrils of hair upon her neck, whose sole object seemed to be to make the white skin more white by contrast.

" Peter," said she suddenly, speaking over her shoulder, " of what are you thinking ? "

" Of a certain steak pasty that was promised for my supper," I answered immediately, mendacious.

" Oh ! "

" And what," I inquired, " what were you thinking ? "

" I was thinking, Peter, that the—shadow in the hedge may not have been Black George, after all."

CHAPTER XII

WHO COMES?

"This table wobbles!" said Charmian.

"It does," said I, "but then I notice that the block is misplaced again."

"Then why use a block?"

"A book is so clumsy——" I began.

"Or a book? Why not cut down the long legs to match the short one?"

"That is really an excellent idea."

"Then why didn't you before?"

"Because, to be frank with you, it never occurred to me."

"I suppose you are better as a blacksmith than a carpenter, aren't you, Peter?" And, seeing I could find no answer worthy of retort, she laughed, and, sitting down, watched me while I took my saw, forthwith, and shortened the three long legs as she had suggested. Having done which, to our common satisfaction, seeing the moon was rising, we went and sat down on the bench beside the cottage door.

"And—are you a very good blacksmith?" she pursued, turning to regard me, chin in hand.

"I can swing a hammer or shoe a horse with any smith in Kent—except Black George, and he is the best in all the South Country."

"And is that a very great achievement, Peter?"

"It is not a despicable one."

"Are you quite satisfied to be able to shoe horses well, sir?"

"It is far better to be a good blacksmith than a bad poet or an incompetent prime minister."

"Meaning that you would rather succeed in the little thing than fail in the great?"

"With your permission, I will smoke," said I.

"Surely," she went on, nodding her permission, "surely it is nobler to be a great failure rather than a mean success?"

"Success is very sweet, Charmian, even in the smallest thing; for instance," said I, pointing to the cottage door that stood open beside her, "when I built that door, and saw it swing on its hinges, I was as proud of it as though it had been——"

"A really good door," interpolated Charmian, "instead of a bad one!"

"A bad one, Charmian?"

"It is a very clumsy door, and has neither bolt nor lock."

"There are no thieves hereabouts, and, even if there were, they would not dare to set foot in the Hollow after dark."

"And then, unless one close it with great care, it sticks—very tight!"

"That, obviating the necessity of a latch, is rather to be commended," said I.

"Besides, it is a very ill-fitting door, Peter."

"I have seen worse."

"And will be very draughty in cold weather."

"A blanket hung across will remedy that."

"Still, it can hardly be called a very good door, can it, Peter? Here I lighted my pipe without answering. "I suppose you make horseshoes much better than you make doors?" I puffed at my pipe in silence. "You are not angry because I found fault with your door, are you, Peter?"

"Angry?" said I; "not in the least."

"I am sorry for that."

"Why sorry?"

"Are you never angry, Peter?"

"Seldom, I hope."

"I should like to see you so—just once." Finding nothing to say in answer to this, I smoked my negro-head pipe and stared at the moon, which was looking down at us through a maze of tree-trunks and branches.

" Referring to horseshoes," said Charmian at last,
" are you content to be a blacksmith all your days? "

" Yes, I think I am."

" Were you never ambitious, then ? "

" Ambition is like rain, breaking itself upon what it
falls on—at least, so Bacon says, and——"

" Oh, bother Bacon ! Were you never ambitious,
Peter ? "

" I was a great dreamer."

" A dreamer ! " she exclaimed with fine scorn ; "are
dreamers ever ambitious ? "

" Indeed, they are the most truly ambitious," I
retorted ; "their dreams are so vast, so infinite, so
far beyond all puny human strength and capacity
that they, perforce, must remain dreamers always.
Epictetus himself——"

" I wish," sighed Charmian, " I do wish——"

" What do you wish ? "

" That you were not——"

" That I was not ? "

" Such a—pedant ! "

" Pedant ! " said I, somewhat disconcerted.

" And you have a way of echoing my words that is
very irritating."

" I beg your pardon," said I, feeling much like a
chidden schoolboy ; "and I am sorry you should think
me a pedant."

" And you are so dreadfully precise and serious,"
she continued.

" Am I, Charmian ? "

" And so very solemn, and austere, and so ponderous, and egotistical, and calm—yes, you are hatefully
calm and placid, aren't you, Peter ? "

And, after I had smoked thoughtfully awhile, I
sighed.

" Yes, I fear I may seem so."

" Oh, I forgive you ! "

" Thank you."

" Though you needn't be so annoyingly humble
about it," said she, and frowned, and, even while she
frowned, laughed and shook her head.

" And pray, why do you laugh ? "

" Because—oh, Peter, you are such a—boy ! "

" So you told me once before,' said I, biting my pipe-stem viciously.

" Did I, Peter ? "

" You also called me a—lamb, I remember—at least, you suggested it."

" Did I, Peter ? " and she began to laugh again, but stopped all at once and rose to her feet.

" Peter ! " said she, with a startled note in her voice, " don't you hear something ? "

" Yes," said I.

" Someone is coming ! "

" Yes."

" And—they are coming this way ! "

" Yes."

" Oh—how can you sit there so quietly ? Do you think——" she began, and stopped, staring into the shadows with wide eyes.

" I think," said I, knocking the ashes from my pipe, and laying it on the bench beside me, " that, all things considered, you were wiser to go into the cottage for a while."

" No—oh, I couldn't do that ! "

" You would be safer perhaps."

" I am not a coward. I shall remain here, of course."

" But I had rather you went inside."

" And I much prefer staying where I am."

" Then I must ask you to go inside, Charmian."

" No, indeed, my mind is made up."

" Then I insist, Charmian."

" Mr Vibart ! " she exclaimed, throwing up her head, " you forget yourself, I think. I permit no one to order my going and coming, and I obey no man's command."

" Then—I beg of you."

" And I refuse, sir—my mind is made up."

" And mine also ! " said I, rising.

" Why, what—what are you going to do ? " she cried, retreating as I advanced towards her.

" I am going to carry you into the cottage."

" You would not dare ! "

" If you refuse to walk how else can you get there ? " said I.

Anger, amazement, indignation, all these I saw in her eyes as she faced me, but anger most of all.

" Oh—you would not dare ! " she said again, and with a stamp of her foot.

" Indeed, yes," I nodded. And now her glance wavered beneath mine, her head drooped, and, with a strange little sound that was neither a laugh nor a sob, and yet something of each, she turned upon her heel, ran into the cottage, and slammed the door behind her.

CHAPTER XIII

A PEDDLER IN ARCADIA

THE cottage, as I have said, was entirely hidden from the chance observer by reason of the foliage: ash, alder and bramble flourished luxuriantly, growing very thick and high, with here and there a great tree; but, upon one side, there was a little grassy glade, or clearing rather, some ten yards square, and it was towards this that my eyes were directed as I reseated myself upon the settle beside the door, and waited the coming of the unknown.

Though the shadows were too deep for my eyes to serve me, yet I could follow the new-comer's approach quite easily by the sound he made; indeed I was particularly struck by the prodigious rustling of leaves. Whoever it was, must be big and bulky, I thought, and clad, probably, in a long, trailing garment.

All at once I knew I was observed, for the sounds ceased, and I heard nothing save the distant bark of a dog and the ripple of the brook near by.

I remained there for, maybe, a full minute, very still, only my fists clenched themselves as I sat listening and waiting—and that minute was an hour.

"You won't be wantin' ever a broom, now?"

The relief was so sudden and intense that I had much ado to keep from laughing outright.

"You won't be wantin' ever a broom, now?" inquired the voice again.

"No," I answered, "nor yet a fine leather belt with a steel buckle made in Brummagem as ever was."

"Oh, it's you, is it?" said the Peddler, and forthwith Gabbing Dick stepped out of the shadows, brooms on shoulder and bulging pack upon his back, at sight of which the leafy tumult of his approach was immediately accounted for. "So it's you, is it?" he

287

repeated, setting down his brooms and spitting
lugubriously at the nearest patch of shadow.

" Yes," I answered, " but what brings you here? "

" I be goin' to sleep 'ere, my chap."

" Oh!—you don't mind the ghost, then? "

" Oh, Lord, no! Theer be only two things as I
can't abide—trees as ain't trees is one on 'em, an'
women's t' other."

" Women? "

" Come, didn't I once tell you I were married? "

" You did."

" Very well then! Trees as ain't trees is bad
enough, Lord knows!—but women's worse—ah!"
said the Peddler, shaking his head, " a sight worse!
Ye see, trees ain't got tongues—leastways not as I
ever heerd tell on, an' a tree never told a lie—or ate a
apple, did it? "

" What do you mean by ' ate an apple '? "

" I means as a tree can't tell a lie, or eat a apple,
but a woman can tell a lie—which she does—frequent,
an' as for apples——"

" But——" I began.

" Eve ate a apple, didn't she? "

" The Scriptures say so," I nodded.

" An' told a lie arterwards, didn't she? "

" So we are given to understand."

" Very well then!" said the Peddler, " there y'
are!" and he turned to spit into the shadow again.
" Wot's more," he continued, " 'twere a woman as
done me out o' my birthright."

" How so? "

" Why, 'twere Eve as got us druv out o' the Gardin
o' Eden, weren't it? If it 'adn't been for Eve I might
ha' been livin' on milk an' 'oney, ah! an' playin' wi'
butterflies, 'stead o' bein' married, an' peddlin' these
'ere brooms. Don't talk to me o' women, my chap, I
can't abide 'em—bah! if theer's any trouble afoot you
may take your Bible oath as theer's a woman about
some'eres—theer allus is! "

" Do you think so? "

" I knows so; ain't I a-'earin' an' a-seein' such

all day, an' every day—theer's Black Jarge, for one."

"What about him?"

"What about 'im!" repeated the Peddler; "w'y, ain't 'is life been ruined, broke, wore away by one o' them Eves?—very well then!"

"What do you mean—how has his life been ruined?"

"Oh! the usual way of it; Jarge loves a gell—gell loves Jarge—sugar ain't sweeter—very well then! Along comes another cove—a strange cove—a cove wi' nice white 'ands an' soft, takin' ways—'e talks wi' 'er—walks wi' 'er—smiles at 'er—an' pore Jarge ain't nowheeres—pore Jarge's cake is dough—ah! an' doughy dough at that!"

"How do you come to know all this?"

"'Ow should I come to know it but from the man 'isself? 'Dick,' says 'e (baptismal name Richard, but Dick for short), 'Dick,' says 'e, 'd'ye see this 'ere stick?' an' 'e shows me a good, stout cudgel cut out o' th' 'edge, an' very neatly trimmed it were too. 'Ah! I sees it, Jarge,' says I. 'An' d'ye see this un?' says 'e, 'oldin' up another as like the first as one pea to its fellow. 'Ah! I sees that un too, Jarge,' says I. 'Well,' says Jarge, 'one's for 'im an' one's for me—'e can take 'is chice,' 'e says, 'an' when we do meet, it's a-goin' to be one or t' other of us,' 'e says, an' wot's more—'e looked it! 'If I 'ave to wait, an' wait, an' foller 'im, an' foller 'im,' says Jarge, 'I'll catch 'im alone, one o' these fine nights, an' it'll be man to man.' "

"And when did he tell you all this?"

"'S' marnin' as ever was."

"Where did you see him?"

"Oh no!" said the Peddler, shaking his head, "not by no manner o' means. I'm married, but I ain't that kind of a cove!"

"What do you mean?"

"The runners is arter 'im—lookin' for 'im 'igh an' low, an'—though married, I ain't one to give a man away. I ain't a friendly cove myself, never was, an' never shall be—never 'ad a friend all my days, an'

T

don't want one—but I likes Black Jarge—I pities, an'
I despises 'im."

" Why do you despise him?"

" Because 'e carries on so, all about a Eve—w'y,
theer ain't a woman breathin' as is worth a man's
troublin' 'is 'ead over, no, nor never will be—yet 'ere's
Black Jarge ready—ah! an' more than willin' to get
'isself 'ung, an' all for a wench—a Eve——"

" Get himself hanged?" I repeated.

" Ah—'ung! w'y, ain't 'e a-waitin' an' a-waitin' to
get at this cove—this cove wi' the nice white 'ands an'
the takin' ways, ain't 'e a-watchin' an' a-watchin' to
meet 'im some lonely night—and when 'e do meet
'im——". The Peddler sighed.

" Well?"

" W'y, there'll be bloodshed—blood!—quarts on it
—buckets on it! Black Jarge'll batter this 'ere cove's
'ead soft, so sure as I were baptised Richard— 'e'll lift
this cove up in 'is great, strong arms, an' 'e'll throw
this cove down, an' 'e'll gore 'im, an' stamp 'im down
under 'is feet, an' this cove's blood'll go soakin' an'
a-soakin' into the grass, some'eres beneath some
'edge, or in some quiet corner o' the woods—and the
birds'll perch on this cove's breast, an' flutter their
wings in this cove's face, 'cause they'll know as this
cove can never do nobody no 'urt no more; ah!
there'll be blood—gallons of it!"

" I hope not!" said I.

" Ye do, do ye?"

" Most fervently!"

" An' 'cause why?"

" Because I happen to be that cove," I answered.

" Oh!" said the Peddler, eyeing me more narrowly; " you are, are ye?"

" I am!"

" Yet you ain't got w'ite 'ands."

" They were white once," said I.

" An' I don't see as your ways is soft—nor yet—
takin'!"

" None the less, I am that cove!"

" Oh!" repeated the Peddler, and, having turned

this intelligence over in his mind, spat thoughtfully
into the shadow again. " You won't be wantin' ever
a broom, I think you said ? "

" No," said I.

" Very well then ! " he nodded, and, lifting his
brooms, made towards the cottage door !

" Where are you going ? "

" To sleep in this 'ere empty 'ut."

" But it isn't empty ! "

" So much the better," nodded the Peddler, "good-
night ! " and, with the words, he laid his hand upon
the door, but, as he did so, it opened, and Charmian
appeared. The Peddler fell back three or four paces,
staring with round eyes.

" By Goles ! " he exclaimed. " So you are married
then ? "

Now, when he said this I felt suddenly hot all over,
even to the very tips of my ears, and, for the life of
me, I could not have looked at Charmian.

" Why—why—— " I began, but her smooth, soft
voice came to my rescue.

" No—he is not married," said she, " far from it."

" Not ? " said the Peddler, " so much the better ;
marriage ain't love, no, nor love ain't marriage—I'm a
married cove myself so I know what I'm a-sayin' ; if
folk do talk, an' shake their 'eads over ye—w'y, let 'em,
only don't—don't go a-spilin' things by gettin'
' churched.' You're a woman, but you're a fine un—a
dasher, by Goles, nice an' straight-backed, an' round, an'
plump—if I was this 'ere cove, now, I know what—— "

" Here," said I hastily, " here—sell me a broom ! "
The Peddler drew a broom from his bundle and
passed it to me.

" One shillin' and sixpence ! " said he, which sum I
duly paid over. " Don't," he continued, pocketing
the money, and turning to Charmian, " don't go
spilin' things by lettin' this young cove go a-marryin'
an' a-churchin' ye—nobody never got married as
didn't repent it some time or other, an' wot's more,
when Marriage comes in at the door, Love flies out up
the chimbley—an' there y' are ! Now, if you loves

this young cove, w'y very good! if this 'ere young cove loves you—which ain't to be wondered at—so much the better, but don't—don't go a-marryin' each other, an'—as for the children——"

"Come—I'll take a belt—give me a belt!" said I, more hastily than before.

"A belt?" said the Peddler.

"A belt, yes."

"Wi' a fine steel buckle made in——"

"Yes—yes!" said I.

"Two shillin' an' sixpence!" said the Peddler.

"When I saw you last time, you offered much the same belt for a shilling," I demurred.

"Ah!" nodded the Peddler, "but belts is riz—'arf-a-crown's the price—take it or leave it."

"It's getting late," said I, slipping the money into his hand, "and I'll wish you good-night!"

"You're in a 'urry about it, ain't you?"

"Yes."

"Ah—to be sure!" nodded the fellow, looking from me to Charmian with an evil leer, "early to bed an'——"

"Come—get off!" said I angrily.

"Wot—are ye goin' to turn me away—at this time o' night!"

"It is not so far to Sissinghurst!" said I.

"But Lord! I wouldn't disturb ye—an' there's two rooms, ain't there?"

"There are plenty of comfortable beds to be had at 'The Bull.'"

"So you won't gi'e me a night's shelter, eh?"

"No," I answered, greatly annoyed by the fellow's persistence.

"An' you don't want to buy nothin' for the young woman—a necklace—or, say—a pair o' garters?" But here, meeting my eye, he shouldered his brooms hastily and moved off. And, after he had gone some dozen yards or so, he paused and turned.

"Very well then!" he shouted, "I 'opes as you gets your' ead knocked off—ah!—an' gets it knocked off—soon!" Having said which, he spat up into the air towards me, and trudged off.

CHAPTER XIV

CONCERNING BLACK GEORGE'S LETTER

IT was with a feeling of great relief that I watched the fellow out of sight, nevertheless his very presence seemed to have left a blight upon all things, for he, viewing matters with the material eye of Common-sense, had, thereby, contaminated them—even the air seemed less pure and sweet than it had been heretofore, so that, glancing over my shoulder, I was glad to see that Charmian had re-entered the cottage.

"Here," said I to myself, "here is Common-sense, in the shape of a half-witted peddling fellow, blundering into Arcadia, in the shape of a haunted cottage, a woman, and a man. Straightway our Peddler, being Common-sense, misjudges us—as, indeed, would every other common-sense individual the world over; for Arcadia, being of itself Abstract and Immaterial, is opposed to, and incapable of being understood by Concrete Common-sense, and always will be—and there's the rub! And yet," said I, "thanks to the Wanderer of the Roads, who built this cottage, and hanged himself here, and thanks to a Highland Scot who performed wonderfully on the bagpipes, there is little chance of any Common-sense Vagrant venturing near Arcadia again—at least until the woman is gone, or the man is gone, or——"

Here, going to rub my chin (being somewhat at a loss), I found that I had been standing, all this while, the broom in one hand and the belt in the other, and now, hearing a laugh behind me, I turned, and saw Charmian was leaning in the open doorway watching me.

"And so you are the—the cove—with the white hands and the taking ways, are you, Peter?"

"Why—you were actually—listening then?"

" Why, of course I was."

" That," said I, " that was very—undignified ! "

" But very—feminine, Peter ! " Hereupon I threw the belt from me one way, and the broom the other, and sitting down upon the bench began to fill my pipe—rather awkwardly, being conscious of Charmian's mocking scrutiny.

" Poor—poor Black George ! " she sighed.

" What do you mean by that ? " said I quickly.

" Really I can almost understand his being angry with you."

" Why ? "

" You walked with her, and talked with her, Peter— like Cæsar, ' you came, you saw, you conquered ' ! "

Here I dragged my tinder-box from my pocket so awkwardly as to bring the lining with it.

" And—even smiled at her, Peter—and you so rarely smile ! "

Having struck flint and steel several times without success, I thrust the tinder-box back into my pocket and fixed my gaze upon the moon.

" Is she so very pretty, Peter ? "

I stared up at the moon without answering.

" I wonder if you bother her with your Epictetus and—and dry-as-dust quotations ? "

I bit my lips and stared up at the moon.

" Or perhaps she likes your musty books and philosophy ? "

But presently, finding that I would not speak, Charmian began to sing, very sweet and low, as if to herself, yet, when I chanced to glance towards her, I found her mocking eyes still watching me. Now the words of her song were these :

> " My love is like a red, red rose
>   That's newly blown in June,
>   My love is like a melody
>   That's softly played in tune."

And so, at last, unable to bear it any longer, I rose and, taking my candle, went into my room and closed the door. But I had been there scarcely five minutes when Charmian knocked.

"Oh, Peter! I wish to speak to you—please." Obediently I opened the door.

"What is it, Charmian?"

"You dropped this from your pocket when you took out your tinder-box so clumsily!" said she, holding towards me a crumpled paper. And looking down at it, I saw that it was Black George's letter to Prudence.

Now, as I took it from her, I noticed that her hand trembled, while in her eyes I read fear and trouble; and seeing this, I was, for a moment, unwontedly glad, and then wondered at myself.

"You—did not read it—of course?" said I, well knowing that she had.

"Yes, Peter—it lay open, and——"

"Then," said I, speaking my thought aloud, "you know that she loves George."

"He means you harm," said she, speaking with her head averted, "and, if he killed you——"

"I should be spared a deal of sorrow, and—and mortification, and—other people would be no longer bothered by Epictetus and dry-as-dust quotations." She turned suddenly, and, crossing to the open doorway, stood leaning there. "But, indeed," I went on hurriedly, "there is no chance of such a thing happening—not the remotest. Black George's bark is a thousand times worse than his bite—this letter means nothing, and—er—nothing at all," I ended, somewhat lamely, for she had turned and was looking at me over her shoulder.

"If he has to 'wait, and wait, and follow you, and follow you'?" said she, in the same low tone.

"Those are merely the words of a half-mad peddler," said I.

"'And your blood will go soaking, and soaking into the grass!'"

"Our Peddler has a vivid imagination!" said I lightly. But she shook her head, and turned to look out upon the beauty of the night once more, while I watched her, chin in hand.

" I was angry with you to-night, Peter," said she at
length, " because you ordered me to do something
against my will—and I—did it; and so, I tried to
torment you—you will forgive me for that, won't
you ? "

" There is nothing to forgive, nothing, and—good-
night, Charmian." Here she turned, and, coming to
me, gave me her hand.

" Charmian Brown will always think of you as
a——"

" Blacksmith ! " said I.

" As a blacksmith ! " she repeated, looking at me
with a gleam in her eyes, " but oftener as a——"

" Pedant ! " said I.

" As a pedant ! " she repeated obediently, " but
most of all as a——"

" Well ? " said I.

" As a—man," she ended, speaking with bent head.
And here again I was possessed of a sudden gladness
that was out of all reason, as I immediately told
myself.

" Your hand is very small," said I, finding nothing
better to say, " smaller even that I thought."

" Is it ? " and she smiled and glanced up at me
beneath her lashes, for her head was still bent.

" And wonderfully smooth and soft ! "

" Is it ? " said she again, but this time she did not
look up at me. Now another man might have stooped
and kissed those slender, shapely fingers—but, as for
me, I loosed them, rather suddenly, and, once more
bidding her good-night, re-entered my own chamber,
and closed the door.

But to-night, lying upon my bed, I could not sleep,
and fell to watching the luminous patch of sky framed
in my open casement. I thought of Charmian, of her
beauty, of her strange whims, and fancies, her swift-
changing moods, and her contrariness, comparing
her, in turn, to all those fair women I had ever read of
or dreamed over in my books. Little by little, however, my thoughts drifted to Gabbing Dick and Black
George, and, with my mind's eye, I could see him as

he was (perhaps at this very moment), fierce-eyed and grim of mouth, sitting beneath some hedgerow, while, knife in hand, he trimmed and trimmed his two bludgeons, one of which was to batter the life out of me. From such disquieting reflections I would turn my mind to sweet-eyed Prudence, to the Ancient, the forge, and the thousand and one duties of the morrow. I bethought me, once more, of the storm, of the coming of Charmian, of the fierce struggle in the dark, of the Postilion, and of Charmian again. And yet, in despite of me my thoughts would revert to George, and I would see myself even as the Peddler pictured me, out in some secluded corner of the woods, lying stiffly upon my back with glassy eyes staring up sightlessly through the whispering leaves above, while my blood soaked and soaked into the green, and with a blackbird singing gloriously upon my motionless breast.

CHAPTER XV

WHICH, BEING IN PARENTHESIS, MAY BE SKIPPED IF
THE READER SO DESIRE

As this life is a Broad Highway along which we must all of us pass whether we will or no; as it is a thoroughfare sometimes very hard and cruel in the going, and beset by many hardships, sometimes desolate and hatefully monotonous, so, also, must its aspect, sooner or later, change for the better, and, the stony track overpassed, the choking heat and dust left behind, we may reach some green, refreshing haven shady with trees, and full of the cool, sweet sound of running waters. Then who shall blame us if we pause unduly in this grateful shade, and, lying upon our backs a while, gaze up through the swaying green of trees to the infinite blue beyond, ere we journey on once more, as soon we must, to front whatsoever of good or evil lies waiting for us in the hazy distance.

To just such a place am I now come in this, my history; the record of a period which I, afterwards, remembered as the happiest I had ever known, the memory of which must remain with me, green and fragrant everlastingly.

If, in the forthcoming pages, you shall find overmuch of Charmian, I would say, in the first place, that it is by her, and upon her, that this narrative hangs; and, in the second place, that in this part of my story I find my greatest pleasure; though here, indeed, I am faced with a great difficulty, seeing that I must depict, as faithfully as may be, that most difficult, that most elusive of all created things, to wit—a woman.

Truly, I begin to fear lest my pen fail me altogether for the very reason that it is of Charmian that I would tell, and of Charmian I understand little more than

298

nothing; for what rule has ever been devised whereby a woman's mind may be accurately gauged, and who of all those wise ones who have written hitherto—poets, romancers or historians—has ever fathomed the why and wherefore of the Mind Feminine?

A fool indeed were I to attempt a thing impossible; I do but seek to show her to you as I saw her, and to describe her in so far as I learned to know her.

And yet, how may I begin? I might tell you that her nose was neither arched nor straight, but perfect, none the less; I might tell you of her brows, straight and low, of her eyes, long and heavy-lashed, of her chin, firm, and round, and dimpled; and yet, that would not be Charmian. For I could not paint you the scarlet witchery of her mouth with its sudden, bewildering changes, nor show you how sweetly the lower lip curved up to meet its mate. I might tell you that to look into her eyes was like gazing down into very deep water, but I could never give you their varying beauty, nor the way she had with her lashes; nor can I ever describe her rich, warm colouring, nor the lithe grace of her body.

Thus it is that I misdoubt my pen of its task, and fear that, when you shall have read these pages, you shall, at best, have caught but a very imperfect reflection of Charmian as she really is.

Wherefore, I will waste no more time or paper upon so unprofitable a task, but hurry on with my narrative, leaving you to find her out as best you may.

CHAPTER XVI

CONCERNING, AMONG OTHER MATTERS, THE PRICE OF BEEF, AND THE LADY SOPHIA SEFTON OF CAMBOURNE

CHARMIAN sighed, bit the end of her pen, and sighed again. She was deep in her housekeeping accounts, adding and substracting and, between whiles, regarding the result with a rueful frown.

Her sleeves were rolled up over her round, white arms, and I inwardly wondered if the much vaunted Phryne's were ever more perfect in their modelling, or of a fairer texture. Had I possessed the genius of a Praxiteles I might have given to the world a masterpiece of beauty to replace his vanished Venus of Cnidus; but, as it happened, I was only a humble blacksmith, and she a fair woman who sighed, and nibbled her pen, and sighed again.

" What is it, Charmian ? "

" Compound addition, Peter, and I hate figures—I detest, loathe, and abominate them—especially when they won't balance ! "

" Then never mind them," said I.

" Never mind them, indeed—the idea, sir ! How can I help minding them when living costs so much and we so poor."

" Are we ? " said I.

" Why, of course we are."

" Yes—to be sure—I suppose we are," said I dreamily.

Lais was beautiful, Thais was alluring, and Berenice was famous for her beauty, but then, could either of them have shown such arms—so long, so graceful in their every movement, so subtly rounded in their lines, arms which, for all their seeming firmness, must (I thought) be wonderfully soft to the touch, and smooth as ivory, and which found a delicate sheen where the light kissed them?

"We have spent four shillings for meat this week, Peter!" said Charmian, glancing up suddenly.

"Good!" said I.

"Nonsense, sir—four shillings is most extravagant!"

"Oh!—is it, Charmian?"

"Why, of course it is."

"Oh!" said I; "yes—perhaps it is."

"Perhaps!" said she, curling her lip at me, "perhaps, indeed!" Having said which, Charmian became absorbed in her accounts again, and I in Charmian.

In Homer we may read that the loveliness of Briseis caused Achilles much sorrow; Ovid tells us that Chione was beautiful enough to inflame two gods, and that Antiope's beauty drew down from heaven the mighty Jove himself; and yet, was either of them formed and shaped more splendidly than she who sat so near me, frowning at what she had written, and petulantly biting her pen?

"Impossible!" said I so suddenly that Charmian started and dropped her pen, which I picked up, feeling very like a fool.

"What did you mean by 'impossible,' Peter?"

"I was—thinking merely."

"Then I wish you wouldn't think so suddenly next time."

"I beg your pardon."

"Nor be so very emphatic about it."

"No," said I, "er—no." Hereupon, deigning to receive her pen back again, she recommenced her figuring, while I began to fill my pipe.

"Two shillings for tea!"

"Excellent!" said I.

"I do wish," she sighed, raising her head to shake it reproachfully at me, "that you would be a little more sensible."

"I'll try."

"Tea at twelve shillings a pound is a luxury!"

"Undoubtedly!"

" And to pay two shillings for a luxury when we are so poor—is sinful ! "

" Is it, Charmian ? "

" Of course it is."

" Oh ! " said I; " and yet, life without tea—more especially as you brew it—would be very stale, flat, and unprofitable, and——"

" Bacon and eggs—one shilling and fourpence ! " she went on, consulting her accounts.

" Ah ?" said I, not venturing on "good," this time.

" Butter—one shilling ! "

" Hum ! " said I cautiously, and with the air of turning this over in my mind

" Vegetables—tenpence ! "

" To be sure," said I, nodding my head, " tenpence, certainly."

" And bread, Peter " (this in a voice of tragedy) "—eightpence."

" Excellent ! " said I recklessly, whereat Charmian immediately frowned at me.

" Oh, Peter ! " said she, with a sigh of resignation, " you possess absolutely no idea of proportion. Here we pay four shillings for meat, and only eightpence for bread; had we spent less on luxuries and more on necessaries we should have had money in hand instead of—let me see ! " and she began adding up the various items before her with soft, quick little pats of her fingers on the table. Presently, having found the total, she leaned back in her chair and, summoning my attention with a tap of her pen, announced :

" We have spent nine shillings and tenpence, Peter ! "

" Good, indeed ! " said I.

" Leaving exactly—twopence over."

" A penny for you, and a penny for me."

" I fear I am a very bad housekeeper, Peter."

" On the contrary."

" You earn ten shillings a week."

" Well ? "

" And here is exactly—twopence left—oh, Peter ! "

" You are forgetting the tea and the beef, and—and the other luxuries," said I, struck by the droop of her mouth.

"But you work so very, very hard, and earn so little—and that little——"

"I work that I may live, Charmian, and lo! I am alive."

"And dreadfully poor!"

"And ridiculously happy."

"I wonder why?" said she, beginning to draw designs on the page before her.

"Indeed, though I have asked myself that question frequently of late, I have as yet found no answer, unless it be my busy, care-free life, with the warm sun about me and the voice of the wind in the trees."

"Yes, perhaps that is it."

"And yet I don't know," I went on thoughtfully, "for now I come to think of it, my life has always been busy and care-free, and I have always loved the sun and the sound of wind in trees—yet, like Horace, have asked 'What is *Happiness*?' and looked for it in vain; and now, here—in this out-of-the-world spot, working as a village smith, it has come to me all unbidden and unsought—which is very strange!"

"Yes, Peter," said Charmian, still busy with her pen.

"Upon consideration I think my thanks are due to my uncle for dying and leaving me penniless."

"Do you mean that he disinherited you?"

"In a way, yes; he left me his whole fortune provided that I married a certain lady within the year."

"A certain lady?"

"The Lady Sophia Sefton of Cambourne," said I.

Charmian's pen stopped in the very middle of a letter, and she bent down to examine what she had been writing.

"Oh!" said she very softly, "the Lady Sophia Sefton of Cambourne?"

"Yes," said I.

"And—your cousin—Sir Maurice—were the conditions the same in his case?"

"Precisely!"

"Oh!" said Charmian, just as softly as before, "and this lady—she will not—marry you?"

" No," I answered.

" Are you quite—sure ? "

" Certain !—you see, I never intend to ask her."

Charmian suddenly raised her head and looked at me.

" Why not, Peter ? "

" Because, should I ever marry—a remote contingency, and most improbable—I am sufficiently self-willed to prefer to exert my own choice in the matter ; moreover, this lady is a celebrated toast, and it would be most repugnant to me that my wife's name should ever have been bandied from mouth to mouth, and hiccoughed out over slopping wineglasses——".

The pen slipped from Charmian's fingers to the floor, and before I could pick it up she had forestalled me, so that when she raised her head she was flushed with stooping.

" Have you ever seen this lady, Peter ? "

" Never, but I have heard of her—who has not ? "

" What have you heard ? "

" That she galloped her horse up and down the steps of St Paul's Cathedral, for one thing.".

" What more ? "

" That she is proud, and passionate, and sudden of temper—in a word, a virago ! "

" Virago ! " said Charmian, flinging up her head.

" Virago ! " I nodded, " though she is handsome, I understand—in a strapping way—and I have it on very excellent authority that she is a black-browed goddess, a peach, and a veritable plum."

" ' Strapping ' is a hateful word, Peter ! "

" But very descriptive.".

" And—doesn't she interest you—a little, Peter ? "

" Not in the least," said I.

" And pray, why not ? ".

" Because I care very little for either peaches or plums."

" Or black-browed goddesses, Peter ? "

" Not if she is big and strapping, and possesses a temper."

" I suppose—to such a philosopher as you—a woman

Charmian rested her round elbows upon the table, and, setting her chin in her hands, stared squarely at me

Face Page 304

or a goddess, black-browed or not, can scarcely compare with, or hope to rival an old book, can she, sir ? "

" Why, that depends, Charmian."

" On what ? "

" On the book ! " said I.

Charmian rested her round elbows upon the table,
and, setting her chin in her hands, stared squarely
at me.

" Peter," said she.

" Yes, Charmian ? "

" If ever you did meet this lady—I think——"

" Well ? "

" I know——"

" What ? "

" That you would fall a very easy victim ! "

" I think not," said I.

" You would be her slave in—a month—three weeks
—or much less——"

" Preposterous ! " I exclaimed.

" If she set herself to make you ! "

" That would be very immodest ! " said I ; " besides,
no woman can make a man love her."

" Do your books teach you that, Peter ? " Here,
finding I did not answer, she laughed and nodded her
head at me. " You would be head over ears in love
before you knew it ! "

" I think not," said I, smiling.

" You are the kind of man who would grow sick
with love, and never know what ailed him."

" Any man in such a condition would be a pitiful
ass ! " said I.

Charmian only laughed at me again, and went back
to her scribbling.

" Then, if this lady married you," said she suddenly, " you would be a gentleman of good position
and standing ? "

" Yes, I suppose so—and probably miserable."

" And rich, Peter ? "

" I should have more than enough."

" Instead of being a village blacksmith——"

" With just enough, and absurdly happy and con-

U

tent," I added, " which is far more desirable—at least
I think so."

" Do you mean to say that you would rather—exist
here, and make horseshoes all your life, than—live,
respected and rich."

" And married to——"

" And married to the Lady Sophia ? "

" Infinitely ! " said I.

" Then your cousin, so far as you are concerned, is
free to woo and win her and your uncle's fortune ? "

" And I wish him well of his bargain ! " I nodded.
" As for me, I shall probably continue to live here,
and make horseshoes—wifeless and content."

" Is marriage so hateful to you ? "

' In the Abstract—no; for in my mind there exists
a woman whom I think I could love—very greatly ;
but, in the Actual, yes, because there is no woman in
all the world that is like this woman of my mind."

" Is she so flawlessly perfect—this imaginary
woman ? "

" She is one whom I would respect for her intellect."

" Yes."

" Whom I would honour for her proud virtue."

" Yes, Peter."

" Whom I would worship for her broad charity, her
gentleness, and spotless purity."

" Yes, Peter."

" And love with all my strength, for her warm,
sweet womanhood—in a word, she is the epitome of
all that is true and womanly ! "

" That is to say—as you understand such things,
sir, and all your knowledge of woman, and her virtues
and failings, you have learned from your books,
therefore, misrepresented by history, and distorted by
romance, it is utterly false and unreal. And, of course,
this imaginary creature of yours is ethereal, bloodless,
sexless, unnatural, and quite impossible ! "

Now, when she spoke thus I laid down my pipe
and stared, but, before I could get my breath, she
began again, with curling lip and lashes that drooped
disdainfully.

" I quite understand that there can be no woman worthy of Mr Peter Vibart—she whom he would honour with marriage must be specially created for him! Ah! but some day a woman—a real, live woman—will come into his life, and the touch of her hand, the glance of her eyes, the warmth of her breath, will dispel this poor, flaccid, misty creature of his imagination, she will fade and fade, and vanish into nothingness. And when the real woman has shown him how utterly false and impossible this dream woman was—then, Mr Peter Vibart, I hope she will laugh at you—as I do, and turn her back upon you—as I do, and leave you—for the very superior, very pedantic pedant that you are—and scorn you—as I do, most of all because you are merely a—creature! " With the word she flung up her head and stamped her foot at me, and turning, swept out through the open door into the moonlight.

" Creature ? " said I, and so sat staring at the table, and the walls, and the floor and the rafters in a blank amazement.

But in a while, my amazement growing, I went and stood in the doorway looking at Charmian, but saying nothing.

And, as I watched, she began to sing softly to herself, and, putting up her hand, drew the comb from her hair so that it fell down, rippling about her neck and shoulders. And, singing softly thus, she shook her hair about her, so that I saw it curled far below her waist; stooped her head, and, parting it upon her neck, drew it over either shoulder, whence it flowed far down over her bosom in two glorious waves, for the moon, peeping through the rift in the leaves above, sent down her beams to wake small fires in it, that came and went, and winked and winked with her breathing.

" Charmian, you have glorious hair! " said I, speaking on the impulse—a thing I rarely do.

But Charmian only combed her tresses, and went on singing to herself.

" Charmian," said I again, " what did you mean when you called me a—creature? "

Charmian went on singing.

" You called me a ' pedant ' once before; to be told that I am superior, also, is most disquieting. I fear my manner must be very unfortunate to afford you such an opinion of me."

Charmian went on singing.

" Naturally I am much perturbed, and doubly anxious to know what you wish me to understand by the epithet, ' creature ' ? "

Charmian went on singing. Wherefore, seeing she did not intend to answer me, I presently re-entered the cottage.

Now it is ever my custom, when at all troubled, or put out in any way, to seek consolation in my books, hence, I now took up my Homer, and, trimming the candles, sat down at the table.

In a little while Charmian came in, still humming the air of her song, and not troubling even to glance in my direction.

Some days before, at her request, I had brought her linen, and lace, and ribands from Cranbrook, and these she now took out, together with needle and cotton, and, sitting down at the opposite side of the table, began to sew.

She was still humming, and this of itself distracted my mind from the lines before me; moreover, my eye was fascinated by the gleam of her flying needle, and I began to debate within myself what she was making. It (whatever it might be) was ruffled, and edged with lace, and caught here and there with little bows of blue riband, and, from these, and divers other evidences, I had concluded it to be a garment of some sort, and was yet casting about in my mind to account for these bows of riband, when, glancing up suddenly, she caught my eye, whereupon, for no reason in the world, I felt suddenly guilty, to hide which I began to search through my pockets for my pipe.

" On the mantelshelf ! " said she.

" What is ? "

" Your pipe ! "

" Thank you ! " said I, and reached it down.

" What are you reading? " she inquired; " is it of
Helen, or Aspasia, or Phyrne? "

" Neither—it is the parting of Hector and Andro-
mache," I answered.

" Is it very interesting? "

" Yes."

" Then why do your eyes wander so often from the
page? "

" I know many of the lines by heart," said I. And
having lighted my pipe, I took up the book, and once
more began to read. Yet I was conscious, all the time,
of Charmian's flashing needle, also she had begun to
hum again.

And, after I had endeavoured to read, and Charmian
had hummed for perhaps five minutes, I lowered my
book, and, sighing, glanced at her.

" I am trying to read, Charmian."

" So I see."

" And your humming confuses me."

" It is very quiet outside, Peter."

" But I cannot read by moonlight, Charmian."

" Then—don't read, Peter." Here she nibbled her
thread with white teeth, and held up what she had
been sewing to view the effect of a bow of riband,
with her head very much on one side. And I inwardly
wondered that she should spend so much care upon
such frippery—all senseless bows and laces.

" To hum is a very disturbing habit! " said I.

" To smoke an evil-smelling pipe is worse—much
worse, Peter! "

" I beg your pardon! " said I, and laid the offend-
ing object back upon the mantel.

" Are you angry, Peter? "

" Not in the least; I am only sorry that my smoking
annoyed you—had I known before——"

" It didn't annoy me in the least! "

" But from what you said I understood——"

" No, Peter, you did not understand—you never
understand, and I don't think you ever will understand anything but your Helens and Phrynes—and
your Latin and Greek philosophies, and that is what

makes you so very annoying, and so—so quaintly original ! ''

" But you certainly found fault with my pipe."

" Naturally !—didn't you find fault with my humming ? ''

" Really," said I, " really, I fail to see——"

" Of course you do ! " sighed Charmian. Whereupon there fell a silence between us, during which she sewed industriously, and I went forth with brave Hector to face the mighty Achilles. But my eye had traversed barely twenty lines when :

" Peter ? "

" Yes ? "

" Do you remember my giving you a locket ?"

" Yes."

" Where is it ? "

" Oh ! I have it still—somewhere."

" Somewhere, sir ? " she repeated, glancing at me with raised brows.

" Somewhere safe," said I, fixing my eyes upon my book.

" It had a riband attached, hadn't it ? "

" Yes."

" A pink riband, if I remember—yes, pink."

" No—it was blue ! " said I unguardedly.

" Are you sure, Peter ? "   And here, glancing up, I saw that she was watching me beneath her lashes.

" Yes," I answered ; " that is—I think so."

" Then you are not sure ? "

" Yes I am," said I ; " it was a blue riband," and I turned over a page very ostentatiously.

" Oh ! " said Charmian, and there was another pause, during which I construed probably fifty lines or so.

" Peter ? "

" Well ? "

" Where did you say it was now—my locket ?"

" I didn't say it was anywhere."

" No, you said it was ' somewhere '—in a rather vague sort of way, Peter."

" Well, perhaps I did," said I, frowning at my book.

" It is not very valuable, but I prized it for association's sake, Peter."

" Ah!—yes, to be sure," said I, feigning to be wholly absorbed.

" I was wondering if you ever—wear it, Peter? "

" Wear it ! " I exclaimed, and glancing furtively down at myself, I was relieved to see that there were no signs of a betraying blue riband; " wear it ! " said I again, " why should I wear it? "

" Why indeed, Peter, unless it was because it was there to wear." Suddenly she uttered an exclamation of annoyance, and, taking up a candle, began looking about the floor.

" What have you lost? "

" My needle ! I think it must have fallen under the table, and needles are precious in this wilderness; won't you please help me to find it? "

" With pleasure ! " said I, getting down upon my hands and knees, and together we began to hunt for the lost needle.

Now, in our search, it chanced that we drew near together, and once her hand touched mine, and once her soft hair brushed my cheek, and there stole over me a perfume like the breath of violets, the fragrance that I always associated with her, faint, and sweet, and alluring—so much so, that I drew back from further chance of contact, and kept my eyes directed to the floor.

And, after I had sought vainly for some time, I raised my head and looked at Charmian, to find her regarding me with a very strange expression.

" What is it? " I inquired. " Have you found the needle? " Charmian sat back on her heels, and laughed softly.

" Oh, yes, I've found the needle, Peter, that is—I never lost it."

" Why then—what—what did you mean——? "

For answer she raised her hand and pointed to my breast. Then, glancing hurriedly down, I saw that the locket had slipped forward through the bosom of my shirt, and hung in plain view. I made an instinctive movement to hide it, but, hearing her laugh, looked at her instead.

" So this was why you asked me to stoop to find your needle ? "

" Yes, Peter."

" Then you—knew ? "

" Of course I knew."

" Hum ! " said I. A distant clock chimed eleven, and Charmian began to fold away her work, seeing which, I rose, and took up my candle. " And— pray—— "

" Well ? "

" And pray," said I, staring hard at the flame of my candle, " how did you happen to—find out—— ? "

" Very simply—I saw the riband round your neck days ago. Good-night, Peter ! "

" Oh," said I. " Good-night ! "

CHAPTER XVII

THE OMEN

"My lady sweet, arise!
My lady sweet, arise
With everything that pretty is,
My lady sweet, arise!"

IT was morning, and Charmian was singing. The
pure, rich notes floated in at my open lattice, and I
heard the clatter of her pail as she went to fetch water
from the brook. Wherefore I presently stepped out
into the sunshine, my coat and neckcloth across my
arm, to plunge my head and face into the brook, and
carry back the heavy bucket for her, as was my
custom.

Being come to the brook I found the brimming
bucket, sure enough, but no Charmian. I was looking about wonderingly, when she began to sing again,
and, guided by this, I espied her kneeling beside the
stream.

The water ran deep and very still, just here, over-
hung by ash, and alder, and willow, whose slender,
curving branches formed a leafy bower wherein she
half knelt, half sat, bending over to regard herself in
the placid water. For a long moment she remained
thus, studying her reflection intently in this crystal
mirror, and little by little her song died away. Then
she put up her hands and began to rearrange her hair
with swift, dexterous fingers, apostrophising her
watery image the while, on this wise:

"My dear, you are growing positively apple-
cheeked—I vow you are! your enemies might almost
call you—strapping—alack! And then your complexion, my dear, your adorable complexion!" she
went on, with a rueful shake of her head. "you are as
brown as a gipsy—not that you need go breaking your

313

heart over it—for, between you and me, my dear, I think it rather improves you; the pity of it is that you have no one to appreciate you properly—to render to your charms the homage they deserve, no one—not a soul, my dear; your hermit, bless you! can see, or think, of nothing that exists out of a book—which, between you, and me, and the bucket yonder, is perhaps just as well—and yet—heigho! To be so lovely, and so forlorn! indeed, I could shed tears for you if it would not make your eyelids swell and your classic nose turn red."

Here she sighed again, and, taking a tendril of hair between her fingers, transformed it, very cleverly, into a small curl.

" Yes, your tan certainly becomes you, my dear," she went on, nodding to her reflection; " not that he will ever notice—dear heart, no! were you suddenly to turn as black as a Hottentot—before his very eyes—he would go on serenely smoking his pipe, and talk to you of Epictetus—heigho!" Sighing thus, she broke off a spray of leaves and proceeded to twine them in among the lustrous coils of her hair, bending over her reflection meanwhile, and turning her head this way and that, to note the effect.

" Yes," said she at last, nodding at her image with a satisfied air, " that touch of green sets off your gipsy complexion admirably, my dear—I could positively kiss you—I vow I could, and I am hard to please. St Anthony himself, meeting you alone in the desert, would, at least, have run away from you, and that would have been some tribute to your charms, but our Philosopher will just glance at you with his slow, grave smile, and tell you, in his solemn, affable way— that it is a very fine morning—heigho!"

Here (somewhat late in the day, perhaps), perceiving that I was playing eavesdropper, I moved cautiously away, and taking up the pail, returned to the cottage. I now filled the kettle and set it upon the fire, and proceeded to spread the cloth (a luxurious institution of Charmian's, on which she insisted) and to lay out the breakfast things. In the midst of which,

however, chancing to fall into a reverie, I became
oblivious of all things till roused by a step behind me,
and, turning, beheld Charmian standing with the
glory of the sun about her—like the Spirit of Summer
herself, broad of hip and shoulder, yet slender, and
long of limb, all warmth, and life, and long, soft
curves from throat to ankle—perfect with vigorous
youth from the leaves that crowned her beauty to the
foot that showed beneath her gown.

And, as I gazed upon her, silent and wondering,
lo! though her mouth was solemn yet there was
laughter in her eyes as she spoke.

"Well, sir—have you no greeting for me?"

"It—is a—very fine morning!" said I. And now
the merriment overflowed her eyes, and she laughed,
yet blushed a little, too, and lowered her eyes from
mine, and said, still laughing:

"Oh, Peter—the teapot—do mind the teapot!"

"Teapot?" I repeated, and then I saw that I still
held it in my hand.

"Pray, sir—what might you be going to do with
the teapot in one hand, and that fork in the other?"

"I was going to make the tea, I remember," said I.

"Is that why you were standing there staring at the
kettle while it boiled over?"

"I—forgot all about the kettle," said I. So Charmian took the teapot from me, and set about brewing
the tea, singing merrily the while. Anon she began
to fry the bacon, giving each individual slice its due
amount of care and attention; but, her eyes chancing
to meet mine, the song died upon her lip, her lashes
flickered and fell, while up from throat to brow there
crept a slow, hot wave of crimson. And in that
moment I turned away and strode down to the brook.

Now it happened that I came to that same spot
where she had leaned and, flinging myself down, I fell
to studying my reflection in the water, even as she
had done.

Heretofore, though I had paid scant heed to my
appearance, I had been content (in a certain imper-
sonal sort of way), had dressed in the fashion, and

taken advantage of such adornments as were in favour, as much from habit as from any set design; but now, lying beside the brook with my chin propped in my hands, I began to study myself critically, feature by feature, as I had never dreamed of doing before.

Mirrored in the clear waters I beheld a face, lean and brown, and with lank, black hair; eyes, dark and of a strange brilliance, looked at me from beneath a steep prominence of brow; I saw a somewhat high-bridged nose with thin, nervous nostrils, a long, cleft chin, and a disdainful mouth.

Truly, a saturnine face, cold, and dark, and un-lovely, and thus—even as I gazed—the mouth grew still more disdainful, and the heavy brow lowered blacker and more forbidding. And yet, in that same moment, I found myself sighing, while I strove to lend some order to the wildness of my hair.

"Fool!" said I, and plunged my head beneath the water, and held it there so long that I came up puffing and blowing; whereupon I caught up the towel and fell to rubbing myself vigorously, so that presently, looking down into the water again, I saw that my hair was wilder than ever—all rubbed into long elf-locks. Straightway I lifted my hands, and would have smoothed it somewhat, but checked the impulse.

"Let be," said I to myself, turning away, "let be. I am as I am, and shall be henceforth—in very truth a village blacksmith—and content so to be—absolutely content."

At sight of me Charmian burst out laughing, the which, though I had expected it, angered me never-theless.

"Why, Peter!" she exclaimed, "you look like——"

"A very low fellow!" said I, "say a village black-smith who has been at his ablutions."

"If you only had rings in your ears, and a scarf round your head, you would be the image of a Spanish brigand—or like the man Mina whose exploits I have read of—a Spanish general, I think."

"A guerrilla leader," said I, taking my place at the table, "and a singularly cold-blooded villain—indeed I think it probable that we much resemble one another; is it any wonder that I am shunned by my kind—avoided by the ignorant and regarded askance by the rest?"

"Why, Peter!" said Charmian, regarding me with grave eyes, "what do you mean?"

"I mean that the country folk hereabout go out of their way to avoid crossing my path—not that, I suppose, they ever heard of Mina, but because of my looks."

"Your looks?"

"They think me possessed of the 'Evil Eye' or some such folly—may I cut you a piece of bread?"

"Oh, Peter!"

"Already, by divers honest-hearted rustics, I am credited with having cast a deadly spell upon certain unfortunate pigs, with having fought hand to hand with the hosts of the nethermost pit, and with having sold my soul to the devil—may I trouble you to pass the butter?"

"Oh, Peter, how foolish of them!"

"And how excusable! considering their ignorance and superstition," said I. "Mine, I am well aware, is not a face to win me the heart of man, woman, or child; they (especially women and children) share, in common with dogs and horses, that divine attribute which, for want of a better name, we call 'instinct,' whereby they love or hate for the mere tone of a voice, the glance of an eye, the motion of a hand, and, the love or hate once given, the prejudice for, or against, is seldom wholly overcome."

"Indeed," said Charmian, "I believe in first impressions."

"Being a woman," said I.

"Being a woman!" she nodded; "and the instinct of dog, and child, and woman has often proved true in the end."

"Surely instinct is always true?" said I—"I'd thank you for another cup of tea—yet, strangely enough, dogs generally make friends with me very readily, and the few children to whom I've spoken have neither screamed nor run away from me. Still, as I said before, I am aware that my looks are scarcely calculated to gain the love of man, woman, or child, not that it matters greatly, seeing that I am likely to hold very little converse with either."

"There is one woman, Peter, to whom you have talked by the hour together——"

"And who is doubtless weary enough of it all—more especially of Epictetus and Trojan Helen."

"Two lumps of sugar, Peter?"

"Thank you! Woman are very like flowers——" I began.

"That is a very profound remark, sir!—more especially coming from one who has studied and knows womankind so deeply."

"—and it is a pity that they should be allowed to 'waste their sweetness on the desert air.'"

"And philosophical blacksmiths, Peter?"

"More so if they be poor blacksmiths."

"I said 'philosophical,' Peter."

"You probably find your situation horribly lonely here?" I went on after a pause.

"Yes; it's nice and lonely, Peter."

"And, undoubtedly, this cottage is very poor and mean, and—er—humble;" Charmian smiled and shook her head.

"But then, Charmian Brown is a very humble person, sir."

"And you haven't even the luxury of a mirror to dress your hair by!"

"Is it so very clumsily dressed, sir?"

"No, no," said I hastily, "indeed I was thinking——"

"Well, Peter?"

"That it was very—beautiful!"

"Why, you told me that last night—come, what do you think of it this morning?"

"With those leaves in it—it is—even more so!"

Charmian laughed, and rising, swept me a stately curtsy.

"After all, sir, we find there be exceptions to every rule!"

"You mean?"

" Even blacksmiths ! "

And in a while, having finished my breakfast, I rose, and, taking my hat, bade Charmian 'Good-morning,' and so came to the door. But on the threshold I turned and looked back at her. She had risen, and stood leaning with one hand on the table; now in the other she held the bread-knife, and her eyes were upon mine.

And lo! wonder of wonders! once again, but this time sudden and swift—up from the round, full column of her throat, up over cheek and brow there rushed that vivid tide of colour; her eyes grew suddenly deep and soft, and then were hidden 'neath her lashes—and, in that same moment, the knife slipped from her grasp, and falling, point downwards, stood quivering in the floor between us—an ugly thing that gleamed evilly.

Was this an omen—a sign vouchsafed of that which, dark and terrible, was, even then, marching to meet us upon this Broad Highway? O Blind, and more than blind!

Almost before it had ceased to quiver I stooped, and, plucking it from the floor, gave it into her hand. Now, as I did so, her fingers touched mine, and, moved by a sudden mad impulse, I stooped and pressed my lips upon them—kissed them quick, and fierce, and so turned, and hurried upon my way.

Yet, as I went, I found that the knife had cut my chin, and that I was bleeding.

O Blind, and more than blind! Surely this was a warning, an omen to heed—to shiver over, despite the warm sun!

But, seeing the blood, I laughed, and strode village-wards, blithe of heart and light of foot.

O Blind, and more than blind!

CHAPTER XVIII

IN WHICH I HEAR NEWS OF SIR MAURICE VIBART

"WHICH I says—Lord love me!"

I plunged the iron back into the fire, and, turning my head, espied a figure standing in the doorway; and, though the leather hat, and short, round jacket had been superseded by a smart groom's livery, I recognised the Postilion.

"So 'elp me Bob, if this ain't a piece o' luck!" he exclaimed, and, with the words, he removed his hat and fell to combing his short, thick hair with the handle of his whip.

"I'm glad you think so," said I.

"You can drownd me if it ain't!" said he.

"And pray, how is the gentleman who—happened to fall, and hurt himself, if you remember—in the storm?"

"'Appened to fall, an' 'urt 'isself?" repeated the Postilion, winking knowingly, "''urt 'isself,' says you—'Walker!' says I, 'Walker!'" with which he laid his forefinger against the side of his nose and winked again.

"What might you be pleased to mean?"

"I means as a gent 'appenin' to fall in the dark may p'r'aps cut 'is 'ead open—but 'e don't give 'isself two black eyes, a bloody nose, a split lip, an' three broken ribs, all at once—it ain't nat'ral, w'ich if you says contrairy, I remarks—'Walker!' Lord!" continued the Postilion, seeing I did not speak, "Lord! it must 'a' been a pretty warm go while it lasted—you put 'im to sleep sound enough, it took me over a hour to Tonbridge, an' 'e never moved till 'e'd been put to bed at 'The Chequers' an' a doctor sent for. Ah! an' a nice time I 'ad of it, what wi' chamber-maids a-runnin' up an' down stairs to see the 'poor gentle-

man,' an' everybody a-starin' at me, an' a-shakin'
their 'eads, an' all a-axin' questions, one atop o' the
other, till the doctor come. ' 'Ow did this 'appen, me
man?' says 'e. 'A haccident!' says I. 'A haccident?' says the doctor, wi' a look in 'is eye as I didn't
just like. 'Ah!' says I, 'fell on 'is 'ead—out o' the
chaise,' says I, 'struck a stone, or summ'at,' says I.
'Did 'e fall of 'is own accord?' says the doctor. 'Ah,
for sure!' says I. 'Humph!' says the doctor, 'what
wi' 'is eyes, an' 'is nose, an' 'is lip, looks to me as if
someone 'ad 'elped 'im.' 'Then you must be a dam'
fool!' says a voice, an' there's my gentleman—Number One, you know, a-sittin' up in bed an' doin' 'is
'ardest to frown. 'Sir?' says the doctor. 'Sir! to
you,' says my gentleman, 'this honest fellow tells the
truth. I did fall out o' the accursed chaise—an' be
damned to you!' says 'e. 'Don't excite yourself,'
says the doctor; 'in your present condition it would
be dangerous.' 'Then be so good as to go to the
devil!' says my gentleman. 'I will!' says the doctor,
an' off 'e goes. 'Hi, there, you,' says my gentleman,
callin' to me as soon as we were alone, 'this accursed
business 'as played the devil with me, an' I need a
servant. 'Ow much do you want to stay wi' me?'
'Twenty-five shillin' a week,' says I, doin' myself
proud while I 'ad the chance. 'I'll give ye thirty,'
says 'e; ''wot's ye name?' 'Jacob Trimble, sir,'
say I. 'An' a most accursed name it is!—I'll call you
Parks,' says 'e, 'an' when I ring let no one answer
but yourself. You can go, Parks—an', Parks—get
me another doctor.' Well," pursued the Postilion,
seating himself near by, "we'd been there a couple o'
weeks, an' though 'e was better, an' 'is face near well
again, 'e still kept to 'is room, when, one day, a smart
phaeton an' blood 'osses drives up, an' out steps a fine
gentleman—one o' them pale, sleepy sort. I was
a-standin' in the yard, brushin' my master's coat—a
bottle-green wi' silver buttons, each button 'avin'
what they calls a monneygram stamped onto it. 'Ha,
me man!' says the sleepy gent, steppin' up to me, 'a
fine coat—doocid fashionable cut, curse me!—your

x

master's?' 'Yes, sir,' says I, brushin' away. 'Silver buttons too!' says the gent, 'let me see—ah yes!—a V, yes, to be sure—'ave the goodness to step to your master an' say as a gentleman begs to see 'im.' 'Can't be done, sir,' says I; 'me master ain't seein' nobody, bein' in indifferent 'ealth.' 'Nonsense!' says the gentleman, yawnin' an' slippin' a guinea into me 'and. 'Just run, like a good feller, an' tell 'im as I bear a message from George!' 'From 'oo?' says I. 'From George,' says the gent, smilin' an' yawnin'—'just say from George.' So, to come to the end of it, up I goes, an' finds me master walkin' up an' down an' a-swearin' to 'isself as usual. 'A gentleman to see you, sir,' says I. 'Why, devil burn your miserable carcass!' say 'e, 'didn't I tell you as I'd see nobody?' 'Ay, but this 'ere gent's a-sayin' 'e 'as a message from George, sir.' My master raised both clenched fists above 'is 'ead an' swore—ah! better than I'd heard for many a long day. 'Ows'ever, down stairs 'e goes, cursin' on every stair. In a time 'e comes back. 'Parks,' says 'e, 'do you remember that—that place where we got lost—in the storm, Parks?' 'Ah, sir,' says I. 'Well, go there at once,' says 'e, 'an',' —well—'e give me certain orders— jumps into the phaeton wi' the sleepy gentleman, an' they drive off together—an' accordin' to orders—'ere I am.''

"A very interesting story!" said I. "And so you are a groom now?"

"Ah!—an' you are a blacksmith, eh?"

"Yes."

"Well, if it don't beat everything as ever I heard— I'm a stiff'un, that's all!"

"What do you mean?"

"I means my droppin' in on you, like this 'ere, just as if you wasn't the one man in all England as I was 'opeful to drop in on.'

"And you find me very busy!" said I.

"Lord love me!" said the Postilion, combing his hair so very hard that it wrinkled his brow. "I comes up from Tonbridge this 'ere very afternoon, an', 'avin' drunk a pint over at 'The Bull' yonder, an' axed questions as none o' they chawbacons could give a answer to, I 'ears the chink o' your 'ammer, an' comin' over 'ere, chance like, I finds—you; I'll be gormed if it ain't a'most onnat'ral!'"

"And why?"

"'Cos you was the very i-dentical chap as I come up from Tonbridge to find."

"Were you sent to find me?'"

"Easy a bit—you're a blacksmith, a'n't you?"

"I told you so before."

"Wot's more, you looks a blacksmith in that there leather apron, an' wi' your face all smutty. To be sure, you're powerful like 'im—Number One as was—my master as now is——"

"Did he send you to find me?"

"Some folks might take you for a gentleman, meetin' you off 'and like, but I knows different."

"As how?"

"Well, I never 'eard of a gentleman turnin' 'isself into a blacksmith, afore, for one thing——"

"Still, one might," I ventured.

"No," answered the Postilion, with a decisive shake of the head, "it's ag'in natur'; when a gentleman gets down in the world, an' 'as to do summ'at for a livin', 'e generally shoots 'isself—ah! an' I've knowed 'em do it too! An' then I've noticed as you don't swear, nor yet curse—not even a damn."

"Seldom," said I; "but what of that?"

"I've seed a deal o' the quality in my time, one way or another—many's the fine gentleman as I've druv, or groomed for, an' never a one on 'em as didn't curse me—ah!" said the Postilion, sighing and shaking his head, "'ow they did curse me!—'specially one—a young lord—oncommon fond o' me 'e were too, in 'is way, to the day 'is 'oss fell an' rolled on 'im. 'Jacob,' says 'e, short like, for 'e were a-goin' fast. 'Jacob!' says 'e, 'damn your infernally ugly mug!' says 'e; 'you bet me as that cursed brute would do for me.' 'I did, my lord,' says I, an' I remember as the tears was a-runnin' down all our faces as we carried

'im along on the five-barred gate, that bein' 'andiest.
'Well, devil take your soul, you was right, Jacob, an'
be damned to you!' says 'e; 'you'll find a tenner in
my coat pocket 'ere, you've won it, for I sha'n't last
the day out, Jacob.' An' 'e didn't either, for 'e died
afore we got 'im 'ome, an' left me a 'undred pound in
'is will. Ah! gentlemen as is gents is all the same.
Lord love you! there never was one on 'em but
damned my legs, or my liver, or the chaise, or the
'osses, or the road, or the inns, or all on 'em together.
If you was to strip me as naked as the palm o' your
'and, an' to strip a lord, or a earl, or a gentleman as
naked as the palm o' your 'and, an' was to place us
side by side—where'd be the difference? We're both
men, both flesh and blood, a'n't we?—then where'd
be the difference? 'Oo's to tell which is the lord an'
which is the postilion?"

"Who indeed?" said I, setting down my hammer.
"Jack is often as good as his master—and a great
deal better."

"Why, nobody!" nodded the Postilion, "not a
soul—till we opened our mouths; an' then 'twould be
easy enough, for my lord, or earl, or gentleman, bein'
naked, an' not likin' it (which would only be nat'ral),
would fall a-swearin' 'eavens 'ard, damning everybody
an' cursin' everything, an' never stop to think, while
I—not bein' born to it—should stand there a-shiverin'
an' tryin' a curse or two myself, maybe—but Lord!
mine wouldn't amount to nothin' at all, me not bein'
nat'rally gifted, nor yet born to it—an' this brings me
round to 'er!"

"Her?"

"Ah—'er! Number Two—'er as quarrelled wi'
Number One all the way from London—'er as run
away from Number One—wot about—'er?" Here he
fell to combing his hair again with his whip-handle,
while his quick, bright eyes dodged from my face to
the glowing forge and back again, and his clean-
shaven lips pursed themselves in a soundless whistle.
And, as I watched him, it seemed to me that this was
the question that had been in his mind all along.

" Seeing she did manage to run away from him—
Number One—she is probably very well," I answered.

" Ah—to be sure ! very well, you say ?—ah, to be
sure ! " said the Postilion, apparently lost in contemplation of the bellows; " an'—where might she be,
now ? "

" That I am unable to tell you," said I, and began
to blow up the fire while the Postilion watched me,
sucking the handle of his whip reflectively.

" You work oncommon 'ard—drownd me if you
don't ! "

" Pretty hard ! " I nodded.

" An' gets well paid for it, p'r'aps ? "

" Not so well as I could wish," said I.

" Not so well as 'e could wish," nodded the Postilion, apparently addressing the sledge-hammer, for
his gaze was fixed upon it. " Of course not—the
'arder a man works the wuss 'e gets paid—'ow much
did you say you got a week ? "

" I named no sum," I replied.

" Well—'ow much might you be gettin' a week ? "

" Ten shillings."

" Gets ten shillin' a week ! " he nodded to the
sledge-hammer, " that ain't much for a chap like 'im
—kick me if it is ! "

" Yet I make it do very well ! "

The Postilion became again absorbed in contemplation of the bellows ; indeed he studied them so intently,
viewing them with his head now on one side, now on
the other, that I fell to watching him, under my brows,
and so, presently, caught him furtively watching me.
Hereupon he drew his whip from his mouth and
spoke.

" Supposing——" said he, and stopped.

" Well ? " I inquired, and, leaning upon my hammer, I looked him square in the eye.

" Supposing—wot are you a-staring at, my feller ? "

" You have said ' supposing ' twice—well ? "

" Well," said he, fixing his eye upon the bellows
again, " supposing you was to make a guinea over an'
above your wages this week ? "

" I should be very much surprised," said I.

" You would? "

" I certainly should."

" Then—why not surprise yourself? "

" You must speak more plainly," said I.

" Well then," said the Postilion, still with his gaze abstracted, " supposin' I was to place a guinea down on that there anvil o' yours—would that 'elp you to remember where Number Two—'er—might be? "

" No! "

" It wouldn't? "

" No! "

" A guinea's a lot o' money! "

" It is," I nodded.

" An' you say it wouldn't? "

" It would not! " said I.

" Then say—oh! say two pun' ten an' 'ave done with it."

" No! " said I, shaking my head.

" What—not—d'ye say ' no ' to two pun' ten? "

" I do."

" Well, let's say three pound."

I shook my head and, drawing the iron from the fire, began to hammer at it.

" Well then," shouted the Postilion, for I was making as much din as possible, " say four—five—ten—fifteen—twenty-five—fifty! " Here I ceased hammering.

" Tell me when you've done! " said I.

" You're a cool customer, you are—ah! an' a rum un' at that—I never see a rummer."

" Other people have thought the same," said I, examining the half-finished horseshoe ere I set it back in the fire.

" Sixty guineas! " said the Postilion gloomily.

" Come again! " said I.

" Seventy then! " said he, his gloom deepening.

" Once more! " said I.

" A 'undred—one 'undred guineas! " said he, removing his hat to mop at his brow.

" Any more? " I inquired.

"No!" returned the Postilion sulkily, putting on his hat," I'm done!"

"Did he set the figure at a hundred guineas?" said I.

"'Im—oh! 'e's mad for 'er, 'e is—'e'd ruin 'isself, body and soul, for 'er, 'e would, but I ain't goin' to offer no more; no woman as ever breathed—no matter 'ow 'andsome an' up-standin'—is worth more'n a 'undred guineas—it ain't as if she was a blood-mare—an' I'm done!"

"Then I wish you good-day!"

"But—just think—a 'undred guineas is a fortun'!"

"It is!" said I.

"Come, think it over," said the Postilion persuasively, "think it over, now!"

"Let me fully understand you then," said I; "you propose to pay me one hundred guineas on behalf of your master, known heretofore as Number One, for such information as shall enable him to discover the whereabouts of a certain person known as Her, Number Two—is that how the matter stands?"

"Ah! that's 'ow it stands," nodded the Postilion, "the money to be yours as soon as ever 'e lays 'ands on 'er—is it a go?"

"No!"

"No?"

"No!"

"W'y, you must be stark, starin' mad—that you must—unless you're sweet on 'er yourself——"

"You talk like a fool!" said I angrily.

"So you are sweet on 'er then?"

"Ass!" said I, "fool!" and, dropping my hammer, I made towards him, but he darted nimbly to the door, where, seeing I did not pursue, he paused.

"I may be a hass," he nodded, "an' I may be a fool—but I don't go a-fallin' in love wi' ladies as is above me, an' out o' my reach, and don't chuck away a 'undred guineas for one as ain't likely to look my way—not me! Which I begs leave to say—hass yourself, an' likewise fool—bah!" With which expletive he set his thumb to his nose, spread out his fingers, wagged them and swaggered off.

Above me, and out of my reach! One not likely to look my way!

And, in due season, having finished the horseshoe, having set each tool in its appointed place in the racks, and raked out the clinkers from the fire, I took my hat and coat, and, closing the door behind me, set out for the Hollow.

CHAPTER XIX

HOW I MET BLACK GEORGE AGAIN, AND WHEREIN THE PATIENT READER SHALL FIND A "LITTLE BLOOD"

IT was evening—that time before the moon is up and when the earth is dark, as yet, and full of shadows. Now as I went, by some chance there recurred to me the words of an old song I had read somewhere, years ago, words written in the glorious, brutal, knightly days of Edward the First, of warlike memory; and the words ran thus:

> "For her love I carke, and care,
> For her love I droop, and dare,
> For her love all my bliss is bare,
> And I wax wan."

"I wonder what poor, love-sick, long-dead-and-forgotten fool wrote that?" said I aloud.

> "For her love in sleep I slake,
> For her love all night I wake,
> For her love I mourning make,
> More than any man!"

Some doughty squire-at-arms, or perhaps some wandering knight (probably of a dark, unlovely look), who rode the forest ways with his thoughts full of Her, and dreaming of Her loveliness. "Howbeit, he was, beyond all doubt, a fool and a great one!" said I, "for it is to be inferred, from these few words he has left us, that his love was hopeless. She was, perhaps, proud and of a high estate, one who was above him, and far beyond his reach—who was not likely even to look his way. Doubtless she was beautiful, and therefore haughty and disdainful, for disdainful pride is an attribute of beauty, and ever was and ever will be— and hence it came that our misfortunate squire, or

329

knight-errant, was scorned for his pains, poor fool!
Which yet was his own fault, after all, and, indeed,
his just reward, for what has any squire-at-arms or
lusty knight, with the world before him, and glory yet
unachieved—to do with love? Love is a bauble—a toy,
a pretty pastime for idle folk who have no thought
above such—away with it!—Bah;" And, in my
mind—that is to say, mentally—I set my thumb to my
nose, and spread my fingers, and wagged them—even
as the Postilion had done. And yet, despite this, the
words of the old song recurred again and again,
pathetically insistent, voicing themselves in my footsteps so that, to banish them, I presently stood still.

And in that very moment a gigantic figure came
bursting through the hedge, clearing the ditch in a
single bound—and Black George confronted me.

Haggard of face, with hair and beard matted and
unkempt, his clothes all dusty and torn, he presented
a very wild and terrible appearance; and beneath one
arm he carried two bludgeons. The Peddler had
spoken truly, then, and, as I met the giant's smouldering eye, I felt my mouth become suddenly parched
and dry, and the palms of my hands grew moist and
clammy.

For a moment neither of us spoke, only we looked at
each other steadily in the eye; and I saw the hair of
his beard bristle, and he raised one great hand to
the collar of his shirt, and tore it open as if it were
strangling him.

" George!" said I at last, and held out my hand.

George never stirred.

" Won't you shake hands, George?"

His lips opened, but no words came.

" Had I known where to look for you, I should have
sought you out days ago," I went on; " as it is I have
been wishing to meet you, hoping to set matters right."

Once again his lips opened, but still no word came.

" You see, Prudence is breaking her heart over you."

A laugh burst from him, sudden, and harsh.

" You'm a liar!" said he, and his voice quavered
strangely.

" I speak gospel truth ! " said I.

" I be nowt to Prue since the day you beat me at th'
'ammer-throwin'—an' ye know it."

" Prudence loves you, and always has ? " said I.
" Go back to her, George, go back to her, and to your
work—be the man I know you are, go back to her—
she loves you. If you still doubt my word—here, read
that ! " and I held out his own letter, the letter on
which Prudence had written those four words :
" George, I love you."

He took it from me—crumpled it slowly in his hand
and tossed it into the ditch.

" You'm a liar ! " said he again, " an' a—coward ! "

" And you," said I, " you are a fool, a blind, gross,
selfish fool, who, in degrading yourself—in skulking
about the woods and lanes—is bringing black shame
and sorrow to as sweet a maid as ever——"

" It don't need you to tell me what she be an' what
she bean't," said Black George in a low, repressed
voice. " I knowed 'er long afore you ever set eyes on
'er—grew up wi' 'er, I did, an' I bean't deaf nor
blind. Ye see, I loved 'er—all my life—that's why
one o' us two's a-goin' to lie out' ere all night—ah ! an'
all to-morrow, likewise, if summ'un don't chance to
find us," saying which, he forced a cudgel into my hand.

" What do you mean, George ? "

" I means as if you don't do for me, then I be
a-goin' to do for 'ee."

" But why ? " I cried ; " in God's name—why ? "

" I be slow, p'r'aps, an' thick p'r'aps, but I bean't
a fule—come, man—if she be worth winnin' she be
worth fightin' for."

" But I tell you she loves Black George, and no
other—she never had any thought of me, or I of her—
this is madness—and worse ! " and I tossed the cudgel
aside.

" An' I tell 'ee," broke in the smith, his repression
giving way before a fury as fierce as it was sudden,
" I tell 'ee—you be a liar, an' a coward—I know, I
know—I've heerd, an' I've seen—your lyin', coward's
tongue sha'n't save 'ee—oh, ecod ! wi' your white face

an' tremblin' 'ands—you be a shame to the woman as loves ye an' the woman as bore ye!—stand up, I say, or by God! I'll do for 'ee!" and he raised his weapon.

Without another word I picked up the cudgel, and pointing to a gate a little farther along the road, I led the way into the meadow beyond. On the other side of this meadow ran the lane I have mentioned before, and beyond the lane was the Hollow, and glancing thitherward, I bethought me that supper would be ready, and Charmian waiting for me, just about now, and I sighed, I remember, as I drew off my coat, and laid it, together with my hat, under the hedge.

The moon was beginning to rise, casting the magic of her pale loveliness upon the world, and, as I rolled up my sleeves, I glanced round about me with an eye that strove to take in the beauty of all things—of hedge, and tree, and winding road, the gloom of wood, the sheen of water, and the far, soft sweep of hill and dale. Over all these my glance lingered yearningly, for it seemed to me that this look might be my last. And now, as I stooped, and gripped my weapon, I remembered how I had, that morning, kissed her fingers, and I was strangely comforted and glad.

The night air, which had been warm heretofore, struck chilly now, and, as I stood up fronting Black George, I shivered, seeing which he laughed, short and fierce, and, with the laugh, came at me, striking downwards at my head as he came, and tough wood met tough wood with a shock that jarred me from wrist to shoulder.

To hit him upon the arm, and disable him, was my one thought and object. I therefore watched for an opening, parrying his swift strokes and avoiding his rushes as well as I might. Time and again our weapons crashed together, now above my head, now to right, or left, sometimes rattling in quick succession, sometimes with pauses between strokes, pauses filled in with the sound of heavy breathing and the ceaseless thud of feet upon the sward. I was already bruised in half-a-dozen places, my right hand and arm felt numb, and with a shooting pain in the shoulder, that grew more acute with every movement; my breath also was

beginning to labour. Yet still Black George pressed
on, untiring, relentless, showering blow on blow,
while my arm grew ever weaker and weaker, and the
pain in my shoulder throbbed more intensely.

How long had we fought? five minutes—ten—half-
an-hour—an hour? I could see the sweat gleaming
upon his cheek, his eyes were wild, his mouth gaped
open, and he drew his breath in great sobbing pants.
But, as I looked, his cudgel broke through my tired
guard, and, taking me full upon the brow, drove me
reeling back; my weapon slipped from my grasp, and,
blinded with blood, I staggered to and fro, like a
drunken man, and presently slipped to the grass. And
how sweet it was to lie thus, with my cheek upon kind
mother earth, to stretch my aching body, and with my
weary limbs at rest. But Black George stood above
me, panting, and, as his eyes met mine, he laughed—
a strange-sounding, broken laugh, and whirled up his
cudgel—to beat out my brains—even as the Peddler
had foretold—to-morrow the blackbird would sing
upon my motionless breast, and, looking into Black
George's eyes—I smiled.

"Get up!" he panted, and, lowered the cudgel.
"Get up—or, by God—I'll do—for 'ee!"

Sighing, I rose, and took the cudgel he held out to
me, wiping the blood from my eyes as I did so.

And now, as I faced him once more all things vanished from my ken save the man before me—he filled
the universe, and, even as he leaped upon me, I leaped
upon him, and struck with all my strength; there was
a jarring, splintering shock, and Black George was
beaten down upon his knees, but as, dropping my
weapon, I stepped forward, he rose, and stood panting, and staring at the broken cudgel in his hand.

"George!" said I.

"You'm a-bleedin', Peter!"

"For that matter, so are you."

"Blood-lettin' be—good for a man—sometimes—it
eases un."

"It does," I panted; "perhaps you are—willing to
—hear reason—now?"

"We be—even so fur—but fists be better nor—sticks any day—an' I—be goin'—to try ye—wi' fists!"

"Have we not bled each other sufficiently?"

"No," cried George, between set teeth, "theer be more nor blood-lettin' 'twixt you an' me—I said as 'ow one on us would lie out 'ere all night—an' so 'e shall—by God!—come on—fists be best arter all!"

This was the heyday of boxing, and, while at Oxford, I had earned some small fame at the sport. But it was one thing to spar with a man my own weight in a padded ring, with limited rounds governed by a code of rules, and quite another to fight a man like Black George, in a lonely meadow, by light of moon. Moreover, he was well acquainted with the science, as I could see from the way he "shaped," the only difference between us being that whereas he fought with feet planted square, and wide apart, I balanced myself upon my toes, which is (I think) to be commended as being quicker, and more calculated to lessen the impact of a blow.

Brief though the respite had been it had served me to recover my breath, and, though my head yet rung from the cudgel-stroke, and the blood still flowed freely, getting, every now and then, into my eyes, my brain was clear as we fronted each other for what we both knew must be the decisive bout.

The smith stood with his mighty shoulders stooped something forward, his left arm drawn back, his right flung across his chest, and, so long as we fought, I watched that great fist and knotted forearm, for, though he struck oftener with his left, it was in that passive right that I thought my danger really lay.

It is not my intention to chronicle this fight blow by blow, enough, and more than enough, has already been said in that regard; suffice it then, that as the fight progressed I found that I was far the quicker, as I had hoped, and that the majority of his blows I either blocked or avoided easily enough.

Time after time his fist shot over my shoulder, or over my head, and time after time I countered heavily —now on his body, now on his face; once he stag-

gered, and once I caught a momentary glimpse of his features convulsed with pain; he was smeared with blood from the waist up, but still he came on.

I fought desperately now, savagely, taking advantage of every opening, for though I struck him four times to his once yet his blows had four times the weight of mine; my forearms were bruised to either elbow, and my breath came in gasps; and always I watched that deadly " right." And presently it came, with arm and shoulder and body behind it—quick as a flash, and resistless as a cannon-ball; but I was ready, and, as I leaped, I struck, and struck him clean and true upon the angle of the jaw; and, spinning round, Black George fell, and lay with his arms wide stretched, and face buried in the grass.

Slowly, slowly he got upon his knees, and thence to his feet, and so stood panting, hideous with blood and sweat, bruised, and cut, and disfigured, staring at me, as one in amaze.

Now, as I looked, my heart went out to him, and I reached forth my right hand.

" George ! " I panted. " Oh, George ! "

But Black George only looked at me, and shook his head, and groaned.

" Oh, Peter ! " said he, " you be a man, Peter ! I've fou't—ah ! many's the time, an' no man ever knocked me down afore. Oh, Peter ! I—I could love 'ee for it —if I didn't hate the very sight of 'ee—come on, an' let's get it over an' done wi'."

So once again fists were clenched and jaws set— once again came the trampling of feet, the hiss of breath, and the thudding shock of blows given and taken.

A sudden, jarring impact—the taste of sulphur on my tongue—a gathering darkness before my eyes, and, knowing this was the end, I strove desperately to close with him; but I was dazed, blind—my arms fell paralysed, and, in that moment, the Smith's right fist drove forward. A jagged flame shot up to heaven— the earth seemed to rush up towards me—a roaring blackness engulfed me, and then—silence.

CHAPTER XX

HOW I CAME UP OUT OF THE DARK

SOMEONE was calling to me, a long way off.

Someone was leaning down from a great height to call to me in the depths; and the voice was wonderfully sweet, but faint, faint, because the height was so very high, and the depths so very great.

And still the voice called, and called, and I felt sorry for that I could not answer, because, as I say, the voice was troubled, and wonderfully sweet.

And, little by little, it seemed that it grew nearer, this voice, was it descending to me in these depths of blackness, or was I being lifted up to the heights where, I knew, blackness could not be? Ay, indeed, I was being lifted, for I could feel a hand upon my brow—a smooth, cool hand that touched my cheek, and brushed the hair from my forehead; a strong, gentle hand it was, with soft fingers, and it was lifting me up and up from the loathly depths which seemed more black and more horrible the farther I drew from them.

And so I heard the voice nearer, and ever nearer, until I could distinguish words, and the voice had tears in it, and the words were very tender.

" Peter—speak !—speak to me, Peter ! "

" Charmian ? " said I, within myself; " why, truly, whose hand but hers could have lifted me out of that gulf of death, back to light and life ? " Yet I did not speak aloud, for I had no mind to, yet a while.

" Ah ! speak to me—speak to me, Peter ! How can you lie there so still and pale ? "

And now her arms were about me, strong, and protecting, and my head was drawn down upon her bosom.

" Oh, Peter !—my Peter ! "

Nay, but was this Charmian, the cold, proud

336

Charmian. Truly I had never heard that thrill in her voice before—could this indeed be Charmian? And lying thus, with my head on this sweet pillow, I could hear her heart whispering to me, and it seemed that it was striving to tell me something—striving, striving to tell me something, could I but understand—ah! could I but understand!

"I waited for you so long—so long, Peter—and—the supper is all spoiled—a rabbit, Peter—you liked rabbit, and—and oh, God! I want you—don't you hear me, Peter—I want you—want you!" and now her cheek was pressed to mine, and her lips were upon my hair, and upon my brow—her lips! Was this indeed Charmian, and was I Peter Vibart? Ah, if I could but know what it was her heart was trying to tell me, so quick and passionately!

And while I lay listening, listening, something hot splashed down upon my cheek, and then another, and another; her bosom heaved tumultuously, and instinctively, raising my arms, I clasped them about her.

"Don't!" I said, and my voice was a whisper; "don't, Charmian!"

For a moment her clasp tightened about me, she was all tenderness and clinging warmth, then I heard a sudden gasp, her arms loosened and fell away, and so I presently raised my head, and, supporting myself upon my hand, looked at her. And then I saw that her cheeks were burning.

"Peter."

"Yes, Charmian?"

"Did you——" She paused, plucking nervously at the grass, and looking away from me.

"Well, Charmian?"

"Did you—hear——" Again she broke off, and still her head was averted.

"I heard your voice calling to me from a great way off, and so—I came, Charmian."

"Were you conscious when—when I—found you?"

"No," I answered; "I was lying in a very deep, black pit." Here she looked at me again.

"I—I thought you—were—dead, Peter."

Y

" My soul was out of my body—until you recalled it."

" You were lying upon your back, by the hedge here, and—oh, Peter! your face was white and shining in the moonlight—and there was—blood upon it, and you looked like one that is—dead! " and she shivered.

" And you have brought me back to life," said I, rising; but, being upon my feet, I staggered giddily, to hide which, I laughed, and leaned against a tree. " Indeed," said I, " I am very much alive still, and monstrously hungry—you spoke of a rabbit, I think——"

" A rabbit! " said Charmian in a whisper, and as I met her eye I would have given much to have recalled that thoughtless speech.

" I—I think you did mention a rabbit," said I, floundering deeper.

" So then—you deceived me, you lay there and deceived me--with your eyes shut, and your ears open, taking advantage of my pity——"

" No, no—indeed, no—I thought myself still dreaming; it—it all seemed so unreal, so——so beyond all belief and possibility and——" I stopped, aghast at my crass folly, for, with a cry, she sprang to her feet, and hid her face in her hands, while I stood dumbfounded, like the fool I was. When she looked up, her eyes seemed to scorch me.

" And I thought Mr Vibart a man of honour—like a knight of his old-time romances, high and chivalrous —oh! I thought him a—gentleman! "

" Instead of which," said I, speaking (as it were), despite myself, " instead of which, you find me only a blacksmith—a low, despicable fellow eager to take advantage of your unprotected womanhood." She did not speak, standing tall and straight, her head thrown back; wherefore, reading her scorn of me in her eyes, seeing the proud contempt of her mouth, a very demon seemed suddenly to possess me, for certainly the laugh that rang from my lips proceeded from no volition of mine.

" And yet, madam," my voice went on, " this

despicable blacksmith fellow refused one hundred guineas for you to-day.''

"Peter!" she cried, and shrank away from me as if I had threatened to strike her.

"Ah!—you start at that—your proud lip trembles —do not fear, madam—the sum did not tempt him— though a large one.''

"Peter!" she cried again, and now there was a note of appeal in her voice.

"Indeed, madam, even so degraded a fellow as this blacksmith could not very well sell that which he does not possess—could he? And so the hundred guineas go a-begging, and you are still—unsold!" Long before I had done she had covered her face again, and, coming near, I saw the tears running out between her fingers and sparkling as they fell. And once again the devil within me laughed loud and harsh. But, while it still echoed, I had flung myself down at her feet.

"Charmian," I cried, "forgive me—you will, you must!" and, kneeling before her, I strove to catch her gown, and kiss its hem, but she drew it close about her, and, turning, fled from me through the shadows.

Heedless of all else but that she was leaving me, I stumbled to my feet and followed. The trees seemed to beset me as I ran, and bushes to reach out arms to stay me, but I burst from them, running wildly, blunderingly, for she was going—Charmian was leaving me. And so, spent and panting, I reached the cottage, and met Charmian at the door. She was clad in the long cloak she had worn when she came, and the hood was drawn close about her face.

I stood panting in the doorway, barring her exit.

"Let me pass, Peter.''

"By God—no!" I cried, and, entering, closed the door, and leaned my back against it.

And, after we had stood thus awhile, each looking upon the other, I reached out my hands to her, and my hands were torn and bloody.

"Don't go, Charmian." I mumbled, "don't go!

Oh, Charmian—I'm hurt—I didn't want you to know, but you mustn't leave me—I am not—well, it is my head, I think. I met Black George, and he was too strong for me. I'm deaf, Charmian, and half blinded —oh, don't leave me—I'm afraid, Charmian!" Her figure grew more blurred and indistinct, and I sank down upon my knees; but in the dimness I reached out and found her hands, and clasped them, and bowed my aching head upon them, and remained thus a great while, as it seemed to me.

And presently, through the mist, her voice reached me.

"Oh, Peter! I will not leave you—lean on me— there—there!" And, little by little, those strong, gentle hands drew me up once more to light and life. And so she got me to a chair, and brought cool water, and washed the blood and sweat from me, as she had once before, only now my hurts were deeper, for my head grew beyond my strength to support, and hung upon my breast, and my brain throbbed with fire, and the mist was ever before my eyes.

"Are you in much pain, Peter?"

"My head—only my head, Charmian—there is a bell ringing there, no—it is a hammer, beating." And indeed I remembered little for a while, save the touch of her hands and the soothing murmur of her voice, until I found she was kneeling beside me, feeding me with broth from a spoon. Wherefore I presently took the basin from her and emptied it at a gulp, and, finding myself greatly revived thereby, made some shift to eat of the supper she set before me.

So she presently came and sat beside me and ate also, watching me at each morsel.

"Your poor hands!" said she, and, looking down at them, I saw that my knuckles were torn and broken, and the fingers much swelled. "And yet," said Charmian, "except for the cut in your head, you are quite unmarked, Peter."

"He fought mostly for the body," I answered, "and I managed to keep my face out of the way; but he caught me twice—once upon the chin, lightly, and

once up behind the ear, heavily; had his fist landed
fairly I don't think even you could have brought me
back from those loathly depths, Charmian."

And in a while, supper being done, she brought my
pipe, and filled it, and held the light for me. But my
head throbbed woefully and for once the tobacco was
flavourless; so I sighed, and laid the pipe by.

"Why, Peter!" said Charmian, regarding me with
an anxious frown, "can't you smoke?"

"Not just now, Charmian," said I, and leaning my
head in my hands, fell into a sort of coma, till, feeling
her touch upon my shoulder, I started, and looked up.

"You must go to bed, Peter."

"No," said I.

"Yes, Peter."

"Very well, Charmian, yes—I will go to bed," and
I rose.

"Do you feel better now, Peter?"

"Thank you, yes—much better."

"Then why do you hold on to the chair?"

"I am still a little giddy—but it will pass." And—
Charmian—you forgive——"

"Yes—yes, don't—don't look at me like that, Peter
—and—oh, good-night!—foolish boy!"

"I am—twenty-five, Charmian!" But as she
turned away I saw that there were tears in her eyes.

Dressed as I was, I lay down upon my bed, and,
burying my head in the pillow, groaned, for my pain
was very sore; indeed I was to feel the effects of
George's fist for many a day to come, and it seems
to me now that much of the morbid imaginings, the
nightly horrors, and black despair, that I endured in
the time which immediately followed, was chiefly
owing to that terrible blow upon the head.

CHAPTER XXI

OF THE OPENING OF THE DOOR, AND HOW CHARMIAN BLEW OUT THE LIGHT

HE bestrode a powerful black charger, and his armour glittered through the green. And, as he rode beneath the leafy arches of the wood, he lifted up his voice, and sang, and the song was mournful, and of a plaintive seeming, and rang loud behind his visor-bars; therefore, as I sat beside the freshet, I hearkened to his song:

> " For her love I carke, and care,
> For her love I droop, and dare,
> For her love my bliss is bare
> And I wax wan!"

Forth he rode from the shadowy woodland, pacing very solemn and slow; and thrice he struck his iron hand upon his iron breast.

> " For her love in sleep I slake,
> For her love all night I wake,
> For her love I mourning make,
> More than any man!"

Now, being come to where I sat beside the brook, he checked his horse, and gazed full long upon me, and his eyes shone from the gloom of his helmet.

" Messire," quoth he, " how like you my song?"

" But little, sir—to be plain with you, not a whit," I answered.

" And, beseech you—wherefore?"

" Because it is folly—away with it, for, if your head be full of such, how shall you achieve any lasting good—Glory, Learning, Power?" But, sighing, he shook his head; quoth he:

" O Blind One!—Glory is but a name, Learning but a yearning emptiness, and whither leadeth

342

Ambition? Man is a mote dancing in a sun-ray—the the world, a speck hanging in space. All things vanish and pass utterly away save only True-love, and that abideth everlastingly; 'tis sweeter than Life, and stronger than Death, and reacheth up beyond the stars; and thus it is I pray you tell me—where is she?"

"She?"

"She whom ye love?"

"I love no woman," said I.

"Liar!" cried he, in a terrible voice, and the voice was the voice of Black George.

"And who are you that says so?" I demanded, and stood upon my feet.

"Look—behold and know thyself, O Blind and more than blind!" And, leaning down, he raised his visor so that the moonlight fell upon his face, and the face I looked upon was—my own, and, while I gazed, he lifted up his voice, and cried:

"Ye Spirits of the Wood, I charge ye—who is he that rideth in the green, dreaming ever of her beauty, and sighing forth his love everlastingly, Spirits of the Wood, I charge ye?"

And out of the gloom of the wood, from every rustling leaf, and opening bud, came a little voice that rose and blended in a soft, hushed chorus, crying:

"Peter Vibart!—Peter Vibart!"

"Spirits of the Wood, I charge ye—who is he that walketh to and fro in the world, and having eyes, seeth not, and ears, heareth not—a very Fool of Love?"

Once again the voices cried in answer:

"Peter Vibart!—Peter Vibart!"

"Spirits of the Wood, I charge ye—who is he that shall love with a love mightier than most—who shall suffer greatly for love and because of it—who shall think of it by day, and dream of it o' nights—who is he that must die to find love and the fulness of life?— O Spirits of the Wood, I charge ye!"

And again from out the green came the soft, hushed chorus:

" Peter Vibart !—Peter Vibart ! "

But, even as I laughed, came one from the wood, with a horse and armour. And the armour he girded on me, and the horse I mounted. And there, in the moonlit glade, we fought, and strove together, my Other Self and I. And, sudden and strong he smote me, so that I fell down from my horse, and lay there dead, with my blood soaking, and soaking into the grass. And, as I watched, there came a blackbird that perched upon my breast, carolling gloriously. Yet, little by little, this bird changed, and lo ! in its place was a new Peter Vibart standing upon the old; and the New trampled the Old down into the grass, and— it was gone. Then, with his eyes on the stars, the new Peter Vibart fell a-singing, and the words I sang were these :

> " For her love I carke, and care,
> For her love I droop, and dare,
> For her love my bliss is bare
> And I wax wan ! "

And thus there came into my heart that which had been all unknown—undreamed of hitherto, yet which, once there, could never pass away.

" O Spirits of the Wood, I charge ye—who is he that counteth True-love sweeter than Life—greater than Wisdom—stronger than Death? O Spirits of the Wood, I charge ye ! "

And the hushed voices chorused softly.

" Peter Vibart !—Peter Vibart ! " And, while I listened, one by one the voices ceased, till there but one remained—calling, calling, but ever soft, and far away, and when I would have gone toward this voice —lo ! there stood a knife quivering in the ground before me, that grew and grew until its haft touched heaven, yet still the voice called upon my name very softly :

" Peter !—Peter !—oh, Peter, I want you !—oh, Peter !—wake ! wake ! " I sat up in bed, and, as I listened, grew suddenly sick, and a fit of trembling shook me violently, for the whisper was still in my ears, and in the whisper was an agony of fear and dread indescribable.

" Peter !—oh, Peter, I am afraid !—wake ! wake ! "

A cold sweat broke out upon me and I glared helplessly towards the door.

" Quick, Peter !—come to me—oh, God ! "

I strove to move, but still I could not. And now, in the darkness, hands were shaking me wildly, and Charmian's voice was speaking in my ear.

" The door ! " it whispered, " the door ! "

Then I arose, and was in the outer room, with Charmian close beside me in the dark, and my eyes were upon the door. And then I beheld a strange thing, for a thin line of white light traversed the floor from end to end. Now, as I watched this narrow line, I saw that it was gradually widening and widening; very slowly, and with infinite caution, the door was being opened from without. In this remote place, in this still, dead hour of the night, full of the ghostly hush that ever precedes the dawn—there was something devilish—something very like murder in its stealthy motion. I heard Charmian's breath catch, and, in the dark, her hand came and crept into mine and her fingers were cold as death.

And now a great anger came upon me, and I took a quick step forward, but Charmian restrained me.

" No, Peter ! " she breathed; " not yet—wait ! " and wound her arms round mine.

In a corner near by stood that same trusty staff that had been the companion of my wanderings, and now I reached, and took it up, balancing it in my hand. And all the time I watched that line of light upon the floor widening, and widening, growing ever broader and more broad. The minutes dragged slowly by, while the line grew into a streak, and the streak into a lane, and upon the lane came a blot that slowly resolved itself into the shadow of a hand upon the latch. Slowly, slowly, to the hand came a wrist, and to the wrist an arm—another minute, and this maddening suspense would be over. Despite Charmian's restraining clasp I crept a long pace nearer the softly moving door.

The sharp angle of the elbow was growing obtuse as the shadowy arm straightened itself. Thirty seconds more! I began to count, and, gripping my staff braced myself for what might be, when—with a sudden cry, Charmian sprang forward, and, hurling herself against the door, shut it with a crash.

"Quick, Peter!" she panted. I was beside her almost as she spoke, and had my hand upon the latch.

"I must see who this was," said I.

"You are mad!" she cried.

"Let me open the door, Charmian."

"No, no—I say no!"

"Whoever it was must not escape—open the door!"

"Never! never—I tell you—death is outside—there's murder in the very air, I feel it—and—dear God—the door has no bolt."

"They are gone now—who ever they were," said I reassuringly; "the danger is over—if danger it could be called."

"Danger!" cried Charmian. "I tell you—it was death."

"Yet, after all, it may have been only some homeless wanderer."

"Then why that deadly, silent caution?"

"True!" said I, becoming thoughtful.

"Bring the table, Peter, and set it across the door."

"Surely the table is too light to——"

"But it will give sufficient warning—not that I shall sleep again to-night. Oh, Peter! had I not been dreaming, and happened to wake—had I not chanced to look towards the door, it would have opened—wide, and then—oh, horrible!"

"You were dreaming?"

"A hateful, hateful dream, and awoke in terror, and, being afraid, glanced towards the door, and saw it opening—and now—bring the table, Peter."

Now, groping about, my hand encountered one of the candles, and taking out my tinder-box, all unthinking, I lighted it.

Charmian was leaning against the door, clad in a flowing white garment—a garment that was wonderfully stitched—all dainty frills and laces, with here and there a bow of blue riband, disposed, it would seem, by the hand of chance, and yet most wonderfully. And up from this foam of laces her shoulders rose, white, and soft, and dimpled, sweeping up in noble lines to the smooth round column of her throat. But as I stared at all this loveliness she gave a sudden gasp, and stooped her head, and crossed her hands upon her bosom, while up over the snow of shoulder, over neck, and cheek, and brow, ebbed that warm crimson tide; and I could only gaze and gaze—till, with a movement swift and light, she crossed to that betraying candle and, stooping, blew out the light.

Then I set the table across the door, having done which I stood looking towards where she yet stood.

" Charmian," said I.

" Yes, Peter."

" To-morrow——"

" Yes, Peter ? "

" I will make a bar to hold the door."

" Yes, Peter."

" Two bars would be better, perhaps ? "

" Yes, Peter."

" You would feel safe, then—safer than ever ? "

" Safer than ever, Peter."

CHAPTER XXII

IN WHICH THE ANCIENT DISCOURES ON LOVE

I AM forging a bar for my cottage door : such a bar as might give check to an army, or resist a battering-ram; a bar that shall defy all the night-prowlers that ever prowled; a stout, solid bar, broad as my wrist, and thick as my two fingers; that, looking upon it as it lies in its sockets across the door, Charmian henceforth may sleep and have no fear.

The Ancient sat perched on his stool in the corner, but for once we spoke little, for I was very busy, also my mind was plunged in a profound reverie.

And of whom should I be thinking but of Charmian, and of the dimple in her shoulder?

"'Tis bewitched you be, Peter!" said the old man suddenly, prodding me softly with his stick, "bewitched as ever was," and he chuckled.

"Bewitched!" said I, starting.

"Ah!—theer you stand wi' your 'ammer in your 'and—a-starin' an' a-starin' at nobody, nor nothin'—leastways not as 'uman eye can see, an' a-sighin', an' a-sighin'——"

"Did I indeed sigh, Ancient?"

"Ah—that ye did—like a cow, Peter, or a 'orse—'eavy an' tired like. An' slow you be, an' dreamy—you as was so bright an' spry; theer's some—fools, like Joel Amos, as might think as 'twere the work o' ghostes, or demons, a-castin' their spells on ye, or that some vampire 'ad bit ye in the night, an' sucked your blood as ye lay asleep, but I know different—you'm just bewitched, Peter!" and he chuckled again.

"Who knows?—perhaps I am, but it will pass, whatever it is, it will pass——"

"Don't ye be too sure o' that—theer's bewitchments and bewitchments, Peter."

348

Hereupon the smithy became full of the merry din
of my hammer, and while I worked the Ancient
smoked his pipe and watched me, informing me
between whiles that the Jersey cow was "in calf," that
the hops seemed more than usually forward, and that
he had waked that morning with a " touch o' the
rheumatics "; but, otherwise, he was unusually silent,
moreover each time that I happened to glance up it
was to find him regarding me with a certain fixity of
eye, which at another time would have struck me as
portentous.

" Ye be palish this marnin', Peter ! " said he, dab-
bing at me suddenly with his pipe-stem; " shouldn't
wonder if you was to tell me as your appetite was
bad—come now—ye didn't eat much of a breakfus'
this marnin', did ye ? "

" I don't think I did, Ancient."

" A course not ! " said the old man with a nod of
profound approval—" it aren't to be expected. Let's
see, it be all o' four months since I found ye, bean't
it ? "

" Four months and a few odd days," I nodded, and
fell to work upon my glowing iron bar.

" Ye'll make a tidy smith one o' these days, Peter,"
said the old man encouragingly as I straightened my
back and plunged the iron back into the fire.

" Thank you, Ancient."

" Ay—you've learned to use a 'ammer purty well,
considerin', though you be wastin' your opportoonities
shameful, Peter, shameful."

" Am I, Ancient ? "

" Ay, that ye be—moon can't last much longer—
she be on the wane a'ready ! "

" Moon ? " said I, staring.

" Ah, moon ! " nodded the old man; " theer's nowt
like a moon, Peter, an' if she be at the full so much
the better."

" But what have the moon and I to do with each
other, Ancient ? "

" Old I be, Peter, a old, old man, but I were young
once, an' I tell 'ee the moon 'as a lot more to do wi' it

than some folks think—why, lord love 'ee! theer wouldn't be near so many children a-playin' in the sun if it wasn't for the moon!".

"Ancient," said I, "what might you be driving at?"

"Love, Peter!"

"Love!" said I, letting go the handle of the bellows.

"An' marriage, Peter."

"What in the world—put—such thoughts into your head?"

"You did, Peter."

"I?"

"Ah!—some men is born lovers, Peter, an' you be one. I never see such eyes as yourn afore, so burnin' 'ot they be. Ah, Peter! some maid will see the love-light aflame in 'em some day, an' droop 'er 'ead an' blush an' tremble—for she'll know, Peter, she'll know —maids was made to be loved, Peter——"

"But, Ancient, I am not the kind of man women would be attracted by, I love books, and solitude, and am called a—pedant! and besides, I am not of a loving sort——"

"Some men, Peter, falls in love as easy as they falls out, it comes to some, soft an' quiet—like the dawn of a summer's day, Peter, but to others it comes like a gert an' tur'ble storm—oh, that it do! Theer's a fire ready to burn up inside o' ye at the touch o' some woman's 'and, or the peep o' 'er eye—ah! a fire as'll burn, an' burn, an' never go out again—not even if you should live to be as old as I be—an' you'll be strong an' wild, an' fierce wi' it—an' some day you'll find 'er, Peter, an' she'll find you—"

"And," said I, staring away into the distance, "do you think that, by any possible chance, she might love me, this woman?"

"Ay, for sure," said the Ancient, "for sure she will; why don't 'ee up an ax 'er? Wi' a fine, round moon over'ead, an' a pretty maid at your elber, it's easy enough to tell 'er you love 'er, aren't it?"

"Indeed yes," said I, beginning to rub my chin "very easy!" and I sighed.

"An' when you looks into a pair o' sweet eyes, an

sees the shine o' the moon in' em—why, it aren't so very fur to 'er lips, are it, Peter?"

"No," said I, rubbing my chin harder than ever; "no—and there's the danger of it."

"Wheer's t' danger, Peter?"

"Everywhere!" I answered; "in her eyes, in her thick, soft hair, the warmth of her breath, the touch of her hand, the least contact of her garments—her very step!"

"I knowed it!" cried the Ancient joyfully, peering at me under his brows; "I knowed it!"

"Knew what?"

"You be in love—good lad! good lad!" and he flourished his pipe in the air.

"In love!" I exclaimed; "in love—I?"

"Sure as sure!"

"But love, according to Aristotle, is——"

"Love, Peter, is what makes a man forget 'is breakfus', an' 'is work, an' 'is——"

"But I work very hard—besides——"

"Love is what makes a man so brave as a lion, Peter, an' fall a-tremblin' like a coward when She stands a-lookin' up at 'im; love makes the green earth greener, an' the long road short—ah! almost too short, sometimes, the love of a woman comes betwixt a man an' all evils an' dangers—why don't 'ee up an ax 'er, Peter?"

"She'd laugh at me, Ancient."

"Not she."

"That soft, low laugh of hers."

"Well, what o' that?"

"Besides, she hardly knows me!"

The Ancient took out his snuff-box and gave two loud double knocks upon the lid.

"A woman knows a man sooner than a man knows a woman—ah, a sight sooner! Why, Lord bless ye, Peter, she 'as 'im all reckoned up long afore 'e knows for sure if 'er eyes be black 'uns or brown 'uns—that she 'as." Here he extracted a pinch of snuff. "As for Prudence—she loves 'ee wi' all 'er 'eart an' soul!"

"Prudence?" said I, staring.

"Ah! Prudence—I be 'er grandfeyther, an' I know."

"Prudence!" said I again.

"She'm a 'andsome lass, an' so pretty as a picter—you said so yourself, an' what's more, she'm a sensible lass, an' 'll make ye as fine a wife as ever was if only——"

"If she only loved me, Ancient."

"To be sure, Peter."

"But, you see, she doesn't."

"Eh—what? What, Peter?"

"Prudence doesn't love me!"

"Doesn't——"

"Not by any means."

"Peter—ye're jokin'."

"No, Ancient."

"But I—I be all took aback—mazed I be—not love ye, an' me wi' my 'eart set on it—are ye sure?"

"Certain."

"Ow d'ye know?"

"She told me so."

"But—why—why shouldn't she love ye?"

"Why should she?"

"But I—I'd set my 'eart on it, Peter."

"It is very unfortunate!" said I, and began blowing up the fire.

"Peter."

"Yes, Ancient?"

"Do 'ee love she?"

"No, Ancient." The old man rose, and, hobbling forward, tapped me upon the breast with the handle of his stick.

"Then who was you a-talkin' of, a while back—'bout 'er eyes, an' 'er 'air, an' 'er dress, an' bein' afraid o' them?"

"To be exact, I don't know, Ancient."

"Oh, Peter!" exclaimed the old man, shaking his head, "I wonders at ye; arter me a-thinkin' and a-thinkin', an' a-plannin' an' a-plannin' all these months—arter me a-sendin' Black Jarge about 'is business——"

" Ancient, what do you mean ? "

" Why, didn't I out an' tell un as you was sweet on Prue——"

" Did you tell him that ? " I cried.

" Aye to be sure I did; an' what's more, I says to 'un often an' often, when you wasn't by : ' Jarge,' I'd say, ' Prue's a lovely maid, an' Peter's a fine young chap, an' they'm beginnin' to find each other out, they be all'us a-talkin' to each other an' a-lookin' at each other, mornin', noon an' night ! ' I says, ' like as not we'll 'ave 'em marryin' each other afore very long ! ' an' Jarge 'ud just wrinkle up 'is brows, an' walk away, an' never say a word. But now—it be tur'ble 'ard to be disapp'inted like this, Peter—arter I'd set my 'eart on it—an' me such a old man—such a very ancient man. Oh, Peter ! you be full o' disapp'intments, an' all manner o' contrairiness ; sometimes I a'most wishes as I'd never took the trouble to find ye at all ! "

And, with this Parthian shot, the old man sighed, and turned his back upon me, and tottered out of the forge.

z

CHAPTER XXIII

HOW GABBING DICK, THE PEDDLER, SET A HAMMER GOING IN MY HEAD

HAVING finished my bars, with four strong brackets to hold them, I put away my tools, and donned hat and coat.

It was yet early, and there was, besides, much work waiting to be done, but I felt unwontedly tired and out of sorts, wherefore, with my bars and brackets beneath my arm, I set out for the Hollow.

From the hedges, on either side of me, came the sweet perfume of the honeysuckle, and beyond the hedges the fields stood high with ripening corn—a yellow, heavy-headed host nodding and swaying lazily, and I stood awhile to listen to its whisper as the gentle wind swept over it, and to look down the long green alleys of the hop-gardens beyond; and at the end of one of these straight arched vistas there shone a solitary, great star.

And presently, lifting my eyes to the sky, already deepening to evening, and remembering how I had looked round me ere I faced Black George, I breathed a sigh of thankfulness that I was yet alive with strength to walk within a world so beautiful.

Now, as I stood thus, I heard a voice hailing me, and, glancing about, espied one, some distance up the road, who sat beneath the hedge, whom, upon approaching, I recognised as Gabbing Dick, the Peddler.

He nodded, and grinned as I came up, but in both there was a vague unpleasantness, as also in the manner in which he eyed me slowly up and down.

"You've stood a-lookin' up into the sky for a good ten minutes!" said he.

"And what if I have?"

354

"Nothin'," said the Peddler, "nothin' at all—though if the moon 'ad been up, a cove might ha' thought as you was dreamin' of some Eve or other; love-sick folk always stares at the moon—leastways, so they tell me. Anyone as stares at the moon when 'e might be doin' summat better is a fool, as great a fool as any man as stares at a Eve, for a Eve never brought any man nothin' but trouble and sorrer, and never will, no'ow? Don't frown, young cove, nor shake your 'ead, for it's true; wot's caused more sorrer an' blood than them Eves? Blood?—ah! rivers of it! Oceans of good blood's been spilt all along o' women, from the Eve as tricked old Adam to the Eve as tricks the like o' me, or say—yourself." Here he regarded me with so evil a leer that I turned my back in disgust.

"Don't go, young cove, I ain't done yet, and I got summ'at to tell ye."

"Then tell it!" said I, stopping again, struck by the fellow's manner, "and tell it quickly."

"I'm a-comin' to it as fast as I can, ain't I?—very well then! You're a fine, up-standin' young cove, and may 'ave white 'ands (which I don't see myself, but no matter) and may likewise be chock-full o' taking ways (which, though not noticin', I won't go for to deny)—but a Eve's a Eve, and always will be—you'll mind as I warned you agin 'em last time I see ye?—very well then!"

"Well?" said I impatiently.

"Well," nodded the Peddler, and his eyes twinkled malevolently. "I says it again—I warns you again. You're a nice, civil-spoke young cove, and quiet, (though I *don't* like the cock o' your eye), and, mind, I don't bear you no ill-will—though you did turn me from your door on a cold, dark night——"

"It was neither a cold nor a dark night!" said I.

"Well, it might ha' been, mightn't it?—very well then! Still, I don't," said the Peddler, spitting dejectedly into the ditch, "I don't bear you no 'ard feelin's for it, no'ow—me always makin' it a pint to forgive them as woefully oppresses me, likewise them as despitefully uses me—it might ha' been cold, and dark, wi' ice and snow, and I might ha' froze to death—but we won't say no more about it."

" You've said pretty well, I think," said I; " supposing you tell me what you have to tell me—otherwise—good-night ! "

" Very well then ! " said the Peddler, " let's talk o' summat else—still livin' in the 'Oller, I suppose ? "

" Yes."

" Ah, well ! I come through there to-day," said he, grinning, and again his eyes grew malevolent.

" Indeed ? "

" Ah !—indeed ! I come through this 'ere very arternoon, and uncommon pretty everything was lookin', wi' the grass so green, and the trees so—so——"

" Shady."

" Shady's the word ! " nodded the Peddler, glancing up at me through his narrowed eyelids, and chuckling, " a paradise you might call it—ah ! a paradise, or a—garden of Eden, wi' Eve, and the serpent and all ! " and he broke out into a cackling laugh. And, in the look, and the laugh, indeed about his whole figure, there was something so repellent, so evil, that I was minded to kick and trample him down into the ditch, yet the leering triumph in his eyes held me.

" Yes ? " said I.

" Ye see, bein' by, I 'appened to pass the cottage—and very pretty that looked to, and nice and neat inside ! "

" Yes ? " said I.

" And, bein' so near, I 'appened to glance in at the winder, and there, sure enough, I see—'er—as you might say, Eve in the gardin. And a fine figure of a Eve she be, and 'andsome wi' it—'tain't often as you see a maid the likes o' 'er so proud and 'aughty like."

" Well ? "

" Well, just as I 'appened to look in at the winder, she 'appened to be standin' wi' an open book in 'er 'and—a old, leather book wi' a broken cover."

"Yes?" said I.

"And she was a-laughin'—and a pretty, soft Eve's laugh it were too."

"Yes?" said I.

"And—'e were a-lookin' at the book—over 'er shoulder!" The irons slipped from my grasp, and fell with a harsh clang.

"Ketches ye, does it?" said the Peddler. I did not speak, but, meeting my eye, he scrambled hastily to his feet, and, catching up his pack, retreated some little way down the road.

"Ketches ye, does it, my cove?" he repeated; "turn me away from your door on a cold, dark night, would ye (not as I bears you any ill-will for it, bein' of a forgivin' natur')? But I says to you, I says—look out!—a fine 'andsome lass she be wi' 'er soft eyes and red lips, and long, white arms—the eyes, and lips and arms of a Eve; and Eve tricked Adam, didn't she?— and you ain't a better man nor Adam, are ye?—very well then!" saying which he spat once more into the ditch, and, shouldering his pack, strode away.

And, after some while, I took up my iron bars, and trudged on towards the cottage. As I went, I repeated to myself, over and over again, the word, "Liar." Yet my step was very slow and heavy, and my feet dragged in the dust; and, somewhere in my head, a small hammer had begun to beat, soft, and slow, and regular, but beating, beating upon my brain.

Now the upper cover of my Virgil book was broken!

CHAPTER XXIV

THE VIRGIL BOOK

A MAN was leaning in the shadow of a tree, looking down into the Hollow.

I could not see him very distinctly because, though evening had scarcely fallen, the shadows, where he stood, were very dense, but he was gazing down into the Hollow in the attitude of one who waits. For what?—for whom?

A sudden fit of shivering shook me from head to foot, and, while I yet shivered, I grew burning hot; the blood throbbed at my temples, the small hammer was drumming much faster now, and the cool night air seemed to be stifling me.

Very cautiously I began creeping nearer the passive figure, while the hammer beat so loud that it seemed he must hear it where he stood: a shortish, broad-shouldered figure, clad in a blue coat. He held his hat in his hand, and he leaned carelessly against the tree, and his easy assurance of air maddened me the more.

As he stood thus, looking always down into the Hollow, his neck gleamed at me above the collar of his coat, wherefore I stooped and, laying my irons in the grass, crept on, once more, and, as I went, I kept my eyes upon his neck.

A stick snapped sharp and loud beneath my tread, the lounging back stiffened and grew rigid, the face showed for an instant over the shoulder, and, with a spring, he had vanished into the bushes.

It was a vain hope to find a man in such a dense tangle of boughs and underbrush, yet I ran forward, nevertheless, but, though I sought eagerly upon all sides, he had made good his escape. So, after a while, I retraced my steps to where I had left my irons and

358

brackets, and taking them up, turned aside to that
precipitous path which, as I have already said, leads
down into the Hollow.

Now, as I went, listening to the throb of the
hammer in my head, whom should I meet but Charmian, coming gaily through the green, and singing
as she came. At sight of me she stopped, and the
song died upon her lip.

"Why—why, Peter—you look pale—dreadfully
pale——"

"Thank you, I am very well!" said I.

"You have not been—fighting again?"

"Why should I have been fighting, Charmian?"

"Your eyes are wild—and fierce, Peter."

"Were you coming to—to—meet me, Charmian?"

"Yes, Peter." Now, watching beneath my brows,
it almost seemed that her colour had changed, and
that her eyes, of set purpose, avoided mine. Could
it be that she was equivocating?

"But I—am much before my usual time, to-night,
Charmian."

"Then there will be no waiting for supper, and I
am ravenous, Peter!"

And as she led the way along the path she began to
sing again.

Being come to the cottage, I set down my bars and
brackets, with a clang.

"These," said I, in answer to her look, "are the
bars I promised to make for the door."

"Do you always keep your promises, Peter?"

"I hope so."

"Then," said she, coming to look at the great bars,
with a fork in her hand, for she was in the middle of
dishing up, "then, if you promise me always to come
home by the road, and never through the coppice—
you will do so, won't you?"

"Why should I?" I inquired, turning sharply to
look at her.

"Because the coppice is so dark, and lonely, and if
—I say, if I should take it into my head to come and
meet you sometimes, there would be no chance of my

missing you." And so she looked at me and smiled, and, going back to her cooking, fell once more a-singing, the while I sat and watched her beneath my brows.

Surely, surely no woman whose heart was full of deceit could sing so blithely and happily, or look at one with such sweet candour in her eyes?

And yet the supper was a very ghost of a meal, for when I remembered the man who had watched and waited, the very food grew nauseous and seemed to choke me. "She's a Eve—a Eve!" rang a voice in my ear; "Eve tricked Adam, didn't she, and you ain't a better man nor Adam—she's a Eve—a Eve!"

"Peter, you eat nothing."

"Yes, indeed!" said I, staring unseeingly down at my plate, and striving to close my ears against the fiendish voice.

"And you are very pale!"

I shrugged my shoulders.

"Peter—look at me."

I looked up obediently.

"Yes, you are frightfully pale—are you ill again— is it your head—Peter—what is it?" and, with a sudden, half-shy gesture, she stretched her hand to me across the table. And as I looked from the mute pity of her eyes to the mute pity of that would-be comforting hand, I had a great impulse to clasp it close in mine, to speak, and tell her all my base and unworthy suspicions, and, once more, to entreat her pardon and forgiveness. The words were upon my lips, but I checked them, madman that I was, and shook my head.

"It is nothing," I answered, "unless it be that I have not yet recovered from Black George's fist—it is nothing!" And so the meal drew to an end, and though, feeling my thoughts base, I sat with my head on my hand and my eyes upon the cloth, yet I knew she watched me, and more than once I heard her sigh. A man who acts on impulse may sometimes be laughed at for his mistakes, but he will frequently attain to higher things, and be much better loved by his fellows than the colder, more calculating logician who rarely makes a blunder; and Simon Peter was a man of impulse.

Supper being over and done, Charmian must needs take my coat, despite my protests, and fall to work upon its threadbare shabbiness, mending a great rent in the sleeve. And, watching her through the smoke of my pipe, noting the high mould of her features, the proud poise of her head, the slender elegance of her hands, I was struck sharply by her contrast to the rough, bare walls that were my home, and the toil-worn, unlovely garment beneath her fingers. As I looked, she seemed to be suddenly removed from me—far above and beyond my reach.

" That is the fourth time, Peter."

" What, Charmian ? "

" That is the fourth time you have sighed since you lighted your pipe, and it is out, and you never noticed it ! "

" Yes," said I, and laid the pipe upon the table, and sighed again, before I could stop myself. Charmian raised her head, and looked at me with a laugh in her eyes.

" Oh, most philosophical, dreamy blacksmith ! where be your thoughts ? "

" I was thinking how old and worn and disreputable my coat looked."

" Indeed, sir," said Charmian, holding it up, and regarding it with a little frown, "forsooth it is ancient, and hath seen better days."

" Like its wearer ! " said I, and sighed again.

" Hark to this ancient man ! " she laughed, " this hoary-headed blacksmith of ours, he sighs, and for ever sighs; if it could possibly be that he had met anyone sufficiently worthy—I should think that he had fallen—*philosophically*—in love—how think you, Sir Knight of the Rueful Countenance ? "

" I remember," said I, " that, among other things, you once called me ' Superior Mr Smith.' " Charmian laughed, and nodded her head at me.

" You had been describing to me some quite impossible, idealistic creature, alone worthy of your regard, sir."

" Do you still think me ' superior,' Charmian ? "

" Do you still dream of your impalpable, blood-
lessly-perfect ideals, sir ? "

" No," I answered; " no, I think I have done with
dreaming."

" And I have done with this thy coat, for behold ! it
is finished," and rising, she folded it over the back of
my chair.

Now, as she stood thus behind me, her hand fell
and, for a moment, rested lightly upon my shoulder.

" Peter."

" Yes, Charmian."

" I wish, yes, I do wish that you were either much
younger or very much older."

"Why ? "

" Because you wouldn't be quite so—so cryptic—
such a very abstruse problem.   Sometimes I think I
understand you better than you do yourself, and sometimes I am utterly lost; now, if you were younger I
could read you easily for myself, and, if you were
older, you would read yourself for me."

" I was never very young ! " said I.

" No, you were always too repressed, Peter."

" Yes, perhaps I was."

" Repression is good up to a certain point, but,
beyond that, it is dangerous," said she with a portentous shake of the head.   " Heigho ! was it a week
or a year ago that you avowed yourself happy, and
couldn't tell why ? "

" I was the greater fool ! " said I.

" For not knowing why, Peter ? "

" For thinking myself happy ! "

"Peter, what is happiness ? "

"An idea," said I, " possessed generally of fools ! "

" And what is misery ? "

" Misery is also an idea."

" Possessed only by the wise, Peter—surely he is
wiser who chooses happiness ? "

"Neither happiness nor misery comes from choice."

" But—if one seeks happiness, Peter ? "

"One will assuredly find misery ! " said I, and,
sighing, rose, and taking my hammer from its place

above my bookshelf, set to work upon my brackets, driving them deep into the heavy framework of the door. All at once I stopped, with my hammer poised, and, for no reason in the world, looked back at Charmian, over my shoulder, looked to find her watching me with eyes that were (if it could well be) puzzled, wistful, shy, and glad at one and the same time, eyes that veiled themselves swiftly before my look, yet that shot one last glance, between their lashes, in which was only joy and laughter.

" Yes? " said I, answering the look. But she only stooped her head and went on sewing, yet the colour was bright in her cheeks.

And, having driven in the four brackets, or staples, and closed the door, I took up the bars and showed her how they were to lie cross-wise across the door, resting in the brackets.

" We shall be safe now, Peter," said she; " those bars would resist—an elephant."

" I think they would," I nodded; " but there is yet something more." Going to my shelf of books I took thence the silver-mounted pistol she had brought with her, and balanced it in my hand. " To-morrow I will take this to Cranbrook, and buy bullets to fit it."

" Why, there are bullets there—in one of the old shoes, Peter."

" They are too large—this is an unusually small calibre, and yet it would be deadly enough at close range. I will load it for you, Charmian, and give it into your keeping, in case you should ever—grow afraid again, when I am not by—this is a lonely place—for a woman—at all times."

" Yes, Peter." She was busily employed upon a piece of embroidery, and began to sing softly to herself again as she worked, that old song which worthy Mr Pepys mentions having heard from the lips of mischievous-eyed Nell Gwynn :

> " In Scarlet Town where I was born
> There was a fair maid dwellin'
> Made every youth cry ' well-a-day ! '
> Her name was Barbara Allen."

" Are you so happy, Charmian ? "

" Oh, sir, indifferent well, I thank you."

> " All through the merrie month of May
>   When green buds were a-swellin',
>   Young Jimmy Grove on his death-bed lay,
>   For love of Barbara Allen."

" Are you so—miserable, Peter ? "

" Why do you ask ? "

" Because you sigh, and sigh—like—poor Jimmy Grove in the song."

" He was a fool ! " said I.

" For sighing, Peter ? "

" For dying."

" I suppose no philosopher could ever be so—foolish, Peter ? "

" No," said I ; " certainly not ! "

" It is well to be a philosopher, isn't it, Peter ? "

" Hum ! " said I, and once more set about lighting my pipe. Anon I rose and, crossing to the open door, looked out upon the summer night, and sighed, and coming back, sat watching Charmian's busy fingers.

" Charmian," said I at last.

" Yes, Peter ? "

" Do you—ever see any—any—men lurking about the Hollow—when I am away ? " Her needle stopped suddenly, and she did not look up as she answered :

" No, Peter."

" Never ?—are you—sure, Charmian ? " The needle began to fly to and fro again, but still she did not look up.

" No—of course not—how should I see anyone ? I scarcely go beyond the Hollow, and—I'm busy all day."

" A Eve—a Eve ! " said a voice in my ear—" Eve tricked Adam, didn't she ?—a Eve ! "

After this I sat for a long time without moving, my mind harassed with doubts and a hideous, morbid dread. Why had she avoided my eye ? Her own were pure and truthful, and could not lie ! Why, why had they avoided mine ? If only she had looked at me !

Presently I rose, and began to pace up and down the room.

" You are very restless, Peter ! "

" Yes," said I; "yes, I fear I am—you must pardon me——"

" Why not read ? "

" Indeed I had not thought of my books."

" Then read me something aloud, Peter."

" I will read you the sorrow of Achilles for the loss of Briseis," said I, and, going into the corner, I raised my hand to my shelf of books—and stood there with hand upraised yet touching no book, for a sudden spasm seemed to have me in its clutches, and once again the trembling seized me, and the hammer had recommenced its beat, beating upon my brain.

And, in a while, I turned from my books, and, crossing to the door, leaned there with my back to her lest she should see my face just then.

" I—I don't think I—will read—to-night ! " said I at last.

" Very well, Peter, let us talk."

" Or talk," said I; " I—I think I'll go to bed. Pray," I went on hurriedly, for I was conscious that she had raised her head and was looking at me in some surprise, "pray excuse me—I'm very tired." So, while she yet stared at me, I turned away, and, mumbling a good-night, went into my chamber, and closing the door, leaned against it, for my mind was sick with dread, and sorrow, and a great anguish, for now I knew that Charmian had lied to me—my Virgil book had been moved from its usual place.

CHAPTER XXV

IN WHICH THE READER SHALL FIND LITTLE TO DO WITH THE STORY, AND MAY, THEREFORE, SKIP

Is there anywhere in the world so damnable a place of torment as a bed? To lie awake through the slow, dragging hours, surrounded by a sombre quietude from whose stifling blackness thoughts, like demons, leap to catch us by the throat; or, like waves, come rolling in upon us, ceaselessly, remorselessly—burying us beneath their resistless flow, catching us up, whirling us dizzily aloft, dashing us down into depths infinite; now retreating, now advancing, from whose oncoming terror there is no escape, until we are once more buried beneath their stifling rush.

To lie awake, staring wide-eyed into a crowding darkness wherein move terrors unimagined; to bury our throbbing temples in pillows of fire; to roll, and toss until the soul within us cries out in agony, and we reach out frantic hands into a void that mocks us by the contrast of its deep and awful quiet. At such times fair Reason runs affrighted to hide herself, and foaming Madness fills her throne; at such times our everyday sorrows, howsoever small and petty they be, grow and magnify themselves until they overflow the night, filling the universe above and around us; and of all the woes the human mind can bear—surely Suspicion gnaws deeper than them all!

So I lay beneath the incubus, my temples clasped tight between my burning palms to stay the maddening ring of the hammer in my brain. And Suspicion grew into Certainty, and with Certainty came Madness; Imagination ran riot: she was a Messalina—a Julia—a Joan of Naples—a veritable Succuba—a thing polluted, degraded, and abominable; and, because of her beauty, I cursed all beautiful things, and because

366

of her womanhood, I cursed all women. And ever the hammer beat upon my brain, and foul shapes danced before my eyes—shapes so insanely hideous and revolting that, of a sudden, I rose from my bed, groaning, and coming to the casement—leaned out.

Oh! the cool, sweet purity of the night! I heard the soft stir and rustle of leaves all about me, and down from heaven came a breath of wind, and in the wind a great rain-drop that touched my burning brow like the finger of God. And, leaning there, with parted lips and closed eyes, gradually my madness left me, and the throbbing in my brain grew less.

How many poor mortals, since the world began, sleepless, and anguish-torn—even as I—have looked up into that self-same sky and sorrowed for the dawn.

> " For her love, in sleep I slake,
> For her love, all night I wake,
> For her love, I mourning make
> More than any man ! "

Poor fool! to think that thou couldst mourn more than thy kind!

Thou'rt but a little handful of grey dust, ages since, thy name and estate long out of mind; where'er thou art, thou shouldst have got you wisdom by now, perchance.

Poor fool! that thou must love a woman—and worship with thy love, building for her an altar in thine heart. If altar crumble and heart burst is she to blame who is but woman, or thou, who wouldst have made her all divine?

Well, thou'rt dead—a small handful of grey dust, long since—perchance thou hast got thee wisdom ere now—poor fool—O Fool Divine!

As thou art now, thy sleepless nights forgot—the carking sorrows of thy life all overpast, and done—so must I, some time, be, and, ages hence, shall smile at this, and reckon it no more than a broken toy—heigho!

And so I presently turned me back to my tumbled bed, but it seemed to me that torment and terror still waited me there, moreover I was filled with a great desire for action, this narrow chamber stifled me, while outside was the stir of leaves, the gentle breathing of the wind, the cool murmur of the brook, with night brooding over all, deep, and soft, and still.

Being now dressed, I stood awhile, deliberating how I might escape without disturbing—her who slumbered in the outer room. So I came to the window, and thrusting my head and shoulders sidewise through the narrow lattice, slowly, and with much ado, wriggled myself out. Rising from my hands and knees, I stood up and threw wide my arms to the perfumed night, inhaling its sweetness in great, deep breaths, and so turned my steps towards the brook, drawn thither by its rippling melody, for a brook is a companionable thing, at all times, to a lonely man, and very full of wise counsel and friendly admonitions, if he but have ears to hear withal.

Thus, as I walked beside the brook it spoke to me of many things, grave and gay, delivering itself of observations upon the folly of Humans, comparing us very unfavourably with the godlike dignity of trees, the immutability of mountains, and the profound philosophy of brooks. Indeed it waxed most eloquent upon this theme, caustic, if you will, but with a ripple, between whiles, like the deep-throated chuckle of the wise old philosopher it was.

" Go to ! " chuckled the brook. " O heavy-footed, heavy-sighing Human—go to ! It is written that Man was given dominion over birds and beasts, and fishes, and all things made, yet how doth Man, in all his pride, compare with even a little mountain ? And, as to birds, and beasts, and fishes, they provide for themselves, day in and day out, while Man doth starve, and famish ! To what end is Man born but to work, beget his kind, and die ? O Man ! lift up thy dull-sighted eyes—behold the wonder of the world, and the infinite universe about thee; behold thyself, and see thy many failings and imperfections, and thy stupendous littleness—go to ! Man was made for the World, and not the World for Man ! Man is a leaf in the forest—a grain of dust borne upon the wind, and, when the wind faileth, dust to dust returneth—out upon thee, with thy puny griefs and sorrows.

"O Man!—who hath dominion over all things save thine own heart, and who, in thy blind egotism, setteth thyself much above me, who am but a runlet of water. O Man! I tell thee, when thou art dusty bones I shall still be here, singing to myself in the sun or talking to some other poor Human Fool, in the dark. Go to!" chuckled the brook, "the Wheel of Life turneth ever faster and faster—the woes of to-day shall be the woes of last year, or ever thou canst count them all—out upon thee—go to!"

CHAPTER XXVI

OF STORM, AND TEMPEST, AND HOW I MET ONE
PRAYING IN THE DAWN

ON I went, chin on breast, heedless of all direction—
now beneath the shade of trees, now crossing grassy
glades or rolling meadow, or threading my way
through long alleys of hop-bines; on and on, skirting
hedges, by haycocks looming ghostly in the dark, by
rustling cornfields, through wood and coppice, where
branches touched me, as I passed, like ghostly fingers
in the dark; on I went, lost to all things but my own
thoughts. And my thoughts were not of Life, nor
Death, nor the world, nor the spaces beyond the world
—but of my Virgil book with the broken cover, and of
him who had looked at it—over her shoulder. And,
raising my hands, I clasped them about my temples,
and leaning against a tree, stood there a great while.
Yet, when the trembling fit had left me, I went on
again, and with every footstep there rose a voice
within me, crying: "Why? Why? Why?"

Why should I, Peter Vibart, hale and well in body,
healthy in mind—why should I fall thus into ague-
spasms because of a woman—of whom I knew nothing,
who had come I knew not whence, accompanied by
one whose presence, under such conditions, meant
infamy to any woman—why should I burn thus in a
fever if she chose to meet another while I was abroad?
Was she not free to follow her own devices—had I any
claim upon her—by what right did I seek to compass
her goings and comings, or interest myself in her
doings? Why? Why? Why?

As I went, the woods gradually fell away, and I
came out upon an open place. The ground rose
sharply before me, but I climbed on, and up, and so,
in time, stood upon a hill.

Now, standing upon this elevation, with the woods looming dimly below me, as if they were a dark tide hemming me in on all sides, I became conscious of a sudden great quietude in the air—a stillness that was like the hush of expectancy; not a sound came to me, not a whisper from the myriad leaves below.

But, as I stood there listening, very faint and far away, I heard a murmur that rose, and died, and rose again, that swelled and swelled into the roll of distant thunder. Down in the woods was a faint rustling, as if some giant were stirring among the leaves, and out of their depths breathed a puff of wind that fanned my cheek, and so was gone. But, in a while, it was back again, stronger, more insistent than before, till, sudden as it came, it died away again and all was hushed and still, save only for the tremor down there among the leaves; but lightning flickered upon the horizon, the thunder rolled nearer and nearer, and the giant grew ever more restless.

Round about me, in the dark, were imps that laughed and whispered together, and mocked me amid the leaves:

" Who is the madman that stands upon a lonely hill at midnight, bare-headed, half clad, and hungers for the storm? Peter Vibart! Peter Vibart! Who is he that, having eyes, sees not, and having ears, hears not? Peter Vibart! Peter Vibart! Blow, Wind, and buffet him! Flame, O Lightning, that he may see! Roar, O Thunder, that he may hear and know!"

Upon the stillness came a rustling, loud, and ever louder, drowning all else, for the giant was awake at last, and stretching himself; and now, up he sprang with a sudden bellow, and, gathering himself together, swept up towards me, through the swaying tree-tops, pelting me with broken twigs and flying leaves, and filling the air with the tumult of his coming.

Oh, the wind!—the bellowing, giant wind! on he came, exulting, whistling through my hair, stopping my breath, roaring in my ears his savage, wild halloo! And, as if in answer, forth from the inky heaven burst a jagged, blinding flame, that zig-zagged down among the tossing trees, and vanished with a roaring thunder-clap that seemed to stun all things to silence. But not for long, for in the darkness came the wind again—fiercer, wilder than before, shrieking a defiance. The thunder crashed above me, and the lightning quivered in the air about me till my eyes ached with the swift transitions from pitch darkness to dazzling light—light in which distant objects started out clear and well defined, only to be lost again in a swirl of blackness. And now came rain—a sudden, hissing downpour, long threads of scintillating fire where the lightning caught it—rain that wetted me through and through.

The storm was at its height, and, as I listened, rain and wind, and thunder became merged, and blended into awful music—a symphony of Life and Death played by the hands of God; and I was an atom—a grain of dust—an insect, to be crushed by God's little finger. And yet, needs must this insect still think upon its little self—for half drowned, deafened, blind, and half-stunned though I was, still the voice within me cried: "Why? Why? Why?"

Why was I here instead of lying soft, and sheltered, and sleeping the blessed sleep of tired Humanity? Why was I here, with death about me—and why must I think, and think, and think of Her?

The whole breadth of heaven seemed torn asunder—blue flame crackled in the air, it ran hissing along the ground—then—blackness, and a thunderclap that shook the very hill beneath me, and I was down upon my knees, with the swish of the rain about me.

Little by little upon this silence stole the rustle of leaves, and in the leaves were the imps who mocked me:

"Who is he that doth love—in despite of himself, and shall do, all his days—be she good or evil, what-ever she was, whatever she is? Who is the very Fool of Love? Peter Vibart! Peter Vibart!"

And so I bowed my face upon my hands, and remained thus a great while, heeding no more the tempest about me. For now indeed was my question answered, and my fear realised.

" I love her !—whatever she was—whatever she is— good or evil—I love her. O Fool !—O most miserable Fool ! "

And presently I rose, and went on down the hill. Fast I strode, stumbling and slipping, plunging on heedlessly through bush and brake until at last, looking about me, I found myself on the outskirts of a little spinney, or copse, and then I became conscious that the storm had passed, for the thunder had died down to a murmur, and the rain had ceased ; only all about me were little soft sounds, as if the trees were weeping silently together.

Pushing on, I came into a sort of narrow lane, grassy underfoot and shut in on either hand by very tall hedges that loomed solid and black in the night ; and, being spent and weary, I sat down beneath one of these and propped my chin in my hands.

How long I remained thus I cannot say, but I was at length aroused by a voice—a strangely sweet and gentle voice at no great distance, and the words it uttered were these :

" O ! give thanks unto the Lord, for He is good, for His mercy endureth for ever ! O Lord ! I beseech Thee look down in Thine infinite pity upon this, Thy world ; for lo ! day is at hand, and Thy children must soon awake to life, and toil, and temptation. O ! Thou who art the Lover of Men, let Thy Holy Spirit wait to meet with each one of us upon the threshold of the dawn, and lead us through this coming day. Like as a father pitieth his children so dost Thou pity all the woeful and heavy-hearted. Look down upon all those who must so soon awake to their griefs, speak comfortably to them ; remember those in pain who must so soon take up their weary burdens ! Look down upon the hungry, and the rich, the evil, and the good, that in this new day, finding each something of Thy mercy, they may give thanks unto the Lord, for He is good, for His mercy endureth for ever."

So the voice ended, and there was silence and a profound stillness upon all things ; wherefore, lifting my eyes unto the east, I saw that it was dawn.

CHAPTER XXVII

THE EPILEPTIC

Now, when the prayer was ended, I turned my back upon the lightening east and set off along the lane.

But, as I went, I heard one hailing me, and glancing round, saw that in the hedge was a wicket-gate, and over this gate a man was leaning. A little, thin man with the face of an ascetic, or mediæval saint, a face of a high and noble beauty, upon whose scholarly brow sat a calm serenity, yet beneath which glowed the full, bright eye of the man of action.

"Good-morning, friend!" said he; "welcome to my solitude. I wish you joy of this new day of ours; it is cloudy yet, but there is a rift down on the horizon—it will be a fair day, I think."

"On the contrary, sir," said I, "to me there are all the evidences of the bad weather continuing. I think it will be a bad day, with rain, and probably thunder and lightning! Good-morning, sir!"

"Stay!" cried he as I turned away, and, with the word, set his hand upon the gate, and, vaulting nimbly over, came towards me with a broad-brimmed straw hat in one hand and a long-stemmed wooden pipe in the other.

"Sir," said he, "my cottage is close by—you look worn, and jaded. Will you not step in and rest awhile?"

"Thank you, sir; but I must be upon my way."

"And whither lies your way?"

"To Sissinghurst, sir."

"You have a long walk before you, and, with your permission, I will accompany you a little way."

"With pleasure, sir!" I answered, "though I fear you will find me a moody companion, and a somewhat

374

silent one; but then, I shall be the better listener, so light your pipe, sir, and, while you smoke, talk."

"My pipe!" said he, glancing down at it; "ah! yes—I was about to compose my Sunday evening's sermon."

"You are a clergyman, sir?"

"No, no—a preacher—or say rather—a teacher, and a very humble one, who, striving himself after Truth, seeks to lend such aid to others as he may."

"Truth!" said I; "what is Truth?"

"Truth, sir, is that which can never pass away; the Truth of Life is Good Works, which abide everlastingly."

"Sir," said I, "you smoke a pipe, I perceive, and should, therefore, be a good preacher, for smoking begets thought——"

"And yet, sir, is not to act, greater than to think?"

"Why, Thought far outstrips puny Action!" said I—"it reaches deeper, soars higher—in our actions we are pigmies, but in our thoughts we may be gods, and embrace a universe."

"But," sighed the Preacher, "while we think, our fellows perish in ignorance and want!"

"Hum!" said I.

"Thought," pursued the Preacher, "may become a vice, as it did with the old-time monks and hermits, who, shutting themselves away from their kind, wasted their lives upon their knees, thinking noble thoughts and dreaming of holy things, but—leaving the world very carefully to the devil. And, as to smoking, I am seriously considering giving it up." Here he took the pipe from his lips and thrust it behind his back.

"Why?"

"It has become, unfortunately, too human! It is a strange thing, sir," he went on, smiling and shaking his head, "that this, my one indulgence, should breed me more discredit than all the cardinal sins, and become a stumbling-block to others. Only last Sunday I happened to overhear two whiteheaded old fellows talking. 'A fine sermon, Giles?' said the one. 'Ah! good enough,' replied the other, 'but it might ha' been better—ye see—'e smokes ! ' So I am seriously thinking of giving it up, for it would appear, that if a preacher prove himself as human as his flock they immediately lose faith in him, and become deaf to his teaching."

"Very true, sir ! " I nodded. " It has always been human to admire and respect that only which is in any way different to ourselves; in archaic times those whose teachings were above men's comprehension, or who were remarkable for any singularity of action, were immediately deified. Pythagoras recognised this truth when he shrouded himself in mystery, and delivered his lectures from behind a curtain, though to be sure he has come to be regarded as something of a charlatan in consequence."

"Pray, sir," said the Preacher, absent-mindedly puffing at his pipe again, " may I ask what you are ?"

" A blacksmith, sir."

" And where did you read of Pythagoras and the like ? "

" At Oxford, sir."

" How comes it then that I find you in the dawn, wet with rain, buffeted by wind, and—most of all—a shoer of horses ? "

But, instead of answering, I pointed to a twisted figure that lay beneath the opposite hedge.

" A man ! " exclaimed the Preacher, " and asleep, I think."

" No," said I, " not in that contorted attitude."

" Indeed, you are right," said the Preacher; " the man is ill—poor fellow ! " and, hurrying forward, he fell on his knees beside the prostrate figure.

He was a tall man, roughly clad, and he lay upon his back, rigid and motionless, while upon his blue lips were flecks and bubbles of foam.

" Epilepsy ! " said I. The Preacher nodded, and busied himself with loosening the sodden neckcloth, the while I unclasped the icy fingers to relieve the tension of the muscles.

The man's hair was long and matted, as was also his beard, and his face all drawn and pale, and very

*We took the man's wasted form between us
and bore it, easily enough, to where stood a
small cottage, bowered in roses*

Face Page 376

We took the man's wasted form between us and bore it, easily enough, to where stood a small cottage, bowered in roses

Face Page 376

deeply lined. Now, as I looked at him, I had a vague
idea that I had somewhere, at some time, seen him
before.

"Sir," said the Preacher, looking up, "will you
help me to carry him to my cottage?—it is not very
far."

So we presently took the man's wasted form between
us and bore it, easily enough, to where stood a small
cottage bowered in roses and honeysuckle. And,
having deposited our unconscious burden upon the
Preacher's humble bed, I turned to depart.

"Sir," said the Preacher, holding out his hand, "it
is seldom one meets with a blacksmith who has read
the Pythagorean Philosophy—at Oxford, and I should
like to see you again. I am a lonely man save for my
books, come and sup with me some evening, and let
us talk——"

"And smoke?" said I. The little Preacher sighed.
"I will come," said I; "thank you! and good-bye!"
Now, even as I spoke, chancing to cast my eyes upon
the pale, still face on the bed, I felt more certain than
ever that I had somewhere seen it before.

CHAPTER XXVIII

IN WHICH I COME TO A DETERMINATION

As I walked through the fresh, green world there ensued within me the following dispute, as it were, between myself and two voices; and the first voice I will call Pro, and the other Contra.

MYSELF. May the devil take that "Gabbing Dick"!
PRO. He probably will.
MYSELF. Had he not told me of what he saw—of the man who looked at my Virgil—over her shoulder——
PRO. Or had you not listened.
MYSELF. Ah yes!—but then, I did listen, and that he spoke the truth is beyond all doubt, the misplaced Virgil proves that. However, it is certain, yes, very certain, that I can remain no longer in the Hollow.
CONTRA. Well, there is excellent accommodation at "The Bull."
PRO. And pray, why leave the Hollow?
MYSELF. Because she is a woman——
PRO. And you love her!
MYSELF. To my sorrow.
PRO. Well, but woman was made for man, Peter, and man for woman——!
MYSELF (sternly). Enough of that—I must go!
PRO. Being full of bitter jealousy.
MYSELF. No!
PRO. Being a mad, jealous fool——
MYSELF. As you will.
PRO. —who has condemned her unheard—with no chance of justification.
MYSELF. To-morrow, at the very latest, I shall seek some other habitation.
PRO. Has she the look of guilt?
MYSELF. No; but then women are deceitful by

378

nature, and very skilful in disguising their faults—at least so I have read in my books——

PRO (contemptuously). Books! Books! Books!

MYSELF (shortly). No matter; I have decided.

PRO. Do you remember how willingly she worked for you with those slender, capable hands of hers——?

MYSELF. Why remind me of this?

PRO. You must needs miss her presence sorely; her footstep, that was always so quick, and light——

MYSELE. Truly wonderful in one so nobly formed!

PRO. —and the way she had of singing softly to herself.

MYSELF. A beautiful voice——

PRO. With a caress in it— and then, her habit of looking at you over her shoulder.

MYSELF. Ah yes!—her lashes a little drooping, her brows a little wrinkled, her lips a little parted.

CONTRA. A comfortable inn is " The Bull."

MYSELF (hastily). Yes, yes—certainly.

PRO. Ah!—her lips—the scarlet witchery of her lips! Do you remember how sweetly the lower one curved upward to its fellow? A mutinous mouth, with its sudden, bewildering changes! you never quite knew which to watch oftenest—her eyes, or her lips——

CONTRA (hoarsely). Excellent cooking at " The Bull"!

PRO. And how she would berate you, and scoff at your Master Epictetus, and dry-as-dust philosophers!

MYSELF. I have sometimes wondered at her pronounced antipathy to Epictetus.

PRO. And she called you a " creature."

MYSELF. The meaning of which I never quite fathomed.

PRO. And, frequently, a " pedant."

MYSELF. I think not more than four times.

PRO. On such occasions, you will remember, she had a petulant way of twitching her shoulder towards you, and frowning, and, occasionally, stamping her foot; and, deep within you, you loved it all, you know you did.

CONTRA. But that is all over, and you are going to " The Bull."

MYSELF (hurriedly). To be sure—" The Bull."

PRO. And, lastly, you cannot have forgotten—you never will forget—the soft tumult of the tender bosom that pillowed your battered head—the pity of her hands —those great, scalding tears, the sudden, swift caress of her lips, and the thrill in her voice when she said——

MYSELF (hastily). Stop! that is all forgotten.

PRO. You lie! You have dreamed of it ever since, working at your anvil, or lying upon your bed, with your eyes upon the stars—you have loved her from the beginning of things!

MYSELF. And I did not know it, I was very blind; the wonder is that she did not discover my love for her long ago, for, not knowing it was there, how should I try to hide it?

CONTRA. O Blind, and more than blind! why should you suppose she hasn't?

MYSELF (stopping short). What? Can it be possible that she has?

CONTRA. Didn't she once say that she could read you like a book?

MYSELF. She did.

CONTRA. And have you not often surprised a smile upon her lips, and wondered?

MYSELF. Many times.

CONTRA. Have you not beheld a thin-veiled mockery in her look? Why, poor fool, has she not mocked you from the first? You dream of her lips. Were not their smiles but coquetry and derision?

MYSELF. But why should she deride me?

CONTRA. For your youth, and—innocence.

MYSELF. My youth! my innocence!

CONTRA. Being a fool ingrain, didn't you boast that you had known but few women?

MYSELF. I did, but——

CONTRA. Didn't she call you boy! boy! boy!—and laugh at you?

MYSELF. Well—even so——

CONTRA (with bitter scorn). O Boy! O Innocent of the innocent! go to, for a bookish fool! Learn that lovely ladies yield themselves but to those who are masterful in their wooing, who have wooed often, and triumphed as often. O Innocent of the innocent! forget the maudlin sentiment of thy books and old romances—thy pure Sir Galahads, thy "vary parfait gentil knightes," thy meek and lowly lovers serving their ladies on bended knee; open thine eyes, learn that women to-day love only the strong hand, the bold eye, the ready tongue; kneel to her, and she will scorn and contemn you. What woman, think you, would prefer the solemn, stern-eyed purity of a Sir Galahad (though he be the king of men) to the quick-witted gaiety of a debonnaire Lothario (though he be but the shadow of a man)? Out upon thee, pale-faced student! thy tongue hath not the trick, nor thy mind the nimbleness for the winning of a fair and lovely lady. Thou'rt well enough in want of a better, but, when Lothario comes, must she not run to meet him with arms outstretched?

"To-morrow," said I, clenching my fists, "to-morrow I will go away!"

Being now come to the Hollow, I turned aside to the brook, at that place where was the pool in which I was wont to perform my morning ablutions; and, kneeling down, I gazed at myself in the dark, still water; and I saw that the night had, indeed, set its mark upon me.

"To-morrow," said I again, nodding to the wild face below, "to-morrow I will go far hence."

Now while I yet gazed at myself I heard a sudden gasp behind me and, turning, beheld Charmian.

"Peter! is it you?" she whispered, drawing back from me.

"Who else, Charmian? Did I startle you?"

"Yes—oh, Peter!"

"Are you afraid of me?"

"You are like one who has walked with—death!"

I rose to my feet, and stood looking down at her.

"Are you afraid of me, Charmian?"

"No, Peter."

"I am glad of that," said I, "because I want to ask you—to marry me, Charmian."

CHAPTER XXIX

IN WHICH CHARMIAN ANSWERS MY QUESTION

" Peter ! "

" Yes ? "

" I wish you wouldn't."

" Wouldn't what, Charmian ? "

" Stir your tea round, and round, and round—it is really most—exasperating ! "

" I beg your pardon ! " said I humbly.

" And you eat nothing—and that is also exasperating."

" I am not hungry."

" And I was so careful with the bacon—see it is fried—beautifully—yes, you are very exasperating, Peter ! "

Here, finding I was absent-mindedly stirring my tea round and round again, I gulped it down out of the way, whereupon Charmian took my cup and refilled it; having done which, she set her elbows upon the table, and, propping her chin in her hands, looked at me.

" You climbed out through your window last night, Peter ? "

" Yes."

" It must have been a—dreadfully tight squeeze ! "

" Yes."

" And why did you go by the window ? "

" I did not wish to disturb you."

" That was very thoughtful of you—only, you see, I was up and dressed; the roar of the thunder woke me. It was a dreadful storm, Peter ! "

" Yes."

" The lightning was awful ! "

" Yes."

" And you were out in it ? "

" Yes."

" Oh, you poor, poor Peter !—how cold you must have been."

" On the contrary," I began, " I——"

" And wet, Peter—miserably wet and clammy ! "

" I did not notice it," I murmured.

" Being a philosopher, Peter, and too much engrossed in your thoughts ? "

" I was certainly thinking."

" Of yourself ! "

" Yes——"

" You are a great egoist, aren't you, Peter ? "

" Am I, Charmian ? "

" Who but an egoist could stand with his mind so full of himself and his own concerns as to be oblivious to thunder and lightning, and not know that he is miserably clammy and wet ? "

" I thought of others besides myself."

" But only in connection with yourself ; everything you have ever read, or seen, you apply to yourself, to make that self more worthy in Mr Vibart's eyes. Is this worthy of Peter Vibart ? Can Peter Vibart do this, that, or the other, and still retain the respect of Peter Vibart ? Then why, being in all things so very correct and precise, why is Peter Vibart given to prowling abroad at midnight, quite oblivious to thunder, lightning, wet and clamminess ? I answer : Because Peter Vibart is too much engrossed by— Peter Vibart. There ! that sounds rather cryptic, and very full of Peter Vibart—but that is as it should be," and she laughed.

" And what does it mean, Charmian ? "

" Good sir, the sibyl hath spoken ! Find her meaning for yourself."

" You have called me, on various occasions, a ' creature,' a ' pedant '—very frequently a pedant, and now, it seems I am an egoist, and all because——"

" Because you think too much, Peter ; you never open your lips without having first thought out just what you are going to say, you never do anything without having laboriously mapped it all out beforehand, that you may not outrage Peter Vibart's tranquillity by any impulsive act or speech—oh! you are always thinking and thinking—and that is even worse than stirring, and stirring at your tea as you are doing now." I took the spoon hastily from my cup, and laid it as far out of reach as possible. " If ever you should write the book you once spoke of, it would be just the very sort of book that I should—hate."

"Why, Charmian?"

" Because it would be a book of artfully turned phrases; a book in which all the characters, especially women, would think and speak, and act by rote and rule—as according to Mr Peter Vibart; it would be a scholarly book, of elaborate finish and care of detail, with no irregularities of style, or anything else, to break the monotonous harmony of the whole—indeed, sir, it would be a most unreadable book! "

" Do you think so, Charmian? " said I, once more taking up the teaspoon.

"Why, of course! " she answered, with raised brows; " it would probably be full of Greek and Latin quotations! and you would polish and rewrite it until you had polished every vestige of life and spontaneity out of it, as you do out of yourself, with your thinking, and thinking."

" But I never quote you Greek or Latin—that is surely something, and, as for thinking, would you have me a thoughtless fool, or an impulsive ass? "

" Anything rather than a calculating, introspective philosopher, seeing only the mote in the sunbeam, and nothing of the glory." Here she gently disengaged the teaspoon from my fingers, and laid it in her own saucer, having done which, she sighed, and looked at me with her head to one side. " Were they all like you, Peter, I wonder—those old philosophers, grim and stern, and terribly repressed, with burning eyes, Peter, and with very long chins? Epictetus was, of course! "

" And you dislike Epictetus, Charmian? "

" I detest him! He was just the kind of person, Peter, who, being unable to sleep, would have wandered out into a terrible thunderstorm, in the middle of the night, and, being cold, and wet, and clammy, Peter, would have drawn moral lessons, and made epigrams upon the thunder and lightning. Epictetus, I am quite sure, was a—person!"

"He was one of the wisest, gentlest, and most lovable of all the Stoics!" said I.

"Can a philosopher possibly be lovable, Peter?" Here I very absent-mindedly took up a fork, but, finding her eye upon me, laid it down again.

"You are very nervous, Peter, and very pale, and worn, and haggard, and all because you habitually— overthink yourself; and indeed, there is something very far wrong with a man who perseveringly stirs an empty cup—with a fork!" And, with a laugh, she took my cup, and, having once more refilled it, set it before me.

"And yet, Peter—I don't think—no, I don't think I would have you very much changed, after all."

"You mean that you would rather I remained the pedantic, egotistical creature——"

"I mean, Peter, that, being a woman, I naturally love novelty, and you are very novel—and very interesting."

"Thank you!" said I, frowning.

"And more contradictory than any woman!"

"Hum!" said I.

"You are so strong, and simple—so wise and brave —and so very weak, and foolish, and timid!"

"Timid?" said I.

"Timid!" nodded she.

"I am a vast fool!" I acknowledged.

"And I never knew a man anything like you before, Peter!"

"And you have known many, I understand?"

"Very many."

"Yes—you told be so once before, I believe."

"Twice, Peter; and each time you became very silent and gloomy! Now you, on the other hand," she continued, "have known very few women?"

"And my life has been calm and unruffled in consequence!"

2 B

"You had your books, Peter, and your horseshoes."

"My books and horseshoes, yes."

"And were content?"

"Quite content."

"Until, one day—a woman—came to you."

"Until, one day—I met a woman."

"And then——?"

"And then—I asked her to marry me, Charmian."

Here there ensued a pause during which Charmian began to pleat a fold in the tablecloth.

"That was rather—unwise of you, wasn't it?" said she at last.

"How unwise?"

"Because—she might—have taken you at your word, Peter."

"Do you mean that—that you won't, Charmian?"

"Oh dear, no! I have arrived at no decision yet—how could I? You must give me time to consider." Here she paused in her pleating to regard it critically, with her head on one side. "To be sure," said she, with a little nod, "to be sure, you need someone to—to look after you—that is very evident!"

"Yes."

"To cook—and wash for you."

"Yes."

"To mend your clothes for you."

"Yes."

"And you think me—sufficiently competent?"

"Oh, Charmian, I—yes."

"Thank you!" said she, very solemnly, and, though her lashes had drooped, I felt the mockery of her eyes; wherefore I took a sudden, great gulp of tea, and came near choking, while Charmian began to pleat another fold in the tablecloth.

"And so Mr Vibart would stoop to wed so humble a person as Charmian Brown?—Mr Peter Vibart would, actually, marry a woman of whose past he knows nothing?"

"Yes," said I.

"That, again, would be rather—unwise, wouldn't it?"

" Why ? "

" Considering Mr Vibart's very lofty ideals in regard to women."

" What do you mean ? "

" Didn't you once say that your wife's name must be above suspicion—like Cæsar's—or something of the kind ? "

" Did I ?—yes, perhaps I did—well ? "

" Well, this woman—this Humble Person has no name at all, and no shred of reputation left her. She has compromised herself beyond all redemption in the eyes of the world."

" But then," said I, " this world and I have always mutually despised each other."

" She ran away, this woman—eloped with the most notorious, the most accomplished rake in London."

" Well ? "

" Oh !—is not that enough ? "

" Enough for what, Charmian ? " I saw her busy fingers falter and tremble, but her voice was steady when she answered :

" Enough to make any—wise man think twice before asking this Humble Person to—to marry him."

" I might think twenty times, and it would be all one ! "

" You—mean—— ? "

" That if Charmian Brown will stoop to marry a village blacksmith, Peter Vibart will find happiness again ; a happiness that is not of the sunshine—nor the wind in the trees—Lord, what a fool I was ! " Her fingers had stopped altogether now, but she neither spoke nor raised her head.

" Charmian," said I, leaning nearer across the table, " speak."

" Oh, Peter ! " said she, with a sudden break in her voice, and stooped her head lower. Yet in a little she looked up at me, and her eyes were very sweet and shining.

Now, as our glances met thus, up from throat to brow there crept that hot, slow wave of colour, and in her face and in her eyes I seemed to read joy, and fear.

and shame, and radiant joy again. But now she bent her head once more, and strove to pleat another fold, and could not; while I grew suddenly afraid of her, and of myself, and longed to hurl aside the table that divided us, and thrust my hands deep into my pockets, and, finding there my tobacco-pipe, brought it out, and fell to turning it aimlessly over and over. I would have spoken only I knew that my voice would tremble, and so I sat mum-chance, staring at my pipe with unseeing eyes, and with my brain in a ferment. And presently came her voice, cool, and sweet, and sane:

" Your tobacco, Peter," and she held the box towards me across the table.

" Ah, thank you! " said I, and began to fill my pipe, while she watched me with her chin propped in her hands.

" Peter! "

" Yes, Charmian? "

" I wonder why so grave a person as Mr Peter Vibart should seek to marry so impossible a creature as—the Humble Person? "

" I think," I answered, " I think, if there is any special reason, it is because of—your mouth."

" My mouth? "

" Or your eyes—or the way you have with your lashes."

Charmian laughed, and forthwith drooped them at me, and laughed again, and shook her head.

" But surely, Peter, surely there are thousands, millions of women with mouths and eyes like—the Humble Person's? "

" It is possible," said I, " but none who have the same way with their lashes."

" What do you mean? "

" I can't tell; I don't know."

" Don't you, Peter? "

" No—it is just a way."

" And so it is that you want to marry this very Humble Person? "

" I think I have wanted to from the very first, but did not know it—being a blind fool! "

" And—did it need a night walk in a thunderstorm to teach you ? "

" No—that is, yes—perhaps it did."

" And—are you quite, quite sure ? "

" Quite—quite sure ! " said I, and, as I spoke, I laid my pipe upon the table, and rose; and, because my hands were trembling, I clenched my fists. But, as I approached her, she started up and put out a hand to hold me off, and then I saw that her hands were trembling also. And standing thus, she spoke, very softly :

" Peter."

" Yes, Charmian ? "

" Do you remember describing to me the—the perfect woman who should be your—wife ? "

" Yes."

" How that you must be able to respect her for her intellect ? "

" Yes."

" Honour her for her virtue ? "

" Yes, Charmian."

" And worship her—for her—spotless purity ? "

" I dreamed a paragon—perfect and impossible—I was a fool ! " said I.

" Impossible ! Oh, Peter ! what—what do you mean ? "

" She was only an impalpable shade quite impossible of realisation—a bloodless thing, as you said, and quite unnatural—a sickly figment of the imagination—I was a fool ! "

" And you are—too wise now, to expect—such virtues—in any woman ? "

" Yes," said I; " no—oh, Charmian ! I only know that you have taken this phantom's place—that you fill all my thoughts—sleeping, and waking——"

" No ! No ! " she cried, and struggled in my arms, so that I caught her hands, and held them close, and kissed them many times.

" Oh, Charmian ! Charmian !—don't you know—can't you see—it is you I want—you, and only you for ever; whatever you were—whatever you are—I love you—love you, and always must ! Marry me,

Charmian !—marry me ! and you shall be dearer than my life—more to me than my soul——" But, as I spoke, her hands were snatched away, her eyes blazed into mine and her lips were all bitter scorn, and at the sight, Fear came upon me.

" Marry you ! " she panted; "marry you ?—no, and no, and no ! " And so she stamped her foot, and sobbed, and turning, fled from me, out of the cottage.

And now to Fear came Wonder, and with Wonder was Despair.

Truly, was ever man so great a fool !

CHAPTER XXX

CONCERNING THE FATE OF BLACK GEORGE

A BROAD, white road; on either hand some half-dozen cottages with roofs of thatch, or red tile, backed by trees gnarled and ancient, among which rises the red conical roof of some oast-house. Such, in a word, is Sissinghurst.

Now, upon the left-hand side of the way there stands a square, comfortable, whitewashed building, peaked of roof, bright as to windows, and with a mighty sign before the door, whereon you shall behold the picture of a bull: a bull rolling of eye, astonishingly curly of horn and stiff as to tail, and with a prodigious girth of neck and shoulder; such a snorting, fiery-eyed, curly-horned bull as was never seen off an inn-sign.

It was at this bull that I was staring with much apparent interest, though indeed, had that same curly-horned monstrosity been changed by some enchanter's wand into a green dragon, or griffin, or swan with two necks, the chances are that I should have continued sublimely unconscious of the transformation.

Yet how should honest Silas Hoskins, ostler, and general factotum of " The Bull " inn, be aware of this fact, who, being thus early at work, and seeing me lost in contemplation, paused to address me in all good faith?

" A fine bull 'e be, eh, Peter? Look at them 'orns, an' that theer tail; it's seldom as you sees 'orns or a tail the like o' them, eh?"

" Very seldom! " I answered, and sighed.

" An' then—'is nose-'oles, Peter, jest cast your eye on them nose-'oles, will ye; why, dang me! if I can't 'ear 'im a-snortin' when I looks at 'em! An' 'e were all painted by a chap—a little old chap wi' grey whiskers—no taller'n your elber, Peter! Think o' that

391

—a little chap no taller'n your elber! I seen 'im do it wi' my two eyes—a-sittin' on a box. Drored t' bull in wi' a bit o' chalk, first; then 'e outs wi' a couple o' brushes; dab 'e goes, an' dab, dab again, an'—by Goles! theer was a pair o' eyes a-rollin' theirselves at me—just a pair o' eyes, Peter. Ah! 'e were a wonder were that little old chap wi' grey whiskers! The way 'e went at that theer bull, a-dabbin' at 'im 'ere, an' a-dabbin' at 'im theer till 'e come to 'is tail—'e done 'is tail last of all, Peter. 'Give 'un a good tail!' says I. 'Ah! that I will,' says 'e. 'An' a good stiff 'un!' says I. 'Ye jest keep your eye on it, an' watch!' says 'e. Talk about tails, Peter! 'E put in that theer tail so quick as nigh made my eyes water, an'—as for stiffness—well, look at it! I tell 'ee that chap could paint a bull wi' 'is eyes shut, ah, that 'e could! an' 'im such a very small man—wi' grey whiskers. No, ye don't see many bulls like that 'un theer, I'm thinkin' Peter?"

"They would be very hard to find!" said I, and sighed again. Whereupon Silas sighed, for company's sake, and nodding, went off about his many duties, whistling cheerily.

So I presently turned about and crossed the road to the smithy. But upon the threshold I stopped all at once, and drew softly back, for, despite the early hour, Prudence was there, upon her knees before the anvil, with George's great hand-hammer clasped to her bosom, sobbing over it, and, while she sobbed, she kissed its worn handle. And because such love was sacred, and hallowed that dingy place, I took off my hat as I once more crossed the road.

Seeing "The Bull" was not yet astir, for the day was still young (as I say), I sat me down in the porch, and sighed.

And after I had sat there for some while, with my chin sunk upon my breast, and plunged in bitter meditation, I become aware of the door opening, and next moment a tremulous hand was laid upon my head, and, looking round, I beheld the Ancient.

"Bless 'ee, Peter—bless 'ee lad!—an' a old man's blessin' be no light thing—'specially such a old, old

man as I be—an' it bean't often as I feels in a blessin'
sperrit—but oh, Peter! 'twere me as found ye, weren't
it?"

"Why, to be sure it was, Ancient, very nearly five
months ago."

"An' I be allus ready wi' some noos for ye, bean't I?"

"Yes, indeed!"

"Well, I got more noos for 'ee, Peter—gert noos!"

"And what is it this time?"

"I be allus full up o' noos, bean't I?" he repeated.

"Yes, Ancient," said I, and sighed; "and what is
your news?"

"Why, first of all, Peter, jest reach me my snuff-
box, will 'ee?—'ere it be—in my back 'ind pocket—
thankee! thankee!" Hereupon he knocked upon the
lid with a bony knuckle. "I du be that full o' noos
this marnin' that my innards be all of a quake, Peter,
all of a quake!" he nodded, saying which he sat
down close beside me.

"Peter."

"Yes, Ancient?"

"Some day—when that theer old stapil be all
rusted away, an' these old bones is a-restin' in the
churchyard—over to Cranbrook, Peter—you'll think,
sometimes, o' the very old man as was always so full
o' noos, won't 'ee, Peter?"

"Surely, Ancient, I shall never forget you," said I,
and sighed.

"An' now, Peter," said the old man, extracting a
pinch of snuff, "now for the noos—'bout Black Jarge,
it be."

"What of him, Ancient?" The old man shook his
head.

"It took eight on' em to du it, Peter, an' now four on
'em's a-layin' in their beds, an' four on 'em's 'obblin'
on crutches—an' all over a couple o' rabbits—though
theer be some fules as says they was pa'tridges!"

"Why—what do you mean?"

"Why, ye see, Peter, Black Jarge be such a gert,
strong man(I were much such another when I were
young)—like a lion, in 'is wrath, 'e be—ah!—a bull

bean't nothin' to Black Jarge! An' they keepers come an' found 'im under a tree, fast asleep—like David in the Cave of Adullam, Peter, wi' a couple o' rabbits as 'e'd snared. An', when they keepers tried to tak' 'im, 'e rose up, 'e did, an' throwed some on 'em this way an' some on 'em that way—'twere like Samson an' the Philistines; if only 'e'd 'appened to find the jaw-bone of a ass lyin' 'andy, 'e'd ha' killed 'em all an' got away, sure as sure. But it weren't to be, Peter, no; dead donkeys be scarce nowadays, an' as for asses' jaw-bones——"

"Do you mean that George is taken—a prisoner?"

The Ancient nodded, and inhaled his pinch of snuff with much evident relish.

"It be gert noos, bean't it, Peter?"

"What have they done with him? Where is he, Ancient?" But, before the old man could answer, Simon appeared.

"Ah, Peter!" said he, shaking his head, "the Gaffer's been tellin' ye 'ow they've took Jarge for poachin', I suppose——"

"Simon!" cried the Ancient, "shut thy mouth, lad—hold thy gab an' give thy poor old feyther a chance—I be tellin' 'im so fast as I can! As I was a-sayin', Peter—like a fur'us lion were Jarge wi' they keepers—eight on 'em, Peter—like dogs, a-growlin' an' growlin' an' leapin', and worryin' all round 'im— ah!—like a lion 'e were——"

"Waitin' for a chance to use 'is ' right,' d'ye see, Peter!" added Simon.

ANCIENT. Wi' 'is eyes a-rollin' an' flamin', Peter, an' 'is mane all bristlin'——

SIMON. Cool as any cucumber, Peter——

ANCIENT. A-roarin' an' a-lashin' of 'is tail——

SIMON. And sparrin' for an openin', Peter, and when 'e sees one—downin' 'is man every time——

ANCIENT. Leapin' in the air, rollin' in the grass, wi' they keepers clingin' to 'im like leeches—ah! leeches——

SIMON. And every time they rushed, tap 'ud go 'is " left," and bang 'ud go 'is " right "——

ANCIENT. An' up 'e'd get, like Samson again, Peter, an' give 'isself a shake; bellerin'—like a bull o' Bashan——

SIMON. Ye see, they fou't so close together that the keepers was afear'd to use their guns——

ANCIENT (indignantly). Guns!—who's a-talkin' o' guns? Simon, my bye—you be allus a-maggin' an' a-maggin'; bridle thy tongue, lad, bridle thy tongue afore it runs away wi' ye.

SIMON (sheepishly). All right, Old 'Un—fire away!

But, at this juncture, Old Amos hove in view, followed by the Apologetic Dutton, with Job, and sundry others, on their way to work, and, as they came they talked together, with much solemn wagging of heads. Having reached the door of " The Bull " they paused and greeted us, and I thought Old Amos's habitual grin seemed a trifle more pronounced than usual.

" So poor Jarge 'as been an' gone and done for 'isself at last, eh? O my soul! think o' that, now! " sighed Old Amos.

" Allus knowed as 'e would! " added Job; "many's the time I've said as 'e would, an' you know it—all on you."

" It'll be the Barbadies, or Austrayley! " grinned Amos, " transportation, it'll be—O my soul! think o' that now—an' 'im a Siss'n'urst man! "

" An' all along o' a couple o'—rabbits! " said the Ancient, emphasising the last word with a loud rap on his snuff-box.

" Pa'tridges, Gaffer!—they was pa'tridges! " returned Old Amos.

" I allus said as Black Jarge'd come to a bad end," reiterated Job, " an' what's more—'e aren't got nobody to blame but 'isself! "

" An' all for a couple o'—rabbits! " sighed the Ancient, staring Old Amos full in the eye.

" Pa'tridges, Gaffer, they was pa'tridges—you, James Dutton—was they pa'tridges or was they not— speak up, James."

Hereupon the man Dutton, all perspiring apology,

as usual, shuffled forward, and, mopping his reeking brow, delivered himself in this wise :

" W'ich I must say—meanin' no offence to nobody, an' if so be, apologisin'—w'ich I must say—me 'avin' seen 'em—they was—leastways," he added, as he met the Ancient's piercing eye, " leastways—they might 'ave been, w'ich—if they ain't—no matter ! "

Having said which, he apologetically smeared his face all over with his shirt-sleeve, and subsided again.

" It do wring my 'eart—ah, that it do ! to think o' pore Jarge a convic' at Bot'ny Bay ! " said Old Amos, "a-workin', an' diggin', an' slavin' wi' irons on 'is legs an' arms, a-jinglin', an' a-janglin' when 'e walks."

" Well, but it's Justice, aren't it ? " demanded Job— " a poacher's a thief, an' a thief's a convic'—or should be ! "

" I've 'eerd," said Old Amos, shaking his head, " I've 'eerd as they ties they convic's up to posts, an' lashes , an' lashes 'em wi' the cat o' nine tails ! "

" They generally mostly deserves it ! " nodded Job.

" But 'tis 'ard to think o' pore Jarge tied up to one o' them floggin'-posts, wi' 'is back all raw an' bleedin' ! " pursued Old Amos ; " crool 'ard it be, an' 'im such a fine, strappin' young chap."

" 'E were allus a sight too fond o' pitchin' into folk, Jarge were ! " said Job ; " it be a mercy as my back weren't broke more nor once."

" Ah ! " nodded the Ancient, " you must be amazin' strong in the back, Job ! The way I've seed 'ee come a-rollin' an' a-wallerin' out o' that theer smithy's won-nerful, wonnerful. Lord ! Job—'ow you did roll ! "

" Well, 'e won't never do it no more," said Job, glowering ; " what wi' poachin' 'is game, an' knockin' 'is keepers about, 'taren't likely as Squire Beverley'll let 'im off very easy——"

" Who ? " said I, looking up, and speaking for the first time.

" Squire Beverley o' Burn'am 'All."

" Sir Peregrine Beverley ? "

" Ay, for sure."

" And how far is it to Burnham Hall ? "

" 'Ow fur ? " repeated Job, staring, " why, it lays 'tother side o' Horsmonden——"

" It be a matter o' eight mile, Peter," said the Ancient.

" Nine, Peter ! " cried Old Amos—" nine mile, it be ! "

" Though I won't swear, Peter," continued the Ancient, " I won't swear as it aren't—seven—call it six an' three quarters ! " said he, with his eagle eye on Old Amos.

" Then I had better start now," said I, and rose.

" Why, Peter—wheer be goin' ? "

" To Burnham Hall, Ancient."

" What—you ? " exclaimed Job ; " d'ye think Squire'll see you ? "

" I think so ; yes."

" Well, 'e won't—they'll never let the likes o' you or me beyond the gates."

" That remains to be seen," said I.

" So you'm goin', are ye ? "

" I certainly am."

" All right ! " nodded Job, " if they sets the dogs on ye, or chucks you into the road—don't go blamin' it on to me, that's all ! "

" What—be ye really a-goin', Peter ? "

" I really am, Ancient."

" Then—by the Lord !—I'll go wi' ye."

" It's a long walk ! "

" Nay—Simon shall drive us in the cart."

" That I will ! " nodded the Innkeeper.

" Ay, lad," cried the Ancient, laying his hand upon my arm, " we'll up an' see Squire, you an' me—shall us, Peter ? There be some fules," said he, looking round upon the staring company, " some fules as talks o' Bot'ny Bay, an' irons, an' whippin'-posts—all I says is—let 'em, Peter, let 'em ! You an' me'll up an' see Squire, Peter, sha'n't us ? Black Jarge aren't a convic' yet, let fules say what they will ; we'll show 'em, Peter, we'll show 'em ! " So saying, the old man led me into the kitchen of " The Bull " while Simon went to have the horses put to.

CHAPTER XXXI

IN WHICH THE ANCIENT IS SURPRISED

A CHEERY place, at all times, is the kitchen of an English inn, a comfortable place to eat in, to talk in, or to doze in; a place with which your parlours and withdrawing-rooms, your salons (*à la* the three Louis) with their irritating rococo, their gilt, and satin, and spindle-legged discomforts, are not (to my mind) worthy to compare.

And what inn kitchen, in all broad England, was ever brighter, neater, and more comfortable than this kitchen of "The Bull," where sweet Prue held supreme sway, with such grave dignity, and with her two white-capped maids to do her bidding and behests?—surely none. And surely in no inn, tavern, or hostelry soever, great or small, was there ever seen a daintier, prettier, sweeter hostess than this same Prue of ours.

And her presence was reflected everywhere, and, if ever the kitchen of an inn possessed a heart to lose, then, beyond all doubt, this kitchen had lost its heart to Prue long since; even the battered cutlasses crossed upon the wall, the ponderous jack above the hearth, with its legend: ANNO DOMINI 1643, took on a brighter sheen to greet her when she came, and, as for the pots and pans, they fairly twinkled.

But to-day Prue's eyes were red, and her lips were all a-droop, the which, though her smile was brave and ready, the Ancient was quick to notice.

"Why, Prue, lass, you've been weepin'!"

"Yes, grandfer."

"Your pretty eyes be all swole—red they be; what's the trouble?"

"Oh! 'tis nothing, dear, 'tis just a maid's fulishness—never mind me, dear."

" Ah! but I love 'ee, Prue—come, kiss me—theer now, tell me all about it—all about it, Prue."

" Oh, grandfer! " said she, from the hollow of his shoulder, " 'tis just—Jarge! " The old man grew very still, his mouth opened slowly, and closed with a snap.

" Did 'ee—did 'ee say—Jarge, Prue? Is it—breekin' your 'eart ye be for that theer poachin' Black Jarge? To think—as my Prue should come down to a poachin'——"

Prudence slipped from his encircling arm and stood up very straight and proud —there were tears thick upon her lashes, but she did not attempt to wipe them away.

" Grandfer," she said, very gently, " you mustn't speak of Jarge to me like that—ye mustn't—ye mustn't —because I—love him, and if—he ever—comes back—I'll marry him if—if he will only ax me; and if he—never comes back, then—I think—I shall—die ! " The Ancient took out his snuff-box, knocked it, opened it, glanced inside, and—shut it up again.

" Did 'ee tell me as you—love—Black Jarge, Prue? "

" Yes, grandfer, I always have and always shall ! "

" Loves Black Jarge! " he repeated; " allus 'as—allus will! Oh, Lord! what 'ave I done? " Now, very slowly a tear crept down his wrinkled cheek, at sight of which Prue gave a little cry, and, kneeling beside his chair, took him in her arms. " Oh, my lass !—my little Prue—'tis all my doin'. I thought—— Oh, Prue, 'twere me as parted you ! I thought——" the quivering voice broke off.

" 'Tis all right, grandfer, never think of it—see—there, I be smilin' ! " and she kissed him many times.

" A danged fule I be ! " said the old man, shaking his head.

" No, no, grandfer ! "

" That's what I be, Prue—a danged fule ! If I do go afore that theer old, rusty stapil, 'twill serve me right—a danged fule I be ! Allus loved 'im—allus will, an' wishful to wed wi' 'im ! Why, then," said

the Ancient, swallowing two or three times, " so 'ee
shall, my sweet—so 'ee shall, sure as sure, so come an'
kiss me, an' forgive the old man as loves 'ee so."

" What do 'ee mean, grandfer ? " said Prue between
two kisses.

" A fine, strappin' chap be Jarge ; arter all, Peter,
you bean't a patch on Jarge for looks, be you ? "

" No, indeed, Ancient ! "

" Wishful to wed 'im, she is, an' so she shall.
Lordy Lord ! Kiss me again, Prue, for I be goin' to
see Squire—ay, I be goin' to up an' speak wi' Squire
for Jarge—an' Peter be comin' too."

" Oh, Mr Peter ! " faltered Prudence, " be this
true ? " and in her eyes was the light of a sudden hope.

" Yes," I nodded.

" D'you think Squire'll see you—listen to you ? "
she cried breathlessly.

" I think he will, Prudence," said I.

" God bless you, Mr Peter ! " she murmured.
" God bless you ! "

But now came the sound of wheels and the voice of
Simon, calling, wherefore I took my hat and followed
the Ancient to the door, but there Prudence stopped
me.

" Last time you met wi' Jarge—he tried to kill you.
Oh, I know, and now—you be goin' to——"

" Nonsense, Prue ! " said I. But, as I spoke, she
stooped, and would have kissed my hand, but I raised
her, and kissed her upon the cheek instead. " For
good luck, Prue," said I, and so turned and left her.

In the porch sat Job, with Old Amos, and the rest,
still in solemn conclave over pipes and ale, who
watched with gloomy brows as I swung myself up
beside the Ancient in the cart.

" A fule's journey ! " remarked Old Amos sententi-
ously, with a wave of his pipe; " a fule's journey ! "

The Ancient cast an observing eye up at the cloudless sky, and also nodded solemnly.

" Theer be some fules in this world, Peter, as mixes
up rabbits wi' pa'tridges, and honest men—like Jarge
—wi' thieves, an' lazy waggabones—like Job—but

" Grandfer," she said, very gently, " you mustn't speak of Jarge to me like that"

Face Page 400

"Grandfather," she said, very gently, "you mustn't speak of Jorge to me like that."

Face Page 400

we'll show 'em, Peter, we'll show 'em—dang 'em!
Drive on, Simon, my bye!"

So, with this Parthian shot, feathered with the one
strong word the Ancient kept for such occasions, we
drove away from the silenced group, who stared
mutely after us until we were lost to view.   But the
last thing I saw was the light in Prue's sweet eyes as
she watched us from the open lattice.

2 C

CHAPTER XXXII

HOW WE SET OUT FOR BURNHAM HALL

"PETER," said the Ancient, after we had gone a little way, "Peter, I do 'opes as you aren't been an' gone an' rose my Prue's 'opes only to dash 'em down again."

"I can but do my best, Ancient."

"Old 'Un," said Simon, " 'twei en't Peter as rose 'er 'opes, 'twere you—Peter never said nowt about bringin' Jarge 'ome——"

"Simon," commanded the Ancient, "hold thy tongue, lad; I says again, if Peter's been an' rose Prue's 'opes only to dash 'em 'twill be a bad day for Prue, you mark my words, Prue's a lass as don't love easy, an' don't forget easy."

"Why, true, Gaffer, true, God bless 'er!"

"She be one as 'ud pine—slow an' quiet, like a flower in the woods, or a leaf in autumn—ah! fade, she would, fade an' fade!"

"Well, she bean't a-goin' to do no fadin', please the Lord!"

"Not if me, an' Peter, an' you, can 'elp it, Simon, my bye—but we'm but poor worms, arter all, as the Bible says, an' if Peter 'as been an' rose 'er 'opes o' freein' Jarge, an' don't free Jarge—if Jarge should 'ave to go a convic' to Austrayley, or—or t'other place, why then—she'll fade, fade as ever was, an' be laid in the churchyard afore 'er poor old grandfeyther!"

"Lord, Old 'Un!" exclaimed Simon, "who's a-talkin' o' fadin's an' churchyards? I don't like it—let's talk o' summat else."

"Simon," said the Ancient, shaking his head reprovingly, "ye be a good bye—ah! a steady, dootiful lad ye be, I don't deny it; but the Lord aren't give you no imagination, which, arter all, you should be

402

main thankful for; a imagination's a troublesome thing—aren't it, Peter?"

"It is," said I, "a damnable thing!"

"Ay—many's the man as 'as been ruinated by 'is imagination—theer was one, Nicodemus Blyte were 'is name——"

"And a very miserable cove 'e sounds, too!" added Simon.

"But a very decent, civil-spoke, quiet young chap 'e were!" continued the Ancient, "only for 'is imagination; Lord! 'e were that full o' imagination 'e couldn't drink 'is ale like an ordinary chap—sip, 'e'd go, an' sip, sip, till 'twere all gone, an' then 'e'd forget as ever 'e'd 'ad any, an' go away wi'out paying for it—if some'un didn't remind 'im——"

"'E were no fule, Old 'Un!" nodded Simon.

"An' that weren't all, neither, not by no manner o' means," the Ancient continued. "I've knowed that theer chap sit an' listen to a pretty lass by the hour together an' never say a word—not one!"

"Didn't git a chance to, p'r'aps?" said Simon.

"It weren't that, no, it were jest 'is imagination a-workin' an' workin' inside of 'im, an' fillin' 'im up. 'Ows'ever, at last, one day, 'e up an' axed 'er to marry 'im, an' she, bein' all took by surprise, said 'yes,' an' went an' married some'un else."

"Lord!" said Simon, "what did she go and marry another chap for?"

"Simon," returned the Ancient, "don't go askin' fulish questions. 'Ows'ever, she did, an' poor Nicodemus growed more imaginative than ever—arter that, 'e took to turnips."

"Turnips?" exclaimed Simon, staring.

"Turnips as ever was!" nodded the Ancient, "used to stand, for hours at a time, a-lookin' at 'is turnips an' shakin' 'is 'ead over 'em."

"But—what for?—a man must be a danged fule to go shakin' of 'is 'ead over a lot o' turnips!"

"Well, I don't know," rejoined the Ancient; "'is turnips was very good 'uns, as a rule, an' fetched top prices in the markets."

At this juncture there appeared a man in a cart, ahead of us, who flourished his whip, and roared a greeting, a coarse-visaged, loud-voiced fellow, whose beefy face was adorned with a pair of enormous fiery whiskers that seemed for ever striving to hide his ears, which last, being very large and red, stood boldly out at right angles to his head, refusing to be thus ambushed, and scorning all concealment.

"W'at—be that the Old 'Un—be you alive an' kickin' yet?"

"Ay, God be thanked, John!"

"And w'at be all this I 'ear about that theer Black Jarge—'e never were much good—but w'at be all this?"

"Lies, mostly, you may tak' your oath!" nodded the Ancient.

"But 'e've been took for poachin', ah! an' locked up at the 'All——"

"An' we'm goin' to fetch 'un—we be goin' to see Squire——"

"W'at—you, Old 'Un? You see Squire—haw! haw!"

"Ah, me!—an' Peter, an' Simon, 'ere—why not?"

"*You* see 'is Worship Sir Peregrine Beverley, Baronet, an' Justice o' the Peace—*you*? Ecod! that's a good 'un—danged if it ain't! An' what might you be wishful to do when ye see 'im—which ye *won't*?"

"Fetch back Jarge, o' course."

"Old 'Un, you must be crazed in your 'ead, arter Jarge killin' four keepers—Sir Peregrine's own keepers too—shootin' 'em stone dead, an' three more a-dyin'——"

"John," said the Ancient, shaking his head, "that's the worst o' bein' cursed wi' ears like yourn——"

"My ears is all right!" returned John, frowning.

"Oh, ah!" chuckled the old man, "your ears is all right, John—prize ears, ye might call 'em, I never seed a pair better grow'd—never, no!"

"A bit large, they may be," growled John, giving a furtive pull to the nearest ambush, "but——"

"Large as ever was, John!" nodded the Ancient—

"oncommon large! an', consequent, they ketches a lot too much. I've kep' my eye on them ears o' yourn for thirty year an' more, John—if so be as they grows any bigger, you'll be 'earin' things afore they're spoke, an'——"

John gave a fierce tug to the ambush, muttered an oath, and, lashing up his horse, disappeared down the road in a cloud of dust.

"'Twere nigh on four year ago since Black Jarge thrashed John, weren't it, Simon?"

"Ah!" nodded Simon, "John were in 'The Ring' then, Peter, an' a pretty tough chap 'e were, too, though a bit too fond o' swingin' wi' 'is 'right' to please me."

"'E were very sweet on Prue then, weren't 'e, Simon?"

"Ah!" nodded Simon again; "'e were allus 'anging round 'The Bull'—till I warned 'im off——"

"An'—'e laughed at 'ee, Simon."

"Ah! 'e did that; an' I were going to 'ave a go at 'im myself; an' the chances are 'e'd 'ave beat me, seein' I 'adn't been inside of a ring for ten year, when——"

"Up comes Jarge," chuckled the Ancient. 'What's all this?' say Jarge. 'I be goin' to teach John 'ere to keep away from my Prue,' says Simon. 'No, no,' says Jarge, 'John's young, an' you bean't the man you was ten years ago—let me,' says Jarge. 'You?' says John, 'you get back to your bellers—you be purty big, but I've beat the 'eads off better men nor you!' 'Why, then, 'ave a try at mine,' says Jarge; an' wi' the word, bang! come John's fist agin' 'is jaw, an' they was at it. Oh, Peter! that were a fight! I've seed a few in my time, but nothin' like that 'ere."

"And when 'twere all over," added Simon, "Jarge went back to 'is 'ammer, an' bellers, an' we picked John up, and I druv 'im 'ome in this 'ere very cart, an' nobody's cared to stand up to Jarge since."

"You have both seen Black George fight, then?" I inquired.

"Many's the time, Peter."

"And have you ever—seen him knocked down?"

"No," returned the Ancient, shaking his head, "I've seed 'im all blood from 'ead to foot, an' once a gert, big sailor-man knocked 'im sideways, arter which Jarge got fu'rus-like, an' put 'im to sleep——"

"No, Peter!" added Simon, "I don't think as there be a man in all England as could knock Black Jarge off 'is pins in a fair, stand-up fight."

"Hum!" said I.

"Ye see—'e be that 'ard, Peter!" nodded the Ancient. "Why, look!" he cried—"look 'ee theer!"

Now, looking where he pointed, I saw a man dart across the road some distance away; he was hidden almost immediately, for there were many trees thereabouts, but there was no mistaking that length of limb and breadth of shoulder.

"'Twere Black Jarge 'isself!" exclaimed Simon, whipping up his horses; but when we reached the place George was gone, and though we called and sought for some time, we saw him no more.

So, in a while, we turned and jogged back towards Sissinghurst.

"What be you a-shakin' your 'ead over, Old 'Un?" inquired Simon after we had ridden some distance.

"I were wonderin' what that old fule Amos'll say when we drive back wi'out Jarge."

Being come to the parting of the ways, I descended from the cart, for my head was strangely heavy, and I felt much out of sorts, and, though the day was still young, I had no mind for work. Therefore I bade adieu to Simon and the Ancient, and turned aside towards the Hollow, leaving them staring after me in wonderment.

CHAPTER XXXIII

IN WHICH I FALL FROM FOLLY INTO MADNESS

IT was with some little trepidation that I descended into the Hollow, and walked along beside the brook, for soon I should meet Charmian, and the memory of our parting, and the thought of this meeting, had been in my mind all day long.

She would not be expecting me yet, for I was much before my usual time, wherefore I walked on slowly beside the brook, deliberating on what I should say to her, until I came to that large stone where I had sat dreaming the night when she had stood in the moonlight, and first bidden me in to supper. And now, sinking upon this stone, I set my elbows upon my knees, and my chin in my hands, and, fixing my eyes upon the ever-moving waters of the brook, fell into a profound meditation.

From this I was suddenly aroused by the clink of iron and the snort of a horse.

Wondering, I lifted my eyes, but the bushes were very dense, and I could see nothing. But, in a little, borne upon the gentle wind, came the sound of a voice, low and soft, and very sweet—whose rich tones there was no mistaking—followed, almost immediately, by another—deeper, gruffer—the voice of a man.

With a bound, I was upon my feet, and had, somehow, crossed the brook, but, even so, I was too late; there was the crack of a whip, followed by the muffled thud of a horse's hoofs, which died quickly away, and was lost in the stir of leaves.

I ground my teeth, and cursed that fate which seemed determined that I should not meet this man face to face—this man whose back I had seen but once—a broad-shouldered back clad in a blue coat.

I stood where I was, dumb and rigid, staring

straight before me, and once again a tremor passed over me, that came and went, growing stronger and stronger, and, once again, in my head was the thud, thud, thud of the hammer.

> "In Scarlet Town where I was born,
>   There was a fair maid dwellin'
>   Made every youth cry 'well-a-day!'
>   Her name was Barbara Allen."

She was approaching by that leafy path that wound its way along beside the brook, and there came upon me a physical nausea, and ever the thud of the hammer grew more maddening.

> "All through the merrie month of May
>   When green buds are a-swellin'
>   Young Jimmy Grove on his death-bed lay
>   For love of Barbara Allen."

Now, as she ended the verse, she came out into the open, and saw me, and, seeing me, looked deliberately over my head, and went on singing, while I—stood shivering:

> "So, slowly, slowly she came up
>   And slowly she drew nigh him,
>   And, all she said when she came near:
>   'Young man, I think you're dyin'!'"

And suddenly the trees and bushes swung giddily round—the grass swayed beneath my feet—and Charmian was beside me with her arm about my shoulders; but I pushed her from me, and leaned against a tree near by, and hearkened to the hammer in my brain.

"Why—Peter!" said she. "Oh—Peter!"

"Please, Charmian," said I, speaking between the hammer-strokes, "do not touch me again—it is—too soon after——"

"What do you mean—Peter? What do you mean?"

"He has—been with you—again——"

"What do you mean?" she cried.

"I know of—his visits—if he was—the same as—last time—in a—blue coat—no, don't, don't touch me."

But she had sprung upon me, and caught me by the

I fall from Folly into Madness   409

arms, and shook me in a grip so strong that, giddy as I
was, I reeled and staggered like a drunken man. And
still her voice hissed : "What do you mean?"   And her
voice, and hands, and eyes were strangely compelling.

"I mean," I answered, in a low, even voice, like one
in a trance, "that you are a Messalina, a Julia, a Joan
of Naples, beautiful as they—and as wanton."

Now at the word she cried out, and struck me twice
across the face, blows that burnt and stung.

"Beast!" she cried.   "Liar!   O that I had the
strength to grind you into the earth beneath my foot.
O! you poor, blind, self-deluding fool!" and she
laughed, and her laughter stung me most of all.   "As
I look at you," she went on, the laugh still curling her
lip, "you stand there—what you are—a beaten hound.
This is my last look, and I shall always remember you
as I see you now—scarlet-cheeked, shamefaced—a
beaten hound!"   And, speaking, she shook her hand
at me, and turned upon her heel; but with that word,
and in that instant, the old, old dæmon leapt up within
me, and, as he leapt, I clasped my arms about her, and
caught her up, and crushed her close and high against
my breast.

"Go?" said I.   "Go—no—no, not yet!"

And now, as her eyes met mine, I felt her tremble,
yet she strove to hide her fear, and heaped me with
bitter scorn; but I only shook my head, and smiled.
And now she struggled to break my clasp, fiercely,
desperately; her long hair burst its fastenings, and
enveloped us both in its rippling splendour; she beat
my face, she wound her fingers in my hair, but my lips
smiled on, for the hammer in my brain had deadened
all else.

And presently she lay still.   I felt her body relax
and grow suddenly pliable and soft, her head fell back
across my arm, and, as she lay, I saw the tears of her
helplessness ooze out beneath her drooping lashes;
but still I smiled.

So, with her long hair trailing over me, I bore her
to the cottage.   Closing the door behind me with my
foot, I crossed the room, and set her down upon the bed.

She lay very still, but her bosom heaved tumultuously, and the tears still crept from beneath her lashes; but in a while she opened her eyes and looked at me, and shivered, and crouched farther from me, among the pillows.

"Why did you lie to me, Charmian; why did you lie to me?" She did not answer, only she watched me as one might watch some relentless, oncoming peril.

"I asked you once if you ever saw men hereabouts—when I was away, do you remember? You told me, ' no,' and, while you spoke, I knew you lied, for I had seen him standing among the leaves, waiting and watching for you. I once asked you if you were ever lonely when I was away, and you answered ' no—you were too busy—seldom went beyond the Hollow '—do you remember? And yet—you had brought him here—here, into the cottage—he had looked at my Virgil—over your shoulder—do you remember?"

"You played the spy," she whispered with trembling lips, yet with eyes still fierce and scornful.

"You know I did not; had I seen him I should have killed him, because—I loved you. I had set up an altar to you in my heart, where my soul might worship—poor fool that I was! I loved you with every breath I drew. I think I must have shown you something of this, from time to time, for you are very clever, and you may have laughed over it together—you and he. And lately I have seen my altar foully desecrated, shattered, and utterly destroyed, and, with it, your sweet womanhood dragged in the mire, and yet—I loved you still. Can you imagine, I wonder, the agony of it, the haunting horrors of imagination, the bitter days, the sleepless nights? To see you so beautiful, so glorious, and know you so base! Indeed, I think it came near driving me mad—it has sent me out into the night, I have held out my arms for the lightning to blast me, I have wished myself a thousand deaths. If Black George had but struck a little harder —or a little lighter; I am not the man I was before he thrashed me, my head grows confused and clouded at times—would to God I were dead! But now—you would go ! Having killed my heart, broken my life, driven away all peace of mind—you would leave me ! No, Charmian, I swear by God you shall not go—yet awhile. I have bought you very dear—bought you with my bitter agony, and by all the blasting torments I have suffered."

Now, as I ended, she sprang from the bed and faced me, but, meeting my look, she shrank a little, and drew her long hair about her like a mantle, then sought with trembling hands to hold me off.

"Peter—be sane. Oh, Peter ! be merciful and let me go—give me time—let me explain."

"My books," said I, " have taught me that the more beautiful a woman's face the more guileful is her heart; and your face is wonderfully beautiful, and, as for your heart—you lied to me before."

"I—oh, Peter !—I am not the poor creature you think me."

"Were you the proudest lady in the land—you have deceived me, and mocked me, and lied to me ! " So saying, I reached out, and seized her by each rounded arm, and slowly drew her closer. And now she strove no more against me, only in her face was bitter scorn, and an anger that cast out fear.

"I hate you—despise you ! " she whispered. " I hate you more than any man was ever hated ! "

Inch by inch I drew her to me, until she stood close, within the circle of my arms.

" And I think I love you more than any woman was ever loved ! " said I ; " for the glorious beauty of your strong, sweet body, for the temptation of your eyes, for the red lure of your lips ! " And so I stooped and kissed her full upon the mouth. She lay soft and warm in my embrace, all unresisting, only she shivered beneath my kiss, and a great sob rent her bosom.

" And I also think," said I, " that, because of the perfidy of your heart, I hate you as much as you do me—as much as ever woman, dead or living, was hated by man—and shall—for ever ! "

And, while I spoke, I loosed her, and turned, and strode swiftly out and away from the cottage.

CHAPTER XXXIV

IN WHICH I FIND PEACE AND JOY AND AN
ABIDING SORROW

I HURRIED on, looking neither to right nor left, seeing only the face of Charmian, now fearful and appealing, now blazing with scorn. And coming to the brook, I sat down, and thought upon her marvellous beauty, of the firm roundness of the arms that my fingers had so lately pressed. Anon I started up again, and plunged, knee-deep, through the brook, and strode on and on, bursting my way through bramble and briar, heedless of their petty stings, till at last I was clear of them, being now among trees. And here, where the shadow was deepest, I came upon a lurking figure—a figure I recognised—a figure there was no mistaking, and which I should have known in a thousand.

A shortish, broad-shouldered man, clad in a blue coat, who stood with his back towards me, looking down into the Hollow, in the attitude of one who waits —for what? for whom?

He was cut off from me by a solitary bush, a bramble, that seemed to have strayed from its kind and lost itself, and, running upon my toes, I cleared this bush at a bound, and, before the fellow had realised my presence, I had pinned him by the collar.

"Damn you!—show your face!" I cried, and swung him round so fiercely that he staggered, and his hat fell off.

Then, as I saw, I clasped my head between my hands, and fell back—staring.

A grizzled man with an honest, open face, a middle-aged man whose homely features were lighted by a pair of kindly blue eyes, just now round with astonishment.

"Lord!—Mr Peter!" he exclaimed.

" Adam ! " I groaned. " Oh, God forgive me, it's Adam ! "

" Lord ! Mr Peter," said he again, " you sure give me a turn, sir ! But what's the matter wi' you, sir ? Come, Mr Peter, never stare so wild like—come, sir, what is it ? "

" Tell me—quick ! " said I, catching his hand in mine, " you have been here many times before of late ? "

" Why—yes, Mr Peter, but——"

" Quick ! " said I ; " on one occasion she took you into the cottage yonder and showed you a book—you looked at it over her shoulder ? "

" Yes, sir—but——"

" What sort of book was it ? "

" A old book, sir, wi' the cover broke, and wi' your name writ down inside of it—'twas that way as she found out who you was——"

" Oh, Adam ! " I cried. " Oh, Adam ! now may God help me ! " And, dropping his hand, I turned and ran until I reached the cottage ; but it was empty, Charmian was gone.

In a fever of haste I sought her along the brook, among the bushes and trees, even along the road. And, as I sought, night fell, and in the shadows was black despair.

I searched the Hollow from end to end, calling upon her name, but no sound reached me, save the hoot of an owl, and the far-off, dismal cry of a corn-crake.

With some faint hope that she might have returned to the cottage, I hastened thither, but, finding it dark and desolate, I gave way to my despair.

O blind, self-deceiving fool ! She had said that, and she was right—as usual. She had called me an egoist—I was an egoist, a pedant, a blind, self-deceiving fool who had wilfully destroyed all hopes of a happiness the very thought of which had so often set me trembling—and now—she had left me—was gone ! The world—my world, was a void—its emptiness terrified me. How should I live without Charmian, the woman whose image was ever before my eyes, whose soft, low voice was ever in my ears?

And I had thought so much to please her! I who had set my thoughts to guard my tongue, lest by word, or look, I might offend her! And this was the end of it!

Sitting down at the table I leaned my head there, pressing my forehead against the hard wood, and remained thus a great while.

At last, because it was very dark, I found and lighted a candle, and came and stood beside her bed. Very white and trim it looked, yet I was glad to see its smoothness rumpled where I had laid her down, and to see the depression in the pillow that her head had made. And, while I stood there, up to me stole a perfume very faint, like the breath of violets in a wood at evening time, wherefore I sank down upon my knees beside the bed.

And now the full knowledge of my madness rushed upon me in an overwhelming flood; but with Misery was a great and mighty Joy, for now I knew her worthy of all respect and honour and worship, for her intellect, for her proud virtue, and for her spotless purity. And thus, with Joy came Remorse, and with Remorse—an abiding Sorrow.

And gradually my arms crept about the pillow where her head had so often rested, wherefore I kissed it, and laid my head upon it, and sighed, and so fell into a troubled sleep.

CHAPTER XXXV

HOW BLACK GEORGE FOUND PRUDENCE IN THE DAWN

THE chill of dawn was in the air when I awoke, and it was some few moments before, with a rush, I remembered why I was kneeling there beside Charmian's bed. Shivering, I rose and walked up and down to reduce the stiffness in my limbs.

The fire was out and I had no mind to light it, for I was in no mood to break my fast, though the necessary things stood ready, as her orderly hands had set them, and the plates and cups and saucers twinkled at me from the little cupboard I had made to hold them : a cupboard whose construction she had overlooked with a critical eye. And I must needs remember how she had insisted on being permitted to drive in three nails with her own hand—I could put my finger on those very nails; how she had tapped at those nails for fear of missing them; how beautiful she had looked in her coarse apron, and with her sleeves rolled up over her round white arms—how womanly, and sweet; yet I had dared to think—had dared to call her—a Messalina ! O that my tongue had withered or ever I had coupled one so pure and noble with a creature so base and common !

So thinking, I sighed and went out into the dawn ; as I closed the door behind me its hollow slam struck me sharply, and I called to mind how she had called it a bad and ill-fitting door. And indeed so it was.

With dejected step and hanging head I made my way towards Sissinghurst (for, since I was up, I might as well work, and there was much to be done), and, as I went, I heard a distant clock chime four.

Now, when I reached the village the sun was beginning to rise, and thus, lifting up my eyes, I beheld one standing before " The Bull," a very tall man,

415

much bigger and greater than most; a wild figure in
the dawn, with matted hair and beard, and clad in
tattered clothes; yet hair and beard gleamed a red gold
where the light touched them, and there was but one
man I knew so tall and so mighty as this. Wherefore
I hurried towards him, all unnoticed, for his eyes were
raised to a certain latticed casement of the inn.

And, being come up, I reached out and touched this
man upon the arm.

" George! " said I, and held out my hand. He
turned swiftly, but, seeing me, started back a pace,
staring.

" George! " said I again. " Oh, George! " But
George only backed still farther, passing his hand
once or twice across his eyes.

" Peter ? " said he at last, speaking hardly above
a whisper; " but you'm dead, Peter, dead—I killed
'ee."

" No," I answered, " you didn't kill me, George—
indeed, I wish you had—you came pretty near it, but
you didn't quite manage it. And, George—I'm very
desolate—won't you shake hands with a very desolate
man ?—if you can, believing that I have always been
your friend, and a true and loyal one, then, give me
your hand; if not—if you think me still the despicable
traitor you once did, then, let us go into the field
yonder, and if you can manage to knock me on the
head for good and all this time—why, so much the
better. Come, what do you say ? "

Without a word Black George turned and led the
way to a narrow lane a little distance beyond " The
Bull," and from the lane into a meadow. Being come
thither I took off my coat and neckerchief, but this
time I cast no look upon the world about me, though
indeed it was fair enough. But Black George stood
half turned from me, with his fists clenched and his
broad shoulders heaving oddly.

" Peter," said he, in his slow, heavy way, " never
clench ye fists to me—don't—I can't abide it. But oh,
man, Peter! 'ow may I clasp 'ands wi' a chap as I've
tried to kill—I can't do it, Peter—but don't—don't

clench ye fists agin me no more. I were jealous of 'ee from the first—ye see, you beat me at th' 'ammer-throwin'—an' she took your part agin me; an' then, you be so takin' in your ways, an' I be so big an' clumsy—so very slow an' 'eavy Theer beant' no choice betwixt us for a maid like Prue—she allus was different from the likes o' me, an' any lass wi' half an eye could see as you be a gentleman, ah! an' a good 'un. An' so, Peter, an' so—I be goin' away—a sojer —p'r'aps I sha'n't love the dear lass quite so much arter a bit—p'r'aps it won't be quite so sharp-like, arter a bit, but what's to be—is to be. I've larned wisdom, an' you an' she was made for each other an' meant for each other from the first; so—don't go to clench ye fists agin me no more, Peter."

" Never again, George! " said I.

" Unless," he continued, as though struck by a bright idea, " unless you'm minded to 'ave a whack at me;—if so be—why, tak' it, Peter, an' welcome. Ye see, I tried so 'ard to kill 'ee—so cruel 'ard, Peter, an' I thought I 'ad. I thought 'twere for that as they took me, an' so I broke my way out o' the lock-up, to come an' say ' good-bye ' to Prue's winder, an' then I were goin' back to give myself up an' let 'em hang me if they wanted to."

" Were you, George? "

" Yes." Here George turned to look at me, and, looking, dropped his eyes and fumbled with his hands, while up under his tanned skin there crept a painful, burning crimson. " Peter! " said he.

" Yes, George? "

" I got summat more to tell 'ee—summat as I never meant to tell to a soul;—when you was down—lyin' at my feet——"

" Yes, George? "

" I—I kicked 'ee—once! "

" Did you, George? "

" Ay—I—I were mad—mad wi' rage an' blood lust, an'—oh, man, Peter!—I kicked 'ee. Theer," said he, straightening his shoulders, " leastways I can look 'ee in the eye now that be off my mind. An' now, if so be

2 D

you'm wishful to tak' ye whack at me—why, let it be a good 'un, Peter."

" No, I shall never raise my hand to you again, George."

" 'Tis likely you be thinkin' me a poor sort o' man, arter what—what I just told 'ee—a coward?"

" I think you more of a man than ever," said I.

" Why, then, Peter—if ye do think that, here's my hand—if ye'll tak' it, an' I—bid ye—good-bye!"

" I'll take your hand—and gladly, George, but not to wish you good-bye—it shall be, rather, to bid you welcome home again."

" No," he cried. " No—I couldn't—I couldn't abide to see you an'—Prue—married, Peter—no, I couldn't abide it."

" And you never will, George. Prue loves a stronger, a better man than I. And she has wept over him, George, and prayed over him, such tears and prayers as surely might win the blackest soul to heaven, and has said that she would marry that man— ah! even if he came back with fetter-marks upon him —even then she would marry him—if he would only ask her."

" Oh, Peter!" cried George, seizing my shoulders in a mighty grip and looking into my eyes with tears in his own, " oh, man, Peter—you as knocked me down an' as I love for it—be this true?"

" It is God's truth!" said I, " and look!—there is a sign to prove I am no liar—look!" and I pointed towards " The Bull."

George turned, and I felt his fingers tighten suddenly, for there, at the open doorway of the inn, with the early glory of the morning all about her, stood Prue. As we watched, she began to cross the road towards the smithy, with laggard step and drooping head.

" Do you know where she is going, George? I can tell you—she is going to your smithy—to pray for you —do you hear, to pray for you? Come!" and I seized his arm.

" No, Peter, no—I durstn't—I couldn't." But he

suffered me to lead him forward nevertheless. Once he stopped and glanced round, but the village was asleep about us. And so we presently came to the open doorway of the forge.

And behold! Prue was kneeling before the anvil with her face hidden in her arms, and her slender body swaying slightly. But all at once, as if she felt him near her, she raised her head and saw him, and sprang to her feet with a glad cry. And, as she stood, George went to her, and knelt at her feet, and raising the hem of her gown, stooped and kissed it.

"Oh, my sweet maid!" said he. "Oh, my sweet Prue!—I bean't worthy—I bean't——" But she caught the great shaggy head to her bosom and stifled it there.

And in her face was a radiance—a happiness beyond words, and the man's strong arms clung close about her.

So I turned, and left them in paradise together.

CHAPTER XXXVI

WHICH SYMPATHISES WITH A BRASS JACK, A BRACE OF CUTLASSES, AND DIVERS POTS AND PANS

I FOUND the Ancient sunning himself in the porch before the inn, as he waited for his breakfast.

"Peter," said he, " I be tur'ble cold sometimes. It comes a-creepin' on me all at once, even if I be sittin' before a roarin' fire or a-baskin' in this good, warm sun—a cold as reaches down into my poor old 'eart—grave-chills, I calls 'em, Peter—ah! grave-chills. Ketches me by the 'eart they do; ye see I be that old, Peter, that old an' wore out."

" But you're a wonderful man for your age!" said I, clasping the shrivelled hand in mine, "and very lusty and strong——"

"So strong as a bull I be, Peter!" he nodded readily, " but then, even a bull gets old an' wore out, an' these grave-chills ketches me oftener an' oftener. 'Tis like as if the Angel o' Death reached out an' touched me—just touched me wi' 'is finger, soft-like, as much as to say: ''Ere be a poor, old, wore-out creeter as I shall be wantin' soon.' Well, I be ready; 'tis only the young, or the fool, as fears to die. Three-score years an' ten, says the Bible, an' I be years an' years older than that. Oh! I sha'n't be afeared to answer when I'm called, Peter. ' Here I be, Lord!' I'll say. ''Ere I be, thy poor old servant'—but oh, Peter! if I could be sure o' that theer old rusty stapil bein' took first, why then I'd go j'yful—j'yful, but—why theer be that old fule Amos—Lord! what a dodderin' old fule 'e be, an' theer be Job, an' Dutton—they be comin' to plague me, Peter, I can feel it in my bones. Jest reach me my snuff-box out o' my 'ind pocket, an' you shall see me smite they Amalekites 'ip an' thigh."

" Gaffer," began Old Amos, saluting us with his usual grin, as he came up, " we be wishful to ax 'ee a question—we be wishful to know wheer be Black Jarge, which you 'avin' gone to fetch 'im, an' bring 'im 'ome again— them was your words."

" Ah ! " nodded Job, " them was your very words, ' bring 'im 'ome again,' says you——"

" But you didn't bring 'im 'ome," continued Old Amos, " leastways, not in the cart wi' you. Dutton 'ere—James Dutton see you come drivin' 'ome, but 'e didn't see no Jarge along wi' you—no, not so much as you could shake a stick at, as you might say. Speak up, James Dutton—you was a-leanin' over your front gate as Gaffer come drivin' 'ome, wasn't you, an' you see Gaffer plain as plain, didn't you ? "

" W'ich, me wishin' no offence, an' no one objectin' —I did," began the Apology, perspiring profusely as usual, " but I takes the liberty to say as it were a spade, an' not a gate—leastways——"

" But you didn't see no signs o' Jarge, did ye ? " demanded Old Amos, " as ye might say, neither 'ide nor 'air of 'im—speak up, James Dutton."

" W'ich, since you axes me, I makes so bold as to answer—an' very glad I'm sure—no; though as to 'ide an' 'air, I aren't wishin' to swear to, me not bein' near enough—w'ich could only be expected, an' very much obliged, I'm sure."

" Ye see, Gaffer," pursued Amos, " if you didn't bring Jarge back wi' you—w'ich you said you would —the question we axes is—wheer be Jarge ? "

" Ah !—wheer ? " nodded Job gloomily. Here the Ancient was evidently at a loss, to cover which, he took a vast pinch of snuff.

" 'Ow be we to know as 'e bean't pinin' away in a dungeon cell wi' irons on 'is legs, an' strapped in a strait-jacket an——"

Old Amos stopped, open-mouthed and staring, for out from the gloom of the smithy issued Black George himself, with Prue upon his arm. The Ancient stared also, but, dissembling his vast surprise, he dealt the lid of his snuff-box two loud, triumphant knocks.

"Peter," said he, rising stiffly, "Peter lad, I were beginnin' to think as Jarge were never comin' in to breakfus' at all. I've waited and waited till I be so ravenous as a lion an' tiger—but 'ere 'e be at last, Peter, 'ere 'e be, so let's go in an' eat summat." Saying which, he turned his back upon his discomfited tormentors, and led me into the kitchen of the inn.

And there were the white-capped maids setting forth such a breakfast as only such a kitchen could produce. And, presently, there was Prue herself, with George hanging back, something shamefaced, till the Ancient had hobbled forward to give him welcome. And there was honest Simon all wonderment and hearty greeting. And (last, but by no means least), there were the battered Cutlasses, the Brass Jack, and the glittering Pots and Pans—glittering, and gleaming, and twinkling a greeting likewise, and with all their might.

Ah! but they little guessed why Prue's eyes were so shy and sweet, or why the colour came and went in her pretty cheeks; little they guessed why this golden-haired giant trod so lightly, and held his tall head so very high—little they dreamed of the situation as yet; had they done so, surely they must, one and all, have fallen upon that curly, golden head and buried it beneath their gleaming, glittering, twinkling jealousy.

And what a meal was that! with those deft, white-capped maids to wait upon our wants, and with Prudence hovering here and there to see that all were duly served, and refusing to sit down until George's great arm—a very gentle arm for one so strong and big—drew her down beside him.

Yes, truly, what a meal that was, and how the Ancient chuckled, and dug me with one bony elbow, and George with the other, and chuckled again till he choked, and choked till he gasped, and gasped till he had us all upon our feet, then demanding indignantly why we couldn't let him "enj'y hisself in peace?"

And now, when the meal was nearly over, he suddenly took it into his head that Prue didn't love

George as she should, and as he deserved to be, and nothing would content him but that she must kiss him then and there.

"An' not on the forr'ud, mind—nor on the cheek, but on the place as God made for it—the mouth, my lass!"

And now, who so shy and blushing as Prue, and who so nervous, for her sake, as Black George, very evidently clasping her hand under the table, and bidding her "never to mind—as he was content, and never to put herself out over such as him." Whereupon Mistress Prue must needs turn, and taking his head between her hands, kissed him—not once, or twice, but three times, and upon "the place God made for it—the mouth."

O gleaming Cutlasses! O great Brass Jack and glittering Pots and Pans! can ye any longer gleam and glitter and twinkle in doubt? Alas! I trow not. Therefore it is only natural, and to be expected, that beneath your outward polish lurk black and bitter feelings against this curly-headed giant, and a bloodthirsty desire for vengeance. If so, then one and all of you have, at least, the good feeling not to show it, a behaviour worthy of gentlemen—what do I say?—of gentlemen?—fie! rather let it be said—of pots and pans.

CHAPTER XXXVII

THE PREACHER

It is a wise and (to some extent) a true saying, that hard work is an antidote to sorrow, a panacea for all trouble, but when the labour is over and done, when the tools are set by, and the weary worker goes forth into the quiet evening—how then? For we cannot always work, and, sooner or later, comes the still hour when Memory rushes in upon us again, and Sorrow and Remorse sit, dark and gloomy, on either hand.

A week dragged by, a season of alternate hope and black despair, a restless fever of nights and days, for with each dawn came hope, that lived awhile beside me, only to fly away with the sun, and leave me to despair.

I hungered for the sound of Charmian's voice, for the quick, light fall of her foot, for the least touch of her hand. I became more and more possessed of a morbid fancy that she might be existing near by— could I but find her; that she had passed along the road only a little while before me, or, at this very moment, might be approaching, might be within sight, were I but quick enough.

Often at such times I would fling down my hammer or tongs, to George's surprise, and, hurrying to the door, stare up and down the road; or pause in my hammer-strokes, fiercely bidding George do the same, fancying I heard her voice calling to me from a distance. And George would watch me with a troubled brow but, with a rare delicacy, say no word.

Indeed the thought of Charmian was with me everywhere, the ringing hammers mocked me with her praises, the bellows sang of her beauty, the trees whispered " Charmian! Charmian! " and Charmian was in the very air.

But when I had reluctantly bidden George " good-night,'' and set out along lanes full of the fragrant dusk of evening; when, reaching the Hollow, I followed that leafy path beside the brook, which she and I had so often trodden together; when I sat in my gloomy, disordered cottage, with the deep silence unbroken save for the plaintive murmur of the brook—then, indeed, my loneliness was well-nigh more than I could bear.

There were dark hours when the cottage rang with strange sounds, when I would lie face down upon the floor, clutching my throbbing temples between my palms—fearful of myself, and dreading the oncoming horror of madness.

It was at this time, too, that I began to be haunted by the thing above the door—the rusty staple upon which a man had choked out his wretched life sixty and six years ago; a wanderer, a lonely man, perhaps acquainted with misery, or haunted by remorse, one who had suffered much, and long—even as I—but who had eventually escaped it all—even as I might do. Thus I would sit, chin in hand, staring up at this staple until the light failed, and sometimes, in the dead of night, I would steal softly there to touch it with my finger.

Looking back on all this, it seems that I came very near losing my reason, for I had then by no means recovered from Black George's fist, and indeed even now I am at times not wholly free from its effect.

My sleep, too, was often broken and troubled with wild dreams, so that bed became a place of horror, and, rising, I would sit before the empty hearth, a candle guttering at my elbow, and think of Charmian until I would fancy I heard the rustle of her garments behind me, and start up, trembling and breathless; at such times the tap of a blown leaf against the lattice would fill me with a fever of hope and expectation. Often and often her soft laugh stole to me in the gurgle of the brook, and she would call to me in the deep night silences in a voice very sweet, and faint,

and far away. Then I would plunge out into the
dark, and lift my hands to the stars that winked upon
my agony, and journey on through a desolate world,
to return with the dawn, weary and despondent.

It was after one of these wild night expeditions that
I sat beneath a tree, watching the sunrise. And yet
I think I must have dozed, for I was startled by a
voice close above me, and, glancing up, I recognised
the little Preacher. As our eyes met he immediately
took the pipe from his lips, and made as though to
cram it into his pocket.

"Though, indeed, it is empty!" he exclaimed, as
though I had spoken. "Old habits cling to one,
young sir, and my pipe, here, has been the friend of
my solitude these many years, and I cannot bear to
turn my back upon it yet, so I carry it with me still,
and sometimes, when at all thoughtful, I find it
between my lips. But though the flesh, as you see, is
very weak, I hope, in time, to forgo even this," and
he sighed, shaking his head in gentle deprecation of
himself. "But you look pale—haggard," he went
on; "you are ill, young sir!"

"No, no," said I, springing to my feet; "look at
this arm, is it the arm of a sick man? No, no—I am
well enough, but what of him we found in the ditch,
you and I—the miserable creature who lay bubbling
in the grass?"

"He has been very near death, sir—indeed his
days are numbered, I think, yet he is better, for the
time being, and last night declared his intention of
leaving the shelter of my humble roof and setting
forth upon his mission."

"His mission, sir?"

"He speaks of himself as one chosen by God to
work His will, and asks but to live until this mission,
whatever it is, be accomplished. A strange being!"
said the little Preacher, puffing at his empty pipe
again as we walked on side by side, "a dark, incomprehensible man, and a very, very wretched one—poor
soul!"

"Wretched?" said I, "is not that our human lot?

' Man is born to sorrow as the sparks fly upward,' and Job was accounted wise in his generation.'

"That was a cry from the depths of Despond; but Job stood, at last, upon the heights, and felt once more God's blessed sun, and rejoiced—even as we should. But, as regards this stranger, he is one who would seem to have suffered some great wrong, the continued thought of which has unhinged his mind, his heart seems broken—dead. I have, sitting beside his delirious couch, heard him babble a terrible indictment against some man, I have also heard him pray, and his prayers have been all for vengeance."

"Poor fellow!" said I, "it were better we had left him to die in his ditch, for if death does not bring oblivion, it may bring a change of scene."

"Sir," said the Preacher, laying his hand upon my arm, "such bitterness in one so young is unnatural; you are in some trouble, I would that I might aid you, be your friend—know you better——"

"Oh, sir! that is easily done. I am a blacksmith, hard-working, sober, and useful to my fellows; they call me Peter Smith. A certain time since I was a useless dreamer; spending more money in a week than I now earn in a year, and getting very little for it. I was studious, egotistical, and pedantic, wasting my time upon impossible translations that nobody wanted —and they knew me as—Peter Vibart."

"Vibart!" exclaimed the Preacher, starting, and looking up at me.

"Vibart!" I nodded.

"Related in any way to—Sir Maurice Vibart?"

"His cousin, sir." My companion appeared lost in thought, for he was puffing at his empty pipe again.

"Do you happen to know Sir Maurice?" I inquired.

"No," returned the Preacher; "no, sir, but I have heard mention of him, and lately, though just when, or where, I cannot for the life of me recall."

"Why, the name is familiar to a great many people," said I; "you see, he is rather a famous character, in his way."

Talking thus, we presently reached a stile beyond

which the footpath led away through swaying corn, and by shady hop-garden, to Sissinghurst village. Here the Preacher stopped, and gave me his hand, but I noticed he still puffed at his pipe.

" And you are now a blacksmith ? "

" And mightily content so to be."

" You are a most strange young man ! " said the Preacher, shaking his head.

" Many people have told me the same, sir," said I, and vaulted over the stile. Yet, turning back when I had gone some way, I saw him leaning where I had left him, and with his pipe still in his mouth.

CHAPTER XXXVIII

IN WHICH I MEET MY COUSIN, SIR MAURICE VIBART

As I approached the smithy, late though the hour was (and George made it a rule to have the fire going by six every morning), no sound of hammer reached me, and coming into the place, I found it empty. Then I remembered that to-day George was to drive over to Tonbridge, with Prudence and the Ancient, to invest in certain household necessities, for in a month's time they were to be married.

Hereupon I must needs contrast George's happy future with my dreary one, and fall bitterly to cursing myself; and, sitting on the Ancient's stool in the corner, I covered my face, and my thoughts were very black.

Now presently, as I sat thus, I became conscious of a very delicate perfume in the air, and also, that some-one had entered quietly. My breath caught in my throat, but I did not at once look up, fearing to dispel the hope that tingled within me. So I remained with my face still covered until something touched me, and I saw that it was the gold-mounted handle of a whip, wherefore I raised my head suddenly and glanced up.

Then I beheld a radiant vision in polished riding-boots and speckless moleskins, in handsome flowered waistcoat and perfect-fitting coat, with snowy frills at throat and wrists; a tall, gallant figure, of a graceful, easy bearing, who stood, a picture of cool, gentlemanly insolence, tapping his boot lightly with his whip. But, as his eye met mine, the tapping whip grew suddenly still; his languid expression vanished, he came a quick step nearer and bent his face nearer my own—a dark face, handsome in its way, pale and aquiline, with a powerful jaw, and dominating eyes and mouth; a face,

429

(nay, a mask rather) that smiled and smiled, but never showed the man beneath.

Now, glancing up at his brow, I saw there a small, newly-healed scar.

" Is it possible? " said he, speaking in that softly modulated voice I remembered to have heard once before. " Can it be possible that I address my worthy cousin? That shirt! that utterly impossible coat and belcher! And yet—the likeness is remarkable! Have I the—honour to address Mr Peter Vibart—late of Oxford? "

" The same, sir," I answered, rising.

" Then, most worthy cousin, I salute you," and he removed his hat, bowing with an ironic grace. " Believe me, I have frequently desired to see that paragon of all the virtues whose dutiful respect our revered uncle rewarded with the proverbial shilling. Egad! " he went on, examining me through his glass with a great show of interest, "had you been any other than that same virtuous Cousin Peter whose graces and perfections were for ever being thrown at my head, I could have sympathised with you, positively—if only on account of that most obnoxious coat and belcher, and the grime and sootiness of things in general. Poof! " he exclaimed, pressing his perfumed handkerchief to his nostrils, " faugh! how damnably sulphur-and-brimstony you do keep yourself, cousin—oh, gad! "

" You would certainly find it much clearer outside," said I, beginning to blow up the fire.

" But then, Cousin Peter, outside one must become a target for the yokel eye, and I detest being stared at by the uneducated, who, naturally, lack appreciation. On the whole, I prefer the smoke, though it chokes one most infernally. Where may one venture to sit here? " I tendered him the stool, but he shook his head, and crossing to the anvil flicked it daintily with his handkerchief and sat down, dangling his leg.

" 'Pon my soul! " said he, eyeing me languidly through his glass again, " 'pon my soul! you are damnably like me, you know, in features."

" Damnably! " I nodded.

He glanced at me sharply, and laughed.

"My man, a creature of the name of Parks," said he, swinging his spurred boot to and fro, "led me to suppose that I should meet a person here—a black-smith fellow——"

"Your man Parks informed you correctly," I nodded; "what can I do for you?"

"The devil!" exclaimed Sir Maurice, shaking his head; "but no—you are, as I gather, somewhat eccentric, but even you would never take such a desperate step as to—to——"

"—become a blacksmith fellow?" I put in.

"Precisely!"

"Alas, Sir Maurice, I blush to say that rather than become an unprincipled adventurer living on my wits, or a mean-spirited hanger-on fawning upon acquaint-ances for a livelihood, or doing anything rather than soil my hands with honest toil, I became a blacksmith fellow some four or five months ago."

"Really it is most distressing to observe to what depths Virtue may drag a man!—you are a very monster of probity and rectitude!" exclaimed Sir Maurice; "indeed I am astonished! you manifested not only shocking bad judgment, but a most deplor-able lack of thought (Virtue is damnably selfish as a rule)—really, it is quite disconcerting to find one's self first cousin to a blacksmith——"

"—fellow!" I added.

"Fellow!" nodded Sir Maurice, "Oh, the devil! to think of my worthy cousin reduced to the necessity of labouring with hammer and saw——"

"Not a saw," I put in.

"We will say, chisel, then—a Vibart with hammer and chisel—deuce take me! Most distressing! and, you will pardon my saying so, you do not seem to thrive on hammers and chisels; no one could say you looked blooming, or even flourishing like the young bay tree (which is, I fancy, an Eastern expression)."

"Sir," said I, "may I remind you that I have work to do?"

"A deuced interesting place though, this," he

smiled, staring round imperturbably through his
glass; "so—er—so devilish grimy, and smutty, and
gritty—quite a number of horseshoes, too. D'ye
know, cousin, I never before remarked what a number
of holes there are in a horseshoe—but live and learn!"
Here he paused to inhale a pinch of snuff, very
daintily, from a jewelled box. "It is a strange thing,"
he pursued as he dusted his fingers on his handkerchief, "a very strange thing that, being cousins, we
have never met till now—especially as I have heard so
very much about you."

"Pray," said I, "pray how should you hear about
one so very insignificant as myself?"

"Oh, I have heard of good Cousin Peter since I was
an imp of a boy!" he smiled. "Cousin Peter was my
chart whereby to steer through the shoals of boyish
mischief into the haven of our Uncle George's good
graces. Oh, I have heard over much of you, cousin,
from dear, kind, well-meaning relatives and friends—
damn 'em! They rang your praises in my ears,
morning, noon and night. And why?—simply that I
might come to surpass you in virtue, learning, wit and
appearance, and so win our Uncle George's regard,
and, incidentally, his legacy. But I was a young
demon, romping with the grooms in the stable, while
you were a young angel in nankeens, passing studious
hours with your books. When I was a scapegrace at
Harrow, you were winning golden opinions at Eton;
when you were an 'honours' man at Oxford, I was
'rusticated' at Cambridge. Naturally enough, perhaps, I grew sick of the name of Peter (and, indeed, it
smacks damnably of fish, don't you think?)—you, or
your name, crossed me at every turn. If it wasn't for
Cousin Peter I was heir to ten thousand a year; but
good Cousin Peter was so fond of Uncle George, and
Uncle George was so fond of good Cousin Peter, that
Maurice might go hang for a graceless dog and be
damned to him!"

"You have my deepest sympathy and apologies!"
said I.

"Still, I have sometimes been curious to meet

worthy Cousin Peter, and it is rather surprising that I have never done so."

"On the contrary——" I began, but his laugh stopped me.

"Ah, to be sure!" he nodded, "our ways have lain widely separate hitherto—you, a scholar, treading the difficult path of learning; I—oh, egad! a terrible fellow! a *mauvais sujet*! a sad, sad dog! But after all, cousin, when one comes to look at you to-day, you might stand for a terrible example of Virtue run riot— a distressing spectacle of dutiful respect and good precedent cut off with a shilling. Really, it is horrifying to observe to what depths Virtue may plunge an otherwise well-balanced individual. Little dreamed those dear, kind, well-meaning relatives and friends—damn 'em! that while the wilful Maurice lived on, continually getting into hot water and out again, up to his eyes in debt, and pretty well esteemed, the virtuous pattern Peter would descend to a hammer and saw—I should say, chisel—in a very grimy place where he is, it seems, the presiding genius. Indeed, this first meeting of ours, under these circumstances, is somewhat dramatic, as it should be."

"And yet, we have met before," said I, "and the circumstances were then even more dramatic, perhaps, —we met in a tempest, sir."

"Ha!" he exclaimed, dwelling on the word, and speaking very slowly, "a tempest, cousin?"

"There was much wind and rain, and it was very dark."

"Dark, cousin?"

"But I saw your face very plainly as you lay on your back, sir, by the aid of a Postilion's lanthorn, and was greatly struck by our mutual resemblance." Sir Maurice raised his glass and looked at me, and, as he looked, smiled, but he could not hide the sudden, passionate quiver of his thin nostrils, or the gleam of the eyes beneath their languid lids. He rose slowly and paced to the door; when he came back again he was laughing softly, but still he could not hide the quiver of his nostrils, or the gleam of the eyes beneath their languid lids.

2 E

"So—it was—you?" he murmured, with a pause between the words. "Oh, was ever anything so damnably contrary! To think that I should hunt her into your very arms! To think that of all men in the world it should be you to play the squire of dames!" and he laughed again, but, as he did so, the stout riding-whip snapped in his hands like a straw. He glanced down at the broken pieces, and from them to me. "You see, I am rather strong in the hands, cousin," said he, shaking his head, "but I was not— quite strong enough, last time we met, though, to be sure, as you say, it was very dark. Had I known it was worthy Cousin Peter's throat I grasped I think I might have squeezed it just—a little—tighter."

"Sir," said I, shaking my head, "I really don't think you could have done."

"Yes," he sighed, tossing his broken whip into a corner. "Yes, I think so—you see, I mistook you for merely an interfering country bumpkin——"

"Yes," I nodded, "while I, on the other hand, took you for a fine gentleman nobly intent on the ruin of an unfortunate, friendless girl, whose poverty would seem to make her an easy victim——"

"In which it appears you were as much mistaken as I, Cousin Peter." Here he glanced at me with a sudden keenness.

"Indeed?"

"Why, surely," said he, "surely you must know——" He paused to flick a speck of soot from his knee, and then continued: "Did she tell you nothing of—herself?"

"Very little beside her name."

"Ah! she told you her name, then?"

"Yes, she told me her name."

"Well, cousin?"

"Well, sir?" We had both risen, and now fronted each other across the anvil, Sir Maurice debonnaire and smiling, while I stood frowning and gloomy.

"Come," said I at last, "let us understand each other once for all. You tell me that you have always looked upon me as your rival for our uncle's good

graces—I never was; you have deceived yourself into
believing that because I was his ward that alone aug-
mented my chances of becoming the heir—it never
did. He saw me as seldom as possible, and, if he ever
troubled his head about either of us, it would seem
that he favoured you. I tell you I never was your
rival in the past, and never shall be in the future."

"Meaning, cousin?"

"Meaning, sir, in regard to either the legacy or the
Lady Sophia Sefton. I was never fond enough of
money to marry for it. I have never seen this lady,
nor do I propose to, thus, so far as I am concerned,
you are free to win her and the fortune as soon as you
will; I, as you see, prefer horseshoes."

"And what," said Sir Maurice, flicking a speck of
soot from his cuff, and immediately looking at me
again, "what of Charmian?"

"I don't know," I answered, "nor should I be
likely to tell you, if I did; wherever she may be she is
safe, I trust, and beyond your reach——"

"No," he broke in, "she will never be beyond my
reach until she is dead—or I am—perhaps not even
then, and I shall find her again, sooner or later,
depend upon it—yes, you may depend upon that!"

"Cousin Maurice," said I, reaching out my hand to
him, "wherever she may be, she is alone and unprotected—pursue her no farther. Go back to London,
marry your Lady Sefton, inherit your fortune, but
leave Charmian Brown in peace."

"And pray," said he, frowning suddenly, "whence
this solicitude on her behalf? What is she to you—
this Charmian Brown?"

"Nothing," I answered hurriedly, "nothing at all,
God knows—nor ever can be——" Sir Maurice leaned
suddenly forward, and, catching me by the shoulder,
peered into my face.

"By Heaven!" he exclaimed, "the fellow—
actually—loves her!"

"Well?" said I, meeting his look, "why not?
Yes, I love her." A very fury of rage seemed suddenly to possess him, the languid, smiling gentleman

became a devil with vicious eyes and evil, snarling
mouth, whose fingers sank into my flesh as he swung
me back and forth in a powerful grip.

"You love her?—you?—you?" he panted.

"Yes," I answered, flinging him off so that he
staggered; "yes—yes! I—who fought for her once, and
am willing—most willing, to do so again, now or at any
other time, for, though I hold no hope of winning her
—ever—yet I can serve her still, and protect her from
the pollution of your presence," and I clenched my fists.

He stood poised as though about to spring at me, and
I saw his knuckles gleam whiter than the laces above
them, but, all at once, he laughed lightly, easily as ever.

"A very perfect, gentle knight!" he murmured,
" *sans peur, et sans reproche*—though somewhat grimy
and in a leather apron—Chivalry kneeling amid
hammers and horseshoes, worshipping Her with a
reverence distant and lowly! How like you, worthy
cousin, how very like you, and how affecting! But"
—and here his nostrils quivered again—"but I tell
you—she is mine—mine, and always has been, and no
man living shall come between us—no, by God!"

"That," said I, " that remains to be seen!"

"Ha?"

"Though, indeed, I think she is safe from you
while I live."

"But then, Cousin Peter, life is a very uncertain
thing at best," he returned, glancing at me beneath
his drooping lids.

"Yes," I nodded, "it is sometimes a blessing to
remember that."

Sir Maurice strolled to the door, and, being there,
paused, and looked back over his shoulder.

"I go to find Charmian," said he, "and I shall find
her—sooner or later, and, when I do, should you take
it upon yourself to—to come between us again, or presume to interfere again, I shall—kill you, worthy cousin,
without the least compunction. If you think this sufficient warning—act upon it, if not——" He shrugged his
shoulders significantly. "Farewell, good and worthy
Cousin Peter, farewell!—or shall we say—'au revoir'?"

CHAPTER XXXIX

HOW I WENT DOWN INTO THE SHADOWS

" PETER," said George one evening, turning to me with the troubled look I had seen so often on his face of late, " what be wrong wi' you, my chap; you be growing paler every day. Oh, Peter ! you be like a man as is dyin' by inches—if 'tis any o' my doin'——"

"Nonsense, George ! " I broke in with sudden asperity, " I am well enough ! "

" Yet I've seen your 'ands fall a-trembling sometimes, Peter—all at once. An' you missed your stroke yesterday—come square down on th' anvil—you can't ha' forgot ? "

" I remember," I muttered; " I remember."

" An' twice again to-day. An' you be silent, Peter, an' don't seem to 'ear when spoke to, an' short in your temper—oh, you bean't the man you was. I've see it a-comin' on you more an' more. Oh, man, Peter ! " he cried, turning his back upon me suddenly, " you as I'd let walk over me—you as I'd be cut in pieces for— if it be me as done it——"

" No, no, George—it wasn't you—of course not. If I am a little strange it is probably due to lack of sleep, nothing more."

" Ye see, Peter, I tried so 'ard to kill 'ee, an' you said yourself as I come nigh doin' it——"

" But then, you didn't quite manage it," I cried harshly—" would to God you had; as it is, I am alive, and there's an end of it."

" 'Twere a woundy blow I give 'ee—that last one ! I'll never forget the look o' your face as you went down. Oh, Peter ! you've never been the same since —it be all my doin'—I know it, I know it," and, sinking upon the Ancient's stool in the corner, Black George covered his face.

437

"Never think of it, George," I said, laying my arm across his heaving shoulders; "that is all over and done with, dear fellow, and I would not have it otherwise, since it gained me your friendship. I am all right, well and strong; it is only sleep that I need, George, only sleep."

Upon the still evening air rose the sharp tap, tap of the Ancient's stick, whereat up started the smith, and, coming to the forge, began raking out the fire with great dust, and clatter as the old man hobbled up, saluting us cheerily as he came.

"Lord!" he exclaimed, pausing in the doorway to lean upon his stick and glance from one to the other of us with his quick, bright eyes. "Lord! theer bean't two other such fine, up-standin', likely-lookin' chaps in all the South Country as you two chaps be—no, nor such smiths! it du warm my old 'eart to look at 'ee. Puts me in mind o' what I were myself—ages an' ages ago. I weren't quite so tall as Jarge, p'r'aps, by about—say 'alf-a-inch, but then, I were wider—wider, ah! a sight wider in the shoulder, an' so strong as— four bulls! and wi' eyes big an' sharp an' piercin'— like Peter's, only Peter's bean't quite so sharp, no, nor yet so piercin'—an' that minds me as I've got noos for 'ee, Peter."

"What news?" said I, turning.

"S'prisin' noos it be—ah! an' 'stonishin' tu. But first of all, Peter, I wants to ax 'ee a question."

"What is it, Ancient?"

"Why it be this, Peter," said the old man, hobbling nearer, and peering up into my face, "ever since the time as I went an' found ye, I've thought as theer was summat strange about 'ee, what wi' your soft voice an' gentle ways; an' it came on me all at once— about three o' the clock 's arternoon, as you might be a dook—in disguise, Peter. Come now, be ye a dook or bean't ye—yes or no, Peter?" and he fixed me with his eye.

"No, Ancient," I answered, smiling; "I'm no duke."

"Ah well!—a earl, then?"

"Nor an earl."

" A barrynet, p'r'aps ? "

" Not even a baronet."

" Ah ! " said the old man, eyeing me doubtfully, " I've often thought as you might be one or t'other of 'em—'specially since 'bout three o' the clock 's arter-noon."

" Why so ? "

" Why, that's the p'int—that's the very noos as I've got to tell 'ee," chuckled the Ancient, as he seated himself in the corner. " You must know, then," he began, with an impressive rap on the lid of his snuff-box, " 'bout three o'clock 's arternoon I were sittin' on the stile by Simon's five-acre field when along the road comes a lady, 'an'some an' proud-looking, an' as fine as fine could be, a-ridin' of a 'orse, an' wi' a servant ridin' another 'orse be'ind 'er. As she comes up she gives me a look out o' 'er eyes, soft they was, an' dark, an' up I gets to touch my 'at. All at once she smiles at me, an' 'er smile were as sweet an' gentle as 'er eyes ; an' she pulls up 'er 'orse. ' W'y, you must be the Ancient ! ' says she. ' W'y, so Peter calls me, my leddy,' says I. ' An' 'ow is Peter ? ' she says, quick-like ; ' 'ow is Peter ? ' says she. ' Fine an' 'earty,' says I ; ' eats well an' sleeps sound,' says I ; ' 'is arms is strong an' 'is legs is strong, an' 'e aren't afeard o' nobody—like a young lion be Peter,' says I. Now, while I'm a-sayin' this, she looks at me, soft an' thoughtful-like, an' takes out a little book an' begins to write in it, a-wrinklin' 'er pretty black brows over it an' a-shakin' 'er 'ead to 'erself. An' presently she tears out what she's been a-writin' an' gives it to me. ' Will you give this to Peter for me ? ' says she. ' That I will, my leddy ! ' says I. ' Thank 'ee ! ' says she, smilin' again, an' 'oldin' out 'er w'ite 'an' to me, which I kisses. ' Indeed ! ' says she, ' I understand now why Peter is so fond of you. I think I could be very fond of 'ee tu ! ' says she. An' so she turns 'er 'orse, an' the servant 'e turns 'is an' off they go ; an' 'ere, Peter—'ere be the letter." Saying which, the Ancient took a slip of paper from the cavernous interior of his hat and tendered it to me.

With my head in a whirl, I crossed to the door, and leaned there awhile, staring sightlessly out into the summer evening; for it seemed that in this little slip of paper lay that which meant life or death to me; so, for a long minute I leaned there, fearing to learn my fate. Then I opened the little folded square of paper, and, holding it before my eyes, read:

"Charmian Brown presents" (This scratched out.) "While you busied yourself forging horseshoes your cousin, Sir Maurice, sought and found me. I do not love him, but——   CHARMIAN."

"Farewell" (This also scored out.)

Again I stared before me with unseeing eyes, but my hands no longer trembled, nor did I fear any more; the prisoner had received his sentence, and suspense was at an end.

And, all at once, I laughed, and tore the paper across, and laughed and laughed, till George and the Ancient came to stare at me.

"Don't 'ee!" cried the old man; "don't 'ee, Peter —you be like a corp' laughin'; don't 'ee!" But the laugh still shook me while I tore and tore at the paper, and so let the pieces drop and flutter from my fingers.

"There!" said I, "there goes a fool's dream! See how it scatters—a little here, a little there; but, so long as this world lasts, these pieces shall never come together again." So saying, I set off along the road, looking neither to right nor left. But, when I had gone some distance, I found that George walked beside me, and he was very silent as he walked, and I saw the trouble was back in his eyes again.

"George," said I, stopping, "why do you follow me?"

"I don't follow 'ee, Peter," he answered; "I be only wishful to walk wi' you a ways."

"I'm in no mood for company, George."

"Well, I bean't company, Peter—your friend, I be," he said doggedly, and without looking at me.

"Yes," said I; "yes, my good and trusty friend."

"Peter," he cried suddenly, laying his hand upon

"Along the road comes a lady, 'an'some an' proud-looking, an' as fine as fine could be"

Face Page 440

my shoulder, " don't go back to that theer ghashly
'Oller to-night——"

" It is the only place in the world for me—to-night,
George." And so we went on again, side by side,
through the evening, and spoke no more until we had
come to the parting of the ways.

Down in the Hollow the shadows lay black and
heavy, and I saw George shiver as he looked.

" Good-bye ! " said I, clasping his hand; " good-
bye, George ! "

" Why do 'ee say good-bye ? "

" Because I am going away."

" Goin' away, Peter—but wheer ? "

" God knows ! " I answered, "but, wherever it be, I
shall carry with me the memory of your kind, true heart—
and you, I think, will remember me. It is a blessed thing,
George, to know that, howso far we go, a friend's kind
thoughts journey on with us, untiring to the end."

" Oh, Peter, man ! don't go for to leave me——"

" To part is our human lot, George, and as well
now as later—good-bye ! "

" No, no ! " he cried, throwing his arm about me,
" not down theer—it be so deadly an' lonely down
theer in the darkness. Come back wi' me—just for
to-night." But I broke from his detaining hand, and
plunged on down into the shadows. And, presently,
turning my head, I saw him yet standing where I had
left him, looming gigantic upon the sky behind, and
with his head sunk upon his breast.

Being come at last to the cottage, I paused, and
from that place of shadows lifted my gaze to the
luminous heaven, where were a myriad eyes that
seemed to watch me with a new meaning, to-night;
wherefore I entered the cottage hastily, and, closing
the door, barred it behind me.

Then I turned to peer up at that which showed above
the door—the rusty staple upon which a man had choked
his life out sixty and six years ago. And I began, very
slowly, to loosen the belcher neckerchief about my throat.

" Peter ! " cried a voice—" Peter ! " and a hand
was beating upon the door.

CHAPTER XL

HOW, IN PLACE OF DEATH, I FOUND THE FULNESS OF LIFE

She came in swiftly, closing the door behind her, found and lighted a candle, and, setting it upon the table between us, put back the hood of her cloak, and looked at me, while I stood mute before her, abashed by the accusation of her eyes.

" Coward ! " she said, and, with the word, snatched the neckerchief from my grasp, and, casting it upon the floor, set her foot upon it. " Coward ! " said she again.

" Yes," I muttered; " yes, I was lost—in a great darkness, and full of a horror of coming nights and days, and so—I would have run away from it all—like a coward——"

" Oh, hateful—hateful ! " she cried, and covered her face as from some horror.

" Indeed, you cannot despise me more than I do myself," said I, " now, or ever; I am a failure in all things, except, perhaps, the making of horseshoes—and this world has no place for failures—and as for horseshoes——"

" Fool," she whispered. " Oh, fool that I dreamed so wise ! Oh, coward that seemed so brave and strong ! Oh, man that was so gloriously young and unspoiled !—that it should end here—that it should come to this." And, though she kept her face hidden, I knew that she was weeping. " A woman's love transforms the man till she sees him, not as he is, but as her heart would have him be; the dross becomes pure gold, and she believes, and believes until—one day her heart breaks——"

" Charmian !—what—what do you mean ? "

" Oh, are you still so blind ? Must I tell you ? "

she cried, lifting her head proudly. "Why did I live beside you here in the wilderness? Why did I work for you—contrive for you—and seek to make this desolation a home for you? Often my heart cried out its secret to you—but you never heard; often it trembled in my voice, looked at you from my eyes— but you never guessed—Oh, blind! blind! And you drove me from you with shameful words—but—oh!— I came back to you. And now—I know you for but common clay, after all, and—even yet——". She stopped, suddenly, and once more hid her face from me in her hands.

"And—even yet, Charmian?" I whispered.

Very still she stood, with her face bowed upon her hands, but she could not hide from me the swift rise and fall of her bosom.

"Speak—oh, Charmian, speak!"

"I am so weak—so weak!" she whispered; "I hate myself."

"Charmian!" I cried—"oh, Charmian!" and seized her hands, and, despite her resistance, drew her into my arms, and, clasping her close, forced her to look at me. "And even yet?—what more—what more—tell me." But, lying back across my arm, she held me off with both hands.

"Don't!" she cried; "don't!—you shame me—let me go."

"God knows I am all unworthy, Charmian, and so low in my abasement that to touch you is presumption, but—oh, woman whom I have loved from the first, and shall, to the end, have you stooped in your infinite mercy, to lift me from these depths—is it a new life you offer me—was it for this you came to-night?"

"Let me go—oh, Peter!—let me go."

"Why—why did you come?"

"Loose me!"

"Why did you come?"

"To meet—Sir Maurice Vibart."

"To meet Sir Maurice?" I repeated dully—"Sir Maurice?" And in that moment she broke from me, and stood with her head thrown back, and her eyes

very bright, as though defying me. But I remained
where I was, my arms hanging.

" He was to meet me here—at nine o'clock."

" Oh, Charmian," I whispered, " are all women so
cruel as you, I wonder?" And, turning my back
upon her, I leaned above the mantel, staring down at
the long-dead ashes on the hearth.

But, standing there, I heard a footstep outside, and
swung round with clenched fists, yet Charmian was
quicker, and, as the door opened and Sir Maurice
entered, she was between us.

He stood upon the threshold, dazzled a little by the
light, but smiling, graceful, debonnaire, and *point de
vice* as ever. Indeed his very presence seemed to make
the mean room the meaner by contrast, and, as he
bent to kiss her hand, I became acutely conscious of
my own rough person, my worn and shabby clothes,
and of my hands, coarsened and grimed by labour;
wherefore my frown grew the blacker and I clenched
my fists the tighter.

" I lost my way, Charmian," he began, " but,
though late, I am none the less welcome, I trust?
Ah?—you frown, Cousin Peter? Quite a ghoulish
spot this, at night—you probably find it most con-
genial, good cousin Timon of Athens—indeed, cousin,
you are very like Timon of Athens——" And he
laughed so that I, finding my pipe upon the mantelshelf, began to turn it aimlessly round and round in
my twitching fingers.

" You have already met, then?" inquired Charmian, glancing from one to the other of us.

" We had that mutual pleasure nearly a week ago,"
nodded Sir Maurice, " when we agreed to—disagree,
as we always have done, and shall do—with the result
that we find each other agreeably disagreeable."

" I had hoped that you might be friends."

" My dear Charmian—I wonder at you!" he
sighed, " so unreasonable. Would you have us con-
travene the established order of things? It was
preordained that Cousin Peter should scowl at me
(precisely as he is doing), and that I should shrug my

shoulders, thus, at Cousin Peter—a little hate with,
say, a dash of contempt, gives a zest to that dish of
conglomerate vapidity which we call Life, and makes
it most palatable.

" But I am not here on Cousin Peter's account," he
went on, drawing a step nearer to her, " at this
moment I heartily wish him—among his hammers
and chisels—I have come for you, Charmian, because
I love you. I have sought you patiently until I found
you—and I will never forgo you so long as life lasts
—but you know all this."

" Yes, I know all this."

" I have been very patient, Charmian, submitting
to your whims and fancies—but, through it all, I
knew, and in your woman's heart—you knew, that
you must yield at last—that the chase must end—
some day; well—let it be to-night—my chaise is
waiting——"

" When I ran away from you, in the storm, Sir
Maurice, I told you, once and for all, that I hated you.
Have you forgotten ?—hated you !—always and ever !
and tried to—kill you——"

" Oh, Charmian ! I have known such hate transfigured into love, before now—such love as is only
worth the winning. And you are mine—you always
were—from the first moment that our eyes met. Come,
my chaise is waiting, in a few hours we can be in
London, or Dover——"

" No—never ! "

" Never is a long time, Charmian—but I am at your
service—what is your will ? "

" I shall remain—here."

" Here ?   In the wilderness ? "

" With my—husband."

" Your—husband ? "

" I am going to marry your cousin—Peter Vibart."

The pipe slipped from my fingers and shivered to
pieces on the floor, and in that same fraction of time
Sir Maurice had turned and leapt towards me; but as
he came I struck him twice, with left and right, and
he staggered backwards to the wall.   He stood for a

moment, with his head stooped upon his hands.
When he looked up his face was dead white, and with
a smear of blood upon it that seemed to accentuate its
pallor; but his voice came smooth and unruffled as
ever.

"The Mind Feminine is given to change," said he
softly, "and—I shall return—yes, I shall come back.
Smile, madam! Triumph, cousin!—but I shall come
between you yet—I tell you, I'll come between you—
living or—dead!"

And so he turned, and was gone—into the shadows.

But as for me, I sat down, and leaning my chin in
my hand, stared down at the broken fragments of my
pipe.

"Peter?"

"You are safe now," said I, without looking up,
"he is gone—but, oh, Charmian! was there no other
way——?"

She was down beside me on her knees, had taken
my hand, rough and grimy as it was, and pressed it
to her lips, and so had drawn it about her neck, holding it there, and with her face hidden in my breast.

"Oh—strong man that is so weak!" she whispered.
"Oh—grave philosopher that is so foolish! Oh—
lonely boy that is so helpless. Oh, Peter Vibart—my
Peter!"

"Charmian?" said I, trembling, "what does it
mean?"

"It means, Peter——"

"Yes?"

"That—the—Humble Person——"

"Yes?"

"Will—marry you—whenever you will—if——"

"Yes?"

"If you will—only—ask her."

CHAPTER XLI

LIGHT AND SHADOW

Now, as the little Preacher closed his book, the sun rose up, filling the world about us with his glory.

And looking into the eyes of my wife, it seemed that a veil was lifted, for a moment, there, and I read that which her lips might never tell; and there, also, was joy, and shame, and a deep happiness.

"See," said the little Preacher, smiling upon us, "it is day and a very glorious one; already a thousand little choristers of God's great cathedral have begun to chant your marriage hymn. Go forth together, Man and Wife, upon this great wide road that we call Life; go forth together, made strong in Faith, and brave with Hope, and the memory of Him who walked these ways before you; who joyed, and sorrowed, and suffered, and endured all things—even as we must. Go forth together, and may His blessing abide with you, and the ' peace that passeth understanding.' "

And so we turned together, side by side, and left him standing amid his roses.

Silently we went together, homewards, through the dewy morning, with a soft, green carpet underfoot, and leafy arches overhead, where trees bent to whisper benedictions, and shook down jewels from their dewy leaves upon us as we passed; by merry brooks that laughed and chattered, and gurgled of love and happiness, while over all rose the swelling chorus of the birds. Surely never had they piped so gladly in this glad world before—not even for the gentle Spenser, though he says:

> " There was none of them that feigned
> To sing, for each of them him pained;
> To find out merry, crafty notes
> They ne spared not their throats."

447

And being come, at length, to the Hollow, Charmian must needs pause beside the pool among the willows, to view herself in the pellucid water. And in this mirror our eyes met, and lo! of a sudden, her lashes drooped, and she turned her head aside.

"Don't, Peter!" she whispered; "don't look at me so."

"How may I help it when you are so beautiful?"

And, because of my eyes, she would have fled from me, but I caught her in my arms, and there, amid the leaves, despite the jealous babble of the brook, for the second time in my life, her lips met mine. And, gazing yet into her eyes, I told her how, in this shady bower, I had once watched her weaving leaves into her hair, and heard her talk to her reflection—and so— had stolen away, for fear of her beauty.

"Fear, Peter?"

"We were so far out of the world, and—I longed to kiss you."

"And didn't, Peter."

"And didn't, Charmian, because we were so very far from the world, and because you were so very much alone, and——"

"And because, Peter, because you are a gentle man and strong, as the old locket says. And do you remember," she went on hurriedly, laying her cool, restraining fingers on my eager lips, "how I found you wearing that locket, and how you blundered and stammered over it, and pretended to read your Homer?"

"And how you sang to prevent me?"

"And how gravely you reproved me?"

"And how you called me a 'creature'?"

"And how you deserved it, sir—and grew more helpless and ill at ease than ever, and how—just to flatter my vanity—you told me I had 'glorious hair'?"

"And so you have," said I, kissing a curl at her temple; "when you unbind it, my Charmian, it will cover you—like a mantle."

Now when I said this, for some reason she glanced up at me, sudden and shy, and blushed, and slipped from my arms, and fled up the path like a nymph.

So we presently entered the cottage, flushed and panting, and laughing for sheer happiness. And now she rolled up her sleeves, and set about preparing breakfast, laughing my assistance to scorn, but growing mightily indignant when I would kiss her, yet blushing and yielding, nevertheless. And while she bustled to and fro (keeping well out of reach of my arm), she began to sing in her soft voice to herself :

> " In Scarlet Town where I was born
> There was a fair maid dwellin'
> Made every youth cry ' well-a-day ! '
> Her name was Barbara Allen."

" Oh, Charmian ! how wonderful you are ! "

> " All in the merrie month of May
> When green buds were a-swellin'——"

" Surely no woman ever had such beautiful arms ! so round, and soft, and white, Charmian." She turned upon me with a fork held up admonishingly, but, meeting my look, her eyes wavered, and up from throat to brow rushed a wave of burning crimson.

" Oh, Peter !—you make me—almost—afraid of you," she whispered, and hid her face against my shoulder.

" Are you content to have married such a very poor man—to be the wife of a village blacksmith ? "

" Why, Peter—in all the world there never was such another blacksmith as mine, and—and—there !— the kettle is boiling over——"

" Let it ! " said I.

" And the bacon—the bacon will burn—let me go, and—oh, Peter ! "

So, in due time, we sat down to our solitary wedding breakfast ; and there were no eyes to speculate upon the bride's beauty, to note her changing colour, or the glory of her eyes ; and no healths were proposed, or toasts drunk, nor any speeches spoken— except, perhaps by my good friend—the brook outside, who, of course, understood the situation, and

2 F

babbled tolerantly of us to the listening trees, like the grim old philosopher he was.

In this solitude we were surely closer together, and belonged more fully to each other, for all her looks and thoughts were mine, as mine were hers.

And, as we ate, sometimes talking, and sometimes laughing (though rarely, one seldom laughs in the wilderness), our hands would stray to meet each other across the table, and eye would answer eye, while, in the silence, the brook would lift its voice to chuckle throaty chuckles and outlandish witticisms, such as could only be expected from an old reprobate who had grown so in years, and had seen so very much of life; at such times Charmian's cheeks would flush and her lashes droop—as though (indeed), she were versed in the language of brooks.

So the golden hours slipped by, the sun crept westwards, and evening stole upon us.

" This is a very rough place for you," said I, and sighed.

We were sitting on the bench before the door, and Charmian had laid her folded hands upon my shoulder, and her chin upon her hands. And now she echoed my sigh, but answered without stirring :

" It is the dearest place in all the world."

" And very lonely ! " I pursued.

" I shall be busy all day long, Peter, and you always reach home as evening falls, and then—then— oh ! I sha'n't be lonely."

" But I am such a gloomy fellow at the best of times, and very clumsy, Charmian, and something of a failure."

" And—my husband."

" Peter !—Peter !—oh, Peter ! " I started, and rose to my feet.

" Peter !—oh, Peter ! " called the voice again, seemingly from the road, and now I thought it sounded familiar.

Charmian stole her arms about my neck.

" I think it is Simon," said I uneasily; " what can have brought him ? And he will never venture down into the Hollow on account of the ghost—I must go and see what he wants."

"Yes, Peter," she murmured, but the clasp of her arms tightened.

"What is it?" said I, looking into her troubled eyes. "Charmian, you are trembling!—what is it?"

"I don't know—but oh, Peter! I feel as if a shadow —a black and awful shadow were creeping upon us— hiding us from each other. I am very foolish, aren't I?—and this our wedding-day!"

"Peter! Pe-ter!"

"Come with me, Charmian; let us go together."

"No, I must wait—it is woman's destiny—to wait— but I am brave again; go—see what is wanted."

I found Simon, sure enough, in the lane, seated in his cart, and his face looked squarer and grimmer even than usual.

"Oh, Peter!" said he, gripping my hand, "it be come at last—Gaffer be goin'."

"Going, Simon?"

"Dyin', Peter. Fell downstairs 's marnin'. Doctor says 'e can't last the day out—sinkin' fast, 'e be, an' 'e be axin' for 'ee, Peter. 'Wheer be Peter?' says 'e over an' over again; 'wheer be the Peter as I found of a sunshiny arternoon, down in th' 'aunted 'Oller?' You weren't at work 's marnin', Peter, so I be come to fetch 'ee—you'll come back wi' me to bid 'good-bye' to the old man?"

"Yes, I'll come, Simon," I answered; "wait here for me."

Charmian was waiting for me in the cottage, and, as she looked up at me, I saw the trouble was back in her eyes again.

"You must—go—leave me?" she inquired.

"For a little while."

"Yes—I—I felt it," she said with a pitiful little smile.

"The Ancient is dying," said I. Now, as I spoke, my eyes encountered the staple above the door, wherefore, mounting upon a chair, I seized and shook it. And lo! the rusty iron snapped off in my fingers—like glass, and I slipped it into my pocket.

" Oh, Peter!—don't go—don't leave me!" cried Charmian suddenly, and I saw that her face was very pale, and that she trembled.

" Charmian!" said I, and sprang to her side. " Oh, my love!—what is it?"

" It is—as though the shadow hung over us—darker and more threatening, Peter; as if our happiness were at an end; I seem to hear Maurice's threat—to come between us—living or—dead. I am afraid!" she whispered, clinging to me, " I am afraid!" But, all at once, she was calm again, and full of self-reproaches, calling herself " weak," and " foolish," and " hysterical "—" though, indeed, I was never hysterical before! "—and telling me that I must go—that it was my duty to go to the " gentle, dying old man "—urging me to the door, almost eagerly, till, being out of the cottage, she must needs fall a-trembling once more, and wind her arms about my neck, with a great sob.

" But oh!—you will come back soon—very soon, Peter? And we know that nothing can ever come between us again—never again—my husband." And, with that blessed word, she drew me down to her lips, and turning, fled into the cottage.

I went on slowly up the path to meet Simon, and, as I went, my heart was heavy, and my mind full of a strange foreboding. But I never thought of the omen of the knife that had once fallen, and quivered in the floor between us.

" 'Twere 'is snuff-box as done it!" said Simon, staring very hard at his horse's ears, as we jogged along the road. " 'E were a-goin' upstairs for it, an' slipped 'e did. ' Simon,' says he, as I lifted of 'im in my arms, ' Simon,' says 'e, quiet like, ' I be done for at last, lad—this poor old feyther o' yourn 'll never go a-climbin' up these stairs no more,' says 'e—' never—no—more.' "

After this Simon fell silent, and I likewise, until we reached the village. Before " The Bull " was a group who talked with hushed voices and grave faces, even Old Amos grinned no more.

The old man lay in his great four-post bed, propped

up with pillows, and with Prue beside him, to smooth his silver hair with tender fingers, and Black George towering in the shade of the bed-curtains, like a grieving giant.

"'Ere I be, Peter," said the old man, beckoning me feebly with his hand, "'ere I be—at the partin' o' the ways, an' wi' summat gone wrong wi' my innards! When a man gets so old as I be, 'is innards be like glass, Peter, like glass—an' apt to fly all to pieces if 'e goes a-slippin' an' a-slidin' downstairs, like me."

"Are you in pain?" I asked, clasping his shrivelled hand.

"Jest a twinge, now an' then, Peter—but—Lord! that bean't nothin' to a man the likes o' me— Peter——"

"You always were so hale and hearty," I nodded, giving him the usual opening he had waited for.

"Ay, so strong as a bull, that I were! like a lion in my youth—Black Jarge were nought to me—a cart-'orse I were."

"Yes," said I, "yes," and stooped my head lower over the feeble old hand.

"But arter all, Peter, bulls pass away, an' lions, an' cart'-orses lose their teeth, an' gets wore out, for all flesh is grass—but iron's iron, bean't it, Peter— rusts it do, but 'tis iron all the same, an' lasts a man out—even such a 'earty chap as I were?"

"Sometimes," said I, without looking up.

"An' I be very old an' tired, Peter, my' eart be all wore out wi' beatin' an' beatin' all these years—'tis a wonder at it didn't stop afore now—but a—a—stapil, Peter, don't 'ave no 'eart to go a-beatin' an' a-wearin' of itself away?"

"No, Ancient."

"So 'ere be I, a-standin' in the Valley o' the Shadow, an' waitin' for God's Angel to take my 'and for to show me the way. 'Tis a darksome road, Peter, but I bean't afraid, an' there be a light beyond Jordan-water. No, I aren't afraid to meet the God as made me, for ' the Lord is merciful—and very kind,' an' I don't s'pose as 'E'll be very 'ard on a old, old man as did 'is best, an' wi' a 'eart all tired an' wore away wi' beatin'—I be ready, Peter—only——"

" Yes, Ancient?"

" Oh, Peter!—it be that theer old stapil—as'll go on rustin' away an' rustin' away arter the old man as watched it so is laid in the earth, an' forgot about——"

" No," said I, without looking up, but slipping my hand into my pocket; " no, Ancient——"

" Peter—Oh, Peter!—do 'ee mean——?"

" I mean that, although it had no heart, the staple was tired and worn out—just as you are, and so I brought it to you," and I slipped the rusty bit of iron into the old man's trembling palm.

" O Lord——!" he began in a fervent voice, " O dear Lord!—I got it, Lord—th' owd stapil—I be ready to come to Thee, an' j'yful—j'yful! an' for this mercy, an' benefit received—blessed be Thy name. Amen!"

He lay very quiet for a while, with the broken staple clasped to his breast, and his eyes closed.

" Peter," said he suddenly, " you won't 'ave no one to bring you noos no more—why, Peter! be 'ee cryin' —for me? 'Tis true 'twere me as found ye, but I didn't think as you'd go to cry tears for me—I be goin' to tak' t' owd stapil wi' me, Peter, all along the road—an' Peter——"

" Yes, Ancient?"

" Be you quiet sure as you aren't a dook?"

" Quite sure."

" Nor a earl?"

" No, Ancient."

" Not even a—barrynet?"

" No, Ancient."

" Ah, well!—you be a man, Peter, an' 'tis summat to ha' found a man—that it be."

And now he feebly beckoned us all nearer.

" Children," said he, " I be a old an' ancient man— I be goin' on—across the river to wait for you—my blessin' on ye. It be a dark, dark road, but I've got t' owd stapil, an' there—be a light beyond—the river."

So, the Ancient sighed, and crossed the dark River into the Land of Light Eternal.

CHAPTER XLII

HOW SIR MAURICE KEPT HIS WORD

NIGHT, with a rising moon, and over all things a great quietude, a deep, deep silence. Air, close and heavy, without a breath to wake the slumbering trees; an oppressive stillness, in which small sounds magnified themselves, and seemed disproportionately loud.

And presently, as I went upon my way, I forgot the old man sleeping so peacefully with the rusty staple clasped to his shrunken breast, and thought only of the proud woman who had given her life into my keeping, and who, henceforth, would walk with me, hand in hand, upon this Broad Highway, over rough places, and smooth—even unto the end. So I strode on, full of a deep and abiding joy, and with heart that throbbed and hands that trembled because I knew that she watched and waited for my coming.

A sound broke upon the stillness—sudden and sharp—like the snapping of a stick. I stopped, and glanced about me—but it had come and gone—lost in the all-pervading calm.

And presently, reaching the leafy path that led steeply down into the Hollow, I paused a moment to look about me and to listen again; but the deep silence was all unbroken, save for the slumberous song of the brook, that stole up to me from the shadows, and I wondered idly what that sudden sound might have been. So I began to descend this leafy path, and went on to meet that which lay waiting for me in the shadows.

It was dark here among the trees, for the moon was low as yet, but, every now and then she sent a kindly ray through some opening amid the leaves, so that as I descended the path I seemed to be wading through small, limpid pools of radiance.

455

But all at once I stopped—staring at something which lay at the edge of one of these pools—a white claw—a hand whose fingers, talon-like, had sunk deep and embedded themselves in the turf. And, beyond this gleaming hand, was an arm, and beyond that again, something that bulked across my path, darker than the shadows.

Running forward, I stood looking down at that which lay at my feet—so very still; and stooped suddenly, and turned it over that I might see the face; and, seeing it, started back in shuddering horror. For, in those features—hideous with blood, stained and blackened with powder, I recognised my cousin—Sir Maurice Vibart. Then, remembering the stick that had snapped, I wondered no more, but a sudden deadly faintness came upon me so that I leaned weakly against a tree near by.

A rustling of leaves—a shuddering breath, and, though I did not raise my head, I knew that Charmian was there.

" Oh, Peter ! " she whispered, " oh, Peter ! " and that was all, but, moved by something in her tone, I glanced up. Her eyes were wide and staring—not at me, but at that which lay between us—her face was pallid, even her lips had lost their colour, and she clasped one hand upon her bosom—the other was hidden in the folds of her gown—hidden as I remembered to have seen it once before, but now it struck me with a horrible significance; wherefore I reached out and caught that hidden hand, and drew the weapon from her nerveless fingers, holding it where the light could play upon it. She started, shivered violently, and covered her eyes, while I, looking down at the pistol in my hand, saw that it had lately been discharged.

" He has kept his word ! " she whispered; " he has kept his word ! "

" Yes, Charmian—he has kept his word ! "

" Oh, Peter ! " she moaned, and stretched out her hands towards me, yet she kept her face turned from that which lay across the path between us, and her hands were shaking pitifully "Peter?" she cried with a sudden break in her voice; but I went on wiping the soot from the pistol-barrel with the end of my neckerchief. Then, all at once, she was beside me, clasping my arm, and she was pleading with me, her words coming in a flood.

"No, Peter, no—oh, God!—you do not think it—you can't—you mustn't. I was alone—waiting for you, and the hours passed—and you didn't come—and I was nervous, and frightened, and full of awful fancies. I thought I heard someone—creeping round the cottage. Once I thought someone peered in at the lattice, and once I thought someone tried the door. And so—because I was frightened, Peter, I took that —that, and held it in my hand, Peter. And while I sat there—it seemed more than ever—that somebody was breathing softly—outside the door. And so, Peter, I couldn't bear it any more—and opened the lattice—and fired—in the air—I swear it was in the air. And I stood there –at the open casement—sick with fear, and trying to pray for you—because I knew he had come back—to kill you, Peter, and, while I prayed, I heard another shot—not close, but faint—like the snapping of a twig, Peter—and I ran out —and—oh, Peter!—that is all—but you believe—oh! —you believe, don't you, Peter?"

While she spoke, I had slipped the pistol into my pocket, and now I held out my hands to her, and drew her near, and gazed into the troubled depths of her eyes.

"Charmian!" said I, "Charmian—I love you! and God forbid that I should ever doubt you any more."

So, with a sigh, she sank in my embrace, her arms crept about my neck, and our lips met, and clung together. But even then—while I looked upon her beauty, while the contact of her lips thrilled through me—even then, in my mind, I saw the murderous pistol in her hand—as I had seen it months ago. Indeed it almost seemed that she divined my thought, for she drew swiftly back, and looked up at me with haggard eyes.

" Peter ? " she whispered, " what is it—what is it ? "

" Oh, Charmian ! " said I, over and over again, " I love you—I love you." And I kissed her appealing eyes, and stayed her questioning lips with my kisses. " I love you more than my life—more than honour— more than my soul ; and, because I so love you—to- night you must leave me——"

" Leave you ?—ah no, Peter—no—no, I am your wife—I must stay with you—to suffer and share your troubles and dangers—it is my right—my privilege. Let us go away together, now—anywhere—anywhere, only let us be together—my—husband."

" Don't ! " I cried, " don't ! Do you think it is so easy to remain here without you—to lose you so soon —so very soon ? If I only loved you a little less ! Ah ! don't you see—before the week is out, my description will be all over England ; we should be caught, and you would have to stand beside me in a court of justice, and face the shame of it——"

" Dear love !—it would be my pride—my pride, Peter, to face them all—to clasp this dear hand in mine——"

" Never ! " I cried, clenching my fists ; " never ! You must leave me ; no one must know Charmian Brown ever existed—you must go ! "

" Hush ! " she whispered, clasping me tighter, " listen—someone is coming ! " Away to the right, we could hear the leaves rustling, as though a strong wind passed through them ; a light flickered, went out, flickered again, and a voice hailed faintly :

" Hallo ! "

" Come," said Charmian, clasping my hand, " let us go and meet him."

" No, Charmian, no—I must see this man—alone. You must leave here, to-night—now. You can catch the London Mail at the cross roads. Go to Black- heath—to Sir Richard Anstruther—he is my friend— tell him everything——"

She was down at my feet, and had caught my hand to her bosom.

" I can't ! " she cried, " I can't go—and leave you

here alone. I have loved you so—from the very first, and it seems that each day my love has grown until it is part of me. Oh, Peter!—don't send me away from you—it will kill me, I think——"

"Better that than the shame of a prison!" I exclaimed, and, while I spoke, I lifted her in my arms. "Oh!—I am proud—proud to have won such a love as yours—let me try to be worthy of it. Good-bye, my beloved!" and so I kissed her, and would have turned away, but her arms clung about me.

"Oh, Peter!" she sobbed, "if you must go—if you will go, call me—your wife—just once, Peter."

The hovering light was much nearer now, and the rustle of leaves louder, as I stooped above her cold hands, and kissed their trembling fingers.

"Some day," said I, "some day, if there is a just God in heaven, we shall meet again; perhaps soon, perhaps late. Until then, let us dream of that glorious, golden some day, but now—farewell, oh, beloved wife!"

With a broken cry, she drew my head down upon her breast, and clasped it there, while her tears mingled with her kisses, and so—crying my name, she turned, and was lost among the leaves.

CHAPTER XLIII

HOW I SET OUT TO FACE MY DESTINY

THE pallid moon shone down pitilessly upon the dead, white face that stared up at me through its grime and blood, with the same half-tolerant, half-amused contempt of me that it had worn in life; the drawn lips seemed to mock me, and the clenched fists to defy me still; so that I shivered, and turned to watch the oncoming light that danced like a will-o'-the-wisp among the shadows. Presently it stopped, and a voice hailed once more:

"Hallo!"

"Hallo!" I called back; "this way—this way!" In a little while I saw the figure of a man whom I at once recognised as the one-time Postilion, bearing the lanthorn of a chaise, and, as he approached, it struck me that this meeting was very much like our first, save for him who lay in the shadows, staring up at me with unwinking eyes.

"So ho!" exclaimed the Postilion as he came up, raising his lanthorn that he might view me the better; "it's you again, is it?"

"Yes," I nodded.

"Well, I don't like it," he grumbled, "a-meeting of each other again like this, in this 'ere ghashly place—no, I don't like it—too much like last time to be nat'ral, and, as you know, I can't abide onnat'ralness. If I was to ax you where my master was, like as not you'd tell me 'e was——"

"Here!" said I, and, moving aside, pointed to the shadow.

The Postilion stepped nearer, lowering his lanthorn, then staggered blindly backwards.

"Lord!" he whimpered, "Lord love me!" and stood, staring, with dropped jaw.

"Where is your chaise?"

"Up yonder—yonder—in the lane," he mumbled, his eyes still fixed.

"Then help me to carry him there."

"No, no—I dursn't touch it—I can't—not me—not me!"

"I think you will," said I, and took the pistol from my pocket.

"Ain't one enough for to-night?" he muttered; "put it way—I'll come—I'll do it—put it away." So I dropped the weapon back into my pocket while the Postilion, shivering violently, stooped with me above the inanimate figure, and, with our limp burden between us, we staggered and stumbled up the path, and along the lane to where stood a light travelling chaise.

"'E ain't likely to come to this time, I'm thinkin'!" said the Postilion, mopping the sweat from his brow and grinning with pallid lips, after we had got our burden into the vehicle; "no, 'e ain't likely to wake up no more, nor yet 'curse my 'ead off '—this side o' Jordan."

"No," I answered, beginning to unwind my neck-cloth.

"Nor it ain't no good to go a-bandagin' and a-bindin' of 'im up—like you did last time."

"No," said I; "no." And stepping into the chaise, I muffled that disfigured face in my neckcloth; having done which, I closed the door.

"What now?" inquired the Postilion.

"Now you can drive us to Cranbrook."

"What—be you a-comin' too?"

"Yes," I nodded; "yes, I am coming too"

"Lord love me!" he exclaimed, and a moment later I heard him chirruping to his horses; the whip cracked and the chaise lurched forward. Whether he had some wild notion that I might attempt to descend and make my escape before we reached our destination, I cannot say, but he drove at a furious pace, taking corners at reckless speed, so that the chaise lurched and swayed most violently, and, more than once, I was compelled to hold that awful figure down upon the seat before me, lest it should slide to the floor. On we sped, past hedge and tree, by field and lonely wood. And ever in my ears was the whir of the wheels, the drumming of hoofs, and the crack of the whip; and ever the flitting moonbeams danced across that muffled face until it seemed that the features writhed, and gibed at me, beneath the folds of the neckerchief.

And so at last came lights, and houses, and the sound of excited voices as we pulled up before the Posting House at Cranbrook. Looking from the window, I saw a ring of faces with eyes that gleamed in the light of the lanthorns, and every eye was fixed on me, and every foot gave back a step as I descended from the chaise. And, while I stood there, the Postilion came with two white-faced ostlers, who, between them, bore a heavy burden through the crowd, stumbling awkwardly as they went; and, as men saw that which they carried, there came a low, deep sound—wordless, inarticulate, yet full of menace. But, above this murmur rose a voice, and I saw the Postilion push his way to the steps of the inn, and turn there, with hands clenched and raised above his head.

"My master—Sir Maurice Vibart—is killed—shot to death—murdered down there in the 'aunted 'Oller!" he cried, "and, if you axes me who done it, I says to you—'e did—so 'elp me God!" and speaking, he raised his whip and pointed at me.

Once more there rose that inarticulate sound of menace, and once more all eyes were fixed upon me.

" 'E were a fine gen'man!" said a voice.

"Ah! so gay an' light-'earted!" said another.

"Ay, ay—a generous, open-'anded gen'man!" said a third.

And every moment the murmur swelled, and grew more threatening; fists were clenched, and sticks flourished, so that, instinctively, I set my back against the chaise, for it seemed they lacked only someone to take the initiative ere they fell upon me.

The Postilion saw this too, for, with a shout, he sprang forward, his whip upraised. But, as he did so, the crowd was burst asunder, he was caught by a mighty arm, and Black George stood beside me, his eyes glowing, his fists clenched, and his hair and beard bristling.

"Stand back, you chaps," he growled, "stand back—or I'll 'urt some on ye; be ye all a lot o' dogs to set on an' worry one as is all alone?" And then, turning to me, "What be the matter wi' the fools, Peter?"

"Matter?" cried the Postilion; "murder be the matter—my master be murdered—shot to death—an' there stands the man as done it!"

"Murder?" cried George, in an altered voice; "murder?" Now, as he spoke, the crowd parted, and four ostlers appeared, bearing a hurdle between them, and on the hurdle lay a figure, an elegant figure whose head and face were still muffled in my neckerchief. I saw George start, and, like a flash, his glance came round to my bare throat, and dismay was in his eyes.

"Peter——?" he murmured; then he laughed suddenly and clapped his hand down upon my shoulder. "Look 'ee, you chaps," he cried, facing the crowd, "this is my friend Peter—an honest man an' no murderer, as 'e will tell ye 'isself—this is my friend as I'd go bail for wi' my life to be a true man; speak up, Peter, an' tell 'em as you'm an honest man an' no murderer." But I shook my head.

"Oh, Peter!" he whispered, "speak! speak!"

"Not here, George," I answered; "it would be of no avail—besides, I can say nothing to clear myself."

"Nothin,' Peter?"

"Nothing, George. This man was shot and killed in the Hollow—I found him lying dead—I found the empty pistol, and the Postilion, yonder, found me standing over the body. That is all I have to tell."

"Peter," said he, speaking hurriedly beneath his breath, "oh, Peter!—let's run for it—'twould be main easy for the likes o' you an' me——"

"No, George," I answered; "it would be worse than useless. But one thing I do ask of you—you who know me so much better than most—and it is,

that you will bid me good-bye, and—take my hand
once more, George—here before all these eyes that
look upon me as a murderer, and——"

Before I had finished he had my hand in both of his
—nay, had thrown one great arm protectingly about
me.

"Why, Peter——" he began in a strangely cracked
voice, "oh! man as I love!—never think as I'd believe
their lies, an'—Peter—such fighters as you an' me!—a
match for double their number—let's make a bolt for
it—ecod! I want to hit somebody. Never doubt me,
Peter—your friend—an' they'd go over like skittles—
like skittles, Peter——"

The crowd, which had swelled momentarily, surged,
opened, and a man on horseback pushed his way
towards me, a man in some disorder of dress, as
though he had clothed himself in a hurry.

Rough hands were now laid upon me; I saw
George's fist raised threateningly, but caught it in my
grasp.

"Good-bye," said I, "good-bye, George, and don't
look so downcast, man." But we were forced apart,
and I was pushed, and pulled, and hustled away,
through a crowd of faces whose eyes damned me
wherever I looked, along panelled passage ways, and
into a long, dim room, where sat the gentleman I had
seen on the horse, busily tying his cravat, to whom I
delivered up the pistol, and answered divers questions
as well as I might, and by whom, after much jotting
of notes and memoranda, I was delivered over to four
burly fellows, who, with deep gravity, and a grip
much tighter than was necessary, once more led me
out into the moonlit street, where were people who
pressed forward to stare into my face, and people who
leaned out of windows to stare down upon my head,
and many more who followed at my heels.

And thus, in much estate, I ascended a flight of
worn stone steps into the churchyard, and so—by a
way of tombs and graves—came at last to the great
square church-tower, into which I was incontinently
thrust, and there very securely locked up.

CHAPTER XLIV

THE BOW STREET RUNNERS

IT was toward evening of the next day that the door of my prison was opened, and two men entered. The first was a tall, cadaverous-looking individual of a melancholy cast of feature, who, despite the season, was wrapped in a long frieze coat reaching almost to his heels, from the pocket of which coat projected a short staff, or truncheon. He came forward with his hands in his pockets, and his bony chin on his breast, looking at me under the brim of a somewhat weather-beaten hat—that is to say, he looked at my feet, and my hands, and my throat, and my chin, but never seemed to get any higher.

His companion, on the contrary, bustled forward, and, tapping me familiarly on the shoulder, looked me over with a bright, appraising eye.

"S'elp me, Jeremy!" said he, addressing his saturnine friend, "s'elp me, if I ever see a pore misfort'nate cove more to my mind an' fancy—nice an' tall an' straight-legged—twelve stone if a pound—a five-foot drop now—or say five foot six, an' 'e'll go off as sweet as a bird; ah! you'll never feel it, my covey—not a twinge; a leetle tightish round the windpipe, p'r'aps—but, Lord, it's soon over. You're lookin' a bit pale round the gills, young cove, but, Lord! that's only nat'ral too." Here he produced from the depths of a capacious pocket something that glittered beneath his agile fingers. "And 'ow might be your general 'ealth, young cove?" he went on affably, "bobbish, I 'ope—fair an' bobbish?" As he spoke, with a sudden dexterous motion he had snapped something upon my wrists, so quickly that, at the contact of the cold steel, I started, and as I did so, something jingled faintly.

2 G   465

"There!" he exclaimed, clapping me on the shoulder again, but at the same time casting a sharp glance at my shackled wrists—"there—now we're all 'appy an' comfortable! I see as you're a cove as takes things nice an' quiet, an'—so long as you do—I'm your friend—Bob's my name, an' bobbish is my natur'. Lord!—the way I've seen misfort'nate coves take on at sight o' them 'bracelets' is something outrageous! But you—why, you're a different kidney—you're my kind, you are—what do you say, Jeremy?"

"Don't like 'is eye!" growled that individual.

"Don't mind Jeremy," winked the other; "it's just 'is per-werseness. Lord! 'e is the per-wersest codger you ever see! Why, 'e finds fault wi' the Pope o' Rome, jest because 'e's in the 'abit o' lettin' coves kiss 'is toe—I've 'eard Jeremy work 'isself up over the Pope, an' a pint o' porter, till you'd 'ave thought——"

"Ain't we never a-goin' to start?" inquired Jeremy, staring out of the window, with his back to us.

"And where," said I, "where might you be taking me?"

"Why, since you ax, my covey, we'm a-takin' you where you'll be took good care on, where you'll feed well, and 'ave justice done on you—trust us for that. Though, to be sure, I'm sorry to take you from such proper quarters as these' ere—nice and airy—eh, Jeremy?"

"Ah!—an' wi' a fine view o' the graves!" growled Jeremy, leading the way out.

In the street stood a chaise and four, surrounded by a pushing, jostling throng, men, women and children, who, catching sight of me between the Bow Street Runners, forgot to push and jostle, and stared at me with every eye and tooth they possessed, until I was hidden in the chaise.

"Right away!" growled Jeremy, shutting the door with a bang.

"Whoa!" roared a voice, and a great, shaggy golden head was thrust in at the window, and a hand reached down and grasped mine.

"A pipe an' baccy, Peter—from me; a flask o' rum

—Simon's best, from Simon; an' chicken sang-widges, from my Prue." This as he passed in each article through the window. " An' I were to say, Peter, as we are all wi' you—ever an' ever, an' I were likewise to tell 'ee as 'ow Prue'll pray for 'ee oftener than before, an'—ecod! " he broke off, the tears running down his face, " there were a lot more, but I've forgot it all, only, Peter, me an' Simon be goin' to get a lawyer chap for 'ee, an'—oh, man, Peter, say the word, an' I'll have 'ee out o' this in a twinklin'—an' we'll run for it——"

But, even as I shook my head, the postboy's whip cracked, and the horses plunged forward.

" Good-bye, George! " I cried, " good-bye, dear fellow! " and the last I saw of him was as he stood rubbing his tears away with one fist and shaking the other after the chaise.

CHAPTER XLV

WHICH CONCERNS ITSELF, AMONG OTHER MATTERS,
WITH THE BOOTS OF THE SATURNINE JEREMY

" A BOTTLE o' rum ! " said the man Bob, and taking
it up, very abstracted of eye, he removed the cork,
sniffed at it, tasted it, took a gulp, and handed it over
to his companion, who also looked at, sniffed at, and
tasted it. " And what d'ye make o' that Jeremy ? "

" Tasted better afore now ! " growled Jeremy, and
immediately took another pull.

" Sang-widges, too ! " pursued the man Bob, in a
ruminating tone, " an' I always was partial to chicken ! "
and, forthwith, opening the dainty parcel, he helped
himself, and his companion also.

" What d'ye make o' them, Jeremy ? " he inquired,
munching.

" I've eat wuss ! " rumbled Jeremy, also munching.

" Young cove, they does you credit," said the man
Bob, nodding to me with great urbanity, " great
credit—there ain't many misfort'nates as can per-jooce
such sang-widges as them, though, to be sure, they
eats uncommon quick—'old 'ard there, Jeremy——"
But, indeed, the sang-widges were already only a
memory, wherefore his brow grew black, and he
glared at the still munching Jeremy, who met his
looks with his usual impenetrable gloom.

" A pipe and 'bacca ! " mused the man Bob, after
we had ridden some while in silence, and, with the
same serene unconsciousness of manner, he took the
pipe, filled it, lighted it, and puffed with an air of
dreamy content.

" Jeremy is a good-ish sort," he began, with a complacent flourish of the pipe, "a good-ish sort, but
cross-grained—Lord ! young cove, 'is cross-grainedness
is ekalled only by 'is per-werseness, and 'cause why ?—

468

'cause 'e don't smoke—(go easy wi' the rum, Jeremy!)
there's nothin' like a pipe o' 'bacca to soothe such
things away—(I got my eye on ye, Jeremy!)—no,
there's nothin' like a pipe o' 'bacca; look at me—I
were the per-wersest infant that ever was, till I took to
smokin', and to-day, whatever I am, I ain't per-werse,
nor yet cross-grained, and many a misfort'nate cove,
as is now no more—'as wept over me at partin'——''

"They generally always do!" growled Jeremy,
uncorking the rum-bottle with his teeth.

"No, Jerry, no," returned the other, blowing out a
cloud of smoke; "misfort'nates ain't all the same—
(arter you wi' that bottle!)—you 'ave Cryers, and
Laughers, and Pray-ers, and Silent Ones, and the
silent coves is the dangerousest—(arter you wi' the
bottle, Jeremy!)—now you, my covey," he went on,
tapping my hand gently with his pipe-stem, "you
ain't exactly talkative, in fact—not wishin' no offence,
I might say as you was inclined to be one o' the Silent
Ones. Not as I 'olds that agin you—far from it, only
you reminds me of a young cove as 'ad the misfort'n
to get 'isself took for forgery, and who—arter me a-
talkin' and a-chattin' to 'im in my pleasant way—went
and managed to commit sooicide—under my very nose
—which were 'ardly nice, or even respectable, considerin'—(arter you wi' the bottle, Jeremy!)"

Jeremy growled, held up the bottle to the failing
light of evening, measured its contents with his
thumb, and extended it unwillingly towards his com-
rade's ready hand; but it never got there, for, at that
instant, the chaise lurched violently—there was a cry,
a splintering of glass, a crash, and I was lying, half
stunned, in a ditch, listening to the chorus of oaths
and cries that rose from the cloud of dust where the
frightened horses reared and plunged.

How long I remained thus I cannot say, but, all at
once, I found myself upon my feet, running down the
road, for, hazy though my mind yet was, I could think
only of escape, of liberty, and freedom—at any price—
at any cost. So I ran on down the road, somewhat
unsteadily as yet, because my fall had been a heavy

one, and my brain still reeled. I heard a shout behind me—the sharp crack of a pistol, and a bullet sang over my head; and then I knew they were after me, for I could hear the patter of their feet upon the hard road.

Now as I ran, my brain cleared, but this only served me to appreciate the difficulty of eluding men so seasoned and hardy as my pursuers; moreover, the handcuffs galled my wrists, and the short connecting chain hampered my movements considerably, and I saw that, upon this straight level, I must soon be run down, or shot from behind.

Glancing back, I beheld them some hundred yards, or so, away, elbows in, heads up, running with that long, free stride that speaks of endurance. I increased the pace, the ground flew beneath me, but, when I glanced again, though the man Bob had dropped back, the saturnine Jeremy ran on, no nearer, but no farther than before.

Now, as I went, I presently espied that for which I had looked—a gate set in the midst of the hedge, but it was closed, and never did a gate, before or since, appear quite so high and insurmountable; but, with the desperation of despair, I turned, ran at it, and sprang, swinging my arms above my head as I did so. My foot grazed the top bar—down I came, slipped, stumbled, regained my balance, and ran on over the springy turf. I heard a crash behind me, an oath, a second pistol barked, and immediately it seemed that a hot iron seared my forearm, and glancing down, I saw the skin cut, and bleeding, but, finding it no worse, breathed a sigh of thankfulness, and ran on.

By that leap I had probably gained some twenty yards; I would nurse my strength, therefore. If I could once gain the woods! How far off were they?—half-a-mile, a mile?—well, I could run that easily, thanks to my hardy life. Stay! what was that sound behind me—the fall of flying feet, or the throbbing of my own heart? I turned my head; the man Jeremy was within twelve yards of me—lean, and spare, his head thrust forward, he ran, with the long, easy stride of a greyhound.

So it was to be a question of endurance? Well, I had caught my second wind by now. I set my teeth, and, clenching my fists, lengthened my stride.

And now, indeed, the real struggle began. My pursuer had long ago abandoned his coat, but his boots were heavier and clumsier than those I wore, but then, again, my confining shackles seemed to contract my chest; and the handcuffs galled my wrists cruelly.

On I went, scattering flocks of scampering sheep, past meditative cows who started up, puffing out snorts of perfume; scrambling through hedges, over gate, and stile, and ditch, with eyes upon the distant woods full of the purple gloom of evening, and, in my ears, the muffled thud! thud!—thud! thud! of the pursuit, sometimes seeming much nearer, and sometimes much farther off, but always the same rhythmic, remorseless thud! thud!—thud! thud!

On, and ever on, climbing steep uplands, plunging down precipitous slopes, past brawling brooks, and silent pools all red and gold with sunset, past oak, and ash, and thorn—on and on, with ever those thudding footfalls close behind. And, as we ran, it seemed to me that our feet beat out a kind of cadence—his heavy shoes, and my lighter ones.

Thud! thud!—pad! pad!—thud! thud!—pad! pad! until they would suddenly become confused, and mingle with each other.

One moment it seemed that I almost loved the fellow, and the next that I bitterly hated him. Whether I had gained or not, I could not tell; to look back was to lose ground.

The woods were close now, so close that I fancied I heard the voice of their myriad leaves calling to me—encouraging me. But my breath was panting thick and short, my stride was less sure, my wrists were raw and bleeding, and the ceaseless jingle of my chain maddened me.

Thud!—thud!—untiring, persistent—thud!—thud!—the pulse at my temples throbbed in time with it, my breath panted to it. And surely it was nearer, more distinct—yes, he had gained on me in the last half-mile

—but how much? I cast a look over my shoulder, it was but a glance, yet I saw that he had lessened the distance between us by half. His face shone with sweat—his mouth was a line—his nostrils broad and expanded—his eye staring, and shot with blood, but he ran on with the same long, easy stride that was slowly but surely wearing me down.

We were descending a long grassy slope, and I stumbled, more than once, and rolled in my course, but on came those remorseless footfalls—thud!—thud!—thud!—thud!—strong and sure as ever.

He was nearing me fast—he was close upon me—closer—within reach of me. I could hear his whistling breaths, and then, all at once, I was down on hands and knees; he tried to avoid me—failed, and, shooting high over me, thudded down upon the grass.

For a moment he lay still, then, with a groan, he rolled over, and, propping himself on his arm, thrust a hand into his bosom; but I hurled myself upon him, and, after a brief struggle, twisted the pistol from his grasp, whereupon he groaned again.

" Hurt ? " I panted.

" Arm broke, I think," he growled, and forthwith burst out into a torrent of curses.

" Does it—hurt—so much ? " I panted.

" Ah! but it—ain't that," he panted back, " it's me—a-lettin' of you—work off a mouldy—old trick on me—like—that there——"

" It was my only chance," said I, sitting down beside him to regain my wind.

" To think," he growled, " o' me bein' took in by a——"

" But you are a great runner! " said I.

" A great fool, you mean, to be took in by a——"

" You have a long walk back, and your arm will be painful——"

" And serve me right for bein' took in by——"

" If you will lend me your neckerchief I think I can make your arm more comfortable," said I. He ceased cursing to stare at me, slowly and awkwardly unwound the article in question, and passed it to me. Thereupon, having located the fracture, I contrived a rough splint with a piece of wood lying near; which done, he thanked me, in a burst of profanity, and rose.

"I've see worse coves nor you!" said he, "and one good turn desarvin' another—lie snug all day, and travel by night, and keep to the byroads—this ain't no common case, there'll be a thousand pound on your 'ead afore the week's out—so look spry, my cove!" saying which he nodded, turned upon his heel, and strode away, cursing to himself.

Now, presently, as I went, I heard the merry ring and clink of hammer and anvil, and, guided by the sound, came to a tumbledown smithy where was a man busily at work, with a shock-headed boy at the bellows. At sight of me, the smith set down his hammer, and stared open-mouthed, as did also the shock-headed boy.

"How long would it take you to file off these shackles?" I inquired, holding out my hands.

"To—to file 'em off?"

"Yes."

"Why, that—that depends——"

"Then do it—as soon as you can." Upon this, the man turned his back to me and began rummaging among his tools, with his head very near that of the shock-headed boy, until, having found a file suitable to the purpose, he set to work upon my handcuffs. But he progressed so slowly, for one reason and another, that I began to grow impatient; moreover, noticing that the shock-headed boy had disappeared, I bade him desist.

"A cold chisel and hammer will be quickest," said I; "come, cut me off this chain—here, close up to the rivets." And, when he had done this, I took his file, and thrusting it beneath my coat, set off, running my hardest, leaving him to stare after me, with his eyes and mouth wider than ever.

The sun was down when I reached the woods, and here, in the kind shadows, I stayed awhile to rest, and rid myself of my handcuffs; but, when I felt for the file to do so—it was gone.

CHAPTER XLVI

HOW I CAME TO LONDON

JUSTLY to narrate all that befell me during my flight, and journey to London, would fill many pages, and therefore, as this book of mine is already of a magnitude far beyond my first expectations, I shall hurry on to the end of my story.

Acting upon the advice of the saturnine Jeremy, I lay hidden by day, and travelled by night, avoiding the highway. But in so doing I became so often involved in the maze of cross-roads, bylanes, cowpaths, and cart-tracks, that twice the dawn found me as completely lost as though I had been set down in the midst of the Sahara. I thus wasted much time, and wandered many miles out of my way; wherefore, to put an end to these futile ramblings, I set my face westward, hoping to strike the highroad somewhere between Tonbridge and Sevenoaks; determined rather to run the extra chance of capture than follow haphazard these tortuous and interminable byways.

It was, then, upon the third night since my escape, that, faint and spent with hunger, I saw before me the welcome sight of a fingerpost, and hurrying forward, eager to learn my whereabouts, came full upon a man who sat beneath the fingerpost, with a hunch of bread and meat upon his knee, which he was eating by means of a clasp-knife.

Now I had tasted nothing save two apples all day, and but little the day before—thus, at sight of this appetising food, my hunger grew, and increased to a violent desire before which prudence vanished and caution flew away. Therefore I approached the man, with my eyes upon his bread and meat.

But, as I drew nearer, my attention was attracted by something white that was nailed up against the fingerpost, and I stopped dead, with my eyes riveted by a word printed in great black capitals, and stood oblivious alike of the man who had stopped eating to stare at me, and the bread and meat that he had set down upon the grass; for what I saw was this:

G, R.

MURDER

£500————REWARD

WHEREAS, PETER SMITH, blacksmith, late of SISSINGHURST, in the county of Kent, suspected of the crime of WILFUL MURDER, did, upon the Tenth of August last, make his escape from his gaolers, upon the Tonbridge road, somewhere between SISSINGHURST and PEMBRY; the above REWARD, namely, FIVE HUNDRED POUNDS, will be paid to such person, or persons who shall give such INFORMATION as shall lead to the ARREST, and APPREHENSION of the aforesaid PETER SMITH. In the furtherance of which, is hereunto added a just and close description of the same—VIZ.—He is six foot tall, and a sizable ROGUE. His hair, black, his eyes dark and piercing. Clad, when last seen, in a worn velveteen jacket, knee-breeches buckled at the knees, grey worsted stockings, and patched shoes. The coat TORN at the RIGHT shoulder. Upon his wrists, a pair of steel HANDCUFFS. Last seen in the vicinity of PEMBRY.

While I yet stared at this, I was conscious that the man had risen, and now stood at my elbow; also, that in one hand he carried a short, heavy stick. He stood very still, and with bent head, apparently absorbed in the printed words before him, but more than once I saw his eyes gleam in the shadow of his hat-brim, as they turned to scan me furtively up and down. Yet he did not speak, or move, and there was something threatening, I thought, in his immobility. Wherefore I, in turn, watched him narrowly from the corner of my eye, and thus it chanced that our glances met.

" You seem thoughtful? " said I.

" Ah !—I be that."

" And what might you be thinking ? "

" Why—since you ax me, I was thinkin' as your
eye was mighty sharp and piercin'."

" Ah ! " said I; " and what more ? "

" That your coat was tore at the shoulder."

" So it is," I nodded; " well ? "

" You likewise wears buckled breeches, and grey
worsted stockings."

" You are a very observant man ! " said I.

" Though, to be sure," said he, shaking his head,
" I don't see no 'andcuffs."

" That is because they are hidden under my sleeves."

" A—h—h ! " said he, and I saw the stick quiver
in his grip.

" As I said before, you are a very observant man ! "
said I, watching the stick.

" Well, I've got eyes, and can see as much as most
folk," he retorted, and here the stick quivered again.

" Yes," I nodded; " you also possess legs, and can
probably walk fast ? "

" Ah !—and run, too, if need be," he added significantly.

" Then suppose you start."

" Start where ? "

" Anywhere, so long as you do start."

" Not wi'out you, my buck ! I've took a powerful
fancy to you, and that there five hundred pounds "—
here his left hand shot out and grasped my collar—
" so—s'posin' you come along o' me. And no tricks,
mind—no tricks, or—ah !—would ye ? " The heavy
stick whirled up, but, quick as he, I had caught his
wrist, and now presented my pistol full in his face.

" Drop that stick ! " said I, pressing the muzzle of
the weapon lightly against his forehead as I spoke.
At the touch of the cold steel his body suddenly
stiffened and grew rigid, his eyes opened in a horrified
stare, and the stick clattered down on the road.

" Talking of fancies," I pursued, " I have a great
mind to that smock-frock of yours, so take it off, and
quick about it."

In a fever of haste he tore off the garment in question, and, he thrusting it eagerly upon me, I folded it
over my arm.

" Now," said I, " since you say you can run, supposing you show me what you can do. This is a good
straight lane—off with you and do your best, and no
turning, or stopping, mind, for the moon is very
bright, and I am a pretty good shot." Hardly waiting
to hear me out, the fellow set off up the lane, running
like the wind ; whereupon, I (waiting only to snatch up
his forgotten bread and meat) took to my heels—down
the lane, so that, when I presently stopped to don the
smock-frock, its late possessor had vanished as though
he had never been.

I hurried on, nevertheless, eating greedily as I went,
and, after some while, left the narrow lane behind, and
came out on the broad highway that stretched like a
great, white riband, unrolled beneath the moon. And
here was another fingerpost with the words :

"To Sevenoaks, Tonbridge, and the Wells.—To Bromley and
London."

And here, also, was another placard, headed by that
awful word : MURDER—which seemed to leap out at
me from the rest. And, with that word, there rushed
over me the memory of Charmian as I had seen her
stand—white-lipped, haggard of eye, and—with one
hand hidden in the folds of her gown.

So I turned and strove to flee from this hideous
word, and, as I went, I clenched my fists, and cried
within myself : " I love her—love her—no doubt can
come between us more—I love her—love her—love
her ! " Thus I hurried on along the great highroad,
but, wherever I looked, I saw this most hateful word ;
it shone out palely from the shadows ; it was scored
into the dust at my feet ; even across the splendour of
the moon, in jagged characters, I seemed to read that
awful word : MURDER.

And the soft night-wind woke voices to whisper it as
I passed ; the sombre trees and gloomy hedgerows were
full of it ; I heard it in the echo of my step—MURDER !

MURDER ! It was always there, whether I walked, or ran, in rough and stony places, in the deep, soft dust, in the dewy, tender grass—it was always there, whispering at my heels, and refusing to be silenced.

I had gone on, in this way, for an hour, or more, avoiding the middle of the road, because of the brilliance of the moon, when I overtook something that crawled in the gloom of the hedge, and approaching, pistol in hand, saw that it was a man.

He was creeping forward slowly and painfully on his hands and knees, but, all at once, sank down with his face in the grass, only to rise, groaning, and creep on once more ; and, as he went, I heard him praying :

" Lord, give me strength—O Lord, give me strength. Angela ! Angela ! It is so far—so far——"
And groaning, he sank down again, upon his face.

" You are ill ! " said I, bending over him.

" I must reach Deptford—she's buried at Deptford, and I shall die to-night—O Lord. give me strength ! " he panted.

" Deptford is miles away," said I.

Now, as I spoke, he lifted himself upon his hands and stared up at me. I saw a haggard, hairy face, very thin and sunken, but a fire burned in the eyes, and the eyes seemed, somehow, familiar.

" You ! " he cried, and spat up in the air towards me ; " devil ! " he cried, " Devil Vibart." I recoiled instinctively before the man's sudden, wild ferocity, but, propping himself against the bank. he shook his hand at me, and laughed.

" Devil ! " he repeated ; "shade !—ghost of a devil ! —have you come back to see me die ? "

" Who are you ? " I cried, bending to look into the pale, emaciated face ; " who are you ? "

" A shadow," he answered, passing a shaking hand up over his face and brow, " a ghost—a phantom—as you are ; but my name was Strickland once, as yours was Devil Vibart. I am changed of late—you said so in the Hollow, and—laughed. You don't laugh now, Devil Vibart, you remember poor John Strickland now."

"You are the Outside Passenger!" I exclaimed, "the madman who followed and shot at me in a wood——"

"Followed? Yes, I was a shadow that was always behind you—following and following you, Satan Vibart, tracking and tracking you to hell and damnation. And you fled here, and you fled there, but I was always behind you; you hid from me among lowly folk, but you could not escape the shadow. Many times I would have killed you—but she was between—the Woman. I came once to your cottage, it was night, and the door opened beneath my hand—but your time was not then. But—ha!—I met you among trees, as I did once before, and I told you my name—as I did once before, and I spoke of her—of Angela, and cried her name—and shot you—just here, above the brow; and so you died, Devil Vibart, as soon I must, for my mission is accomplished——"

"It was you!" I cried, kneeling beside him, "it was your hand that shot Sir Maurice Vibart?"

"Yes," he answered, his voice growing very gentle as he went on, "for Angela's sake—my dead wife," and, fumbling in his pocket, he drew out a woman's small, lace-edged handkerchief, and I saw that it was thickened and black with blood. "This was hers," he continued, "in her hand, the night she died—I had meant to lay it on her grave—the blood of atonement—but now——"

A sudden crash in the hedge above; a figure silhouetted against the sky; a shadowy arm, that, falling, struck the moon out of heaven, and, in the darkness, I was down upon my knees, and fingers were upon my throat.

"Oh, Darby!" cried a voice, "I've got him—this way—quick—oh, Darb——" My fist drove into his ribs; I struggled up under a rain of blows, and we struck, and swayed, and staggered, and struck—trampling the groaning wretch who lay dying in the ditch. And before me was the pale oval of a face, and I smote it twice with my pistol-butt, and it was gone, and I—was running along the road.

" Charmian spoke truth ! O God, I thank thee ! "

I burst through a hedge, running on, and on—careless alike of being seen, of capture or escape, of prison or freedom, for in my heart was a great joy.

I was conscious of shouts and cries, but I heeded them no more, listening only to the song of happiness my heart was singing :

" Charmian spoke truth, her hands are clean. O God, I thank thee ! "

And, as I went, I presently espied a caravan, and before it, a fire of sticks, above which a man was bending, who, raising his head, stared at me as I approached. He was a strange-looking man, who glared at me with one eye and leered jocosely with the other ; and, being spent, and short of breath, I stopped, and wiping the sweat from my eyes I saw that it was blood.

" How—is Lewis ? " I panted.

" What," exclaimed the man, drawing nearer, " is it you ?—James ! but you're a picter, you are—hallo ! " he stopped, as his glance encountered the steel that glittered upon my wrist ; while upon the silence the shouts swelled, drawing near and nearer.

" So—the Runners is arter you, are they, young feller ? "

" Yes," said I ; " yes. You have only to cry out, and they will take me, for I can fight no more, nor run any farther, this knock on the head has made me very dizzy."

" Then—take a pull at this 'ere," said he, and thrust a flat bottle into my hand. The fiery spirit burned my throat, but almost immediately my strength and courage revived.

" Better ? "

" Much better," I answered, returning the bottle, " and I thank you——"

" Don't go for to thank me, young feller," said he, driving the cork into the bottle with a blow of his fist, " you thank that young feller as once done as much for me—at a Fair. An' now—cut away—run !—the 'edge is good and dark, up yonder—lay low a bit, and leave these damned Runners to me." I obeyed without more ado, and, as I ran up the lane, I heard him shouting and swearing as though engaged in a desperate encounter; and, turning in the shadow of the hedge, I saw him met by two men, with whom, still shouting and gesticulating excitedly, he set off, running—down the lane.

And so I, once more, turned my face London-wards.

The blood still flowed from the cut in my head, getting often into my eyes, yet I made good progress notwithstanding. But, little by little, the effect of the spirits wore off, a drowsiness stole over me, my limbs felt numbed and heavy. And with this came strange fancies, and a dread of the dark. Sometimes it seemed that odd lights danced before my eyes, like marsh-fires, and strange voices gabbled in my ears, furiously unintelligible, with laughter in a high-pitched key; sometimes I cast myself down in the dewy grass, only to start up again, trembling, and run on till I was breathless; but ever I struggled forward, despite the throbbing of my broken head, and the gnawing hunger that consumed me.

After a while, a mist came on, a mist that formed itself into deep valleys, or rose in jagged spires and pinnacles, but constantly changing; a mist that moved, and writhed, within itself. And in this mist were forms, nebulous and indistinct, multitudes that moved in time with me, and the voices seemed louder than before, and the laughter much shriller, while, repeated over and over again I caught that awful word: MURDER, MURDER.

Chief among this host walked one whose head and face were muffled from my sight, but who watched me, I knew, through the folds, with eyes that stared fixed and wide.

But now, indeed, the mist seemed to have got into my brain, and all things were hazy, and my memory of them is dim. Yet I recall passing Bromley village, and slinking furtively through the shadows of the deserted High Street, but thereafter all is blank save a memory of pain, and toil, and deadly fatigue.

2 H

I was stumbling up steps—the steps of a terrace; a great house lay before me, with lighted windows here and there, but these I feared, and so came creeping to one that I knew well, and whose dark panes glittered palely under the dying moon. And now I took out my clasp-knife, and, fumbling blindly, put back the catch (as I had often done as a boy), and so, the window opening, I clambered into the dimness beyond.

Now as I stumbled forward my hand touched something, a long, dark object that was covered with a cloth, and, hardly knowing what I did, I drew back this cloth and looked down at that which it had covered, and sank down upon my knees, groaning. For there, staring up at me, cold, contemptuous, and set like marble, was the smiling, dead face of my Cousin Maurice.

As I knelt there, I was conscious that the door had opened, that someone approached, bearing a light, but I did not move or heed.

" Peter ?—good God in heaven !—is it Peter ? " I looked up and into the dilated eyes of Sir Richard. " Is it really Peter ? " he whispered.

" Yes, sir—dying, I think."

" No, no—Peter—dear boy," he stammered. "You didn't know—you hadn't heard—poor Maurice—murdered—fellow—name of Smith——!!"

" Yes, Sir Richard, I know more about it than most. You see, I am Peter Smith." Sir Richard fell back from me, and I saw the candles swaying in his grasp.

"You?" he whispered, "you? Oh, Peter!—oh, my boy!"

' But I am innocent—innocent—you believe me—you who were my earliest friend—my good, kind friend—you believe me?" and I stretched out my hands appealingly, but, as I did so, the light fell gleaming upon my shameful wristlets; and, even as we gazed into each other's eyes, mute and breathless, came the sound of steps and hushed voices. Sir Richard sprang forward, and, catching me in a powerful hand, half led, half dragged me behind a tall leather screen beside the hearth, and thrusting me into a chair, turned, and hurried to meet the intruders.

They were three, as I soon discovered by their voices, one of which I thought I recognised.

" It's a devilish shame ! " the first was saying; " not a soul here for the funeral but our four selves— I say it's a shame—a burning shame ! "

" That, sir, depends entirely on the point of view," answered the second, a somewhat aggressive voice, and this it was I seemed to recognise.

" Point of view, sir ? Where, I should like to know, are all those smiling nonentities—those fawning sycophants who were once so proud of his patronage, who openly modelled themselves upon him, whose highest ambition was to be called a friend of the famous ' Buck ' Vibart—where are they now ? "

" Doing the same by the present favourite, as is the nature of their kind," responded the third; " poor Maurice is already forgotten."

" The Prince," said the harsh voice, " the Prince would never have forgiven him for crossing him in the affair of the Lady Sophia Sefton; the day he ran off with her he was as surely dead—in a social sense— as he is now—in every sense."

Here the mist settled down upon my brain once more, and I heard nothing but a confused murmur of voices, and it seemed to me that I was back on the road again, hemmed in by those gibbering phantoms that spoke so much, and yet said but one word: " Murder."

" Quick—a candle here—a candle—bring a light——" There came a glare before my smarting eyes, and I struggled up to my feet.

" Why—I have seen this fellow's face somewhere— ah !—yes, at an inn—a hang-dog rogue—I threatened to pull his nose, I remember, and—by Heaven !— handcuffs ! He has been roughly handled, too ! Gentlemen, I'll lay my life the murderer is found— though how he should come here of all places—extraordinary. Sir Richard—you and I, as magistrates—

duty——'' But the mist was very thick, and the voices grew confused again; only I knew that hands were upon me, that I was led into another room, where were lights that glittered upon the silver, the decanters and glasses of a supper table.

' Yes,'' I was saying, slowly and heavily; '' yes, I am Peter Smith—a blacksmith—who escaped from his gaolers on the Tonbridge Road—but I am innocent—before God—I am innocent. And now—do with me as you will—for I am—very weary——''

Sir Richard's arm was about me, and his voice sounded in my ears, but as though a great way off :

'' Sirs,'' said he, '' this is my friend—Sir Peter Vibart.'' There was a moment's pause, then—a chair fell with a crash, and there rose a confusion of excited voices, yet which grew suddenly silent, for the door had opened, and on the threshold stood a woman, tall, and proud, and richly dressed, from the little dusty boot that peeped beneath her habit to the wide-sweeping hat-brim that shaded the high beauty of her face. And I would have gone to her but that my strength failed me.

'' Charmian ! ''

She started, and, turning, uttered a cry, and ran to me.

'' Charmian,'' said I; oh, Charmian ! '' And so, with her tender arms about me, and her kisses on my lips, the mist settled down upon me, thicker and darker than ever.

CHAPTER XLVII

IN WHICH THIS HISTORY IS ENDED

A BRIGHT room, luxuriously appointed; a great wide bed with carved posts and embroidered canopy; between the curtained windows, a tall oak press with grotesque heads carved thereon, heads that leered and gaped and scowled at me. But the bed and the room and the oak press were all familiar, and the grotesque heads had leered and gaped and frowned at me before, and haunted my boyish dreams many and many a night.

And now I lay between sleeping and waking, staring dreamily at all these things, till roused by a voice near by, and starting up, broad awake, beheld Sir Richard.

"Deuce take you, Peter!" he exclaimed; "I say—the devil fly away with you, my boy!—curse me!—a nice pickle you've made of yourself, with your infernal Revolutionary notions—your digging, and blacksmithing, your walking-tours——"

"Where is she, Sir Richard?" I broke in; "pray, where is she?"

"She?" he returned, scratching his chin with the corner of a letter he held; "she?"

"She whom I saw last night——"

"You were asleep last night, and the night before."

"Asleep?—then how long have I been here?"

"Three days, Peter."

"And where is she—surely I have not dreamed it all—where is Charmian?"

"She went away—this morning."

"Gone!—where to?"

"Gad, Peter!—how should I know?" But seeing the distress in my face, he smiled, and tendered me the letter. "She left this 'For Peter, when he awoke'—

485

and I've been waiting for Peter to wake all the morning."

Hastily I broke the seal, and, unfolding the paper with tremulous hands read:

"DEAREST, NOBLEST, AND MOST DISBELIEVING OF PETERS,—Oh, did you think you could hide your hateful suspicion from me—from me who know you so well? I felt it in your kiss, in the touch of your strong hand, I saw it in your eyes. Even when I told you the truth, and begged you to believe me, even then, deep down in your heart you thought it was my hand that had killed Sir Maurice, and God only knows the despair that filled me as I turned and left you.

"And so, Peter—perhaps to punish you a little, perhaps because I cannot bear the noisy world just yet, perhaps because I fear you a little—I have run away. But I remember also how, believing me guilty, you loved me still, and gave yourself up, to shield me, and, dying of hunger and fatigue—came to find me. And so, Peter, I have not run so very far, nor hidden myself so very close, and if you understand me as you should your search need not be so very long. And dear, dear Peter, there is just one other thing, which I hoped that you would guess, which any other would have guessed, but which, being a philosopher, you never did guess. Oh, Peter—I was once, very long ago it seems, Sophia Charmian Sefton, but I am now, and always was, Your Humble Person,   CHARMIAN."

The letter fell from my fingers, and I remained staring before me so long that Sir Richard came and laid his hand on my shoulder.

"Oh, boy!" said he, very tenderly; "she has told me all the story, and I think, Peter, I think it is given to very few men to win the love of such a woman as this."

"God knows it!" said I.

"And to have married one so very noble and high in all things—you should be very proud, Peter."

"I am," said I; "oh, I am, sir."

" Even, Peter—even though she be a—virago, this Lady Sophia—or a termagant——"

" I was a great fool in those days," said I, hanging my head, " and very young ! "

" It was only six months ago, Peter."

" But I am years older to-day, sir."

" And the husband of the most glorious woman—the most—oh, curse me, Peter, if you deserve such a goddess ! "

" And—she worked for me ! " said I; " cooked, and served, and mended my clothes—where are they ? " I cried, and sprang out of bed.

" What the deuce——" began Sir Richard.

" My clothes," said I, looking vainly about; " my clothes—pray, Sir Richard, where are they ? "

" Burnt, Peter."

" Burnt ? "

" Every blood-stained rag ! " he nodded; " her orders."

" But—what am I to do ? "

Sir Richard laughed, and, crossing to the press, opened the door.

" Here are all the things you left behind you when you set out to—dig, and—egad !—make your fortune. I couldn't let 'em go with all the rest—so I—er—had 'em brought here, to—er—to keep them for you—ready for the time when you should grow tired of digging, and come back to me, and—er—oh, dammit !—you understand—and Grainger's waiting to see you in the library—been there hours—so dress yourself. In Heaven's name dress yourself ! " he cried, and hurried from the room.

It was with a certain satisfaction that I once more donned buckskin and spurred boots, and noticed moreover how tight my coat was become across the shoulders; yet I dressed hastily, for my mind was already on the road, galloping to Charmian.

In the library I found Sir Richard, and Mr Grainger, who greeted me with his precise little bow.

" I have to congratulate you, Sir Peter," he began, " not only on your distinguished marriage, and

accession to fortune, but upon the fact that the—ah—
unpleasantness connecting a certain Peter Smith with
your unfortunate cousin's late decease has been
entirely removed by means of the murderer's written
confession, placed in my hands some days ago by the
Lady Sophia——"

"A written confession—and she brought it to
you?"

"Galloped all the way from Tonbridge, by Gad!"
nodded Sir Richard.

"It seems," pursued Mr Grainger, "that the—ah—
man, John Strickland, by name, lodged with a certain
preacher, to whom, in Lady Vibart's presence, he confessed his crime, and willingly wrote out a deposition
to that effect. It also appears that the man, sick
though he was, wandered from the Preacher's cottage,
and was eventually found upon the road, and now lies
in Maidstone gaol, in a dying condition."

Chancing, presently, to look from the window, I behold a groom who led a horse up and down before the
door; and the groom was Adam, and the horse——

I opened the window, and, leaning out, called a
name. At the sound of my voice the man smiled,
and touched his hat, and the mare ceased her pawing
and chafing, and turned upon me a pair of great, soft
eyes, and snuffed the air, and whinnied. So I leapt
out of the window, and down the steps, and thus it
was that I met "Wings."

"She be in the pink o' condition, sir," said Adam
proudly; "Sir Richard bought 'er——"

"For a song!" added the baronet, who, with Mr
Grainger, had followed to bid me good-bye. "I really
got her remarkably cheap," he explained, thrusting
his fists deep into his pockets, and frowning down my
thanks. But, when I had swung myself into the
saddle, he came and laid his hand upon my knee.

"You are going to—find her, Peter?"

"Yes, sir."

"And you know—where to look?"

"I think so——"

"Because, if you don't—I might——"

" I shall go to a certain cottage," said I tentatively.

" Then you'd better go boy—the mare's all excitement—good-bye, Peter—and cutting up my gravel most damnably—good-bye ! " So saying, he reached up and gripped my hand very hard, and stared at me also very hard, though the tears stood in his eyes. " I always felt very fatherly towards you, Peter—and—you won't forget the lonely old man—come and see me now and then—both of you, for it does get damnably lonely here sometimes, and oh, curse it ! Good-bye ! dear lad." So he turned, and walked up the steps into his great, lonely house.

' O Wings ! with thy slender grace, and tireless strength, if ever thou didst gallop before, do thy best to-day ! Spurn, spurn the dust 'neath thy fleet hoofs, stretch thy graceful Arab neck, bear me gallantly to-day, O Wings, for never shalt thou and I see its like again."

Swift we flew, with the wind before, and the dust behind, past wayside inns where besmocked figures paused in their grave discussions to turn and watch us by ; past smiling field and darkling copse ; past lonely cottage and village green ; through Sevenoaks and Tonbridge, with never a stop ; up Pembry hill, and down, galloping so lightly, so easily, over that hard, familiar road, which I had lately tramped with so much toil and pain ; and so, as evening fell, to Sissinghurst.

A dreamy, sleepy place is Sissinghurst at all times, for its few cottages, like its inn, are very old, and great age begets dreams. But, when the sun is low, and the shadows creep out, when the old inn blinks drowsy eyes at the cottages, and they blink back drowsily at the inn, like the old friends they are ; when distant cows low at gates, and fences ; when sheep-bells tinkle faintly ; when the weary toiler, seated sideways on his weary horse, fares homewards, nodding sleepily with every plodding hoof-fall, but rousing to give one a drowsy " good-night," then who can resist the somnolent charm of the place, save only

the " Bull " himself, snorting down in lofty contempt
—as rolling of eye, as curly of horn, as stiff as to tail
as any indignant bull ever was, or shall be.

But as I rode, watching the evening deepen about
me, soft and clear rose the merry chime of hammer
and anvil, and, turning aside to the smithy, I paused
there, and stooping my head, looked in at the door.

" George ! " said I. He started erect, and dropping
hammer and tongs, came out, running, then stopped
suddenly, as one abashed.

" Oh, friend ! " said I, " don't you know me ? "

" Why—Peter——" he stammered, and broke off.

" Have you no greeting for me, George ? "

" Ay, ay—I heerd you was free, Peter, and I was
glad—glad, because you was the man as I loved, an' I
waited—ay, I've been waitin' for 'ee to come back.
But now—you be so changed—so fine an' grand—an'
I be all black wi' soot from the fire—oh man ! ye
bean't my Peter no more——"

" Never say that, George—never say that," I cried,
and leaping from the saddle, I would have caught his
hand in mine, but he drew back.

" You be so fine an' grand, Peter, an' I be all sooty
from the fire ! " he repeated. " I'd like to just wash
my 'ands first."

" Oh, Black George ! " said I, " dear George."

" Be you rich now, Peter ? "

" Yes, I suppose so."

" A gentleman wi' 'orses, an' 'ouses, an' servants ? "

" Well—what of it ? "

" I'd—like to—wash my 'ands first, if so be you
don't mind, Peter."

" George," said I, " don't be a fool ! " Now, as
we stood thus, fronting each other in the doorway, I
heard a light step upon the road behind me, and
turning, beheld Prudence.

" Oh, Prue ! George is afraid of my clothes, and
won't shake hands with me ! " For a moment she
hesitated, looking from one to the other of us—then,
all at once, laughing a little, and blushing a little, she
leaned forward and kissed me.

"Why, George!" said she, still blushing, "how fulish you be. Mr Peter were as much a gentleman in his leather apron as ever he is in his fine coat—how fulish you be, George!" So proud George gave me his hand, all grimy as it was, rejoicing over me because of my good fortune and mourning over me because my smithing days were over.

"Ye see, Peter, when men 'as worked together—and sorrowed together—an' fou't together—an' knocked each other down—like you an' me—it bean't so easy to say ' good-bye '—so, if you must leave us—why—don't let's say it."

"No, George, there shall be no ' good-byes ' for either one of us, and I shall come back—soon. Until then, take my mare—have her made comfortable for me, and now—good-night—good-night!"

And so, clasping their loving hands, I turned away, somewhat hurriedly, and left them.

There was no moon, but the night was luminous with stars, and, as I strode along, my eyes were often lifted to the "wonder of the heavens," and I wondered which particular star was Charmian's and which mine.

Reaching the Hollow, I paused to glance about me, as I ever did, before descending that leafy path; and the shadows were very black and a chill wind stirred among the leaves, so that I shivered, and wondered, for the first time, if I had come right—if the cottage had been in Charmian's mind when she wrote.

Then I descended the path, hurrying past a certain dark spot. And, coming at last within sight of the cottage, I paused again, and shivered again, for the windows were dark and the door shut. But the latch yielded readily beneath my hand, so I went in, and closed and barred the door behind me.

For, upon the hearth a fire burned with a dim, red glow that filled the place with shadows, and the shadows were very deep.

"Charmian!" said I, "oh, Charmian, are you there—have I guessed right?" I heard a rustle close

beside me, and, in the gloom, came a hand to meet
and clasp my own; wherefore I stooped and kissed
those slender fingers, drawing her into the fireglow,
and her eyes were hidden by their lashes, and the
glow of the fire seemed reflected in her cheeks.

"The candles were so—bright, Peter," she
whispered.

"Yes."

"And so—when I heard you coming——"

"You heard me?"

"I was sitting on the bench, outside, Peter."

"And, when you heard me—you put the candles
out?"

"They seemed so—very bright, Peter."

"And shut the door?"

"I only—just—closed it, Peter." She was still
wrapped in her cloak, as she had been when I first
saw her, wherefore I put back the hood from her face.
And behold! as I did so, her hair fell down, rippling
over my arm, and covering us both in its splendour,
as it had done once before.

"Indeed—you have glorious hair!" said I. "It
seems wonderful to think that you are my wife. I
can scarcely believe it—even yet!"

"Why, I had meant you should marry me from the
first, Peter."

"Had you?"

"Do you think I should ever have come back to
this dear solitude otherwise."

Now when I would have kissed her, she turned her
head aside.

"Peter."

"Yes, Charmian?"

"The Lady Sophia Sefton never did gallop her
horse up the steps of St Paul's Cathedral."

"Didn't she, Charmian?"

"And she couldn't help her name being bandied
from mouth to mouth, or—'hiccoughed out over
slopping wineglasses,' could she?"

"No," said I, frowning; "what a vasty young fool
I was!"

" And, Peter——"

" Well, Charmian?"

" She never was—and never will be—buxom, or strapping—will she;'buxom' is such a—hateful word, Peter! And you—love her?—wait, Peter—as much as ever you loved Charmian Brown?"

" Yes," said I; " yes——"

" And—nearly as much as—your dream woman?"

" More—much more, because you, are the embodiment of all my dreams—you always will be Charmian. Because I honour you for your intellect; and worship you for your gentleness, and spotless purity; and love you with all my strength for your warm, sweet womanhood; and because you are so strong, and beautiful, and proud——"

" And because, Peter, because I am—just—your loving—Humble Person."

And thus it was I went forth a fool, and toiled, and suffered, and loved, and, in the end, got me some little wisdom.

And thus did I, all unworthy as I am, win the heart of a noble woman whose love I pray will endure, even as mine will, when we shall have journeyed to the end of this Broad Highway, which is Life, and into the mystery of the Beyond.

THE RIVERSIDE PRESS LIMITED, EDINBURGH.